THERE'S SOMETHING
ABOUT LADY MARY

Also by Sophie Barnes

Lady Alexandra's Excellent Adventure
How Miss Rutherford Got Her Groove Back

THERE'S
SOMETHING
ABOUT
LADY MARY

A Summersby Tale

SOPHIE BARNES

AVONIMPULSE
An Imprint of HarperCollinsPublishers

Excerpt from *The Secret Life of Lady Lucinda* copyright © 2012 by Sophie Barnes.

Excerpt from *Three Schemes and a Scandal* copyright © 2012 by Maya Rodale.

Excerpt from *Skies of Steel* copyright © 2012 by Zoë Archer.

Excerpt from *Further Confessions of a Slightly Neurotic Hitwoman* copyright © 2012 by JB Lynn.

Excerpt from *The Second Seduction of a Lady* copyright © 2012 by Miranda Neville.

Excerpt from *To Hell and Back* copyright © 2012 by Juliana Stone.

Excerpt from *Midnight in Your Arms* copyright © 2012 by McKinley Hellenes.

Excerpt from *Seduced by a Pirate* copyright © 2012 by Eloisa James.

EPub Edition NOVEMBER 2012 ISBN: 9780062225375

Print Edition ISBN: 9780062225382

10 9 8 7 6 5 4 3 2 1

To my mother-in-law,
who gave me my first romance novel—you've changed my life!

Introduction

There was a time in the not so distant past when an Englishwoman's fortune, social status, and every other aspect of her life were governed entirely by men. Not many exceptions to this situation existed, though there were some ways that a woman could be granted the freedom and independence that so many desired: becoming a peeress in her own right.

There were three ways in which to achieve this much sought after place in society, though just one that is of interest to you, dear reader:

A father could bequeath his title to his daughter by issuing a request to the king and Parliament. Once approved, the peerage would be reissued to the desired female heir by parliamentary and royal warrant.

Yet even if a woman did somehow manage to become a peeress in her own right, her property would still be written over to her husband in the event that she chose to marry.

CHAPTER ONE

London, 1816

Mary stared in disbelief at the thin, little man who sat across from her behind the heavy mahogany desk. His hair had receded well beyond his ears, and his face was pinched. His eyes, lacking any definition due to his pale eyelashes, were set on either side of a nose that would have been perfect had it not been for a slight bump upon the bridge.

Mary watched quietly as he adjusted his spectacles for the hundredth time. She then posed the only reasonable question that she could think to ask: "Are you quite certain that an error of monumental proportions has not been made, Mr. Browne?"

In response to her question, Mr. Browne nodded so profusely that Mary couldn't help but envision his head suddenly popping off his neck and bouncing across the Persian carpet that lay stretched out upon the floor. She stifled a smirk to the best of her abilities but feared that her eyes betrayed her. In any event, Mr. Browne did not look pleased.

"Quite certain, your ladyship. Your father was very adamant about his wishes, and as you can see for yourself," he added as he handed her the final amendment to John Croyden's will, "he made certain that there would be no doubt about his intentions. Indeed, it's really quite plain to see."

"So it is," Mary muttered, still unsure of how to respond to the enormity of what her father's lawyer had just told her. She leafed through the crisp white pages of her father's last wishes before pausing at the one that bewildered her the most. There, right before her very eyes, was a petition made by her father and signed by none other than the Prince Regent himself. Her gloved fingers traced the outline of the royal insignia as she read the request: that John Croyden's daughter, Mary, be made his sole heir and a peeress in her own right, inheriting all of her father's worldly goods, including his title.

His title?

A half hour ago, Mary hadn't even known that he had one. She'd grown up in a modest house in Stepney, a suburb of London where she doubted few aristocrats had ever set foot. The place had served as her father's medical practice until she was old enough to accompany him on his never-ending travels, his constant companion in his quest for knowledge. Still, they'd kept that two-story house with its much-too-low ceilings and worm-eaten beams, returning to it whenever they happened to be passing through the city. It was home to her, yet here she now was, sitting in a lawyer's office, smack in the middle of Mayfair. A part of her wanted to jump up and down with delight, while another, much stronger, part wanted to scream at her father for lying to her all of these years. As an image of his kind and honest eyes came to mind, she couldn't help but wonder how he'd managed to keep something like this from her. It must have been a herculean effort. She let out a deep sigh of frustration. "You mentioned my father's title," she said, as she leafed through the pages. In spite of her efforts to make sense of it all, she was finding herself too distressed to focus. "Which title did he hold, if you don't mind my asking?"

Mr. Browne looked momentarily startled. "Why, he was a marquess, my lady—of Steepleton, to be precise."

Mary gave Mr. Browne a blank stare. "And that would make me what exactly?"

A couple of creases appeared on Mr. Browne's forehead from out of nowhere. Clearly, he wasn't accustomed to explaining the ranks of nobility to the daughters of his clients. He adjusted his spectacles once more. "It makes you a marchioness, my lady; not quite as prestigious a title as that of duchess perhaps, but more esteemed than that of countess, to be sure."

"I see," Mary said, though she was sure it was quite obvious she didn't see at all. She'd never had the slightest interest in the nobility, least of all in understanding which titles outranked others.

Mr. Browne coughed slightly into his fist as if he hoped to somehow fill the silence that followed. "Shall we discuss the financial aspects of the will?" he eventually asked as he leaned forward to rest his folded arms on the desk.

Mary's head snapped to attention at that question. "What financial aspects? My father was a man who made an honest living as a physician and later as a surgeon. He had a respectable income, but he was by no means wealthy. Even so, he did his best to set aside whatever he could for me, and I have legal rights to those funds. If you're about to suggest otherwise, then I promise you that I will contest it in a court of law. Other than that, I don't quite see what—"

"No. . .it is becoming increasingly clear to me that you obviously do not," Mr. Browne blurted out.

Mary's eyes widened with astonishment. She was momentarily taken aback by his remark, but quickly recovered, noting that he too seemed rather shocked. She said nothing, however, but merely watched as he leaned back in his chair and drew a deep breath.

"Lady Steepleton, I am not suggesting that you must forfeit any of the money that your father left you." He spoke in a measured tone that told of more patience than he truly possessed. "I'm merely trying to inform you that your inheritance is substantially larger than you believe it to be."

"How much larger?" Mary asked with a great deal of caution as she shifted uneasily in her seat. She twisted the coarse, graphite-colored cotton of her dress between her fingers and waited solemnly for Mr. Browne to continue, conscious of the fact that her simple appearance hardly made her look the part of an heiress.

"Lady Steepleton, your late father has left you with a sum of no less than fifty thousand pounds," Mr. Browne announced, in a manner that might suggest that he himself was somehow personally responsible for her dramatic increase in wealth. "He has also left you with a very comfortable house on Brook Street, not to mention Steepleton House in Northamptonshire, which I gather is a rather large estate. Suffice it to say, you are now a very affluent woman, Lady Steepleton."

Mary simply gaped at the man as if he'd sprouted a second

head, a pair of horns, or perhaps even both. Her mouth had fallen open at the mention of the fifty thousand pounds, but by the time Mr. Browne was finished, her eyes felt as though they were about to leap out of their sockets at any given moment. "You must be joking," she stammered, for want of anything better to say.

"I assure you that I am *not*," Mr. Browne told her in a tone that conveyed just how offended he was by her suggestion that he might actually consider joking about such a thing. "I take this matter quite seriously, and as you can see for yourself, it is really quite plain—"

"To see," Mary finished with a lengthy sigh as she stared down at the page to which Mr. Browne pointed. Sure enough, there was the indisputable bank statement valuing her father's assets at just over fifty thousand pounds, including a brief mention of his properties. At the very bottom of the page was a quickly scrawled note, identifying the members of the staff who were currently employed at the two locations.

Mary shook her head in quiet bewilderment. "Could I perhaps trouble you for a glass of water?" she asked as she sank back against her chair, her mind buzzing with an endless amount of questions that would in all likelihood never be answered. "Or better yet, make that a brandy."

Returning home from Oxford for the holidays, Ryan Summersby was comfortably seated in his father's landau as it swayed gently from side to side before taking a sharp turn onto Duke Street. He gazed out of the window as it continued on to Grosvenor Square, where it slowed to a steadier pace before finally coming to a complete halt outside a white brick town house that was separated from the pavement by a black, wrought iron fence. The coachman stepped down from his seat, hurrying around to the side to open the carriage door and set down the steps with speedy efficiency. A moment later, Ryan appeared. He handed his travel bag to the awaiting coachman and stepped down slowly, fully aware that his height might otherwise make him appear clumsy. Instead, he reached the ground with remarkable grace, his lips edging upward in a smile of boyish anticipation.

"Welcome home, sir," Hutchins remarked as he reached for Ryan's bags. The aging butler, who'd been with the Summersbys since Ryan's older brother, William, had been born, still maintained a youthful spring to his step.

"Thank you. It's good to be back," Ryan said as he started up the front steps of his father's London home. "Has Papa arrived yet?"

"No, not yet, but he should be here no later than tomorrow evening. He's just tying up a few loose ends back at Moorland—the usual business when he's planning on remaining in town for an extended length of time," Hutchins replied. "And your brother will most likely be unable to join you before next week at the earliest. He was recently called away on an urgent assignment, which I believe has taken him to Scotland. But there's a guest waiting for you in the drawing room. I won't say who, as I've no desire to spoil the surprise, though I'll wager you won't be too disappointed."

Ryan eyed the butler with a large degree of suspicion as he peeled off his calfskin gloves and handed them to Hutchins together with his hat. "What are you up to, old chap?"

"Oh, nothing but the usual," Hutchins told him, his face completely lacking any kind of emotion. Still, there was a twinkle in his wise old eyes. "Just keeping you on your toes, sir."

"Then by all means, carry on," Ryan told him cheerfully as he headed for the drawing room door.

It took him only a second to spot the man who was standing by one of the tall bay windows looking out onto the street as he waited patiently for Ryan to arrive. He was almost as tall as Ryan, though his frame was frailer. His hair, which had turned gray in the space of one week roughly six years earlier, had surprisingly enough retained its thickness. Turning his head away from the window at the sound of the door opening, a pair of light brown eyes came into view, creasing slightly at the corners as they locked onto Ryan.

"Sir Percy!" Ryan exclaimed, unable to hide his enthusiasm as he crossed the floor and reached out to shake the older gentleman's hand. "It's so good to see you again. By Jove it's been far too long."

"Almost a full year," Percy agreed, allowing his mouth to widen into a broad smile. "You look well, though. It does appear as if Oxford agrees with you."

"In some aspects, it certainly does," Ryan agreed with a lopsided smirk.

"And would that be the social aspects, by any chance?"

"You know me too well," Ryan replied. He sighed as he made his way across the room to the side table. "Can I perhaps offer you a glass of claret?"

"Certainly, but only if you'll join me."

Ryan curled his fingers around the cool neck of a crystal

carafe. "I do believe a drink might serve me well after suffering through all those bumps in the road for hours on end."

"Whatever excuse works for you," Percy quipped. "As far as I'm concerned, it's essential to my good health. In fact, I'm quite convinced it's what keeps me from knocking at death's door."

"I'll be sure to keep that in mind," Ryan said with a smile as he handed Percy his glass. He studied the man who'd always been like an uncle to him. Percy was one of his father's oldest and closest friends and if that wasn't enough, he was also the permanent secretary of the Foreign Office. It was unlikely that, with Ryan's father out of town, he would pay a visit for no other reason than to be sociable. Something was afoot; Ryan was certain of it.

"As glad as I am to see you again, Percy, I have the distinct feeling that you're not here to inquire about my health," Ryan said as he gestured toward one of two green silk-clad armchairs. "Please have a seat and tell me why you're really here."

Percy paused for a moment while the hint of a smile played upon his lips. He gave Ryan a short nod. "Very well then," he said as he sat down in the proffered chair and placed his glass on the small, round side table next to him. "I admit that I have an ulterior motive for coming here today."

"I am listening," Ryan told him with genuine interest as he sat down in the other chair and turned an expectant gaze on Percy.

"A number of years ago," Percy began, "I made a promise to an old friend that if anything were to happen to him, I'd keep a watchful eye on his daughter. Apparently, this friend of mine was under the impression that his daughter would be in some sort of terrible danger if anything did happen." A pensive look came over Percy's face. He paused, narrowing his eyes on Ryan. "As it happens, he passed away almost a year ago from a gunshot wound he sustained at Waterloo. From what I understand, he was hit by a stray bullet while attending to a wounded soldier—dratted business, really. He was a good man and an excellent surgeon, the best I've ever seen. Such an unfortunate and unnecessary loss.

"The funny thing is, in spite of my inquiries, there hasn't been the slightest trace of his daughter since then. I sent word out to a couple of agents who were already stationed in Belgium at the time, but they were unable to find her. It almost seemed as though she'd evaporated into thin air—until yesterday, that is, when she finally resurfaced right here in Mayfair after a two-year absence from England." Percy paused for emphasis as his eyes met Ryan's. "I was hoping I might be able to convince you to assist in this matter."

"You do realize I no longer work for the Foreign Office, right?"

"First of all, if this were an official matter, it wouldn't be handled by the Foreign Office. The Home Office would take care of it. And second of all, this is a private matter regarding a promise I'm honor bound to keep. I'd like for it to remain classified."

"You're leaving me with very little choice here, Percy," Ryan argued. "I was hoping to sow some oats this summer, perhaps even attend a few mandatory balls if I have to. What you're suggesting hardly sounds like any fun at all."

"Oh, do stop complaining, Ryan," Percy told him fiercely. "I'll wager you've sown a whole granary full of oats by now—

enough, at any rate, for you to wait a while before jumping into bed with the next actress who comes along. Damn it, boy, I'm asking you for a personal favor here."

"Very well then," Ryan said, still lacking any enthusiasm for this unexpected venture. "What's the chit's name? And more importantly, who is she?"

Percy took another sip of his claret. A slow smile began to spread its way across his face. There was an impish gleam in his eyes as he turned his gaze on Ryan. "I'd be careful about calling her a chit if I were you," he said. "After all, being the Marchioness of Steepleton, she *is* a couple of steps above you on the social ladder. And to answer your question, her name is Mary Croyden."

Ryan stared at Percy with the very unpleasant feeling that he'd just been had. He should have known that Percy would keep an ace like this up his sleeve until he'd already agreed to help. If there was one thing Percy loved, it was the element of surprise. But Ryan was not about to be played the fool, especially when he very much doubted that the Marchioness of Steepleton was even a real title. "How on earth is that even possible?" he asked dubiously.

"Do I really have to explain it to you, Ryan? I would have thought that your father might have seen to the matter by now."

Ryan groaned. "You know perfectly well what I mean, Percy. I've never heard of a Marquess of Steepleton, and now there's suddenly a marchioness? Forgive me if I'm reluctant to believe such a thing, but it hardly makes much sense."

"Hm. . .I suppose you're right. You see, here's the thing of it: the title went into obscurity for a number of years through lack of usage. For whatever reason he might have had, Lady Steepleton's father was determined to make his own way in life, as far away from the social constraints of the upper classes as humanly possible. All the same, he did manage to ensure that his daughter would one day inherit the title from him.

"The point is, if he believed her to be in danger, for whatever reasons he might have had, then she's more likely to be so now that she's returned to London and claimed her inheritance. The sudden appearance of a marchioness is going to make the headline in every gossip column this country has to offer. If someone's out to get her, they'll be crawling out of the woodwork before you know it, mark my word."

Ryan nodded thoughtfully. Perhaps this wouldn't be so boring after all, he mused. He rather liked the image he envisioned of himself dodging bullets as he saved the marchioness from imminent danger. There might even be a swordfight or two, perhaps a race across the countryside at breakneck speed while a group of ruffians chased after them and. . .He suddenly blinked when he heard Percy's voice practically yelling at him.

"Ryan? Are you even listening to what I'm saying?"

"Hm? Oh, I was just wondering how I might best handle the matter."

"Yes, I'm sure you were," Percy told him with a frown. "You need not worry yourself about that, however. I will ensure that Lady Steepleton receives an invitation to the first ball of the season, which happens to be this Saturday evening at Richmond House, by the way. As charming as you are, I'm confident you'll have no trouble at all in befriending her."

"And once I find her, may I tell her why I suddenly have such a keen interest in her?"

"Ryan, you and I both know that women hate the feeling of being watched, even if it is for their own good. If she so much as suspects that your interest in her lies only in protecting her from supposed harm, she'll most likely make it her mission in life to avoid you for the remainder of her days."

"I see your point," Ryan muttered as he mulled that over.

"You're a handsome lad, Ryan. Surely it won't be impossible for you to convince her that you are genuinely interested."

"But I'm not," Ryan said with a frown. "Am I to understand that you wish for me to give this woman a false impression of my true intentions?"

"It is for her own good, you know," Percy remarked.

"Look, you know how much I despise dishonesty, Percy, and to take advantage of any woman's desire to form an attachment just feels wrong."

"Well, I hate to break it to you, Ryan, but spying is a pretty dishonest business."

"Must you always mock me?" The frustration in Ryan's voice was practically scratching at the walls. "Fine; if it will keep her alive, then I'll agree to do whatever it takes—though I'm by no means pleased about it, I'll have you know."

"I am so happy to hear it," Percy remarked rather drily as he drained his glass of its last few drops before jumping to his feet. He looked eager to be gone, no doubt before Ryan changed his mind. "I'll see to it you get an invitation to Richmond House as well then, shall I?"

"That would certainly be an excellent idea," Ryan replied,

his words dripping with sarcasm as he walked his father's friend to the door.

"Listen," Percy said, turning back around on the threshold and placing a solid hand on Ryan's shoulder, "I know this isn't exactly the sort of thing you want to get tangled up in right now, so I appreciate your help."

Ryan nodded. "It's my pleasure."

"Oh, I hardly think so," Percy chuckled, turning about and starting down the steps that led toward the pavement. "But thank you for saying so."

Ryan remained in the doorway a moment longer until Percy had hailed himself a hackney and climbed in. Well, perhaps he ought to ask Hutchins to press one of his black tailcoats. After all, he now had a marchioness to impress.

Chapter Two

Mary stood at the edge of the wide marble terrace behind Richmond House, looking out over the garden and enjoying the feel of the cool night air as it wafted against her skin. She'd gone out there to escape the oppressive heat of the ballroom, which she imagined to be far worse than in the hottest of the British colonies. But to be perfectly honest, the stifling heat was not her only reason. She'd also come outside to escape the hoard of overly eager gentlemen who, it seemed, had swooped down upon her like vultures the moment she'd made her entrance. Each of them wanted to dance with her, or if not dance, then at least bring her something to drink or eat—anything at all that she might be in need of. One gentleman had even offered to bring her an ice from Gunter's in Berkeley Square, declaring that it wouldn't be any trouble at all and that she'd be sure to find it refreshing. Before Mary had managed to speak a single word to anyone, she was juggling three glasses of Champagne and a plate piled high with canapés.

Then, of course, there were all the unmarried ladies who,

feeling threatened by the overwhelming amount of interest the men were showing the new marchioness, had begun their critical dissection of her. They had started at the top of her head and worked their way down to her shoes, conveying each of their opinions to one another in a low whisper that had snaked its way around the room. Apparently they'd concluded that her hair was the color of mud, her eyes the size of teacups, and her mouth too vulgar to appear in polite society, while her figure bore too much resemblance to an upside down pear. And if that weren't enough, the word *plain* was mentioned so repeatedly and with such a degree of intonation that Mary couldn't help but feel herself the most flawed woman in the whole wide world.

The worst of it was that she'd been looking forward to this evening ever since both her housekeeper, Mrs. Hodges, and her maid, Emma, had told her how vital it was to her social standing that she make an appearance at the first ball of the season. She'd initially thought to shy away at home, but when the two women had insisted, she'd decided to trust their judgment.

Once it had been decided that she would attend, she and Emma had truly enjoyed shopping for just the right dress to wear to the occasion. They'd found a small shop on Bond Street, where Mary had settled upon a white muslin gown with a yellow ribbon running just below the bustline. It wasn't the most extravagant dress perhaps, but Mary felt that it suited her quite well. She hadn't felt at all plain in it when she'd admired herself in the mirror earlier that evening; it was a very refreshing change from the mourning colors she'd been wearing since her father had died. In fact, she'd actually

SOPHIE BARNES

felt rather regal. But the evening wasn't turning out the way
she'd envisioned it. Instead of making a few friends as she
had hoped, she was now standing by herself on the terrace,
terrified of going back inside. In truth, all she wanted to do
right now was flee.

*Perhaps I ought to jump the garden wall and make a run for
it*, she thought wistfully, eyeing the eight-foot-high, ivy-clad
barrier. Taking her own height into consideration, she decided that she would definitely need some assistance—a table
to stand on perhaps, or even a bench. She was so busy considering how she might accomplish this great escape of hers that
the sudden sound of a low male voice saying "May I join you?"
from behind her right shoulder completely startled her.

She literally leaped into the air, her right arm rising of
its own accord as she spun around, so fast that she couldn't
stop her hand from making contact with the man behind her.
With a loud thwack it slapped across his face.

"Good Lord!" the man exclaimed as he rubbed his cheek
with his hand. "Do you make a habit out of striking people
with whom you are not even acquainted?"

Mary stared at him, openmouthed and paralyzed. Not
only was he the most handsome man she'd ever laid eyes on,
with his light brown hair, chiseled jawline, patrician nose, and
the bluest eyes imaginable, he was also quite possibly the tall-
est. And his shoulders. . .good God, she'd never thought it
possible for anyone to have such broad shoulders. "I. . .I. . ."
she stammered.

Oh, for heaven's sake.

She squeezed her eyes shut. It was just an accident, nothing more. All she had to do was apologize to the poor man.

Besides, if he hadn't snuck up on her like that, it very likely wouldn't have happened.

"This is all your fault," she said before she could stop herself. Her hand flew to cover her mouth. Had she really said that out loud?

"I beg your pardon?" the man asked, clearly as stunned as she. "Did you really just blame me for getting in the way of your hand?"

"When you put it like that. . ." She bit her lip and paused for a moment. "I apologize for hitting you, but if you would only have made your presence known a bit sooner, I very much doubt that this would have happened."

"I see," the man said, taking on a look of serious contemplation. "Then it seems that I must apologize to you for being so inconsiderate. Perhaps I ought to introduce myself while I am at it. My name is Ryan Summersby."

"Ah, yes," Mary remarked as she nodded knowingly. "The man who is forever getting in the way of flailing limbs."

He grinned. "The one and only."

"And what exactly do you do when you are *not* getting in the way of someone's hand, my. . .lord?"

Could I possibly sound more ridiculous?

She didn't even know how to address this Ryan Summersby person. To top it off, she was jabbering on about nonsensical rubbish. He must think her a complete twit. At least he was laughing, which must mean that he found her remarks somewhat amusing—unless, of course, he was laughing *at* her. She let out a lengthy sigh. Life had been so much easier and far less complicated in the middle classes.

The gentleman paused for a moment and regarded her.

Then he said, "I have been studying medicine for the past year at Oxford. And since I am the Earl of Moorland's second son, I fear that you are incorrect in your form of address, though I am flattered. You see, I am merely Mr. Summersby. My older brother, William, enjoys the title of lord. However, I do hope that you will one day call me Ryan."

Mary felt the heat rise in her cheeks. She'd never been one to blush, yet she was certain that she was turning bright red at that very moment.

Is he flirting with me?

She had no experience with such things at all and as a result could not be at all sure, though it did feel as though he might be. After all, the only reason she could think of for a man like Mr. Summersby to one day expect her to address him so cordially would be if they'd been spending a lot of time together. And the only reason they might do that would be if. . .

"Sir, you overstep yourself," she practically gasped, as if he'd just attempted to touch her inappropriately.

"Have I offended you in some way?" he asked with a note of sincerity that would have melted the arctic tundra.

"Not yet," Mary whispered as she tried to still the erratic pounding of her heart. "But before you jump to any conclusions about me, I must warn you that I am *not* trying to snag a husband."

Mr. Summersby stared at her in a bewildered sort of way before finally erupting into a fit of laughter. "My dear woman, I was merely suggesting that you and I might one day be friends, and all my friends call me Ryan. I know it's unconventional, but I insist upon it.

"One brief conversation on a terrace—as entertaining as it might be—is hardly enough to merit a courtship, you know. Trust me, you mustn't worry yourself about that."

"Oh," Mary muttered, feeling quite embarrassed and perhaps even a little disappointed. "I am terribly sorry, I—"

"No need to apologize. The truth of the matter is that I have very much enjoyed talking to you and that I hope to see you again one day. After all, it seems to me that we have at least one thing in common."

"And what might that be?" Mary asked, relaxing now that the threat of Mr. Summersby's advances had been removed.

"I believe that we both abhor these sorts of events and that we both decided to come out here to get away from it all."

"I was actually rather looking forward to it," Mary admitted. "Though I must say that it is not at all what I had expected."

"And what did you expect?" Mr. Summersby asked, moving up beside her.

"That people would be nicer," she said simply, staring off into the garden, where lanterns flickered close to the ground, illuminating the pathways.

Mr. Summersby chuckled. "They can be quite rude, can't they?"

"Surprisingly so."

"And because of that, you were wondering if you might be able to make the jump?"

"The jump?"

"Over the garden wall," he said, his voice was quite serious. "Though I do not imagine that you would get far, judging from your height."

"And what, pray tell, is wrong with my height?" she asked, vexed that he'd seen right through her, and even more annoyed that he'd touched on the greatest flaw in her plan.

"Nothing at all," he muttered. He was quiet for a moment before saying, "I can give you a foot up if you like."

Mary turned her head to stare at him. She expected him to be grinning from ear to ear, yet he just stood there with a rather solemn expression on his face, as if he were contemplating how high he would have to lift her. "However, I would much prefer it if you would remain here, since I should detest to be left alone."

"And why is that?" Mary asked, turning toward him and placing both hands on her hips.

"Because the minute that I am not otherwise occupied, one of the anxious mamas in there will drag her unmarried daughter before me like a prize cow. I shall have no choice but to endure an account of all the daughter's very fine attributes, and I shall have to do so with a smile upon my face."

He was so grave that Mary couldn't help but pity him. Still, it was difficult not to laugh at the image he'd managed to conjure in her mind. "Sounds awful," she said, making a stoic attempt at holding back the giggles that were cramming together in her throat.

He frowned. "Yes, I can clearly see that you think it is."

"Sorry," she gasped as the first roll of laughter escaped her. There was nothing she could do about it, and before she knew it, she was grinning like a complete lunatic—far too exaggeratedly to merit the humor in what he had said.

"Dear me," she remarked, wiping her eyes with the back of her hand. "You must forgive me. I am generally not at all like this."

"And yet I would hope that you are," Mr. Summersby told her. "The ladies of the *ton* do not generally engage in laughter, you see, and when they do, it is somewhat forced—no real joy lies behind it."

"Hm. . .I see," Mary said, her forehead creasing ever so slightly. "By the way, how long do you suppose we can remain out here before it is considered rude or, even worse, inappropriate?"

"I believe ten minutes might be acceptable."

"Then I think I must consider venturing back inside, for it must surely have been twenty by now, and I should hate for my hosts to think that I am not enjoying myself."

"You are not," Mr. Summersby pointed out.

"No, I am not, or at least I was not until. . ." With no desire to give him the wrong idea, she chose not to finish that sentence, finishing instead with a firm "All the same."

"Very well then," he agreed, pinning her with a solemn stare. "But first things first: I believe it would be rude of me to let you leave without at least asking you to dance. Besides, it would be rather shameful not to make use of all this space." He swept his arm in a wide arc to indicate the vast emptiness of the terrace.

In truth, there was nothing that Mary would have liked more, if she had only known how. Nobody had ever taken the time to teach her how to dance; there simply hadn't been a need for it. She'd seen the ladies inside the ballroom, though, twirling elegantly about as if floating on air while their partners guided them about. And now, as her eyes flittered over Mr. Summersby, taking in the solid strength of him, she simply couldn't help but wonder what it might be like to have him dance with her in such a way.

Before she could manage a response, however, he'd taken her hand in his and led her to the middle of the terrace. "Imagine that—I hear a waltz starting," he said with a cheeky grin as he pulled her toward him.

Her breath caught, and her stomach became a tight knot at the feel of his hand clasped firmly about her waist. She'd thought it strange when her maid had suggested that she get permission to dance the waltz, but this was no longer the case, for her vicinity to Mr. Summersby could only be described as scandalous. He was so close to her that she could breathe in his scent. It was like that of moist morning air after a storm, so intoxicatingly masculine that her sudden desire to be near him outweighed her fear of making a complete cake of herself—which was precisely what she ended up doing the minute he tried twirling her into his arms. For whatever reason, her feet refused to cooperate. Instead, they twisted themselves about one another most awkwardly, which was enough to make her trip on the hem of her gown, propelling her straight forward with an alarming amount of speed until her face slammed right into Mr. Summersby's chest with a thump. It hurt like blazes.

Mary didn't move. She couldn't move, because if she did, she was confident that once she lifted her head, she'd find him laughing at her, and that wasn't something that she was prepared to endure just yet. What she silently prayed for was a means by which to avoid having to look at him ever again. If she could only find a way in which to freeze time forever and thus avoid the humiliation entirely.

The touch of his fingers against her chin brought her hurtling back from her daydream. They nudged her gently as if trying to ease her away, but she held fast, squeezing her eyes tightly shut while hot waves of embarrassment flowed toward her cheeks. "You cannot stay like this forever, you know," he told her softly, then added, "I promise not to tell anyone."

A mere squeak was all that escaped her lips at that remark. Who cared if anyone else might discover that she had two left feet when the most handsome man in all of Christendom had just had a front row seat to her complete lack of elegance? But his hands were on her shoulders now, and with a little push, he managed to add a little space between them.

Taking courage, she slowly opened her eyes, discovering that not only was he not laughing at her, he was watching her with what could only be described as a great deal of concern. "Are you all right?" he asked.

Of course she wasn't all right—she was completely mortified, if anything, but she'd never been a coward either, so, straightening her back and looking him squarely in the eye, she nodded and said, "Yes, thank you. I am perfectly fine."

"Good." He reached for her hand once more and gave it a slight squeeze. "Now then, how about if we try that again?"

She was about to protest, but the sharp look of determination in his eyes stopped her. Besides, it was highly unlikely that she would ever be presented with such an opportunity again, so she might as well make the most of it. "Very well," she said. "Though I would greatly appreciate it if we could perhaps move at a more leisurely pace."

For a brief moment they just stood there, staring at each other. Then something indecipherable flickered behind Mr. Summersby's eyes, and Mary was left with the distinct feeling that he was doing his utmost to refrain from laughing. With a quick nod, he agreed to her suggestion, then carefully pulled her back into his arms. She remained upright this time, to her great relief, and soon discovered that all she had to do was follow him wherever he happened to lead her. What could possibly be more simple than that? All right, her posture wasn't exactly perfect, and her steps were occasionally too wide or too narrow, but by God it was a long time since she'd had this much fun.

With practiced ease, he guided her slowly about the terrace, picking up speed so gradually that Mary never even noticed how fast they were going. She loosened up, forgot herself, and, throwing her head back with careless abandon, laughed with joy as they twirled about to the strains of music that drifted through an open window. It faded much sooner than she would have hoped, forcing their pace to slow until they were once more quite still.

"Thank you," Mr. Summersby told her, offering her a slight bow.

Mary smiled broadly. "I do believe that it is I who should thank you," she replied in a breathless voice as she gazed up at him with her big brown eyes. "You have been quite the gentleman, for which I am truly grateful."

Mr. Summersby paused for a moment before releasing her. He looked as though he was pondering something. "It occurs to me that you know my name, but I have no idea of yours. Would you perhaps be so kind as to tell me whose company I have had the pleasure of enjoying this evening?"

Mary stepped back. Had she really forgotten to introduce herself? Was it possible that Mr. Summersby really didn't know who she was? She suddenly dreaded having to tell him.

She'd enjoyed spending time with him, had even considered the possibility of seeing him again, but once he knew her true identity, he'd probably treat her no differently than all the other gentlemen had done: like a grand pile of treasure with which to pay off his debts and house his mistresses. And who could blame him? He'd already admitted that he was a second son and thus unlikely to be able to rely on an inheritance to sustain the high standards of living he'd undoubtedly acquired as a member of the upper class. Nevertheless, in spite of her own misgivings, he'd been nothing but pleasant toward her, and because of that, she honestly felt that she owed him the truth.

Squaring her shoulders and straightening her spine, she mustered all her courage and turned a serious gaze upon him. "My name is Mary Croyden, and I am the Marchioness of Steepleton." Ryan's response was instantaneous. His mouth dropped open, allowing for a clear view of the back of his throat, while his eyes widened in complete and utter disbelief. He stared at the slender woman who stood before him, doing her best to play the part of a peeress. Was it really possible that she was the very marchioness he'd been looking for when he'd stepped outside for some fresh air only a half hour earlier? The very same one that Percy had asked him to protect? She seemed much too young for such a title, too unpolished and far too simple. It wasn't that he found her unattractive in any way, though he had thought her plain at first glance. No, she merely didn't have that air of prestige about her that all the typical duchesses, marchionesses, and countesses oozed from their very pores.

"What?" she asked with a large degree of annoyance as she

crossed her arms and cocked an eyebrow. "Not what you expected the infamous Marchioness of Steepleton to look like?"

"Not exactly, no," he admitted. "You are just not—"

"Not what? Not pretty enough? Not sophisticated enough? Or is it perhaps the way in which I speak that fails to equate with your ill-conceived notion of what a marchioness ought to sound like?" He had no chance to reply before she said, "Well, you do not exactly strike me as a stereotypical medical student either."

"And just what exactly would you know about that?" he asked, a little put out by her sudden verbal attack.

"Enough," she remarked in a rather clipped tone. "My father was a skilled physician. I know the sort of man it takes to fill such a position, and you, sir, do not fit the bill."

For the first time in his life, Ryan Summersby found himself at a complete loss for words. Not only could he not comprehend that this slip of a woman before him, appearing to be barely out of the schoolroom, was a peeress in her own right, not to mention a woman of extreme wealth. But that she was actually standing there fearlessly scolding him with such vigor. . .He knew that a sane person would be offended, yet he couldn't help but be enthralled.

In addition, he'd managed to glimpse a side of her that he very much doubted few people had ever seen. "You do not think too highly of yourself, do you?" he suddenly asked.

That brought her up short. "I have no idea what you could possibly mean by that," she told him defensively.

"Well, you assume that I do not believe you to be who you say you are. Next, you think the reasoning behind my not believing you might have something to do with the way you look. Finally, you feel the need to assert yourself by finding fault with me, for which I must commend you, since I do not have very many faults at all."

"You arrogant. . ." The marchioness wisely clamped her mouth shut before uttering something that she would be bound to regret. Instead, she turned away and walked toward the French doors that led toward the ballroom. "Thank you for the dance, Mr. Summersby. I hope you enjoy the rest of your evening," she called over her shoulder in an obvious attempt at sounding dignified.

"May I call on you sometime?" he asked, ignoring her abrupt dismissal of him as he thought of the task that Percy had given him. It really wouldn't do for him to muck things up so early in the game. Besides, he wasn't sure he'd ever met a woman who interested him more than Lady Steepleton did at that very moment. He had to admit that the woman had character.

She paused in the middle of her exit, turned slightly, and looked him dead in the eye. "You most certainly may not, Mr. Summersby." And before Ryan had a chance to dispute the matter, she had vanished back inside, the white cotton of her gown twirling about her feet.

CHAPTER THREE

"**A** letter arrived for you no more than a half hour ago, my lady," Mary's butler, Thornton, told her as she handed him her cloak.

Mary spotted the white envelope immediately. It was lying on the silver tray that Thornton always used when delivering the mail. She picked it up and turned it over in her hand. It was completely blank, save for a burgundy wax seal with a smudged insignia stamped into it. Mary frowned as she tore open the envelope, removed the letter, and silently read:

> It has been brought to my attention that you have returned. As it happens, I am in desperate need of your immediate assistance. Please come to the following address as soon as you can.
>
> Yours,
> H

Mary stared down at the piece of paper, mesmerized by its contents. She suddenly snapped to attention. "There is not a single moment to lose, Thornton. Have my horse brought around immediately," she said tersely as she started toward the stairs.

Thornton didn't move. "You are going out again, my lady? At this late hour?" He wore an unmistakable look of disapproval. "Do you think that is wise?"

Mary scowled at him. "Please do not question me, Thornton. I am in a great hurry."

"Very well, my lady." Thornton gave a short bow before setting about his task.

"Oh, and Thornton?" Mary called after him.

"Yes, my lady?"

"I shall be riding astride."

The poor butler looked as if she might as well have slapped him. For a moment it seemed as if he would say something, but he just nodded sheepishly and replied, "Very well, my lady."

Confident of Thornton's dependability, Mary practically flew up the stairs to her bedroom, where she found Emma asleep in a chair. She regretted having to wake her, but she knew she'd never manage to get out of her gown on her own.

"Emma," she said softly as she walked across to the large trunk that stood propped against the wall. Emma snorted slightly in her sleep, turning her head as her mouth opened on a long sigh.

Mary lifted the heavy lid of the trunk. "Emma!" she said again, this time louder. Emma groaned in apparent annoyance as she shifted her whole body in the chair, snuggling back against the headrest.

Oh, for heaven's sake.

"Wake up Emma!" Mary finally exclaimed in a louder voice than she'd intended.

Emma's eyes sprang open. The befuddled maid jumped to her feet as if someone had just jabbed her with a fireplace poker. "I am so sorry, my lady," she managed to say. "I must have dozed off."

"It is quite all right. In truth, I did not expect to return so early. However, I do need your help right away. Would you please unbutton my dress for me?"

"Certainly, my lady." Moving to stand behind her mistress, Emma went to work on the tiny buttons immediately. "Did you have a pleasant evening?"

"I will tell you all about it later, Emma, but right now I am running terribly late."

"You are going out again?" She sounded only a tad bit less appalled than Thornton.

"Yes," Mary replied without elaborating on why or where she might be off to. "Emma?" she then asked in a very serious tone. "Have you ever tied a cravat before?"

Emma paused for a moment as if wondering whether or not this might be a test of some sort. "Only once or twice when my brother asked me to," she replied, opting for an honest response as she pushed the last button through the tight buttonhole. "There," she said. "All done."

"Good." Mary stepped quickly out of her dress and hurried back over to the trunk. She began pulling out a variety of clothes, all of them in somber tones of brown and gray. Removing her petticoat and chemise, she stepped deftly into a pair of tight breeches while Emma looked on in horror, her face growing paler by the second.

"My lady. . .this really is not very. . .ahem. . .appropriate. You cannot possibly mean to leave the house dressed like. . .like that," Emma stammered.

"That is precisely what I mean to do. Now, hand me that shirt over there." She pointed to a rumpled piece of white fabric that lay bunched together on the floor. With just enough hesitation to mark her disapproval, Emma did as she was told.

"I suppose I ought to ready myself as well," Emma said as she handed Mary the shirt.

"No need, Emma; I'm going alone."

"But. . .but. . .but. . ." Emma looked clearly perplexed. "You can't!"

"I can and I will." Mary gave Emma a hard stare. "More importantly, I must."

"Consider your reputation, my lady, and your safety. Whatever this urgent matter might be, I would never forgive myself if anything were to happen to you."

Mary couldn't help but smile at Emma's loyalty. "I appreciate your concern, but this is something that I must do alone." The hapless maid looked ready to protest yet again. "Please trust me, Emma. You can lecture me as much as you like when I return."

"You may count on it, my lady," Emma responded, her eyes filled with worry. But she must have understood that time was of the essence, because she didn't dally any further. Instead, she quickly sprang to assistance, helping her mistress prepare for this mad endeavor.

Rummaging through the trunk for Mary's boots, Emma retrieved them just as Mary finished buttoning up her shirt. Having squeezed her mistress into the tight pair of brown Hessians, Emma made short work of tying the most solemn cravat that Mary had ever seen. "Good Lord, Emma! Is your brother perhaps a cleric?"

"Yes," Emma replied, sounding somewhat surprised by the question. "He is a rector. How did you know?"

"Just a hunch," Mary said and grinned. She patted Emma affectionately on the arm and looked about the room with a searching eye. "Now, where on earth is my hat?"

"Right here," Emma told her, handing her a conical riding hat that had once belonged to Mary's father. She eyed it skeptically. "Not exactly de rigueur, is it?"

"It does not have to be," Mary replied. "It just has to hide my hair, that is all."

Five minutes later, she was running down the front steps of her house, grabbing the reins of a gray-speckled mare from a startled groom, and climbing nimbly into the saddle with the confidence of someone who was not a stranger to riding. She kicked her heels against the horse's flanks, spurring him toward Bedford Square.

Ryan watched from beyond the shadows, uncertain of whether to follow the young man who'd just ridden off or remain behind and watch the house instead. What on earth was Lady Steepleton up to?

The soft rustling of fabric being teased by the breeze, accompanied by the precise click of approaching footsteps, caught his attention. He turned to find a cloaked figure, dressed entirely in black from head to toe, striding toward him with long, even steps. A hood was pulled down over his head, and over his mouth and nose he wore a black scarf, concealing his most prominent features entirely from view.

"What do you want?" Ryan asked in a confident tone, his

fingers curling firmly around the smooth metal of the pistol he held concealed in his pocket.

The stranger chuckled ever so slightly at the question, but it was enough to send a chill down Ryan's spine. "That very much depends on what your little friend wants."

"Explain yourself, sir," Ryan demanded, his voice conveying the tone of a man who was not to be trifled with.

There was another eerie chuckle. "Am I to understand that you, Mr. Summersby, the very man who has been sent to protect the marchioness, has no idea of why she might be in trouble?"

"I do not suppose that you are about to enlighten me," Ryan said. He tightened his grip on his pistol while his eyes bored into the stranger's with enough vehemence to make Lucifer shudder.

But the stranger seemed not to notice. "I would not dream of spoiling the fun for you," he replied. There was a slight pause. "But know this: if she starts looking for answers to questions that do not concern her or investigating matters that ought to be left untouched, then there *are* those who will seek to silence her."

Ryan could scarcely believe he was having this conversation. Mary, the plain, simple woman he'd met only a couple of hours earlier, had just been threatened on her life. "Are you one of them?" Ryan asked, contemplating whether or not he should just kill the man and be done with it.

"I am merely the Messenger," the man said as he bowed before Ryan in an exaggerated show of reverence, twirling his arm as he did so, his head almost reaching as low as his knees before he straightened himself again. Offering another slight chuckle, he then turned on his heel and strode away, calling over his shoulder, "Keep a watchful eye on her, Summersby, and all will be well."

Running a shaky hand through his hair, Ryan stared off into the darkness at the space where the figure had just stood. There was nothing but emptiness now. He dropped his hands to his sides and threw another glance in the direction of her ladyship's front door. Clearly, this whole situation was far more involved than he would ever have thought imaginable.

CHAPTER FOUR

"I must say that you look very pretty tonight, my lady. The cut of your gown is most flattering, and the emeralds look absolutely marvelous; they really bring out the green in your eyes."

Rosemary Dorset, the Viscountess of Arlington, gazed at herself in the full-length mirror and then glanced across at her maid. "Thank you, Lucy. It is entirely your doing, you know." She touched her hand against her forehead. Now, if only the unbearable headache that had been bothering her all day would go away so that she might be able to enjoy the evening with her husband. True, it would be only the two of them, but with his busy schedule, she always looked forward to their time together.

Lucy smiled at the compliment. "You are too kind, my lady," she said as she handed Rosemary her favorite bottle of perfume.

Rosemary reached for it, her hand closing tightly around the cold glass, just as a sharp pain tore through her midsection. She let out a quick gasp, squeezing her eyes together and pressing her hand against her belly as she doubled over in pain.

"My lady!" Lucy exclaimed, wrapping an arm about her mistress for support.

"Call my husband, Lucy, and hurry," Rosemary groaned as she sank onto her bedroom floor, tears welling in her startled eyes. "And tell Firth to send for Dr. Helmsley. I think the baby must be on its way."

It took less than an hour for Helmsley to arrive at the Arlington residence. He was greeted there by Lady Arlington's terrified husband. "Thank God you are here, Doctor. I have no idea what to do. I. . .She is not making any sense, and. . .oh God. . .help her, please help her!"

Helmsley took a firm grip of the viscount's lapels. "My lord, I know that this must be an extremely frightening experience for you, but you must get a hold of yourself; the servants are beginning to stare. Remember, you are the captain, and this is your ship. You will get through this storm one way or another."

Lord Arlington nodded in understanding. Having captained many an oceangoing vessel, Helmsley hoped his words would have the necessary effect. It seemed they did, for the viscount immediately transformed into a man of command, straightening his spine and rising to his full height of just over six feet. "This way, if you please," he said, leading Helmsley up the steep stairs that would take them to Lady Arlington's bedroom. Neither man spoke a word, the only sound being that of their feet treading softly upon the plush runner and the occasional scrape of Lord Arlington's wedding band as it rubbed against the banister.

As soon as he entered her ladyship's bedroom, Helmsley's throat tightened at what he saw. There, in the middle of her imposing canopy bed, her hair spread out about her head, lay the viscountess. She tossed her head jerkily from side to side, her eyes in constant motion as if they were searching for something. Her maid sat by her side, holding her hand in the hope of giving her mistress some small measure of comfort. Occasionally she would take a damp cloth and wipe the beads of sweat that were presently forming on her mistress's brow. "You must help her," the maid pleaded with a glimmer of hope in her eyes.

Helmsley steeled himself as he moved toward the bed, setting his bag on a nearby chair. "My lady?" he asked cautiously. "Can you hear me? I need for you to tell me how you are feeling—if you can."

A few seconds crept by before Lady Arlington's head stopped moving, her gaze suddenly fixed upon Helmsley. She looked momentarily confused. "I had no idea that there were two of you, Doctor. You must introduce me to your twin. Are you a doctor as well?" she asked, addressing the man only she could see.

Helmsley picked up a book that was lying on the bedside table and held it up before her. "How many books am I holding?" he asked.

"Two," she replied. "Though they do appear to be a bit fuzzy around the edges."

"And does it hurt anywhere?"

"Every now and again I feel an unbearable pain in my belly, almost as if. . ." She didn't manage to complete her sentence before a blank look captured her face. Her eyes stared off into the distance, as if she were deep in thought.

"My lady?" Helmsley asked in an urgent voice, though he knew he wouldn't get a response. With no time to lose, he grabbed the book he'd been holding a moment earlier and jammed it into her mouth, just as her eyelids began to flutter. A second later, her eyes rolled back into her head, displaying only the whites, and her whole body began to convulse.

With both his lordship's and the frightened maid's help, they managed to hold her down until the spasms subsided. This was as bad as it got, Helmsley knew. Lady Arlington was eight and a half months pregnant with puerperal eclampsia, and he did not have the surgical experience required to save her or her child. There was only one thing for it: he needed help.

"My lord?" he said, turning to Lord Arlington. "A word if I may."

Although he was clearly uncertain about leaving his wife at such a moment, the viscount nodded his head and instructed the maid to call for help if she needed. He then followed Helmsley out into the hallway. "Will she die?" he asked with a note of anguish.

"There is a very real possibility that she might," Helmsley told him honestly. "Her condition is quite severe, and we are really not left with very many options, I am afraid."

"But there are options?" Lord Arlington asked hopefully.

"I cannot promise anything, but if you are willing to keep an open mind, then perhaps there might be one solution."

Lord Arlington turned a sharp gaze on Helmsley. "Do whatever you can. My mind is open to anything as far as my wife's and child's safety is concerned."

"Very well, my lord. Then I will send for someone to help us without further delay."

Mary burst into Lady Arlington's bedroom like a jack popping out of its box. "I came as soon as I could," she gasped, hurrying over to the bedside. She met Helmsley's gaze. "It is so good to see you again," she told him with a tight smile.

"You too," Helmsley replied, "though I do wish that it had been under different circumstances."

Lord Arlington looked not only shocked but extremely distressed. He addressed Helmsley in a clipped voice. "You brought a woman here to save my wife? *That* is your solution?"

"She is the best surgeon there is," Helmsley told him defensively. "I know how unorthodox this is, but you need to trust my decision if you want your wife and child to live."

The annoyance on the viscount's face was quite apparent. "What are you planning to do?" he asked Mary irritably.

Ignoring the frustrated viscount, Mary turned toward Helmsley instead. "What is your assessment of the patient, Doctor?"

"That she is showing severe signs of puerperal eclampsia. She has complained of abdominal pains and has had four seizures since I arrived on the scene roughly three hours ago."

Mary nodded thoughtfully as she looked over her ladyship's fragile body, noting the swelling that had occurred in both her wrists and ankles. "Can you confirm these seizures?" she asked Lord Arlington.

He nodded as if in a daze.

"Here is what we are going to do," she said in a sharp

tone of authority. She looked across at the maid, who was still clutching her mistress's hand. "I will need a clean white sheet, a pot of boiling water, and plenty of towels. Have it all brought into the kitchen. Go."

The young woman didn't miss a beat. Jumping to her feet, she ran out of the door to set about her task as quickly as she could manage, visibly relieved to finally be of some assistance.

"Now then," Mary continued, turning her attention back to Lord Arlington, "we are going to have to move her downstairs to the kitchen. And to answer your question, I intend to give your wife a cesarean. Do I have your consent?"

"I. . .er. . .a cesarean?" Lord Arlington muttered, looking more confused than ever.

Mary sympathized, knowing full well that the speed with which she'd taken hold of the wheel must have completely thrown him. However, they had to hurry. She opted for complete honesty. "To put it bluntly, my lord, I will have to cut your wife open just below the navel, remove the child, then stitch her back up again. If all goes well, she and the baby will both survive."

Lord Arlington stared at Mary with a look of unsurpassed horror. He began to shake his head, slowly at first and then with more vigor. "No," he said. "Absolutely not." He turned on Helmsley in anger. "What kind of a doctor are you? To bring a. . .a woman into my house who plans to. . .to cut open my wife like a butcher? No, I tell you, I will not allow it!" He was shaking.

Mary had expected this reaction Taking a deep breath to calm her own ragged nerves, she placed a soothing hand on Lord Arlington's arm. "I understand your distress, but you have to understand that this is the only chance your wife has of survival. If I do not perform the procedure, she will die."

"And you are sure of this?" His eyes were wide with fear and worry. "Absolutely and undeniably sure?"

"Yes," she said.

He let out an anguished sigh. His shoulders slumped as if he'd just accepted an unacceptable defeat. "And is this something that you have done before?" he asked her hesitantly.

Mary studied him for a brief moment. She'd watched her father do it once, but she'd never actually had the opportunity to do it herself. Of course, there was the possibility that Lady Arlington might not live through the surgery, but Mary knew that her chances of survival were nonexistent if she didn't go ahead with it. It had to be done, no matter what she had to say in order to convince her patient's husband. "Yes, I have," she lied. He still looked dubious, so she decided to add, "Quite successfully."

"Very well then," Lord Arlington agreed, wiping his hand shakily across his perspiring forehead. "You have my consent."

Once in the kitchen, Mary took the white sheet that the maid had provided and spread it over the sturdy oak table that stood in the center of the room.

"Shall I lay her down?" Lord Arlington asked, eyeing the makeshift operating table.

"Not yet. We will need to get her out of that dress first," Mary said before turning to the maid and handing her a large pair of scissors. "Perhaps you can help with that."

"But it is one of her favorites," the maid protested.

"And it will not do her an ounce of good if she is not alive to wear it, now, will it?" Mary snapped. Time was of the essence, which was something that these people clearly did not seem to understand. She let out a sigh of relief when the maid followed her orders without further delay. "Just leave her chemise," she said.

Once this was done, Lord Arlington placed his wife on the table, grabbing one of the fresh towels and placing it across her pelvis to protect her modesty as much as possible. Her hair, soaked in her own sweat, was matted against her forehead, her eyelids fluttering ever so gently while her breath came in hoarse and shallow bursts.

Opening her bag, Mary pulled out a pair of retractors, a clamp, a pair of forceps, and a scalpel, all of which she dropped into the pot of water that the maid had put to boil. Removing a bottle of brandy from her bag, she pulled out the stopper and tossed it to Helmsley. She then proceeded to pour a generous amount of the amber liquid over Lady Arlington's quivering belly. Some of it dribbled down her sides, pooling in the small spaces where her body failed to touch the table. With the tip of a clean towel, Mary wiped away the excess before turning a keen eye on the rest of the group. "Now, I want each of you to spend the next couple of minutes washing your hands—thoroughly. Take your time and remember to make good use of the soap. I want the lather to reach all the way up to your elbows."

Lord Arlington stared at her as if she'd just turned green. "I hardly think that is necessary," he said. "After all, you yourself have said that we are short on time. Should we not then try to get this over with as quickly as possible, or do you really mean to prolong my wife's suffering while we stand about playing with water?"

"Lord Arlington," Mary told him sternly, "I take very little pleasure in your wife's suffering, and I assure you that I have no desire to prolong it more than necessary. However, since you do wish for me to explain myself to you, I will tell you this: while the majority of the physicians and surgeons in this country may be deaf to new ideas and innovative ways of thinking, I am not, and neither was my father."

The viscount responded with nothing but a blank stare. Clearly, she would have to elaborate, however reluctant she was to waste what little time they had in doing so.

"Forty seven years ago," she said, filling a washbasin with water and reaching for the soap, "a Scottish physician named William Buchan published a book that focused on personal hygiene. It was called *Domestic Medicine*, and although the original work was first sold in Edinburgh, it quickly grew in popularity and was reprinted in London only five years later." She paused for a moment as she dipped the soap in the water and started working it between her hands until foamy bubbles began to appear. She then looked up to see if the name of the book she'd just mentioned had registered with anyone but was greeted by yet another round of vacant gazes. Only Helmsley bore a knowing smile upon his face, for he had heard her speak of Buchan many times before. Returning her gaze to her hands, she said, "In this book of his, Buchan advises everyone to wash their hands after handling the sick or anything else that might have become contaminated. He also advises that we do so before we eat our meals or enter into company with others. His reasoning for doing so was that he believed we would run less risk of becoming infected ourselves or of conveying an infection to others. Unfortunately, however, his advice has been greatly ignored within the medical community."

Mary let out a lengthy sigh. "I don't presume to understand why it is of such monumental importance, my lord, I only know that it is. My father and I have always done it before a surgery, and I do believe that it is part of the reason why the mortality rate of our patients has always been far lower than that of other surgeons.

"So, if your wife's health is of any importance to you, then you will wash your hands without further complaint, and once you are done, you will refrain from touching anything else in this room unless I specifically give you permission to do so. Do I make myself clear?"

Lord Arlington stared back at her for only a fraction of a second before rushing over to the washbasin and grabbing the soap that she'd just now finished with. Mary caught Helmsley's eye. There was a very distinct smirk upon his face as he gave her a quiet nod of approval. Good. She'd hate having to waste time arguing with him as well.

When Lord Arlington returned to his wife's side a few minutes later, Mary looked at him and said, "I have taken the liberty of administering some laudanum. It should make it easier on her, but this is not going to be a painless procedure. I hope I can count on you to hold her down and keep her steady for me. Dr. Helmsley will help you while. . ." She turned to the maid. "I am terribly sorry, but I do not know your name."

"It is Lucy Pinksworth, my lady."

Mary acknowledged her with a quick nod. "Answer me honestly, Miss Pinksworth. Are you likely to faint at the sight of blood?"

"N...no, my lady. I believe I shall be quite all right."

"Good, because I am going to need someone to keep the bladder out of the way while I open up the uterus. Do you think you can manage that?"

Lucy's face paled momentarily, but then she appeared to pull herself together "I...yes, I believe I can," she replied with a surprising amount of conviction as she watched Mary fish her tools out of the boiling water before setting them side by side on a clean white towel.

"All right," Mary said as she drew a long breath. "Then let us get started."

It took about an hour for Mary to complete the operation, and since the viscountess fainted from the pain very early on, Lord Arlington and Helmsley were left with very little to do. Lucy, on the other hand, performed admirably. She followed Mary's instructions to the letter, without flinching as much as once.

"Congratulations, Lord Arlington," Mary said as she lifted a squealing baby from its mother's womb. "It looks as though you have a very healthy baby boy." She handed the child over to Lucy and began the monotonous process of stitching up her patient.

As she finished the last of the stitches, Mary finally allowed herself to relax. She looked up at Helmsley, who was showing marked signs of relief. Lady Arlington and the baby were both alive for now. She knew that they weren't out of danger yet, but a strong feeling told her that all would be well with both mother and child.

A soft sniffle caught Mary's attention. "Thank you," Lord Arlington choked as he looked at her through misty eyes. "Thank you, thank you, thank you."

"You are most welcome, my lord," Mary said as she placed a reassuring hand upon his arm. "Of course, we will need to monitor your wife closely for the next few days, but I do believe that she will be all right. The internal suture was done using catgut, so it will dissolve on its own, but I shall have to take out the external stitches once the wound is fully healed. In the meantime, I will stay with you until she wakes up. Depending on how she is feeling, we will decide on a time for me to return and check up on her."

Chapter Five

It was five thirty in the morning by the time Mary made her way to bed, so exhausted that she collapsed fully clothed on top of her covers, her feet dangling precariously over the edge. When she eventually woke up again, it was past noon, and by the time she made it downstairs, fully dressed and with her hair styled to perfection, it was almost one.

The minute she walked into the parlor, she froze. There were flowers not only on every surface but on the floor as well: roses in a wide array of colors, chrysanthemums, lilies, and carnations, all beautifully arranged in bouquets of varying sizes. Mary just stood there and stared. "Thornton?" The butler appeared at her side instantaneously. "What on earth is going on?"

"Well, I can take it to mean only one thing, my lady. You must have made quite an impression last night at Richmond House—these flowers have been arriving all morning. And now that it is past lunch time, you will probably be receiving your first caller at any—" The doorbell rang. "Moment," he finished.

Mary stared at Thornton in horror. "You don't mean to tell me that. . .but I just got out of bed. I cannot possibly receive anyone now."

"I can fend them off for a while, my lady, but I cannot keep them at bay forever. There is a plate of food for you in the dining room, which will no doubt do you a world of good after all that gallivanting about last night." He gave her a disapproving look. "In the meantime, I shall see who is at the door; after all, it is the polite thing to do."

Mary paused only long enough to realize that once the front door was opened, whoever had decided to call upon her would be likely to spot her straight away, leaving her with little choice but to invite them in. With a soft rustle of her skirts, she immediately fled down the hallway and into the dining room, almost grateful to discover that no ostentatious bouquets of flowers had made it that far yet.

She'd just pulled out her chair when the sound of loud voices arguing caught her attention. It sounded as if Thornton was yelling at somebody. *Good heavens.* Ten seconds later, the door flew open, admitting none other than Mr. Summersby.

"I am terribly sorry, my lady," Thornton apologized. "I tried to explain to him that you are not receiving visitors at the moment, but the gentleman just would not listen."

Mary scowled at Mr. Summersby. "It is quite all right, Thornton. Would you please send in another cup in case he would care for some tea."

"Very well, my lady," Thornton replied, glaring at the unwelcome guest. "Should you otherwise need me, I shall not be far."

"Thank you, Thornton, but I am sure that I shall be just fine. You may, however, ask Emma to join us."

"Yes, my lady."

Once Thornton was gone, Mary turned her full attention to the man before her. "Well, this is an unexpected surprise," she remarked. "Although Thornton did say that I could expect callers at any moment."

Mr. Summersby gave her a lopsided grin. "No true gentleman would dare to call upon a lady before three in the afternoon."

"Then I take it that you are not a true gentleman. Or are you perhaps a bit thickheaded? I thought I was quite clear about not wanting to see you again."

Mr. Summersby's mouth made an awkward twist at that remark, as if he were doing his best to refrain from laughing. "You are mistaken, Lady Steepleton," he told her. "I am the very epitome of a true gentleman. In fact, I am your knight in shining armor, come to rescue you from the horde of young pups that are sure to assault you with wagging tails and adoring eyes at any given moment. I shall vouch that they will slobber all over you."

"And just how exactly are you hoping to accomplish such a heroic feat?" Mary asked, unable to help herself from being taken in by Mr. Summersby's charms.

Will our conversations always border on the bizarre?

Thornton returned just then with another cup that he placed upon the table across form Mary's place setting. He was accompanied by Emma, who quickly bobbed a curtsy in her mistress's direction. Mary took her seat, gestured for her guest to do the same, and watched in silence as Thornton poured each of them a steaming hot cup of tea. Emma perched herself on a chair in the corner, her face turned slightly away as if to offer some measure of privacy. Mary couldn't help but be impressed by her thoughtfulness and quickly told Thornton to offer her a cup of tea as well. She then turned an expectant gaze on Mr. Summersby. "Well?"

"Well, I was thinking that a ride in the park might be just the thing to make you want to keep my company." Mary's brows rose. The gentleman certainly didn't waste his time. "I brought my carriage along, you see, and since the weather is as fine as it is today, we could perhaps even take a stroll along the Serpentine."

It did sound very tempting, yet Mary hadn't forgotten why she'd dismissed the handsome man in the first place. Well, of course there was the problem of all the lies she'd probably end up weaving, but mostly it had something to do with the way he had looked at her when she'd told him that she was a marchioness. She knew she wasn't exactly the prettiest of God's creations, but that he'd been so shocked had actually hurt her quite a bit—quite possibly more than she cared to admit.

Now, as far as her profession was concerned, perhaps she was underestimating Mr. Summersby. Was she really all that certain that he wouldn't be supportive of her? She ignored the answer that came to mind, for it wasn't at all the one she was hoping for. She contemplated the issue for a moment, knowing full well that she was probably about to make a very big mistake. But somehow, in that instant, and with him focusing his deep blue eyes on her so expectantly, she simply forgot to care. She wanted to go for that ride and to walk along the Serpentine with him. She wanted a friend, someone to talk to. "I shall join you on one condition," she told him. "Tell me, as honestly as you can, why you did not believe me when I told you that I am the Marchioness of Steepleton."

"As far as I can recall, I never said that I did not believe you," he said, his grin dimpling his cheeks.

"You implied it by staring at me like a gawking imbecile," she retorted, her eyes widening slightly as if she couldn't quite believe she'd just said that out loud.

"And you, my lady, are sure to offend somebody one day with that tongue of yours." He took a sip of tea as he looked at her from over the brim of his cup. He could practically see the steam coming out of her ears. "But, in answer to your question, you just looked too ordinary to fit the part. Your dress, for instance, as pretty as it was, lacked any form of luxury. You wore no expensive baubles, and you just did not have that air of wealth about you. You were not at all like any of the other ladies present; in fact, I quite thought that you might have been someone's distant relation, visiting from the country. I am sorry if that offends you, but that is the truth of it."

Lady Steepleton stared back at him from across the table. "There is no need for you to apologize, Mr. Summersby," she finally said in a delicate voice. "Having seen what all of those other women are like—how snooty and aggressive they can be—I do believe that you have just now given me a compliment."

"They are not all like that," Ryan assured her. "My sister, Alexandra, for instance, is very different."

"Then I shall very much like to meet her," the marchioness told him with a bright smile that instantly forced him to catch his breath. No, Lady Steepleton wasn't at all what he had expected. If anything, she was like a breath of fresh air in a baking summer heat. Now, if he could only figure out why someone might wish to harm her.

They drove Ryan's landau along a number of different paths in the park before making a turn onto Rotten Row. Given the time of day and the splendid weather, the road was packed with people in a variety of carriages or merely on horseback. "Is it always this busy?" Lady Steepleton asked as she adjusted the green ribbon on her bonnet.

"On a day like today? Yes, especially since the weather has been terribly dismal of late," Ryan told her with a smile. He'd taken the seat across from her, while her maid, who'd been brought along for the sake of propriety, sat quietly at her mistress's side, her face averted as if she were taking a remarkable interest in the scenery. Ryan had to give the woman credit for her discretion. "You see, most members of the *ton* enjoy being seen wearing a newly acquired hat or in the company of a particular gentleman or lady. In fact, it is often the way in which a courtship is made public."

Lady Steepleton's lips parted slightly in surprise. Ryan met her gaze and knew what she must be thinking. A smile tugged at his lips as he watched her turn her head away and apply a great deal of interest to the trees that they were just now passing. However, he couldn't help but notice how red she'd suddenly gotten.

"I see," she whispered. "A bit conceited. . .would you not agree?"

Ryan shrugged as he leaned back against his seat, pretending not to have noticed her discomfiture. "Perhaps, my lady, but such is the life of the rich; it often lacks substance."

Lady Steepleton's head snapped around in astonishment. "Do you really mean that?"

"Oh, absolutely. It is one of the foremost reasons why my family withdrew to the country. In fact, we have only recently begun returning to London during the season." He tipped his hat as they passed another carriage.

"Why the sudden change?" she asked, sending a smile toward the couple whom Ryan had just greeted. "If you were happier in the country, then why come to London now?"

Ryan let out a lengthy sigh. "Well, it appears as though my father has determined that it is time for my brother and me to start scouring the marriage mart a bit more thoroughly. Until now, we've been present for only part of the season, attending the occasional ball; and while it is true that my brother is the one facing the greatest amount of pressure due to his being elder, he is, unfortunately, out of town at the moment, leaving me as the sole target of my father's attempts at matchmaking."

Lady Steepleton grinned. "What about your sister?"

Ryan rolled his eyes. "She married the Earl of Trenton last year. Not only was she determined never to get hitched, but considering the type of woman she is, it just seemed very unlikely that she ever would. Now that she is settled with a husband and a child, my father is even more confident that my brother and I will both succeed in finding wives."

"I see. Then you certainly do have a very busy season ahead of you, it would seem."

"It does appear so, doesn't it?" he replied, locking his gaze with hers.

Turning away from Rotten Row, the carriage continued along an alley for a while before slowing to a steady halt. "There is a nice patch of grass over there where I thought we might be able to sit and enjoy a bit of a picnic," Ryan said, stepping down from the carriage and turning to offer first her ladyship and then her maid his hand.

"I hope you did not pack too much," Lady Steepleton said, smoothing her skirts while Emma stepped down onto the gravelly path. "After all, I just ate. Remember?"

"Just some tea and cake," Ryan replied. Taking the basket in one hand and draping a large rolled up blanket across his other arm, he walked over to a patch of sunshine and proceeded to spread the blanket on the ground. It wasn't as warm as he'd hoped; in fact, whenever the clouds blocked out the sun, it was really quite chilly. A good thing he'd settled on tea rather than wine.

"So, tell me about your studies, Mr. Summersby," Lady Steepleton asked with genuine interest once they were seated on the ground. "When we last spoke, you mentioned that you have been studying medicine at Oxford."

"And you told me that I do not strike you as a typical medical student. As I recall, you mentioned that your father was quite the physician."

"That is true," Lady Steepleton agreed. "And I am sorry about what I said; I was upset."

"Then perhaps I ought to be the one apologizing," Ryan told her with a warm smile. She returned it, and his heart swelled. It would seem that her firm facade was already beginning to crack a little, and while he still didn't know her well enough to form a detailed opinion of her, he had to admit that their conversations thus far had sparked his interest with alarming speed. He glanced at Emma. "More tea?" he offered.

"Thank you, my lord." Presenting her cup, the young woman suddenly raised her hand and waved.

Ryan turned, spotting two women approaching along the path. "Someone you know?"

"It is my younger sister with one of her friends." Emma turned her attention toward her mistress. "Would you perhaps permit me to go and greet them, my lady? I shall not go far; I promise."

"I. . ." Lady Steepleton hesitated as she darted a look in Ryan's direction, but if she had any misgivings about being left alone with him, she quickly hid them and forced a smile. "Yes, of course," she told her maid, with a pink blush to her cheeks.

Thanking her mistress, Emma got up and went to speak with her sister and her friend.

Ryan sat in silence for a while, acutely aware of the fact that their chaperone was no longer within earshot. He regarded Lady Steepleton with growing interest. She looked frazzled. Her cheeks were flushed, her eyes averted, and she was nervously toying with the fabric of her dress. "Does it bother you?" he asked her suddenly.

She looked startled at the sound of his voice, as if he'd just intruded on a private thought. "What?" she asked.

"Being alone with me; does it bother you?"

"No," she chuckled, albeit with an underlying hint of nervousness. "Not at all."

"Good. Because you are perfectly safe with me, you know. I would not dream of doing anything that might damage your reputation or compromise you in any way. You have my word on that, as a gentleman."

She stared back at him as if surprised by his sudden declaration. Her mouth formed the shape of an O. "It never occurred to me that you would," she told him at last.

Did he detect the sound of disappointment in her voice? She'd said she didn't think he'd act inappropriately, but had she secretly hoped? A rush of unexpected heat buzzed through him at the thought of it. He regarded her quietly as he tried to make sense of what he was feeling. He had a job to do: that was the only reason why he was even sitting there talking to her in the first place. After all, she wasn't at all the type of woman to strike his fancy. The sort of women he'd been with in the past were far more striking and alluring than Lady Steepleton.

Yet there was something that he couldn't quite define, an attraction so strong that he felt an urgent need to push her down onto the blanket and kiss her breathless.

"Mr. Summersby?"

Ryan blinked, then noticed that she was looking at him in wonder. Her hand was gently touching his arm. When had that happened? He didn't know, but it felt wonderful. "My apologies," he said. "I fear I got a bit lost in my own thoughts there for a moment."

"That is quite all right," she told him with a smile. "As I recall, you were just about to tell me about your studies."

"Well, the truth of it is that I have been studying for years without finding the discipline to focus on any one topic."

"The eternal student on his quest for knowledge," she remarked with a twinkle in her eyes. "It is a journey that knows no end, you know; each time you find the answer to a question, another problem presents itself, and you end up tossed about between any number of different subjects, always searching and never quite satisfied."

Ryan stared at her for a moment as if she'd just discovered the key to unlocking the universe. Perhaps she had—to his universe, at least. Nobody else had ever shown more understanding of him as a person than this woman whom he'd only just met. It was absolutely astounding.

He took a moment to compose himself before continuing. "I have covered practically everything from mathematics to art history, law to literature. My brother eventually insisted that I get a degree in something, and since I would like to make a comfortable living for myself, it really came down to a tie between law and medicine."

"So then, what was the deciding factor?" Lady Steepleton asked with growing interest.

"Well, in the end I suppose that medicine won out because it will always be able to present me with something new. It also incorporates a variety of different areas of expertise: anatomy, biology, chemistry, botany, perhaps even philosophy, to some extent. In short, it is the one area of expertise that I am least likely to grow weary of."

Lady Steepleton laughed at that, and there was a ring to her voice that lifted his soul. "You certainly have thought this through, haven't you?"

"To some degree," he admitted as he took a sip of tea.

"Would you mind if I tried a piece of the cake?" Lady Steepleton asked rather suddenly.

"Oh, how terribly rude of me; I quite forgot to offer." He

quickly reached for the knife and cut a slice of cake that he then placed on a white plate, offering it to her with a tentative smile.

She studied him as he did so, the trace of a smile beginning to tug at the edge of her lips. "Are you always this forgetful and preoccupied?" she asked.

He frowned. "Why, Lady Steepleton, I do believe that you are mocking me."

"Surely not," she said, grinning, before turning quite serious. "I would never dream of it."

"I see," he muttered rather skeptically. "Then perhaps, in answer to your question, I ought to confess that I do not generally find myself in such remarkable company—hence the tendency for my mind to wander."

"Is that an attempt at flattery?" she asked, as if surprised he'd bothered to make the effort.

"That depends on whether or not it is working," he told her slyly.

"Well, it is certainly a better attempt than the one you made last night," she said. "In fact, I daresay that you hardly made any attempt at all."

"My apologies once again, my lady." He'd been a damned fool when she'd finally introduced herself to him the previous evening. Indeed, he'd looked at her as if she'd just dropped from the sky, but the truth of it was he'd been confounded. Looking at her now, he still considered her a conundrum. Her dress was quite plain, while her hair was pulled back so sharply he imagined the roots must be screaming. Her hands were folded neatly in her lap. Truthfully, she looked prim and unapproachable, but when she opened her mouth and spoke, he couldn't help but be impressed by her sharp rejoinders and wit. She clearly had character.

The marchioness suddenly laughed. "I am merely jesting with you," she said. "Although I must admit that your initial reaction to my true identity was somewhat upsetting, I really cannot blame you. In fact, you were quite right to be surprised. After all, I do not exactly look like a lady of the *ton*, much less a marchioness."

Ryan was momentarily startled by her sudden show of self-deprecation. "Well, at least that is something that can easily be rectified by a visit to Bond Street," he said. "All you need are a few extravagant gowns."

Lady Steepleton let out a short sigh. "I suppose that might help." She started fidgeting again, and it occurred to him that he'd not only drawn direct attention to her attire, but voiced his disapproval, when all he'd meant to do was offer her a little help and advice. He groaned inwardly. It was remarkable that she was still sitting there and hadn't decided to storm off.

Hoping to draw her attention to something else, he decided to make an attempt at changing the subject. "You seemed to be quite understanding of my predicament in regards to settling upon one singular area of study. It forces me to wonder if you are to some degree a student too." Well, what was she to say to that? Of course she was, for she had never stopped studying. She nodded faintly in response, unwilling to be completely dishonest with the poor man who, it seemed, was eagerly attempting to make her happy.

"Really?" Mr. Summersby remarked with renewed enthusiasm. "And what, pray tell, has a lady such as yourself determined to study? The arts, perhaps?"

Mary could have choked on her cake at that question. Not only could she not imagine herself studying anything as dull as paintings or poetry, but she would now have to come up with an appropriate answer that wouldn't be nearly as appalling as the truth. After all, they didn't know each other well enough for her to drop *that* cannonball in his lap just yet. "I. . .er. . .I study people, Mr. Summersby," she told him, hoping he might be content with that answer, however vague it might be.

He looked at her quizzically. "People?" he asked. He seemed momentarily confused, but when she didn't elaborate any further, he eventually chose to draw his own conclusion. "Oh, I see; you have an interest in philosophy and the inner workings of the mind, I take it?"

Mary forced herself to hold back her reply. As it happened, she'd studied quite a bit of philosophy, but it was more of a hobby of hers than anything else. There was no doubt about the fact that Mr. Summersby had made a serious error in judgment. However, it was an error not only that she had helped him make, but one that she was not about to correct— at least not yet. "Yes," she heard herself say, increasingly horrified at how easy it had become for her to lie.

"Then you must be quite familiar with Descartes," he said as he took a sip of tea.

"Indeed, I am," she replied, brightening at the possibility of telling him something truthful for once. "I have read several of his works."

Mr. Summersby nodded appreciatively. "Then at least we have that much in common," he told her with a smile as he put his cup down. He glanced over her shoulder, and, following his line of sight, she spotted Emma, still busily chatting with her sister and her friend. Uneasiness wafted over her; they seemed to be farther away than before.

"How do you feel about that walk?" Mr. Summersby asked, forcing her attention back to him. He'd begun piling their things into the picnic basket.

"To be honest, I think I will be relieved to get up off the ground before I catch a chill," she said, waving for Emma to return. She could hardly walk off with him alone.

He gave her a sidelong glance as he carefully arranged the teacups next to the cake. He seemed so unexpectedly gentle. "I am sorry about that. I did not realize that it would be quite so cold. Perhaps we would have been better served if we had remained in the carriage."

"Whoever heard of a picnic in a carriage?" She looked back at him, her eyes meeting his in a deadpan stare. "If you and I are to get along, Mr. Summersby, then you really must stop apologizing all the time. Though I do appreciate your attempts at gallantry, I am not a fragile porcelain doll in need of constant coddling. In fact, I would rather enjoy good banter—if you are up to it."

"You don't mince words, do you?" His voice was serious, but she detected a smile behind his eyes.

"Direct conversation has always served me rather well," she quipped.

"Then I shall endeavor to refrain from apologizing further." He offered her his arm, which she quickly accepted with a warm smile, and led her down toward the path that ran along the embankment of the Serpentine. The wind had picked up a bit, making the few ducks on the river bob even more, while the ribbons on Mary's bonnet had begun to wave with increasing fury. "Do you think that we are at all likely to have a few warm days this summer?" Mr. Summersby asked as he watched her pull the shawl she'd brought along more tightly about her shoulders.

"Do you really wish for us to discuss the weather?" she asked with no attempt at hiding the smirk that played upon her lips.

"Not particularly," he told her plainly. "But since that is what most young ladies prefer to talk about, I fear that I have made a habit of it."

Mary chuckled. "Please refrain from doing so with me. I would be much obliged if we might discuss something of a little more substance than whether or not there will be clouds in the sky tomorrow."

"I see," Mr. Summersby muttered, frowning a little at her remark.

Oh, dear.

Had she been too forward?

"Would you mind telling me what you *would* like to discuss?"

She pondered that for a moment, then turned her face to look at him, her skin tingling with sudden excitement. "Do you believe in chance, Mr. Summersby, or do you suppose that things happen for a reason?"

The question must have stunned him, for his eyes widened in response. She knew it was an odd question to ask, but what better way to discover his true character than through thought-provoking conversation?

"If I am to understand you correctly, you are asking if I

think there is a predetermined purpose to everything that occurs, one we cannot alter."

She shot him a sly smile. "Precisely."

"I think that we mere mortals often presume ourselves to be of far greater import than we actually are. The universe is a grand place, and we, but tiny specs within it. However, I do believe that I am lord of my own actions. Are these actions manipulated somehow through circumstance and my surroundings? I am confident of it. But to think that I am unwillingly moving in one particular direction, unable to veer left or right—I dread to think of it."

"You certainly are a philosopher, Mr. Summersby. Indeed, I. . .Oh, look!" she suddenly exclaimed, as she pointed ahead of them. "That little dog over there appears to have lost its master."

"I say, that looks like one of Lady Cassandra's terriers," Mr. Summersby remarked. "Let us see if we can fetch him for her. She will be ever so pleased."

Before either of them had a chance to make any such attempt, a cloud of lace came tumbling through the bushes. It landed awkwardly in the middle of the path, while a pair of arms protruding from it did their best to grab the terrified critter. Mary just stared at the spectacle, quite agog, until the ball of fabric straightened itself enough to reveal a pretty face framed by dark brown curls.

"Dear me," Mary finally managed to get out. "Are you all right? That was quite a tumble you just took."

The young lady, who was now holding the struggling terrier firmly against her chest, returned an awkward smile that told of her immediate embarrassment. Not only was one side of her straw bonnet torn open, but there were also mud and grass stains on the front of her gown. In fact, she looked quite frightful. "Yes, thank you," she told Mary, then turned her attention to Mr. Summersby. "Fancy meeting you here."

"Lady Cassandra," Mr. Summersby said politely, tipping his hat in greeting, "may I present the Marchioness of Steepleton."

"Oh, you certainly may," Lady Cassandra cried with much enthusiasm as she turned her attention back to Mary. "I have heard so much about you."

Mary groaned inwardly, for the only thing that anyone might have heard about her as of yet was just how *ordinary* and *dull* she was. She made an effort to smile politely.

"Lady Cassandra is one of my brother-in-law's five sisters," Mr. Summersby said, then added, "She is the daughter of the Duke and Duchess of Willowbrook."

"It is a pleasure to make your acquaintance," Mary told Lady Cassandra graciously. "Can we perhaps assist you in any way? We have our carriage just over there if you would like for us to take you home."

"Thank you, but that really will not be necessary," Lady Cassandra replied, slipping the terrier's leash onto its collar. "Naturally, I did not come alone. I brought my maid along with me, you see, but when Trevor suddenly took off, I had no choice but to follow him, leaving poor Miss Baxter behind. I really ought to go and find her; she must be quite worried. But it was delightful meeting you, Lady Steepleton. I do hope that our paths will cross again soon so that we may become better acquainted."

Mary barely managed a faint nod and a smile before Lady Cassandra had bidden them both a good day and hurried off, holding the remainders of her bonnet in place with one hand, while dragging a stubborn Trevor along by the other.

"I daresay that poor Miss Baxter will have something to see to once they arrive home," Mary remarked as she and Mr. Summersby continued on their way.

"Who?" he asked with a perplexed look on his face.

"Lady Cassandra's maid, Mr. Summersby," Mary said, mildly annoyed that she had to explain that much. He clearly had not paid the least bit of attention. "She will have a gown to clean and a bonnet to mend."

"I will wager that she is quite accustomed to doing so by now," Mr. Summersby remarked. "After all, Lady Cassandra is notorious for spoiling her clothes."

"I see," Mary said. How curious, but what a relief: a young lady, similar in age to herself, who'd been raised among the *ton*, but who appeared to be just as far from perfection as she was. What a wonderful discovery. Perhaps the two of them could one day be friends. The wind tugged at her gown once more. She turned to Mr. Summersby. "It's getting rather nippy. Shall we return to the carriage?"

He nodded, turning them about, but not before she caught a glimpse of regret flashing behind his eyes. Curiously, she realized that she felt the same. She hadn't expected to enjoy their outing as much as she had. He had surprised her, forcing her to wonder when they might meet again. She dared not ask, for fear of giving him the wrong impression. She merely enjoyed his company, that was all. But her heart still skipped a beat when she turned her head in his direction and caught him gazing down at her. He smiled, and she caught her breath. He truly was a handsome devil.

Friends, she reminded herself, just friends.

CHAPTER SIX

"Another letter has arrived for you, my lady," Thornton said the minute Lady Steepleton walked through the front door of her house with Emma in tow. Ryan followed at a respectable distance, his only intention being that of seeing her ladyship home safely.

"Thank you, Thornton," she said, taking the white envelope and opening it before she'd even removed her gloves. As she unfolded the piece of paper and began to read, she drew a tight breath.

"Are you all right?" Ryan asked with marked concern.

Lady Steepleton nodded numbly, but there was terror in her eyes. "I. . ." she managed to get out in a raspy voice. "I. . .er. . .Thank you for a lovely day, Mr. Summersby. It was most pleasant."

"Are you quite certain that there is nothing I can do?" Ryan asked. "You look suddenly quite unwell."

"No, thank you," she told him firmly. "My maid will attend to me. I am just a bit tired, that is all."

Ryan knew that she was dismissing him with a lie. He gave

her a curt nod. What else was there to do when the woman wouldn't turn to him for help? "I will call on you tomorrow then," he told her. "If I may."

"Yes," she whispered. "I shall look forward to it."

What the devil did that letter say, Ryan wondered as he walked back to his carriage, annoyed that she had so easily turned him away. He knew he had no right to feel that way; after all, they'd only just met. It would be presumptuous of him to think that she might share her worries with him so soon. Perhaps it was because of the connection they'd shared at the park. He thought of it and realized how extraordinary it had been, perhaps because it was unlike anything he'd ever experienced before. He shook his head, unwilling to dwell on it further. Devil take it, he had a job to do.

"Take the horses home," he told his coachman. "I will walk back from here." But instead, he went to the corner of James Street and waited, keeping a steady gaze pinned on Lady Steepleton's front door. There was no question that she was hiding something, and he had every intention of figuring out what that something might be—before she managed to get herself killed.

It didn't take more than ten minutes before she emerged from her home once more. A carriage drew up to the pavement, and she quickly climbed inside.

Where the devil is she off to now?

Ryan watched as the carriage rolled into motion. There wasn't a moment to lose if he wanted to find out where she was headed. Running into the street, he hailed the first hackney he could find. "Follow that carriage!" he called out to the driver. "And be quick about it, my good man."

Having been shown into the Earl of Woodbridge's drawing room and offered a cup of tea, Mary waited expectantly for his lordship to appear. She'd known him all her life, for he had been one of her father's closest friends and therefore more like an uncle to her than anything else. To her relief, she didn't have to wait long. "Mary," Lord Woodbridge said upon his arrival as he closed the space between them and took her hand in his, pressing a soft kiss to her knuckles. "It is so good to see you again."

"It is good to see you too, Robert. I am sorry I did not contact you sooner, but there has been so much to see to since my return, and, well. . .to be perfectly honest, it has all been a little overwhelming."

"I understand," Robert told her mildly, taking the seat across from her. "It cannot have been easy for you to discover that your father kept so many secrets from you."

"No, it has not been." She met his gaze. "Did you know about it all along?"

"Let's just say that it would have been highly unlikely for us to have been such close friends if we had not shared the same social background—even if we did share the same profession."

Mary nodded with understanding but couldn't stop the feeling of betrayal that washed over her. She'd always wondered about her father's relationship with the earl, but whenever she'd questioned it, her father had explained it away with the shrug of his shoulders or the wave of his hand, claiming that they'd simply known each other forever, and that in their case their friendship transcended social status and material wealth. Lies. . .all of it.

Looking at Robert, she noticed that he was studying her with a cautious gaze. "Your father and I did not always see eye to eye, as you well know, but I was very sorry to hear about his death, Mary. I do hope that you realize that."

"Yes, of course. Thank you. I actually was hoping that you might be able to tell me if there is anything else that he might have kept from me."

He gave her an assessing look. "I am not sure I follow. Your father was a colleague of mine and a truly dependable friend. I knew him for over twenty years, Mary, and in that time he was always working on one theory or another, some more successful than others, I suppose."

"But was there nothing that stood out? Perhaps something that he spoke of with more frequency or with greater passion?"

He frowned. "What is this about, exactly?"

"To tell you the truth, I am not at all sure," she said with a sigh, pulling a piece of paper out of her reticule. "But I received this letter this afternoon, and I am just trying to make some sense of it."

Taking it from her, Robert read it. *"Heed our warning...do not involve yourself in matters that don't concern you."* He looked at Mary with much concern in his dark brown eyes. "This is quite alarming, to say the least. I daresay you ought to take this very seriously." His eyes narrowed. "I hope you haven't done something reckless."

"No! Of course not." Mary tried to compose herself. "I have no idea what they might be referring to. I have not been toying with anything that does not concern me. Though my father may have taught me everything he knows, he never shared his notes with me."

Robert paused for a moment, mulling something over in his head. "Perhaps he was trying to protect you."

"From what?"

"I cannot tell you that, my dear, but if, as you say, he did not share his notes with you, then perhaps it might be wise of you to read them. Your father was a meticulous man, Mary. He passed the piece of paper back to her. "I daresay that whatever this letter is about, it is possible that you might find the answers you are looking for in his journals."

The instant Mary returned home, she hurried upstairs to her room in search of Emma, who was busy polishing Mary's boots. The shirt and breeches were already laid out on the bed. Following her discussion with Robert, Mary was itching to take a look at her father's journals, hoping that she might find some answers. It would have to wait, however; Lady Arlington came first.

"I have no idea what it is that you are up to, my lady," Emma said as she handed Mary her hat after helping her get dressed. "Just promise me that you will be careful."

"Not to worry, Emma. I just have to pay a visit to a friend of mine, that is all."

Emma looked at her skeptically but apparently knew better than to pry into her mistress's affairs and simply nodded, for which Mary was grateful. "I will be here waiting for you to return, my lady."

With only her patient's welfare in mind, Mary walked her horse briskly toward the street corner. She stopped for a moment, glanced about, and when she was certain that she was quite alone, she placed her left foot in the stirrup.

"Excuse me, sir!"

Mary froze, her heart taking off with a gallop. She knew that voice. What in the world was Mr. Summersby doing there so late in the evening? More importantly, what the devil was she supposed to do now? She'd told Lord Arlington that she'd be back to check on his wife, and so she would—not even Mr. Summersby would stop her from keeping such a promise. She continued to mount her horse, hoping to be gone before he could catch up with her.

"Sir!" His voice echoed more insistently through the night as his footsteps broke into a run, his heels clicking loudly against the pavement.

Oh hell, he was coming after her.

Why?

Mary didn't have time to ponder that question. In another couple of seconds he'd be upon her, and then she'd really have some explaining to do. Gritting her teeth and muttering an apology he'd never hear, she swung herself into the saddle and tightened her grip on the reins. Then, without a backward glance, she dug her heels into her horse's sides and rode off, disappearing quickly out of sight.

Ryan stood for a long while after in the middle of the street, staring after the young man who'd just ridden off, the same young man he'd seen the previous evening. He'd hoped to ask him a few questions to find out what he was up to so late. What sort of errands was Lady Steepleton sending him on, and were they related to the letter she'd received? One thing was for sure: the emissary hadn't wanted to stop for a chat.

He glanced at Lady Steepleton's house, wishing he could talk to her and perhaps find out more. Damn. There was more to it than his desire to keep her safe; he was merely looking for an excuse to see her again. Ryan raked his fingers through his hair in frustration. God help him if he wasn't falling for the woman. He'd do well to keep this growing fancy under control, especially since she appeared to be far more trouble than he ever would have imagined. She certainly wasn't as demure as he'd initially thought her to be. He reflected on that for a moment. Would he really care for the companionship of a sedate woman? Absolutely not, although he was hoping for someone a little less willful and unruly than his sister. He grinned at the very thought of it: the Marchioness of Steepleton dressed in a shirt and breeches, gallivanting about like the hoydenish Alexandra.

Not bloody likely.

Lady Steepleton might have a sharp tongue on her, but she wasn't at all the hoydenish type. Still, something was awry, and he intended to get to the bottom of it as quickly as possible.

"Not very astute, are you, Mr. Summersby?" a dry voice asked from behind his left shoulder.

Ryan turned to find the Messenger standing but a few paces away from him. In fact, with just one step, he could probably have reached out and touched him. His eyes narrowed with irritation. "What do you mean?"

"You haven't figured out who it is that keeps leaving Lady Steepleton's house in the middle of the night, running errands that are still as elusive to you as the rider's identity."

Ryan glared back at the black-hooded figure. "And what do you know of it?"

"Enough to tell you that Lady Steepleton is finding it difficult to do as she is told."

"Meaning?" If only they weren't standing on a public street in the middle of London, he'd take much pleasure in wringing this man's neck, no matter whom he might turn out to be.

"Meaning that, if I were you, Mr. Summersby, I would tell Lady Steepleton that if it is a hobby she is looking for, she ought to pick something less likely to draw awareness."

The sound of hooves clicking on the cobbles nearby drew Ryan's attention for the briefest of moments. When he looked back, the Messenger was gone.

Damn!

He needed someone to talk to, not to mention a stiff drink to calm his mood. Picking up his pace, he headed down David Street, toward Berkeley Square. He knew exactly where he wanted to go.

"Can I offer you some more claret?" Alexandra asked as she regarded her brother closely. She couldn't recall the last time she'd seen him so out of sorts.

Ryan nodded, taking the bottle from his sister and filling his glass. He took a long sip. "I need your opinion on something," he finally said after a lengthy moment of silence. "Percy came to me a few days ago, asking that I keep an eye on Lady Steepleton."

"The marchioness that everyone has been so busy talking about?"

"The very one." Ryan sighed. He then went on to tell

Alexandra about his conversation with Percy and about the hooded stranger he'd encountered in the street.

"And what about Lady Steepleton herself?" Alexandra asked. "Has she not given you any clue as to what might be going on?"

Ryan shook his head somewhat sheepishly, forcing a troubled sigh from his sister. She knew that he'd always felt less suited for a career in intelligence than she and William. Not that he couldn't hold his own when it came to fighting or thinking on his feet, but he just didn't have the same feel for uncovering information that had come so naturally to both William and herself. It was one of the key factors in his decision to give up on a career in the Foreign Office and continue with his studies instead. What irked Alexandra was that he seemed to consider the lack of this quality a shortcoming. On the contrary, she'd give anything for the ability to soak up knowledge the way Ryan did.

"All right," Alexandra said thoughtfully. "Let us consider everything that we know so far. You say that her father was a physician and that he was killed at Waterloo. We also know that she received a letter, which appears to have alarmed her in some way, and that upon having read it, she went to meet with Lord Woodbridge, who, by the way, also happens to be the Master of the Royal College of Surgeons. If you ask me, Ryan, whatever it is that your marchioness may be involved in, I am strongly inclined to believe that it is medically related."

"I have to agree, but I just fail to see why that would pose a threat to her in any way."

Alexandra was quiet for a moment. An idea had begun to manifest itself in her head, but it was only a guess, and to verify it, she would have to meet Lady Steepleton in person and take a good look at her. "What if I accompany you on your next visit to the marchioness?" she suggested with a bright smile. "I have a feeling that the two of us will get along famously."

"That is an excellent idea, Alex. I was planning on going over there tomorrow afternoon for tea, but if you are coming along, then perhaps we might take Lady Steepleton shopping. There are a multitude of balls this season, and she is in dire need of some proper gowns to wear."

Alexandra made a sour face, as if she'd just bitten into a lemon.

"Actually," Ryan continued, shifting nervously in his seat, "I thought you might perhaps be able to act as our chaperone."

Alexandra flashed her brother a cheeky grin. "Why, Ryan, I do believe her ladyship has you smitten!"

Ryan sent his sister a scowl, but it made very little difference to her. Not once in all her life could she recall having seen her brother blush, yet there he was, as red as a ripe tomato and looking more uncomfortable than a fish out of water. "Not to worry," she told him kindly. "I promise to be on my very best behavior. I simply cannot wait to meet her."

CHAPTER SEVEN

By the time the clock in the hallway struck two on the following afternoon, Mary had managed to convince herself that Mr. Summersby simply must have recognized her the previous evening, and that, as a consequence, he would never want to call on her again. She'd also managed to drive herself half mad, worrying about whom he might have spoken to regarding what he'd seen. In all truth, she scarcely knew the man, and judging by the way in which gossip tended to spread like wildfire among the *ton*, it wouldn't take much to ruin her reputation, even if he hadn't recognized her. All it would take was a good imagination on his part, and if that was the case, then she might very well have to face the possibility of never touching a scalpel again.

So when Thornton came to announce the arrival of Mr. Summersby and the Countess of Trenton, she was so startled that all she could do was stare in befuddlement at her two visitors for a good three seconds.

"I do apologize for coming unannounced like this," Mr. Summersby said as he strode toward her with his sister in tow. "Apparently, it seems to have become a habit of mine."

"There is no need for you to apologize," Mary stammered, desperately trying to get her fluttering heart under control. What on earth was the matter with her? "In truth, you are most welcome."

"Thank you, my lady. You are too kind." He moved aside to make way for his sister. "May I present to you my sister, formally known as her ladyship, the Countess of Trenton."

"Good heavens, Ryan," Lady Trenton exclaimed as she stepped forward, brushing him aside in the process. "There is no need for all that." She graced Mary with a big smile. "It is a pleasure to make your acquaintance, Lady Steepleton. My brother has told me so much about you."

"Has he?" Mary asked warily.

And just what exactly had he told her? That he'd seen her ride off last night, disguised as a man? She studied Mr. Summersby who looked to be in a wonderful mood, not as though he'd just discovered her greatest secret. Was it possible that he hadn't? She began to relax a little. "May I offer you some tea?" she asked.

"Actually, we were rather hoping to take you shopping," Lady Trenton said. "I understand that you might be in need of a gown for the Glendale ball on Friday."

"Is that so?" Mary asked in a clipped tone as she turned a frosty gaze on Mr. Summersby. Apparently, he'd shared his opinion on her attire with the remarkably fashionable countess. What could possibly make her feel grimmer than that?

"Please do not take offense," Mr. Summersby told her, picking up on her discomfort. "We are only trying to help, and I do assure you that we have your best interests at heart."

Mary let out a quiet sigh of defeat. She nodded slowly as

she shifted her gaze from one sibling to the other. "If you'll please wait a moment, I'll just go and fetch my reticule."

They visited three different fabric shops before finally arriving at one on Fleet Street, where Mary's breath was taken away by the most beautiful selection of fabrics, lace, and ribbons she'd ever seen. Bolts of shimmering silks and satins were neatly arranged in two wide mahogany cabinets that loomed like the Pillars of Hercules from behind the counter. Rolls of the finest muslins and linens were neatly stacked on shelves running from floor to ceiling along one wall, while the plushest velvets lined another.

Mary stepped gingerly forward as if in a daze, her fingers reaching out on their own accord to skim across a piece of abandoned satin that had been left out on the cutting table. She drew a breath and turned her bright eyes on her two companions. "I never imagined that such fabrics existed," she said as she continued to gaze about in wonder.

"Come," Lady Trenton told her gently, taking her by the arm and leading her farther into the shop, while Mr. Summersby followed behind in their wake. "Let's start by looking over here."

It took Mary all of fifteen minutes to decide upon a light blue silk and an overlay of lace that met the approval of both the countess and Mr. Summersby. Once this was done, she and Lady Trenton were rapidly swept through to a private sitting room, where the modiste handed them each a large pile of fashion plates.

"Take your time, ladies," Mr. Summersby told them with a smile as he put on his hat. "I am just going to run a quick errand."

As soon as he had left, Mary and Lady Trenton settled to their task and began leafing through the fashion plates. "I know it seems daunting," the countess said, "but after a while, you decide on the styles that you like, and then it goes much quicker."

"I don't have the faintest idea of what sort of gown might suit me." Mary shook her head, completely overwhelmed by the task at hand. "I never imagined that there might be so many ways in which to fashion a gown."

Lady Trenton grinned. "I know precisely how you feel. A little over a year ago I owned only two dresses, and I certainly didn't have much interest in what they looked like. They were more of a requirement than anything else."

Mary raised her eyes and looked at her as if she were speaking a foreign language. "I don't understand; you are so fashionable and elegant."

"That was not the case before my husband came along, you know. In fact, I have always favored a white shirt and a pair of breeches to the restraining garments that women are encouraged to wear. Not only were they more practical in a swordfight—after all, long gowns do have a tendency to get in the way—but they were just so much more comfortable.

"However, when I met Ashford, and I wanted to draw his attention—you know, open his eyes a little to the feminine side of me—well, let's just say that there's much to be said for a bit of lace and a low décolletage."

Mary looked at Lady Trenton in dumbfounded dismay. "You know how to handle a sword?"

"Indeed, I do. And pistols too, if you must know."

"But how did you learn?" She lowered her voice to a conspiratorial whisper. "I mean, it is completely unheard of for a woman to engage in such things—is it not?"

Lady Trenton looked up from the fashion plate she was presently admiring and fixed Mary with a meaningful look. "Not more so than it is for a woman to practice surgery, Lady Steepleton."

If Mary was the fainting sort, she would have done so that very instant. Had she heard right, or were her ears deceiving her? Whatever the case, she could barely breathe as she sat there clutching the fashion plates so tightly in her hands that her knuckles had begun to turn white.

"It's all right," Lady Trenton assured her as she casually pointed to an illustration of an exquisite gown. "Your secret is safe with me. In fact, I quite admire your efforts. You are a very brave woman, Lady Steepleton."

"H. . .how did you know?" Mary practically choked on the words as they came out of her mouth. She felt feverish; her whole body was trembling.

"Well, it didn't take me too long to figure it out. You see, about a year ago, when my brothers and I were passing through Ghent on our way back to England, I stumbled into a young woman at the inn where we were staying. She was looking for her father at the time, and although I failed to notice, my brother William later remarked on how odd it was that she was wearing a surgeon's badge on her arm. When Ryan mentioned that your father was a surgeon and that he was killed at Waterloo, I thought perhaps you might be the same woman I met in Ghent. Of course, I couldn't be certain until I saw you in person, but once I did, there really was no mistaking it."

"But I don't recognize you at all. You look entirely different from the woman I remember speaking to."

Lady Trenton smiled. "Yes, I imagine that I do." She was quiet for a moment, as if deciding on whether or not to broach a delicate topic or not. "Lady Steepleton—"

"Oh, please, call me Mary. I have a feeling that you and I are going to be fast friends, and having you call me Lady Steepleton not only makes me uncomfortable, but it makes me feel positively ancient."

Alexandra grinned. "Very well, but only if you will call me Alexandra. Agreed?"

"Agreed."

"Well then, Mary," Alexandra said, lowering her voice to a whisper, "I have to say that it is impossible for me to dislike you, for I do believe that you and I have very much in common. However, I would like to know if you plan to pursue an attachment with my brother. As it is, I've heard rumors that the two of you were spotted in the park together yesterday. I hope you'll forgive me for the intrusion, but I only wish for him to be happy. I hope you understand."

As forward as the question was, it didn't bother Mary in the slightest. After all, she could be quite direct herself and therefore considered the question very seriously for a moment before answering. She hadn't spent much time analyzing her feelings for Mr. Summersby yet, but she couldn't help but acknowledge the growing attraction she felt for him. Her heart would start to pound whenever he was near, her stomach flipped whenever he touched her, and when she'd wondered. . .Oh hell, she'd wondered what it might be like to kiss him. Undoubtedly splendid.

"Do you promise not to repeat what I say, even to him?"

"I swear it," Alexandra told her solemnly.

"Then I must tell you that I had absolutely no intention of encouraging anyone's advances when I returned to London two weeks ago. I felt—and I still do—that marriage would be the end of my career since it will be impossible for any man to accept a wife who does what I do.

"But then I met your brother, and I would be lying if I were to tell you that I am not drawn to him in a way that I never thought possible. I want to learn everything there is to know about him. I find myself eagerly awaiting his company, and when he's near, I feel so jittery that I've no idea what to do with myself. If he desires to court me, I daresay I'd be unable to resist."

Alexandra smiled as she wrapped her arms around Mary and gave her a tight squeeze. "I cannot tell you how happy that makes me. However, it does mean that you will have to tell him the truth about yourself, and, if I may give a suggestion, you should do so quickly, before he has the chance to feel deceived."

"I know, I just—"

"I realize that you are worried about the way he will react, but you and I are friends now, and I want you to know that you have my full support. We shall work on Ryan together, and, who knows, perhaps the two of you can even find a way in which to collaborate. After all, you both share the same area of expertise."

"I hadn't thought of that," Mary said, her eyes suddenly sparkling with enthusiasm. "Oh, do you really think that such a thing might be possible? That we might open a practice together? Oh, Alexandra, nothing would thrill me more; really, it wouldn't."

"I am glad to see that the two of you are getting along so wonderfully well," a familiar voice sounded. It was Mr. Summersby who'd just returned and was now casually making his way toward them. "Have you decided on a design for your gown yet?"

"Oh, dear," Mary muttered. "I completely forgot what we came here for."

"How about this one?" Alexandra asked, pointing to the same one that she'd pointed at earlier.

"Oh, yes," Mary said. "That really is quite elegant. A bit risqué at the neckline, perhaps, but I suppose that we can have that altered. Mr. Summersby, what do you think?"

"Well," Mr. Summersby began hesitantly, "while I do think that this particular model will suit you remarkably well, I will give it my seal of approval only if you promise *not* to alter the neckline."

"Good heavens!" Alexandra exclaimed with a wide smile, while her eyes twinkled with delight. "I never pegged you to be such a rogue. You have made poor Mary blush."

"I do beg your pardon, Lady Steepleton. It was not my intention to make you feel uncomfortable."

"There's really no need to apologize," Mary began, feeling the heat all the way to her earlobes. "I—"

"Why, Mr. Summersby," a melodious voice interjected. "I never imagined finding you here."

Ryan turned his head to find none other than Stephanie Maplewood gliding toward him with a brilliant smile pasted on her porcelain face. If a woman had ever looked as though she was cast from plaster, then it was truly she. He'd always considered her to be pretty, though in a somewhat unusual sort of way—the unusual part being that neither a single blemish nor the trace of a fine line marked her face. If they had, she might actually have looked human.

Upon seeing her now, his first instinct was to turn and run. After all, the woman had been chasing after him since her debut two years ago, though he couldn't imagine what had her so obsessed; he'd repeatedly made it clear that whatever she hoped for would never be. However, he was a gentleman, and as such, he did what all well-bred gentlemen were raised to do. He slapped on his most charming smile and said, "Always a pleasure, Lady Stephanie."

"I hope that I am not intruding," she remarked. "But when I saw you, I simply had to come right over."

"And we are so glad that you did," Ryan said. "Have you perhaps met my sister, the Countess of Trenton, and her ladyship, the Marchioness of Steepleton?"

"How do you do, Lady Trenton. It is always such a pleasure to see you."

"Yes, I am quite sure that it is, Lady Stephanie," Alexandra remarked in a dry tone that did very little to hide her displeasure of the other woman's sudden appearance. "It is unfortunate that we do not have more time to stop and chat, but we really are very busy, as you can see."

"Then by all means, I shall not disturb you any longer." Lady Stephanie turned to Ryan with a silky smile. "I do hope to see you again soon, Mr. Summersby—at the ball on Friday, perhaps?" And without as much as acknowledging Lady Steepleton's existence even once, she strolled off.

"Did I offend her in any way?" Lady Steepleton asked Alexandra as soon as she was gone.

Alexandra rolled her eyes heavenward and waved her hand in dismissal. "I wouldn't worry overly much about it if I were you. Stephanie Maplewood has been trying to sink her talons into my brother for years and will shun any woman he spends time with, unless she happens to be a blood relative. She is relentless in her pursuit of him." She looked up at Ryan. "Promise me that I will not have to suffer with her as my sister-in-law

"You have my word on it," he promised, as his eyes strayed to the marchioness.

CHAPTER EIGHT

"We'll drop you off first, Alex," Ryan said as they got back inside the carriage after placing Lady Steepleton's order at the dressmaker's. The woman they'd spoken to there, a Madame Bessette, had assured them that the gown would be ready on Friday morning, just in time for the Glendale ball.

Ryan spotted the look of mischief on his sister's face and warned her with a frown. All he wanted was to have some time alone with Lady Steepleton so they could talk, but with the way things were, there was never a moment of privacy.

"As you wish," Alexandra replied. She looked as if she might erupt with laughter. Ryan rolled his eyes. Well, at least she wasn't enough of a stickler to stand in his way, for which he should probably count his lucky stars.

Lady Steepleton on the other hand, looked visibly shocked, her lips parting as if she were readying herself to protest. Ryan's heart hammered as he watched her most expectantly, but when Alexandra said no more, the marchioness apparently decided not to force the subject and settled back against the seat instead. Ryan's heart rate slowed. He knew he was risking her reputation, but it couldn't be helped; they would simply have to be careful. Whatever it was that was happening between them had to be explored—he could ignore it no longer. And if at the end of their conversation it appeared as though their acquaintance with one another might progress, he vowed to tell her about his assignment. Better to be honest now than to deceive.

They arrived at Trenton House within fifteen minutes. Ryan watched as Alexandra gave her ladyship a quick embrace, gathered her skirts, and offered him her hand so he could help her alight. "Don't do anything untoward," Alexandra warned him as he led her up the front steps of her home. "It wouldn't do to ruin her. As it is, you're riding alone with her in a closed carriage." Ryan opened his mouth to speak, but she cut him off. "I'm not judging you or telling you what to do; the choice is yours. I'm merely advising you to use caution."

"And this should come from you," he said, grinning, and she responded with a smile.

Her eyes, however, were a touch more serious. "You're not away in some foreign city where nobody knows you. This is Mayfair, Ryan. If you decide to ravish her, you'd best pick your locations wisely."

He knew she was right, of course. "I've no idea of ravishing her in a carriage, Alex. I merely thought we might talk."

Alexandra stared back at him with vast amounts of doubt in her eyes. "Talk?"

"As it happens, I enjoy our conversations immensely."

Stepping inside her foyer, Alexandra squeezed his arm and lowered her voice to a whisper. "If that was all you meant to do, you'd hardly need to risk scandal by getting her alone."

She had a point, and she was right, of course. Bidding her a pleasant afternoon, he strode back down the walkway and popped his head inside the carriage. "I know this is not quite proper," he said, offering Lady Steepleton a means of escape, "but I was hoping for a little more time with you than it might take for us to drive up David Street. Would you mind terribly if we asked the driver to take us about for a while?"

Again she hesitated. He ought to take her directly home if he knew what was good for both of them, but the temptation of having her to himself was too great to resist, and so he had offered her the ultimate decision.

"No," she finally said on a gush of air. "No, I don't think I would mind it in the least."

Ryan wasn't about to give her the chance to change her mind. With a curt nod, he issued directions to the driver as quickly and concisely as possible, then climbed up inside and took his seat beside her ladyship. For the next five minutes, neither one of them said a word. Instead, they both stared straight ahead. Ryan was beginning to feel more and more like a naughty child who'd deliberately thwarted his parents' wishes. Lady Steepleton shifted restlessly in her seat. He became instantly aware of her thigh brushing against his. Dear God, he really should have seated himself across from her. Whatever had he been thinking? She moved again, and it had the inexplicable effect of sending warm waves of heat scurrying through him to places he dared not even consider, for fear that other shameful thoughts might enter into his head. Too late. *Blast!*

She made an attempt to turn in her seat, apparently hoping to face him more directly, but she eventually gave up and let out a deep sigh of what he could only presume to be frustration. Hell, he really ought to move to the opposite bench.

"Mr. Summersby," Lady Steepleton suddenly said, turning only her head this time. She leaned back against the side of the carriage to avoid hitting him in the head with her bonnet. "There is something that I absolutely must tell you."

"And there is something that I must tell you," Ryan replied, his eyes locking onto hers. He forced a weak smile to hide his embarrassment at the subject that he was about to address. They were finally alone, and he'd already wasted precious time plucking up the courage. Well, he might as well say what needed saying and pray she wouldn't gape at him with incomprehension afterward. "I. . .I don't quite understand it, but I feel. . ." He let out a sigh, not knowing quite how to go about putting his feelings into words. "I feel this constant need to be with you. And whenever I am not with you, I cannot think of anything else but our next encounter. I understand that we have only just met and that this may sound rash, but I simply cannot seem to get you out of my mind. And then, whenever you grace me with that lovely smile of yours, or I hear you laugh. . .I just want to pull you into my arms and. . ."

He noticed her flustered expression. Oh blast; he'd shocked her. It hadn't been his intention to do so; he'd merely hoped for her to understand the way he felt, had hoped she might reciprocate in some manner. But clearly. . .Oh hell, if only he'd kept his mouth shut and taken her home. He took a deep breath and raked his fingers through his hair in frustration. "Forgive me. This is not the sort of thing that a gentleman ought to tell a lady. I cannot imagine what I was thinking."

"I wonder if you know," she said quietly, so quietly that Ryan had to strain to hear her, "that, as unfathomable as I find it myself, I happen to feel precisely the same way." She then allowed her hand to slide from her lap and onto the seat, where it came to rest right next to his, their two fingers brushing ever so gently against one another.

Heat rushed through him at the point of contact, and his heart leaped. He turned a steady gaze on her, knowing full well that he was flirting with disaster. But how could he resist in light of what she'd just revealed? "Do you mean that?" His voice was hushed, as his finger traced its way along hers.

She offered him an awkward little smile, refusing to meet his eyes as her cheeks turned crimson. "I do," she told him in little more than a whisper.

Ryan drew a ragged breath. He could feel his blood pumping furiously through his veins and wondered if Lady Steepleton was in any way aware of his need. She couldn't possibly be, a woman like her, so composed and demure. It hadn't been his intention to force his desires on her in the carriage. All he'd essentially wanted to do was talk, but when she'd said that she felt the same way, it was almost as if all his primeval urges had suddenly been unleashed.

His eyes drifted over the swell of her breasts, so taut against her bodice from the strain of her anxious breathing that the faint outline of her nipples became clearly visible beneath the muslin. He immediately felt his groin tighten at the thought of what he wanted to do to her and consequently drew a deep breath in an attempt to steady himself. Lifting his hand carefully to her cheek so as not to startle her, he waited quietly for her to relax against him, the soft contours of her cheek pressed against his palm, while her eyes drifted shut and a blissful smile played upon her lips.

How curious it was that when he'd first seen her, she'd struck him as ordinary and plain. Yet looking at her now—her hair slightly tussled beneath her bonnet, her long black eyelashes fluttering against her flushed cheeks, and her full, crimson lips—he realized that she was anything but that. In fact, she was absolutely perfect in every way: a diamond of the first water, in his eyes.

"I have no desire to do anything that you might not wish for me to do," he told her softly as he stroked his thumb against her cheek. "So I would like to ask for your permission first. May I kiss you?"

She caught her breath the moment he asked her, her gaze meeting his in one of puzzlement, as if she couldn't quite fathom what he had just asked her, and it dawned on him, with a massive amount of regrettable sadness, that this remarkable woman did not think herself worthy. She hesitated, studying him as if to ascertain his reasons behind such a request, and for a long unbearable moment, he thought she might decline. But he held her gaze, and somehow, as if by some miracle, he watched as her misgivings subsided and were replaced by longing. On a quivering breath, she managed a small nod of approval.

Ryan didn't need a second telling. Unwilling to give her the chance to reconsider the implications of what she'd just agreed to, he leaned toward her and brushed his lips ever so slightly against hers. It was a feathery soft kiss that lasted no more than a few seconds, gentle and tender in every way. Even so, he could have sworn that his heart stopped beating, while glowing embers ignited in the pit of his belly, a slow blaze that grew in strength until it became a roaring fire.

When he pulled away to gauge her reaction, he saw that same fire reflected in her eyes, her yearning written plainly upon her face, and just like that, he lost what little restraint he'd had. Taking her firmly by the waist, he pulled her onto his lap in one easy sweep. A swift pull on the bow beneath her chin sent her bonnet toppling backward onto the carriage floor only seconds before he crushed his lips against hers.

She quivered against him when he traced his tongue along her lower lip, her posture stiff, as if she might protest at any moment. And though she surely must have considered doing so, she made no attempt to push him away. But Ryan sensed her uncertainty and knew that he must force himself to proceed at a slower pace. Pulling back a little, he placed soft kisses upon her eyelids, and then her cheeks, while his fingers worked their way through her hair, toying with the pins until her dark brown locks tumbled over her shoulders.

He kissed her chin and then her neck, inhaling the sweet scent of her lilac perfume while his hand moved up her side to rest beside her breast. He paused there, inhaling her, then exhaling her, while her pulse drummed beneath his lips, her breathing low and ragged. But then she shifted. It was ever so slight, and quite subtle, so subtle, in fact, that a less experienced man might not have noticed. But Ryan was no fledgling, and he certainly had no intention of denying either one of them when an invitation had just been offered.

With slow deliberation, his fingers crept over one breast

and then over the other in soft strokes. Again she stiffened, her breath caught in her throat until a small groan of pleasure squeezed its way between her lips. So exquisite was the sound that it almost had him spending himself right then and there like a callow youth who'd never lain with a woman before. Taking courage in her response, he took one breast in his hand, squeezing it gently and testing the feel of it. She bowed her head against his, kissing his brow, then his temple, his cheek, until her lips finally found his in a deep and scorching kiss.

Once again, he ran his tongue against her lips, but this time it lasted only a moment. On a soft sigh, she parted her lips and pressed herself closer against his embrace. A low growl rose from Ryan's throat as this first hurdle was overcome. Tightening his grip to keep her steady as the carriage lurched sideways, he eased his tongue inside her mouth, tasting her warmth before coaxing her to follow his lead.

It didn't take long to discover that she was a nimble student, her passion matching his own as she raked her fingers through his hair and tugged him closer in obvious desperation. Nothing could have pleased him more, yet it wasn't enough; he wanted more. With trembling fingers, he eased her sleeves from her shoulders and lowered his head to place soft kisses against the dip of her shoulder blade. Emboldened by her quiet murmur, he allowed himself to go a step further. Hooking his thumbs on the neckline of her bodice, he ran them slowly against her smooth flesh, brushing her gently aroused nipples. Her back arched on a loud groan, and he tugged the fine fabric away, baring her to his greedy gaze. He eased back a little so he could take a better look at her lovely delights: each breast so plump and full, and with a dark, perky nipple at its crest. It was impossible for him to look away. Instead, a devilish grin drew its way across his face. "So beautiful," he whispered as he slid his fingers across them. She responded with a sharp intake of breath. He looked her straight in the eye as he took one tender nipple between his fingers and gently squeezed. She gasped and closed her eyes. "Do you like that?" he asked, knowing full well that she did.

Still, he waited for her response: a small nod, followed by a soft "yes."

"Then I am quite certain that you will like this too." He leaned forward and licked the hardened flesh with a slowness that would have driven any warm-blooded woman half mad. "Oh God," she whimpered, pulling him against her with a fierceness that caught him completely unaware. It excited him to no end. There was a passion within her that he'd just unleashed, an urgent need as desperate as his own. Yes, Lady Steepleton would make an ardent lover; of that he was now completely certain.

He wanted her. There was no longer any inkling of doubt in his mind. *Not now*, he reminded himself, forcing back the desire that threatened to overwhelm him. He'd made a vow, not only to her, but to himself, that he would not take her innocence—not now, at least—not in a lurching carriage. No, he would have to wait for his own release, even if it meant that he'd have to wait for the wedding night. One thing was now quite clear in his mind, however: he *would* marry her.

Easing away from her, he gently lifted her bodice, returning her to some measure of decency as he did his best to avoid the look of disappointment that shone in her eyes.

Moving her off his lap, he bent to pick up her bonnet, then helped her arrange her hair in an orderly fashion. "Thank you," he muttered, taking her hand in his and pressing a tender kiss against her knuckles, "for allowing me such liberties."

She blushed deeply in response, then favored him with a dazzling smile. "It was a pleasure."

Tapping the roof of the carriage to signal the driver that it was time to take her ladyship home, he placed his arm around her shoulders, pulled her close to him, and took courage from the intimacy of the moment. "As I said before, I know that we have scarcely known one another for more than a week, but I do hope that I have just made my intentions quite clear. I plan to marry you, my lady, if you will have me, that is." Mary couldn't get a single word out of her mouth; it seemed as if they were all jammed together in her throat all at once. So she just sat there as the idea of marrying Mr. Summersby manifested itself in her mind. He was right, of course; they didn't know each other well at all, and she still had to tell him about. . .heavens, she'd meant to do it before, but he'd completely led her off track. She opened her mouth in an attempt to speak, more horrified now by his potential response than ever before, because the truth of the matter was that becoming his wife didn't trouble her in the least. In fact, it felt incredibly right.

"And if you will let me," Mr. Summersby continued, stopping her short once more, "hell, even if you will not, I promise to do whatever I can to keep you safe. Nobody is going to hurt you, not as long as I have anything to say about it."

Mary stiffened in her seat as the world around her came

to a screeching halt. "What do you mean?" she asked numbly as she eased herself away from him.

He let out a heavy sigh and squeezed her hand as if he meant to reassure her. Instead, a slow dread swept over her as she waited to hear what he wished to tell her. "I saw the look on your face the other day when you opened that letter," he said, turning to her with deep concern in his light blue eyes. "For whatever reason, you were terrified of its contents."

"That is hardly enough for you to assume that I might be in danger," she told him cautiously. "You have no idea of what that letter said." She looked at him imploringly, hoping that he'd merely been jumping to conclusions.

"No," he agreed, "it is not. But before you and I met, I was approached by a good friend of my family's, a man whom, it appears, was also a close friend of your father's. His name is Sir Percy Foxstone." He was silent for a moment, as if waiting for her to confirm her knowledge of this gentleman, but she'd never heard of this Foxstone fellow, so she just sat there, offering Mr. Summersby a blank stare, her every nerve on sensitized alert. "He asked, on behalf of your father, that I keep an eye on you. Apparently, your father was under the impression that you would be in grave danger if anything were to happen to him; he asked Percy to ensure your protection, as a personal favor to him."

Mary gazed back at Mr. Summersby, while tears began to prickle behind her eyes. How could she have been such a fool? He hadn't sought her company because of how attractive he found her, or because he liked her company more than the next woman's. As it turned out, she was nothing more than an assignment to him—possibly a nuisance even. With startling clarity, she saw that he'd begun calling on her for no other reason than to keep a watchful eye on her at all times and perhaps even to gain access to whatever information he might need.

She should have known that a man like Mr. Summersby would never be drawn to a woman like her. Circumstance had thrown them together, and they'd allowed themselves to get carried away by it. The worst of it was that he was no innocent and that he would very likely have carried on in much the same way with a Covent Garden nun if his need had been great enough. But now, because she was a lady of the *ton*, he was planning to sacrifice himself on the wedding altar in order to save her reputation. There was no other explanation for it—unless, of course, he was after her money and had just laid a very neat trap. Her heart sank at the very thought of such a possibility.

"Why you?" she asked in a tight voice that conveyed the extent of her growing anger. "Why would this man. . .Sir Percy was it? Why would he ask this of you?"

Mr. Summersby hesitated for only a moment. "Because," he said simply, "I used to work for him as an agent for the Foreign Office. But after my last mission, I chose to return to Oxford instead, in order to finish my studies and get a degree. The fact of it is, Sir Percy wanted this matter to be kept private and confidential, so he enlisted me rather than an agent already employed by the Home Office."

Mary gaped at him. She simply did not know what to say. Clearly, they had rushed when it came to considering something as permanent as marriage; they really didn't know each other at all, yet she'd practically been prepared to toss away her innocence only five minutes earlier. It didn't even bear thinking about.

"I know you must be shocked by all of this," he told her apologetically. "I hope it does not change anything between us too drastically."

"Ryan, I. . .Mr. Summersby," she amended. "How can you possibly think that this will not change anything between us? This changes *everything*. Your only interest in me was based entirely on your assignment. You do not really want me, sir, but you appear to be stuck with me all the same, and somehow that has clouded your better judgment. So, in answer to your previous question, no, I will not marry you. I want someone who truly cares for me, not someone who is prepared to go blindly to the altar because society dictates that he must."

Mr. Summersby stared back at her in bewilderment. A slow frown had begun to mar his handsome features. "I am sorry if you see it that way, my lady," he told her in a clipped tone. "I assure you that I meant no offense. In fact, I genuinely like you and—"

"If such a bland word is the best you can think of to describe the way you feel about me," she shot back with growing agitation, "then we truly are ill-suited for one another."

"Well, you are entitled to your own opinion, of course." He crossed his arms in a highly annoyed fashion. "However, there is still the matter of your safety to discuss. As it is, I have already encountered a stranger prowling about outside your house on two separate occasions. He asked that you stop meddling with matters that do not concern you."

Mary's eyes narrowed into two angry slits. "You've been watching my house at night?"

"My lady, I cannot help but find it rather vexing that the point which seems to have you most aggrieved is not the presence of a dubious stranger outside your home, but rather the fact that I have been trying to keep you safe from harm."

Mary grimaced. She couldn't deny that he had a point. "What did he look like?" she asked.

"I do not know. It was dark, and he was using a scarf to conceal his face."

Mary clenched her jaw. "In short, you have nothing useful to tell me, other than admitting that you've been spying on me."

"I was not spying on you, my lady. I was merely trying to determine why somebody might wish to harm you," he told her defensively.

"Well, your answer is as good as mine," she snapped as the carriage rolled to a sudden halt. Not bothering to wait for a footman, she reached for the handle and opened the door to get out.

"Then at least tell me who the young man is that I have seen leaving your house on two separate occasions. Is he a messenger of some sort?"

Mary gave him a frosty glare. "That, Mr. Summersby, is absolutely none of your concern."

He grabbed hold of her wrist before she managed to alight, forcing her to stay and listen. "I only want to help you, Mary. That is all."

Mary paused in the doorway of the carriage. She couldn't hold back the tears any longer, and against her will, they spilled over and poured down her cheeks. "Is that so? Because only a moment ago, you were telling me that you wanted to do a whole lot more." She snatched her arm away. "And in the future, you will please refrain from using my Christian name. I am Lady Steepleton to you. I suggest you try to remember that. Good day, Mr. Summersby."

Unwilling to be detained by him a moment longer, she quickly snatched her arm away, stepped down onto the pavement, and ran inside her house, fleeing from the ridiculous hope she'd allowed her mind to foster: that a man like him might genuinely care for a woman like her.

CHAPTER NINE

Mary raced up the stairs to her bedroom, locking the door firmly behind her. She didn't care that Thornton had gawked at her or that Emma had made a heroic attempt to follow. No, she needed to be alone for a while; she needed to think. Her heart raced as she contemplated her time alone with Mr. Summersby in the carriage. There was no doubt in her mind that she'd behaved in the most deplorable manner, but God help her, she'd liked it. But then to discover that he'd sought her companionship, not out of choice, but because it had been his job to do so left her heart close to the point of breaking.

Still, he'd told her something that she had to consider. The letter that she had received hadn't been the only threat. There was the stranger Mr. Summersby had mentioned. Mary contemplated this for a moment, then thought back on the conversation she'd had with Lord Woodbridge. He'd advised her to consult her father's journals, but until now she hadn't had the opportunity to do so.

Moving quickly toward her wardrobe, she yanked the door open and sank down onto her knees, pushing her shoes

aside as she began pulling out the boxes that she'd brought
with her from Belgium. She paused for a long while on a
couple of the ones containing her father's more personal effects: his pocket watch, a monogrammed handkerchief, his
favorite pipe, and a few other knickknacks.

Wiping the sentimental tears from her eyes, she put the
boxes carefully aside and grabbed hold of a larger one that
had been shoved into one corner. Dragging it out onto the
floor, she took a deep breath before slowly lifting the lid and
setting it aside on the carpet. Inside were ten leather-bound
books, all arranged in two neat rows, their spines all facing
up. Mary just stared at them, almost too afraid to touch.
These had been her father's most prized possession, notes
that he'd accumulated over a span of thirty years relating his
trials and tribulations, his successes and aspirations, all with
one purpose in mind: to advance medicine.

She traced her fingers over them in wonder. Was it possible that they held a secret so powerful that people she'd never
even met felt threatened by it? It seemed ridiculous, yet she
had the letter and had also been made aware that someone
was keeping a watchful eye on her. She shook off the shudder that threatened to run down her spine and returned her
attention to the books. Each volume had been branded with
a gold number. Mary picked up a dark green edition with
the number 1 etched into it and, opening it to the first page,
began to read.

It was almost ten in the evening when Mary found herself
awakened by Emma, who was kneeling beside her and ur-

gently shaking her shoulder. "What is it?" she asked, looking about with sleepy eyes and seeing that she'd fallen asleep on the floor. Her father's journal had slipped from her fingers and was lying snugly in her lap.

"I'm terribly sorry to disturb you, my lady, but it appears that the Dowager Duchess of Warwick is here to see you. She claims that it is a matter of utmost importance."

Mary was confused. "Is it not the middle of the night, Emma?"

"Not quite, my lady, though I must say that it is rather late for a social call. I did attempt to tell her so, but she's a rather formidable woman and refused to take no for an answer. When she insisted upon seeing you this very instant, I found it hard to refuse her once she explained that Lady Arlington had told her about you and that she has come to seek your help. I am sorry, my lady, truly I am, but I really did not know what else to do, short of sending her on her way, which I fear would have been rather rude—especially if the matter is as urgent as she claims."

"It is quite all right, Emma. Would you please show her ladyship into the parlor and offer her some tea. I will be down shortly to greet her."

"Yes, my lady." Emma offered Mary her hand and helped her mistress off the floor before smoothing her skirts with her hands. "Should I call upon any of the other servants?"

Mary had no desire to disturb any of her staff. Still, she knew she'd probably be hungry later, having missed her supper, so rather than answer Emma's question, she asked, "You wouldn't happen to know if Thornton left a plate for me in the dining room, would you?"

"He did—some ham and cheese with bread and pickles, I believe."

"Then I do believe that we shall manage just fine without disturbing anyone else, as long as you will see to the tea. After that, you may go back to bed."

Emma bobbed a small curtsy and went to see about her business, while Mary removed her spencer. She'd been in such a hurry upon arriving home earlier that she'd quite forgotten to take it off. She thought of Mr. Summersby again and sighed in annoyance. What an infuriating man he was! Well, she was better off without him, she decided, grabbing a shawl and winding it about her shoulders. A man like that would only get in the way of her work, no matter how appealing she might find him.

I will not think of it, she told herself as she made her way downstairs to greet her uninvited guest, pausing for a brief moment in the hallway to glance at her reflection in the mirror. No, she wouldn't think of the handsome Mr. Summersby at all.

Groaning at the impossibility of the task that she was setting for herself, she quickly adjusted a few stray hairs, took a deep breath, and opened the door to the parlor. "How do you do," she said politely as she took in the slim figure of the elderly woman who was sitting on the sofa. Lady Warwick's posture was exceedingly dignified as she gracefully balanced her saucer in one hand, while holding her teacup in the other.

"I apologize for troubling you at such an unseemly hour, Lady Steepleton, but I wish to discuss a matter that requires complete discretion. I hope you will forgive me." Her voice held a distinguished tone that spoke of true aristocracy, while the intensity behind her eyes told Mary that she was in the company of a highly intelligent woman. She was immediately curious to know what had brought her ladyship to her home so late in the evening.

"Lady Arlington is my grandniece, you see, so when I visited her earlier today and discovered what you did for her. . .well, I immediately knew that I must seek your advice. You cannot begin to imagine how many physicians I've spoken to about my predicament." A deep frown creased her forehead, and her lips drew together in a thin line as she shook her head in open frustration. "They all claim that an operation will be far too risky, especially with my age taken into account. If you ask me, they're all a bunch of cowards. Still, the matter remains that I refuse to live with the pain a moment longer. I dearly hope that you will be able to help me."

Mary walked quietly over to one of the armchairs and took a seat across from Lady Warwick. "You know, it would help me a great deal if you could tell me precisely what it is that's troubling you," she told her kindly as she refilled Lady Warwick's teacup before pouring herself a cup as well.

Folding her hands in her lap, her ladyship took a deep breath before saying, "I have been told that I have an unpleasantly large kidney stone lodged inside me, and frankly. . ." She suddenly scrunched her face and gasped as she gritted out, "It's a rather unforgiving bugger."

Momentarily startled by the dowager's use of profanity, it took Mary a second longer than usual to react to what was happening, but once she did, she quickly produced a bottle of laudanum from a cabinet designed to house carafes filled with brandy and other such drinks. Instead, it contained most of Mary's medical equipment. She understood that Lady Warwick was enduring an intense amount of pain and consequently added as much of the medicine to her tea as she deemed safe. "Here, drink this," she told her quietly. "It will ease your suffering."

The dowager obediently complied. It took a few minutes for the laudanum to take effect, but once it did, she drew a deep breath and returned her cup to Mary, settling back against the sofa with a drained expression upon her face. "Thank you," she said. "I don't usually agree with taking that stuff, but it was necessary this time. It seems as if the pain is getting worse—unbearably so."

"If it is a kidney stone that you are suffering from, then I will most likely have to operate in order to have it removed." Mary met the dowager's gaze. "It will be not only an uncomfortable procedure, but a painful one as well, I'm afraid."

The dowager gave her a hard stare of determination. "I have never been the sort to be bowled over by anything, Lady Steepleton, not by men, not by the pestilent rules of society, and not by the difficulties of life itself. Consequently, I simply refuse to allow such an insolent little stone to dictate my level of well-being when I am otherwise in perfectly good health. I have reached the point where I will happily endure whatever I must, if it will only free me from this constant torture."

Mary nodded her head sympathetically. "I must also warn you that the opinion of the other physicians you've consulted must not be entirely dismissed. Such an operation is not without risk." The dowager opened her mouth as if to protest, but Mary quickly continued. "I'm not trying to dissuade you, but since you are contemplating putting your life in my hands, I do feel obligated to tell you this. My track record is good. I've lost very few patients, and none after performing a lateral lithotomy—which is what this situation will call for—of which I've done five. In addition, you will require one to three months to recover, so if we do it now, you shall be forced to miss the remainder of the season."

"Pfft. . ." The dowager waved her hand dismissively. "As it is, I haven't attended a social function in over two years due to my ailment. But if you are able to help me, then, who knows? Perhaps I'll be able to dance a jig next year."

Mary smiled. She really liked the older woman. "If you feel up to it," she said. "I can examine you right away, and then tomorrow evening, I can come to your home and perform the procedure, if that is agreeable to you. Do you have a maid or a lady-in-waiting whom you would trust enough to assist?"

The dowager nodded. "Mrs. Harper will do; she was there when my children were born, so I know she's not the squeamish sort."

Mary blinked, realizing that Mrs. Harper must be a trusty servant if she'd been in her mistress's employ for so many years. Composing herself, she got ready to examine her ladyship. It didn't take long for her to confirm that a kidney stone was indeed the culprit. "Will nine p.m. tomorrow evening suit your ladyship?" she asked as she walked the dowager to the door.

"I think it would be splendid," Lady Warwick replied. She smiled, and as she did, Mary couldn't help but notice that her eyes were sparkling with the onset of tears. "I cannot possibly thank you enough. Really, Lady Steepleton, I don't know what I would have done without your help."

Upon seeing her out, Mary retrieved the tray of food that Thornton had left for her in the dining room and then made her way back upstairs to her bedroom, completely exhausted. She was almost at her door when a soft thud, followed by a rustling sound, brought her to a halt. She paused to listen, but no other sound followed. Convincing herself that it was probably nothing, she eased her bedroom door open and instinctively glanced around the room. Nothing looked particularly out of place until a cold wind gripped her and she saw that her window stood gaping wide open. Setting down her tray, she ran across to it and looked out, just in time to see a dark shadow disappearing over the garden wall. "Oh God," she murmured as her stomach tied itself into a tight knot of despair.

Swallowing hard, she pulled the window shut with trembling fingers and locked it firmly back in place, then closed the curtains to block out the darkness. She turned around to glance about the room once more. He eyes went straight to her dresser, where she'd left her father's journal. It was gone. Anger, accompanied by an overwhelming sense of loss, poured through her. This was her father's life, written in his own words and by his own hand, that someone had stolen from her. Whatever their reason, it wasn't justified.

A thought struck her, and gripped by fear she ran over to the wardrobe and threw open the door. The boxes were still there where she'd left them, but what about the books? She lifted the lid. There they were, all of them, save for the very first volume. Mary breathed a sigh of relief. Whatever it was that the intruder had been after, she still had a chance of finding it before he did. She would need a plan, though. It was no longer safe for her to remain in her own house, at least not with the books stashed away in her wardrobe and with very little with which to protect herself. Whoever it was that had taken the first book would almost certainly return soon in search of the rest. She couldn't very well guard them every hour of every day.

But where could she possibly go on such short notice? She considered her other property in Northamptonshire, but did she really want to shy away to a lonely castle where she knew even fewer people than she did in London? The truth of the matter was that, outside of her staff, she had only two friends: Mr. Summersby and his sister, Alexandra.

Mr. Summersby had told her that he wanted to help, and in spite of everything, she believed him. However, after what had happened between them and the things she'd said to him, he was just about the last person she wanted to crawl to for help.

That left only one person: the Countess of Trenton. With a heavy sigh, Mary began piling her father's journals into a bag, along with a few items of clothing that she placed on top. Wishing to be gone before Emma and Thornton awoke, she hurried out of the house, leaving behind a quick note, explaining to them that she'd gone to visit a friend for a few days. She then pulled her hood over her head and walked quickly toward Berkeley Square, intent on waiting by the servant's entrance to avoid waking the household too early.

When Alexandra eventually walked into breakfast at ten, she was more than a little surprised to find Mary waiting for her at the table. "I am so sorry," she said. "I do hope that I haven't kept you waiting for too long."

Mary gave her a weak smile. "Not at all, Alexandra. Your husband asked if he should wake you before he went out, but I asked him not to disturb you."

Alexandra eyed her quizzically. "You must have been here for quite some time if you managed to run into him. He usually leaves by eight."

Mary lowered her eyes to her lap, in an almost embarrassed fashion that instantly piqued Alexandra's interest. "The truth is that I have been here since four."

"Good heavens!" Alexandra exclaimed. "Has something happened? Are you all right?"

Mary nodded. "Yes, yes, I am quite all right, thank you. However, there was an intruder at my house during the night. I believe I must have startled him, for he ran off. Nonetheless, I didn't feel comfortable remaining there and hoped that you wouldn't mind overly much if I came here. Forgive me, but I could think of nowhere else to go."

Alexandra dropped onto a chair, completely speechless. "You poor thing," she finally managed to say. "Of course I don't mind. But this intruder you mention: do you have any idea why he was there?"

"He was after my father's journals, I believe, for I had left one of them out on my nightstand, and it was the only thing he took." Alexandra spotted the glistening tears before they began to fall. A moment later, Mary was shaking with grief. "I am terribly sorry," she said, sobbing.

Alexandra was beside her in a second. "You mustn't be. It is quite understandable for you to be shaken, especially when something so personal and so dear to you was taken." She poured Mary a cup of tea. "Here, this will help soothe you."

Alexandra watched while Mary drank and her breathing returned to normal. "Do you have any idea why someone would want to take your father's journal, Mary?" she eventually asked.

Mary shook her head and let out a heavy sigh. "No, but I received a threat the other day, warning me not to follow in my father's footsteps. And Ryan. . .er, Mr. Summersby. . .told me that he encountered a stranger who gave a similar warning. Whatever this is about, it must be linked to my father's work in some way. I just fail to see how."

Alexandra considered that for a moment before she asked the next question. "Have you told Ryan that you are a surgeon?"

Mary looked as though she might cry again. "I wanted to, but we had a horrible fight. He told me he'd been assigned to protect me. I know that if it were not for that, he wouldn't have given me a second glance, so I refused him after he. . .Oh dear, I have made such a mess of everything."

"After he what?" Alexandra asked with mounting curiosity. She had a good mind to throttle her brother if what she suspected was true. He'd been so bloody righteous in Paris when he'd caught her together with Michael, and now. . .She took a deep breath to calm herself. "Tell me what he did."

Mary sniffed and looked away. "I couldn't possibly," she groaned. "And even if I did, I cannot pretend that he is entirely to blame; we were equally responsible for what happened. It is no matter, really, only that he now believes he *must* marry me, and I just won't have it. I refuse to marry somebody just because he has some nitwit notion that he must, simply because society decrees it has to be so. Nobody saw us, so nobody needs to know about it." She met Alexandra's gaze. "And if you tell anyone, then I shall only deny it."

Alexandra nodded. Yes, Mary Croyden was indeed very similar to herself. She couldn't help but like her, and in spite of what Mary might think, Alexandra knew that Ryan cared about her and that he wasn't just favoring her with his attention because of the assignment. But she would leave Ryan to convince her ladyship of that. As for now, there was still the matter of Mary's safety to consider. "Naturally, you are more than welcome to stay here until this whole thing resolves itself," she told Mary. "We have plenty of space and shall be more than happy to have you."

"Thank you, Alexandra," Mary told her with a grateful smile. "I truly appreciate that."

"In the meantime, I think it might be a good idea for you to read your father's journals. He must have left a clue for you somewhere in there, or if not, then you must at least try to find whatever it is this person was looking for. If he was so intent on getting his hands on it, then it must be important. But be careful, Mary, because whatever it is that he's up to, I'm afraid that he might just be getting started. Once he discovers that you have no intention of heeding his warnings, he may become far more vigilant."

Mary swallowed hard and nodded. "I understand."

"Good," Alexandra told her with a bright smile. "Then after breakfast, I shall teach you how to fire a pistol, and you must promise me that you will go nowhere without it."

Mary gaped at Alexandra as if she were completely mad.

"Can't I just. . ." She took a sharp breath. "I'm sure that a dagger will serve just fine."

Alexandra pinned her with a hard gaze. "You need to get very close to your attacker for that to work. Most people would lose their nerve before they managed to deliver a fatal wound. A pistol is much more reliable. In any event, it is my condition for helping you." She offered her a sly smile. "Are we agreed?"

Mary responded with a slow nod. "Yes," she muttered. "We are agreed."

CHAPTER TEN

Later that day, after taking a much needed nap, Mary went in search of Alexandra. She found her in the parlor with her son, Richard, on her lap, tickling the chortling infant with a feather. It was such a delightful scene that Mary couldn't help but laugh. "You certainly appear to be enjoying yourselves," she said.

Looking up, Alexandra immediately favored her with a warm smile. "We certainly are; this is one of his favorite games," she said as she handed Richard over to his nurse. "Did you sleep well?"

"Oh yes, I feel quite rested now, thank you."

"Good. Then let's have some lunch before we head out," Alexandra said.

"Head out? And where, may I ask, are we going?"

"Just a little way out of town," Alexandra replied, taking Mary's arm and steering her toward the dining room. "I know of a very secluded spot where you can have your first lesson."

"Good heavens!" Mary exclaimed, recalling their earlier conversation. "I was hoping you might have forgotten."

"Well, as you can see, I have not," Alexandra said, taking

her seat at the long mahogany dining table and suggesting that Mary do the same. The food was brought in a moment later: grilled trout bathed in a creamy lemon and dill sauce, small potatoes, and a tomato and onion salad.

"I'm not at all sure that I will be any good at it," Mary complained as one of the servants placed a piece of trout on her plate. She took a sip of her wine. "Not to say that you aren't an excellent teacher, for indeed I am quite certain that you are, but I've never even held a pistol in my hands before, and. . .well, to be perfectly honest, it rather frightens me."

Alexandra chuckled. "It isn't nearly as difficult as you might think. It requires practice to get your aim right, but we're not attempting to make you the finest shot there ever was. The sole purpose of this is for you to have some means of protection. Oftentimes there isn't even a need to fire; the mere fact that you are holding a pistol in your hands can be enough to deter an attacker."

"But—"

"No more buts, Mary," Alexandra told her sternly. "This was my condition for letting you stay here, remember?"

Mary nodded reluctantly as she took another sip of wine. They'd made an agreement, and there was no way for her to back out of it now unless she wanted Alexandra to think her a coward—not a favorable option, by any means. No, she would simply have to calm her nerves and follow Alexandra's lead.

"This is it," Alexandra said a couple of hours later. They'd ridden through the woods on the outskirts of the city, veering off the road until they'd eventually arrived at a small clearing.

Dismounting, they tied their horses to a birch that stood to one side. "Here, take this," Alexandra said, holding a pistol out toward Mary. "Get a feel for it."

Mary hesitantly took the pistol from her. It was heavier than she'd expected. Turning it over in her hands, she studied it with growing curiosity, unable to wonder how many lead shots she'd pulled out of bleeding soldiers at Waterloo. This was the first time she was taking a close look at the sort of weapon that had delivered all those patients to her. The fact that she would soon attempt firing it made her feel slightly odd, as if she were about to commit a sin of some sort.

"How do you like it?"

Mary looked up to find Alexandra watching her with a crooked smile. "I'm not sure," she admitted. "Something about it feels wrong."

Alexandra grinned. "You'll get used to it. Here, I'll show you how to load it." She opened a leather pouch and measured a small quantity of black powder. "Pour this down the barrel—yes, just like that. Now, take the shot and wrap it in this bit of cloth. There's a ramrod right there, just beneath the barrel; take it, and ram the shot home."

Mary followed Alexandra's instructions to the letter and was swiftly met with a nod of approval, even though she'd never felt more awkward in her life. Yet she had to admit that in spite of her reluctance to learn about firearms, she was really quite grateful for the lesson.

"Now then," Alexandra said, stepping up beside her, "stand like this."

"Like this?" Mary asked, copying Alexandra's wide stance.

"Yes, just like that. Good. Now, put your right hand here and hold it firmly in place. Your index finger goes on the trigger. Then take your left hand and use it to support your right—no, not like that." She moved Mary's hand to the correct position. "Like this."

Mary glanced at Alexandra with renewed enthusiasm. "Should I try to fire?" she asked.

"You can," Alexandra told her, stepping away to a safe distance. "Aim for that tree over there and—"

A loud crack split the air as Mary pulled the trigger. But her stance had slackened in the meantime, making her completely unprepared for the sudden force that hit her. In fact, it knocked her completely off her feet and onto the ground while the pistol itself went flying.

Silence followed, and then a loud burst of laughter. "Are you all right?" Alexandra said, standing over her breathless friend, who was now lying smack on her back in the lush grass.

"I think so," Mary murmured, still mildly startled by the situation.

"Heavens, that looked funny," Alexandra said, covering her mouth with both hands in an obvious attempt to contain her giggles. "You're not hurt, I hope? Here, let me give you a hand up."

Mary frowned as she took the proffered hand. "No, I'm fine. I had no idea that it would be so difficult," she muttered, smoothing out the wrinkles in her gown. "Did I at least hit my mark?"

"You certainly did," Alexandra cheered, pointing to the tree that was now split open on the side. "So your aim is pretty decent. Now we just need to work a little on your footing."

They continued practicing for the next couple of hours, before deciding that they'd had enough for the day and that it was time to head back home.

Upon their arrival, they handed over their horses to the grooms at the mews. As they made their way toward the front of the house, Mary suddenly caught Alexandra by the arm. "Is that not Lady Cassandra, your sister-in-law?" she asked.

"It is," Alexandra said. She glanced at Mary. "I didn't realize that the two of you were acquainted with one another."

"I met her the day before yesterday when your brother took me for a ride in the park. She was chasing after her dog."

Alexandra chuckled. "That sounds just like Cass," she said.

"But who is that lady she is with? She looks so extravagant and stylish."

"That, Mary, is my mother-in-law, the Duchess of Willowbrook. Now, come along and I shall introduce you to her straight away. Lady Willowbrook!" she then called out, drawing the attention of the duchess, a woman who still looked remarkably young for her age.

Lady Willowbrook and Lady Cassandra quickly waved in acknowledgment as they began heading toward them. "We were just considering stopping by your house for a visit," Lady Willowbrook said as they drew nearer.

"Well, you are most welcome," Alexandra replied. "In fact, I would like to introduce you to a dear friend of mine, the Marchioness of Steepleton."

"Hello again," Lady Cassandra told Mary with a quick smile.

"No Trevor today?" Mary asked cheerfully.

"Not today." Lady Cassandra leaned closer and lowered her voice to a conspiratorial whisper. "If he were to take off like that while I'm out with Mama, I'd never hear the end of it."

"I see that the two of you have already met," Lady Willowbrook said brightly, casting a chastising glance in her daughter's direction. "Well, it is a pleasure to make your acquaintance, my dear."

"The pleasure is all mine, Your Grace," Mary told her.

Lady Willowbrook immediately responded with a girlish giggle as she waved her hand dismissively. "Oh no, you must not call me that. Heavens, it makes me feel rather antiquated." She took Mary firmly by the arm and began steering her toward Alexandra's front door. "We are all friends here, or at least we shall be once we have finished our tea, so I really must insist that you call me Isabella."

"Very well then," Mary said and grinned, delighting in the other woman's high spirits. "But only if you will return the favor by calling me Mary."

As soon as they were all comfortably seated in the parlor, Isabella turned to Mary and Alexandra. "We ordered some new gowns for Cassandra this morning. I daresay she'll be the belle of the ball for the remainder of the season; no young gentleman with a pair of eyes in his head will be able to resist her."

"Thank you, Mama," Cassandra said with a note of embarrassment. "But the truth of the matter is, I don't have very many gowns left for the remainder of the season, after spilling punch down the front of my green one at the last ball I went to. So Mama decided to take me shopping for some new ones in hopes of replenishing my wardrobe."

"And were you successful?" Mary asked as she took a sip of her tea.

"We picked out some lovely fabrics for five new gowns, one of which should be ready just in time for the ball on Friday—the one at Glendale House," Isabella said. "It will be a light pink one, which I daresay will go extremely well with Cassandra's complexion."

"That is, of course, if I even make it to the ball without ruining it somehow," Cassandra moaned as she picked at a tear in her neckline. "I don't understand why this is always happening to me. No man in his right mind will marry someone as disorderly as I."

"Well, my dear, you shall just have to be extra careful then," Isabella told her despairing daughter. "However, you are fortunate enough to be graced with both good looks and charm. Any gentleman would be a fool not to have you, unless, of course, he cannot afford a maid to mend your gowns, in which case he isn't worth having anyway."

"I couldn't agree more," Alexandra said as she bit into a strawberry tart.

"Have you managed to form any attachments yet, Mary?" Isabella then asked with much interest. "I suppose the whole London season is rather new to you, but as an eligible marchioness, I would imagine that the young gentlemen are quite eager for your attention."

Mary shook her head sadly. She had received enough flowers to open up her own shop, but what did that matter when the only man who interested her had sought her companionship with an ulterior motive in mind? "No," she said. "But I am perfectly content with that, since I have very little desire to marry."

Isabella grinned. "I do believe that Alexandra was of the same opinion until she met my son. Is that not so?"

Looking a little startled as all eyes turned to her, Alexandra just nodded. "It is indeed," she told the duchess, then shrugged a little. "In fact, the thought of falling so deeply in love terrified me. It was my father who made me realize how empty my life would be without love in it, and when the right man came along. . .well, what can I say? I had a change of heart, I suppose."

"But when I came across you and Mr. Summersby in the park the other day, you looked to be quite taken with him— and he with you," Cassandra said as she looked across at Mary.

Mary took a deep breath. This was really a topic that she'd much rather avoid, but now that all eyes in the room were on her, she would have to address the issue. "In a way you are quite correct, Cassandra. It is true that I have enjoyed Mr. Summersby's company on more than one occasion. However, we do have our differences, and, unfortunately, I have come to believe that it will be rather difficult, if not impossible, for us to overcome them."

"Well," Isabella remarked with a twinkle in her eyes, "sometimes it can be a great deal of fun overcoming such differences."

"Mama!" Cassandra exclaimed, jerking around so suddenly that half of her tea landed in her lap.

"Oh come now, my dear, we are all grown women here.

Besides, judging from the sudden color in Mary's cheeks, I daresay that she agrees with me." Isabella handed her clumsy daughter a napkin.

Mary dropped her gaze to the floor. How mortifying that a woman as refined as the duchess would have picked up on her true feelings. For no matter how disappointed she was at discovering that Mr. Summersby did not share her sentiments, she simply couldn't stop thinking about him and hoping that she'd somehow misjudged him.

"Whatever the case," Alexandra said, "it does appear as though our dear Mary has already gotten herself an archenemy."

"And who might that be?" Isabella asked with a sudden frown.

"Oh, it must be Lady Stephanie," Cassandra said. "Everyone knows that she's been pining for Mr. Summersby for the longest time."

"Well, you are correct in your assumption, Cass," Alexandra told her. "We had the misfortune of running into her only yesterday. She practically gave poor Mary the cut direct."

"Is that so?" Isabella ground out. She was clearly quite vexed by Lady Stephanie's audacity. "I am sorry that you had to experience such a rude encounter, Mary. There is no question that Lady Stephanie could do with some discipline. She has not only developed a rather distasteful character, she is also far too spoiled."

"Well, as far as I am concerned," Mary said, "she can have Mr. Summersby all to herself. He is not the one for me."

"Oh, you mustn't say that!" Alexandra cried in horror. "I would surely die if she were to be my new sister-in-law. I would so much rather have you."

"Well, although I am not altogether sure that I like the idea of having such a responsibility placed upon my shoulders, I must admit that am quite flattered," Mary said, her cheeks already dimpling with the beginnings of a playful smile. "But, as I have already said, that is neither here nor there since I do not plan on becoming his wife."

"You will not even give him another chance?" Alexandra asked with a note of desperation.

Mary considered that for a moment. It was difficult to ignore the imploring look in Alexandra's eyes, especially after she'd been so kind to her. And Mr. Summersby was her brother, after all. "Very well, I will perhaps consider giving him one more chance," Mary said. Alexandra immediately clapped her hands together with excitement. "But before you get too carried away, I have to tell you that I cannot promise anything."

"Oh, how fabulous," Cassandra said. "We are soon to have another society wedding."

Mary groaned. "Have you not listened to a single word I have said? I just told you that—"

Cassandra dismissed her with a flick of her wrist. "You are welcome to say whatever you like, Mary. I know what I saw with my very own eyes. And I must say that it didn't take much imagination to envision little hearts and cherubs floating about both of your heads."

Well, what could she possibly say to that? Not a great deal, unless she wished to embarrass herself even further. Instead, she merely sat there quietly, sipping her tea, all the while praying that Mr. Summersby had noticed no such thing.

CHAPTER ELEVEN

"Where the devil can she be?"

"Who?" Bryce asked, regarding his younger son through hooded eyes while he puffed on his cigar.

"Lady Steepleton, of course. Who else?" Ryan looked about the crowded ballroom. Well, it certainly appeared as though the Glendales were having quite the squeeze. Ryan turned to his father. "Every time I went to call on her for the past few days, I was told that she had gone out, which leads me to believe that either she is avoiding me or she has simply left town."

"You seem very wound up about it," Bryce remarked with a slight smirk.

"Of course I am," Ryan snapped. "Percy specifically asked that I keep an eye on her, yet for the past three days I have not seen as much as her shadow. It is really quite disgraceful on my part, wouldn't you agree?"

Bryce grinned. "I am sure that you will find her soon enough, my boy. And I am willing to bet that when you do, you will see that she is perfectly fine."

"How can you possibly be so sure?" Ryan craned his neck in hopes of getting a better view.

"Because I do believe it must be she who is coming our way right now, together with your sister."

Ryan turned to look in the same direction as his father. He didn't see them at first because of the dense crowd, but when his eyes finally found Lady Steepleton's, his mouth fell open in utter amazement. She looked spectacular. Her hair had been fashioned into a mass of curls, all neatly arranged at the back of her head, with a few loose strands gracefully framing her face. And her gown. . .Ryan could scarcely breathe as he watched her approach. Her gown showed off a figure that every woman within a thousand-mile radius would surely envy. The combination of the light blue silk, beneath the cream-colored lace, and a deep blue silk ribbon tied beneath her breasts had an effect that was both elegant and alluring all at the same time. In fact, Ryan couldn't help but notice that all the male heads turned to stare at her as she passed. His stomach tightened at the thought of any other man favoring her with his attention and immediately stepped forward to claim her before somebody else decided to do so. "Good evening, Lady Steepleton." He offered her a slight bow before turning to his sister. "Alexandra, it is good to see you again."

"Thank you, Ryan," Alexandra replied as she took him by his right arm, placing him between herself and the marchioness.

Ryan offered Lady Steepleton his other arm. "May I say that you look absolutely ravishing this evening. That gown is most becoming on you."

"Thank you, Mr. Summersby," Mary said as she began to

fan herself in hopes of concealing the blush that she now felt spreading its way over her entire body. She'd never been so self-conscious of her appearance before in her life. Regardless of having left off on bad terms the last time they'd spoken, she'd still been hoping to make an impression on him this evening. No matter what she kept telling everyone, including herself, the truth of the matter was that she quite enjoyed his attention.

Well, it seemed as though she'd achieved her goal, and the way that made her feel left much to be considered. She still felt her legs turn to goo whenever he looked at her, and her stomach fluttered uncontrollably whenever he touched her in the slightest way. Still, she couldn't let herself forget that his only interest in her had been in regards to his assignment, in spite of the fact that she'd recently promised Alexandra that she'd give him another chance. But at least she'd managed to show him that she wasn't as plain as he and the rest of the *ton* had initially thought. She felt triumphant now as he guided her toward an older gentleman whom she'd never seen before.

"Lady Steepleton," Mr. Summersby announced with much flair, "I would like to present you to my father, the Earl of Moorland."

"It is a pleasure to make your acquaintance at long last," Lord Moorland remarked as he took Mary's hand in his, bent over it, and placed a kiss upon her knuckles. "My son has told me so much about you. In fact, I fail to believe that he has ever admired anyone more—except perhaps for me," he said, grinning, as he gave Mary a good-humored wink.

Mary looked at Mr. Summersby who appeared to be turning a bright shade of red. He gave her a loopy grin. "Well, she certainly has many commendable qualities," he said.

"You are too kind," Mary replied, wondering if he would still hold her in as high a regard once he discovered that she was his superior, not only in title, but professionally as well. Would he even be willing to accept such a thing? Whatever the case might be, it seemed as though she may have misjudged his intentions. If it was true that he admired her as much as his father claimed, then perhaps his reason for courting her hadn't been entirely based on his obligations toward Sir Percy.

"Perhaps I can persuade you to dance the next dance with me," Mr. Summersby suggested her in a voice so full of hope that Mary's heart swelled for him.

"I don't. . ." she began to say, fear setting in at the thought of the entire *ton* watching her dance, when in fact, the only time she'd ever danced before was on the terrace of Richmond House one week ago. And that had certainly not gone as well as she would have hoped. But she stopped herself at the pained expression that had come over Mr. Summersby's face. "I would be delighted to," she said, then leaned toward him and lowered her voice to a whisper. "But you will have to help me, for I don't know a single step."

"Well," Lord Moorland said, grinning, "you certainly are a brave girl,, willing to make a spectacle of yourself before the entire peerage, and for the sake of a simple dance. I can see why you like her, Ryan."

"You mustn't worry yourself overly much, Mary," Alexandra said, giving her arm a reassuring squeeze. "Ryan is a wonderful dancer, and if I am not mistaken, then this next one will be a waltz. Just hold on tight and let him guide you."

"Shall we?" Mr. Summersby asked, offering Mary his arm

before she could conjure up that proverbial hole in the ground that she hoped might swallow her up at any given moment. Instead, she straightened her spine, smiled back at him, and allowed him to guide her toward the dance floor.

Mary felt as if she were flying. They were moving so much faster than when they'd danced before on the terrace at Richmond House. Thankfully, her feet had obeyed her this time, and she'd managed to avoid embarrassing herself or Mr. Summersby. Had they been alone, she would have squealed with delight for all the fun she was having. Instead, she simply enjoyed the feel of Mr. Summersby's hands holding her firmly in his arms as he guided her about the dance floor. She felt safe and oddly relaxed. In fact, aside from her career, nothing had ever felt more right than being together with him at that very moment. It both surprised her and terrified her all at once, especially since she very much doubted that the two would ever be able to coexist.

"What are you thinking?" Mr. Summersby asked as he tightened his hold on her waist and led her about in a wide circle. "You look quite serious."

She sought his eyes and stared back into them, startled once again by their blueness. "I am merely trying to concentrate," she told him with a slight frown. "I should hate to trip and fall in the middle of the ballroom."

He grinned. "That is very unlikely to happen, my lady, for I have quite a solid hold on you, and I have no intention of letting you go. Besides, as I have told you before, you dance rather well, particularly given the fact that this is only your second attempt at it."

"Well, you're not so bad yourself," Mary told him with a hint of mischief in her words.

"What a relief," he replied. "I should hate to think that all those hours spent with that infuriating instructor of mine had gone to waste."

When the music faded, Mr. Summersby leaned forward to whisper in Mary's ear, "I need to speak with you in private." His voice was urgent.

"I'm not entirely sure that that is wise," Mary replied with an impish grin. "The last time you wished to speak with me in private, you showed a remarkable lack of restraint."

"Perhaps I may remind you that you did no better."

"Quite so," Mary conceded. "And that is precisely why I am a trifle worried about being alone with you once again."

"In that case, I promise that I shall do my very best to behave," he teased as he began leading her toward a pair of closed mirrored doors at the far end of the ballroom. "But this is a matter of great importance. It really cannot wait."

Opening one of the doors just enough for them to slip through, Mr. Summersby guided Mary into the room beyond, closing the door quickly behind them so as not to draw attention. Turning to face him, Mary's eyes met his, and she instantly knew that her concerns had not been unfounded. He was watching her in precisely the same manner as he'd done in the carriage; a scalding and possessive gaze that made her heart race and her skin tingle. If she didn't know any better, he was presently contemplating lowering her onto one of the sofa's the room had to offer and. . .

"Lady Steepleton," he said, startling her. Good heavens, whatever had she been thinking? "I'm sorry about the way we parted the last time we spoke. I realize that you were hurt and angry by what I told you, but you must believe me when I say that I do consider you to be the most remarkable woman I have ever known.

"I want you to understand that I didn't offer to marry you out of obligation alone. I realize how absurd this sounds..." He took a deep breath as if to steady himself, while Mary watched with keen interest. Apparently, she wasn't the only one feeling out of sorts—a pleasing discovery, indeed. "I spoke with my father. You may not be aware of this, but he's a close friend of Wellington's and has several other important connections within the military."

Mary raised an eyebrow, curious as to why it might matter to her whom Lord Moorland's friends might be. Reaching out, Mr. Summersby took her hand in his. "For a while now I have had a nagging suspicion. I asked my father to make a few inquiries and discovered that I may have been correct in my assumption. Lady Steepleton, it seems as though your father's death was no accident. The evidence that I've managed to piece together strongly suggests that he was murdered."

Mary stood as if nailed to the floor. She couldn't move, couldn't blink, couldn't speak. But her lips did form a very distinct "no." This wasn't possible. She'd seen him when they'd brought him in from the field on a stretcher. He'd been tending to a wounded soldier and had been caught directly in the line of fire—a shot straight to his head. It didn't make any sense.

"I realize how alarming this must be for you, but from what I gather, another physician who was present at the time, and who examined your father, made a note of his neck having been broken. The shot he sustained was likely delivered at a later time, for the sake of authenticity."

"Good God!" Mary exclaimed, burying her face in her hands. "I never knew. There was so much chaos, and seeing Papa like that. . .I left as fast as my feet could carry me. I knew that it was wrong of me and that I should have stayed, but I just couldn't do it. All my life he's loved me and cared for me, and I couldn't even stay and see to it that he was properly buried." She felt her throat close and her heart ache as her eyes began to burn. She didn't want Mr. Summersby to see her like that, but it was too late, and as she drew a shaky breath, she found herself pulled toward him until his arms were around her in a tight embrace.

"You were in shock," he whispered against the top of her head. "You mustn't blame yourself, my lady. As it is, I can't imagine what your father was thinking, taking you along with him to war. Even if you were at a safe distance from the battlefield, bringing a young woman like yourself, surrounded by so many soldiers and so much carnage, not only is unseemly, but it must have been very traumatic."

Mary pushed herself away from him, accepting the handkerchief that he offered with a wobbly smile. The tears stung, but she wiped them away with a brisk hand. "Who would do such a thing?" she asked, hoping to address the more important issue at hand, yet knowing that she was using it as an excuse to divert the conversation away from herself. "It seems they went to a lot of trouble."

"Yes, it appears that whoever planned this followed you and your father to Waterloo with the intention of using the battle as a means by which to cover up his murder." Mr. Summersby paused. "I hope you understand the significance of this. You mustn't go anywhere alone. You have already been threatened, and if the person behind this was willing to kill your father, then he won't hesitate to kill you as well. Promise me that you will be careful."

Mary nodded in disbelief. Could it possibly be that her father, the man who'd bounced her on his knee when she was a child, had pursued something of so great importance that it had cost him his life? She was suddenly having a very difficult time connecting the man she'd known and loved with this apparent stranger who, it seemed, had kept nothing but secrets from her.

Her eyes met Mr. Summersby's. "I promise," she told him. "But in return, you have to give me your word of honor that you will help me find whoever did this and bring him to justice."

He gave her his word without hesitation. "As I see it, you'll never be completely safe until this man is found." He suddenly frowned and looked at her far too intensely for her liking. "I feel that there's something you're not telling me. What is it?" he asked.

She couldn't lie to him. "Somebody broke into my house a few nights ago and stole the first volume of my father's journals," she told him hesitantly.

Anger sprang to life behind his eyes. "Did you happen to see who it was?"

She shook her head. "No," she said. "I only caught the glimpse of a fleeting shadow. But it was enough to make me understand that I must not dismiss these threats. It seems that they are quite serious. The fact is that I do not have very many people I can turn to for help, so I went to your sister. I have been staying with her ever since."

"So that is why you were never able to receive me," Mr. Summersby muttered. "You were staying with Alex all along."

"Yes, she has been very kind to me. I have told her everything—more than I have told you, in fact." Mary took a deep breath. This was it, the moment of truth. "You see, you don't know me very well at all. I have done some things that I am quite sure that you would never approve of. I believe not only will you be terribly shocked, but it may alter your opinion of me forever."

Mr. Summersby stared at her quizzically. "Whatever it is, my lady, I am certain that it is not as bad as you think. These things never are, and I assure you, there is nothing you can possibly tell me that might alter my opinion of you." As if to prove his point, he pulled her closer, wrapped her in a tight embrace, and kissed her with enough passion and desperation to make her whole body melt with pleasure.

As it happened, it was at this precise moment that Lady Glendale ordered her footmen to open the doors to the game room, the exact same room where Mr. Summersby had taken Mary for their private chat. Needless to say, an immediate hush fell over the entire ballroom at the sight of him standing there kissing the Marchioness of Steepleton in full view of the entire *ton*.

Turning her head, Mary gasped, horrified by all the shocked faces that were presently staring back at her in disbelief. What to do? They couldn't very well deny what had happened; that would be absurd.

One thing was for certain: she wanted to run from the room as fast as her feet could carry her and never, ever look back. This was precisely the sort of thing that would make the headlines in every gossip column. Oh, she could see it now, all the people whispering about her disgraceful behavior every time she stepped out in public. It was without question the most mortifying experience of her life.

She looked to Mr. Summersby, who suddenly appeared rather determined, as if he were planning either to flee or to face full-on battle. A scandal of monumental proportions was about to erupt, so if there was even the slightest chance of them leaving the Glendale ball that evening with their reputations intact, she hoped he'd come up with a way to make it happen—soon. He looked at her for one brief second and squeezed her hand. "Have courage," he whispered. "And follow my lead, wherever it takes us."

He then stepped forward. "Ladies and gentlemen," he said, "since you have practically found us out already, I see no reason for any of us to wait for a formal announcement in the paper. As it happens, Lady Steepleton has just made me the happiest man in London by accepting my offer of marriage."

There was only a moment's silence—the second or two that it took for the information to sink in—and then, all at once, the entire ballroom erupted into a roar of cheers and clapping.

"Well, your engagement certainly came a little sooner than I had expected," Alexandra remarked as she and Lord Moorland squeezed through the crowd to where Mr. Summersby and Mary were standing. "However, we all expected it to happen eventually. I must commend Cassandra for her astuteness, though; she was quite correct in predicting that the two of you would tie the knot this season. As for myself, I am absolutely thrilled."

"Well done, Ryan!" Lord Moorland exclaimed. "I knew it would happen sooner or later. She is a keeper, this one; I couldn't be happier for you." He turned to Mary. "Welcome to the family, my dear."

"Oh, and Mary," Alexandra continued, "I am certain that both Isabella and my father's sister will be most delighted to assist you with all of the preparations."

Mary could scarcely believe what was happening. Had Mr. Summersby really just announced their engagement before the entire *ton*? It was unfathomable. He didn't even know who it was he had just gotten engaged to. She felt ill at the prospect of having to tell him now when there was no longer any turning back. In a split second and without thinking, he'd sealed both of their fates with his reckless-ness.

Damn!

Why did he have to kiss her? It was infuriating, really, especially after he'd promised to restrain himself. Well, there was no point in agonizing over it now. But blast him if she wasn't going to have a very thorough chat with him once they managed to find a moment to themselves. An apology was the very least she would expect from him. For now, however, she simply pasted a smile on her face and thanked Lord Moorland for his kindness. If only she could get out of there as quickly as possible. Some fresh air was bound to do her a world of good.

"Mr. Summersby!"

Mary froze at the sound of Lady Stephanie's silky voice drifting toward them. If she'd been as keen on snagging Mr. Summersby as Alexandra had suggested, then what could she possibly have to say to them now? An eerie sense of uneasiness crept slowly up Mary's spine.

"Ah, Lady Stephanie," Mr. Summersby remarked in a dry tone that showed very little emotion. "So good to see you again."

"Thank you, Mr. Summersby, you are most kind. I heard your little announcement and decided that I simply must come over to congratulate both of you." She cast a brief, disapproving glance in Mary's direction. "And I brought someone with me. It seems that Lord Warwick could scarcely contain his enthusiasm to make the acquaintance of your future bride."

Mary's attention went straight to the gentleman at Lady Stephanie's side. There was anger and contempt in his eyes as he glared back at her, ignoring Mr. Summersby completely. Mary stiffened. This did not bode well.

"Philip," Mr. Summersby said, turning his attention on Lord Warwick, "it has certainly been a while. I don't believe that we have seen one another since last season. How is your lovely family doing?"

Lord Warwick's gaze remained on Mary. "Emma and the children are doing quite well, though I cannot say the same for Mama."

"She is in pain again?" Mr. Summersby spoke with anguish, while Lord Moorland and Alexandra both looked very concerned.

Mary shuddered with foreboding.

"As you know, she has been for some time, but a few nights ago, she decided to take matters into her own hands without a word of warning to anyone."

"With her personality, that's hardly surprising," Lord Moorland muttered.

"The most interesting part of all, however," Lady Stephanie remarked in an annoyingly victorious voice, "is that Lady Steepleton can be found at the very center of this little intrigue."

Mr. Summersby looked confused. He turned to Mary, who was watching the scene unfold with sheer terror. He must have seen that something was amiss, for he leaned toward her with a frown. "What is it?" he whispered. But Mary couldn't speak. Her life was falling apart, and she couldn't say a single word to stop it from doing so. She hadn't considered that the dowager might have a son who'd be appalled at the idea of his mother undergoing surgery at the hands of a woman. When she'd last seen Lady Warwick, they'd agreed that she'd only allow Mrs. Harper to tend to her so as not to alert any of the other servants. Yet somehow Lord Warwick had found her out. Catching Lady Stephanie's venomous gaze, she was convinced that she must have had something to do with it. Whatever the case, it was a disaster far worse than any she could have contemplated.

"It appears that my mother underwent an unauthorized operation," Lord Warwick added as he continued to glare at Mary. "I would like to know what you might know about the matter, Lady Steepleton."

Mary took a sharp breath. Her eyes flitted from Mr. Summersby, to Alexandra, to Lord Moorland, then to Lady Stephanie, who favored her with a triumphant smirk. So that was her big plan, to discredit her and ruin her before the people that she cared about? Well, she wouldn't be called a liar as well, so there really wasn't anything else to be done but to tell the truth. And as for Mr. Summersby. . .this wasn't at all the way she'd planned on his finding out, but at least it would be done with before they headed up the aisle. Perhaps he'd even find a miraculous means by which to escape marrying her if that was what he desired to do once the truth was out.

Straightening her spine and squaring her shoulders as if she were about to head off into battle, she turned a brazen stare on Lord Warwick. "Your mother came to me for help, my lord. She was in severe pain and asked me to do whatever I could in order to alleviate it."

Mary felt Mr. Summersby stiffen by her side. She dared not look at him for fear of what she might see. *He must be truly horrified.*

"I have a good mind to press charges," Lord Warwick said as a look of glee spread its way across Lady Stephanie's face. It seemed that the woman could barely contain her enthusiasm. "In fact, having consulted other surgeons about the procedure in the past, I eventually deemed it far too dangerous for Mama to take such a risk. However, since the operation does appear to have been a success, and since Mama claims she'll have my head if word about this gets out, I have decided to let the matter rest. Besides, we are soon to be related since Mama is your fiancé's great-aunt."

Mary felt the blood drain from her face. Mr. Summersby was related to the dowager countess *and* to Lord Warwick? Heaven help her!

Lord Warwick then turned to Lady Stephanie, whose venomous smile was rapidly fading. "I thank you for bringing this matter to my attention, Lady Stephanie. But in the future, I trust that you will speak of this to no one."

Lady Stephanie's jaw dropped. "But. . .but. . ." She looked at him in desperation.

"If you do, I shall not only deny every bit of it, but I shall also have you besmirched as the worst slanderer and liar that the *ton* has ever seen. Do I make myself clear?"

Lady Stephanie's eyes grew cold with anger. "Perfectly," she ground out, making no attempt to hide her displeasure at this sudden turn of events. Turning sharply on her heel, she stalked off with an arrogant tilt to her chin.

Once Lady Stephanie was out of sight, Lord Warwick turned to Ryan with a stony expression. "I shall take my leave of you. Do try to keep her ladyship under control; she's your responsibility now." And without further ado, he marched off at a brisk pace, no doubt in search of a large brandy.

Chapter Twelve

It took a while for any of them to react to what had just happened, but eventually Mr. Summersby stirred, releasing his hold on Mary's arm. "I am going to White's," he told his father decisively, dismissing Mary's existence entirely. "Don't wait up for me."

Mary clenched her jaw firmly shut, struggling to fight back the onset of tears that threatened to burst from her eyes at any moment. Mr. Summersby never as much as glanced in her direction as he walked off, not even bothering to say goodnight to his hosts.

"Keep an eye on Lady Steepleton," Alexandra told her father. "Find Michael and have him escort her safely back to my house. I am going after Ryan to knock some sense back into him."

Lord Moorland nodded. "Ay, the boy's a bigger fool than I would have thought him to be if he discredits Lady Steepleton for her obvious success. It's about time that somebody helped that poor woman; she's suffered long enough."

Mary gaped at her soon-to-be father-in-law. "You heard what Lord Warwick said. I am an unlicensed surgeon, and as a woman, I daresay no court would be very forgiving of my actions if they were to become known." She gave him a half-hearted smile. "I think it would be completely understand-able if your son were to decide never to speak to me again."

Lord Moorland halted a pacing footman and picked two glasses of Champagne from his tray. He gave one to Mary. "My dear, I have been around long enough to know an honorable person when I see one, and you, Lady Steepleton, are indeed an honorable person. Not only did you disregard the risk to your own reputation, choosing instead to help a dear old woman in need, you also didn't deny a single thing when you were con-fronted. Instead, you faced your persecutors head on, knowing full well what the risk would be. If that is not admirable, then I do not know what is." Mary opened her mouth to say some-thing, but Lord Moorland stopped her. "My dear woman, you are exactly the sort of wife my son needs, even if he is too preoc-cupied with his own anger right now to realize it. He will come around, though; I shall make damn sure of it. So don't worry about it any further, and just enjoy your Champagne."

Well, there wasn't much else she could do, she supposed, as she linked her arm with the one Lord Moorland offered her. After all, she couldn't scream in frustration in the middle of Glendale House, which was what she really wanted to do. So instead she took a large gulp of Champagne and allowed Lord Moorland to lead her about as they began their search for Lord Trenton.

"Ryan!" Alexandra yelled with complete disregard for how unladylike she might appear, racing down the steps of

Glendale House in pursuit of her brother. Seeing the back of him disappear inside a carriage, she quickened her step and leaped in after him, landing on the opposite seat with a thump.

Ryan glared at her. "What do you want?" he asked.

"Don't be a fool, Ryan," Alexandra told him, ignoring his question. "You have treated Mary very badly, walking off the way you did after having just asked her to marry you."

Ryan pinned his sister with a deadpan stare. "I have treated *her* badly? Alex, she is the one who has been dishonest, leading a secret life—one that she clearly had no intention of ever telling me about."

"Are you quite sure about that, Ryan? Because as far as I know, she had every intention of telling you."

"You knew about this?" Ryan asked incredulously. Alexandra nodded. "Since when?"

"Since I recalled seeing her once before. Do you remember the female surgeon William told you about? The one I practically knocked over in Ghent last year on our way back to England?"

"That was Lady Steepleton?" Ryan asked in astonishment as he sank back against the seat of the carriage. Again, Alexandra nodded. "I don't generally consider myself a stickler, but this is completely intolerable."

"Ryan, I think you are making a Cheltenham tragedy out of all of this. It may be true that you haven't known her for very long, but listen to your gut instinct. Does she strike you as the sort of woman who would do what she has apparently been doing unless she knew what she was about? I hear her father was a very skilled surgeon. Do you really believe that he would have allowed his daughter to practice unless he was confident that she would do an excellent job?"

"As if that matters," he protested. "Even if she is the best surgeon in the world, it does not change the fact that she deliberately kept it from me, or that she is breaking the law in the process. The woman is no better than a common criminal."

Alexandra glared back at her brother. "How dare you talk about her like that! Honestly, Ryan, I realize that you are angry, but resorting to insults is surely beneath you. Why not look at it like this: she knows that what she is doing might land her in a world of trouble, yet she does it all the same because of her desire to help those in need. If anything, you ought to be proud of her, just as you have always been proud of me. And stop getting so angry about the fact that she kept it from you. She only recently met you, Ryan. Did you really expect her to trust you with something of such immense importance after a few amicable conversations? One can hardly blame her for being cautious, especially after discovering that you were not exactly who you claimed to be either."

"I don't know," Ryan said with a sigh, shaking his head in frustration. "This is not at all what I bargained for: a wife who claims to be a surgeon. It is—"

"It is what, Ryan?" Alexandra asked. "Unthinkable? Preposterous? Absurd?"

"Yes!"

"And what about me, Ryan? You never had an issue with the fact that I chose to wear breeches instead of a gown, or that I learned to fight with a sword."

"I have always admired you, Alex; you know that."

Alexandra smiled. "Well, I can assure you that Michael

was not nearly as accepting of my behavior when we first met, and I can guarantee that most people would be quite appalled if they knew of all the things that I have been up to." She paused for a moment. "If you care about Mary as much as I think you do, then I would strongly advise you to talk to her, give her a chance to explain herself to you. And don't condemn her just because it is what society expects you to do. You are better than that, Ryan; I know you are. Think for yourself and make your own decision."

"I will consider it," he assured her. "But for now I am going to White's to have a drink in the hopes of clearing my head a bit. I will ask the driver to take you home after he drops me off."

"Lady Steepleton, a word if we may?"

Mary turned her head to find Robert navigating his way through the crowd that filled the Glendale ballroom. He was accompanied by two other gentlemen. Mary smiled warmly in greeting. "How lovely to see you again, Lord Woodbridge."

Lord Moorland nodded politely at each of the men. "It has been a while since you and I have had a round of faro, old chap," he told Robert. "If I am not mistaken, I made off with quite a bit of your blunt last time, and having recently looked over my expenses, I do believe that it is time for us to play again soon."

Robert grinned. "I fear you will take the shirt from off my back. Never mind, Moorland, I shall be happy to keep you out of the poorhouse."

Lord Moorland merely responded by taking a puff of his newly lit cigar.

Mary regarded Robert and the two other gentlemen whom he'd brought along with him. "Forgive me, my lord, but I do not believe that I have ever had the pleasure of meeting your friends."

"How very thoughtless of me," Robert said. "After all, our reason for coming over here was not only to congratulate you on your engagement, but also to introduce these fine gentlemen to you—they were good friends and colleagues of your father's." He paused for emphasis. "May I present Sir Bosworth and Mr. Clemens. In fact, Sir Bosworth is working on developing a means by which the patient may experience an entirely painless surgery. He will not tell me much more, but perhaps you can coerce it out of him."

"My lips are sealed, you scoundrel," Bosworth said, grinning.

"It is a pleasure to meet both of you," Mary told them sincerely. "I wonder if you might be able to shed some light on a matter that has been plaguing me of late. It appears as though my father may have been working on a theory of some sort before he died. Do either of you have any idea as to what it may have been? Lord Woodbridge says he has no idea on the matter, but perhaps—"

"I am terribly sorry," Clemens remarked, shaking his head. "I am not aware of any such theory."

"Unfortunately, your father never really discussed his work with anyone," Bosworth added. "He was always very secretive about his work."

"Yes." Mary sighed, feeling more discouraged than ever. "I have gathered as much."

"What about the journals?" Robert asked. "Did you have

a chance to read through them yet? I am certain that whatever it is you are looking for must be in there somewhere."

Mary frowned. "Yes," she said. She considered Mr. Summersby's warning. The thought of any of these gentlemen being involved in the threats against her was preposterous, but news did travel on the wind, and if they found out, it was possible that the man who'd stolen her father's journal would too. She simply could not trust anybody. "But there was only the one, an account of his apprenticeship. That is all."

"I see," Robert replied, giving her a broad smile. "Well then, perhaps we shall never know what he was working on in the last few years."

"A pity," Bosworth stated.

Clemens nodded in agreement.

"Well, it was a pleasure as always, Lady Steepleton," Robert told her, offering her a bow. "We shall not keep you any longer."

"Thank you, my lord. I shall have to invite you for tea one day, perhaps together with Helmsley, whom you may recall."

"Yes, of course," Robert replied as he nodded his head in recollection of the physician who'd been like a brother to Mary's father. "I shall look forward to the invitation."

"It appears you know them well," Mary told Moorland as they walked away to continue in their search for Lord Trenton.

"Oh, yes," he remarked. "Lord Woodbridge and I are old friends—even used to visit us at Moorland Park when Lady Moorland was still alive. She would throw the most extravagant house parties, you know."

Mary gave him a sympathetic smile. He spoke of his wife

with such affection that Mary knew he must still miss her terribly. "I am so sorry," she said as she gently squeezed his arm.

"There is no need for you to be," he told her mildly. "I am fortunate to have known that kind of love—few people ever do, you know. They mostly settle, marrying for the sake of convenience. I only hope that my own children will not be among them, but that they will find love matches just as I did." He gave Mary a meaningful look that had her blushing right away.

"And what of Bosworth and Clemens?" she asked in an attempt to change the subject. She really had no desire to think of Mr. Summersby at all right now. It only made her feel miserable.

"I have met them both before," Lord Moorland commented. "But I really do not know too much about either one of them, truth is. As I recall, I read about Bosworth about five years ago in the *Times*. It seems there was some dispute about a surgery he had performed where the patient had died. Rumor had it he made a tragic error in judgment, but the whole incident was quickly hushed up and followed by an article clearing his name of any wrongdoing."

"I see," Mary said, pondering that bit of information. "Then I take it no charges were pressed against him?"

"Oh no; it was all hearsay. It took a while for the gossip to cease, but I must say he made a full recovery. He is now one of the most respected and sought after physicians in London." Bryce took a puff of his cigar. "Ah look, there is Trenton right now."

They walked across to where Lord Trenton was standing. He appeared to be in the midst of a very animated conversation with another gentleman. "Trenton," Lord Moorland boomed when they were within three yards of him, "stop pulling caps, will you? Lady Steepleton is in need of your assistance."

"Ah, Lord Moorland, perhaps you can settle our little dispute." Lord Trenton greeted Mary politely, introducing her to his companion before turning once again to his father-in-law. "Townsend here insists that the volcanic eruption in the Dutch East Indies last year has nothing to do with the dismal climate we are experiencing this summer. I, on the other hand, agree with what the men of science are claiming: that it not only has everything to do with it, but that our economy is likely to suffer as a result."

"Come now, Lord Moorland," Townsend said. "You must admit that such a theory sounds quite absurd. That volcano is on the other side of the planet, for heaven's sake. Do you seriously expect us to believe that it would have such a dramatic effect on the British climate—a whole year later, no less?"

"Hm. . .I must admit that I agree with Trenton on this one," Lord Moorland announced after a moment's reflection. "In fact, there are still ships arriving from as far away as Australia claiming that the air there was thick with dust and ash when they embarked five months ago. I do believe it is more than likely for such a geological event to have had profound effects on the climate all over the planet. Besides, you must admit that it is rather unusual for it to snow as late as May, and we *did* have snow in May, if you will recall."

Townsend sighed. "I don't suppose that you are willing to side with me, Lady Steepleton?"

"I am afraid not," Mary chuckled, delighting in the conversation. "In fact, you need only look at a history book to be reminded that the climatic effect was quite similar when the Icelandic volcano—I forget its name now—erupted in the late 1700s."

All three men stared at her. "That is an odd bit of trivia to be lugging around with you," Lord Moorland finally remarked.

Mary shrugged. "I suppose I do have a tendency to remember the most absurd pieces of information. But actually, the reason that I recall it so well is because I recently read the memoirs of Benjamin Franklin. He theorized that the dramatic drop in temperature at that time was due to the blocking out of sunlight by volcanic dust and ashes."

"Well, there you are then," Trenton exclaimed triumphantly. "If one of America's most notable thinkers says it is so, then it surely must be."

"Yes," Townsend admitted. "Although I would like to point out that it was the lovely Lady Steepleton who won your case." He smiled wryly at Mary, who in turn was feeling quite pleased with herself.

"Now that that has been settled," Lord Moorland said, turning to Trenton, "Your wife requested that you escort Lady Steepleton back to your house; it seems she had to have a little discussion with Ryan."

Trenton raised an eyebrow. "I see. I hope it doesn't involve a duel."

"One never can be sure," Lord Moorland noted. "That woman is as feisty as they come, but then again, I am the one who raised her."

Townsend looked just about ready to choke on his Champagne at that exchange of dialogue, while Mary felt quite shaken at the prospect of Alexandra and Mr. Summersby drawing swords against one another. "You cannot be serious," she muttered.

"Lady Steepleton, I am always quite serious," Lord Moorland remarked with a devilish grin. "In fact, I have always prided myself on my grave demeanor."

Mary's face relaxed into a warm smile. "Well, in that case, I shall simply have to take your word for it, my lord," she told him with an edge of sarcasm.

"Yes," Lord Moorland chuckled. "Do that, Lady Steepleton, and you and I will get along just fine."

Later that evening, in a house not far from Berkeley Square, six gentlemen convened to discuss the matter of Lady Steepleton and her father's missing journals. The Raven regarded his guests with an intense stare as he took a seat in his favorite leather armchair. "Well, gentlemen," he announced, "it does appear as though we have a slight problem on our hands." A soft murmur made its way around the room. "We have but one of Lord Steepleton's journals in our possession, and the bloody thing is as good as useless. I demand an explanation."

"Apparently, our agent was caught off guard by Lady Steepleton herself. As it is, we were fortunate to recover as much as we did," one man remarked.

"And from what we have been able to gather, the marchioness is not in possession of the rest, my lord," another commented.

"She is lying," the Raven grumbled as he took a sip of his brandy.

"Then how do you suggest we proceed?" the Messenger asked as he leaned forward in his seat.

The Raven turned to him with a smirk. "Now, there is a question for us to consider." He looked at the other gentlemen who were gathered around him. "I have an idea, but it may require a great deal of patience."

"That may be a luxury we do not have," a third man said.

"Perhaps, but at least we know that her ladyship has no idea of what she is looking for. That ought to give us a bit of extra time."

"But now that she is engaged to Mr. Summersby," the second put in, "she will soon be under the protection of that entire family. They will not make our task any easier."

"Which is why we must act soon," the Raven told him as he drummed his fingers against his armrest. "However, that is not to say that we ought to be rash about it. The right moment will present itself. Of that, I am quite certain."

CHAPTER THIRTEEN

"Where the devil do you think you're going?"

Mary turned to find Mr. Summersby staring down at her with stormy eyes. After Lord Trenton had seen her back to his and Alexandra's home in Berkeley Square, she'd waited for him to head back out again before slipping out the front door and running as fast as her feet would carry her back to her own home on Brook Street. She'd stayed for only as long as it had taken her to get out of her evening gown and into her shirt and breeches. Then she'd given her apologies to Emma and Thornton, who'd both looked quite alarmed by their mistress' sudden antics.

"Spying on me again, are we?" she asked in a mocking tone. Her eyes were hard as steel.

"Not that I enjoy it much," he told her coolly. "But apparently it is necessary for me to keep a vigilant eye on you. You clearly have very little common sense in that stubborn head of yours." Reaching out, he grabbed her arm.

"Unhand me, you fiend," Mary snapped, matching his anger. She had a job to attend to, and nothing, not even Mr. Summersby's ill temper, was going to stand in her way.

"Not until you answer my question," he said sternly. "And while you are at it, you may as well tell me why you are dressed like that."

"I have no time for this, Ryan," Mary said irritably, letting his Christian name slip as she struggled to get her arm free from his grip. "And I certainly don't owe you an explanation."

"Oh, I believe you owe me a very good explanation, my dear. You are now my fiancée, whether you like it or not. I will not have you running about London dressing like a man and prescribing any number of harmful remedies for only God knows what. It is no longer your name alone that you are dishonoring, but mine as well."

"And whose recklessness was it that landed us in this mess to begin with? I told you I did not wish to marry you when you asked me, yet you still have the audacity to complain about the situation that you are suddenly in after recklessly kissing me before the entire *ton*. If anyone ought to complain, it should be me. You, on the other hand, only have yourself to blame."

Ryan pierced her with his bright blue eyes. Heaven help her if her legs weren't turning to jelly no matter how angry she was. She took a deep breath to steady herself. "What would you have me do, Mary?" he asked as he held her gaze.

"End the betrothal," she told him sharply.

A shadow flickered across his eyes, but it was gone in a heartbeat. "I cannot do that. Not now that it has been publically announced."

"That is regrettable," she told him rather coolly. But it was her wounded pride and anger that were doing all the talking. Her heart wasn't nearly as convinced of what she was saying.

"It appears as though we find ourselves in quite an awkward situation."

"It certainly does," he muttered.

There was a look of defeat in his eyes that Mary had never seen before. It pained her to know how much she'd disappointed him. Then again, it wasn't as if she'd claimed to be something else. After all, she'd wanted to tell him, planned it even, but somehow she hadn't quite managed it before it was too late.

Too late.

Too late for what, exactly? For them to live happily ever after? It was folly to even consider such an outcome. Of course, they were attracted to one another physically, but a lifelong affection would require so much more. It would require love—the very thing that was built on trust—not exactly something that the two of them had in high commodity.

Mary almost laughed at the very idea of it all. There she was, with a man she barely knew and who barely knew her, and the foolish fellow kept insisting that they get married! Well, if such a union was to have any chance in hell of being an amicable one, then perhaps it was time for her to start being completely honest.

She gave a lengthy sigh. "I have an appointment that I must keep. But if you have a genuine interest in discovering what it is that I am up to, then you are certainly welcome to come along."

Ryan looked as though she were telling him to jump off a cliff. "You will not tell me what this is about before we get there, will you?"

She shook her head. "No, it is best if you see it for yourself."

"In that case," he told her. "I will join you."

"Summersby," Lord Arlington remarked as Ryan and Mary stepped through the front door of Arlington House. "This certainly is quite a surprise."

"Trust me, Arlington, I am just as surprised to be here as you apparently are to have me." He cast a frown at Mary. "I only hope to shed some light on what her ladyship has been up to."

It was Lord Arlington's turn to look surprised.

"Mr. Summersby has taken it upon himself to make me his fiancée," Mary explained. "It seems that he now has a misplaced notion of ownership, which he is quite keen on exercising."

"I am not entirely sure if I ought to congratulate you or. . .Well, I hope that the two of you will be very happy with one another," Lord Arlington told them. "Lady Steepleton," he then continued, "on a more serious note, won't it be somewhat inappropriate for Summersby to attend?"

"I see your point, my lord. However, Mr. Summersby has studied medicine at Oxford for a year now and shall be accompanying us as my assistant. I therefore see no reason why he may not join us, unless you or your wife is uncomfortable with it, of course, in which case we shall naturally respect your wishes."

Lord Arlington regarded Ryan, who looked positively stunned by Mary's tactical maneuvering. He must have decided that there couldn't be much harm in Ryan's seeing his wife's abdomen as long as his interest was of a medical nature alone. Either that, or he had no desire for further discussion and simply wanted to get on with the matter, for he finally said, "This way, if you will," as he directed Mary and Ryan toward the stairs.

Once they reached the top of the landing, Mary paused at the door to Lady Arlington's bedroom. "You will tell nobody about what you experience after stepping into this room," she said, her eyes pinned on Ryan's. "Do I make myself clear?"

He nodded, his curiosity shining bright in his eyes.

She eyed him skeptically. "You will also refrain from saying something that might alarm the patient."

Once again, Ryan nodded.

"Very well then, Lord Arlington, you may show us in," Mary said.

Lord Arlington, who appeared to be far calmer than when Mary had last seen him, opened the door to his wife's bedroom and ushered Mary and Ryan inside. The lighting was dim, but they could clearly make out Lady Arlington, who'd been comfortably propped up against a large pile of pillows on her bed. She looked up from the book she was reading as soon as she heard them enter.

"How are you feeling this evening, my lady?" Mary asked as she approached the wide bed.

Lady Arlington closed the book she was holding, one that Ryan instantly recognized as *Gulliver's Travels*. "That is quite an adventure story you have there, my lady."

Lady Arlington smiled. "What a pleasant surprise to have you visit, Mr. Summersby." She then looked at him conspiratorially. "I think my husband would prefer it if I read something more serious. In fact, I do believe he suggested Homer's *Iliad* as the greatest work of fiction ever written."

"It may well be," Ryan agreed. "Though I must admit that it might take a trifle longer for you to get through."

"It's a poem," Lady Arlington mouthed as if her husband weren't standing right there in front of her.

"All I wanted was to introduce a bit of culture into your life, my dear," Lord Arlington remarked, as if he'd taken huge offense to her heartless dismissal of his favorite literary work.

"Then you may invite me to the theater as soon as I am fully recovered and our son is old enough to stay with his nurse for the evening."

Ryan hadn't noticed the crib until then. He now saw that Mary was standing by it, completely ignoring their verbal banter, her entire attention focused on the small creature that lay peacefully asleep inside. "I must congratulate you, Arlington. I had no idea that your wife had given birth already."

"We haven't made the formal announcement just yet," Lord Arlington admitted. "Once we do, we are bound to be overrun by people from near and far, all eager to have a look at my heir. We thought it best to wait a while, until Lady Arlington is fully recovered."

"Was it a difficult birth?" Ryan asked before he could stop himself.

He was just about to apologize for asking when Mary turned to him. "You could say that." She gave him a crooked smile, while her eyes sparkled with mischief.

"Wait. . .did you. . .?"

"I did indeed," Mary said, looking just about as pleased as a cat that had just caught a canary.

Ryan let out a sigh of relief. "You have no idea how glad I am to hear it. For a while there I was quite convinced you might actually have operated on the poor woman, when in fact, all you did was deliver a baby—a healthy looking one, I might add."

Lady Arlington chuckled ever so slightly. "You haven't told him, have you?"

Mary shook her head.

"Told me what?" Ryan asked, feeling slightly puzzled. He was clearly missing something.

"Before you say anything, Lady Steepleton," Lord Arlington added, "I want you to know how grateful my wife and I are for what you have done for us." He turned to Ryan with a very serious expression, but when he spoke, his voice was gentle and reassuring. "I had my doubts at first too, you know. But Lady Steepleton truly deserves to be recognized for her accomplishment. She is quite a remarkable woman, Summersby; you are lucky to have her."

"Would someone please explain to me what the devil you are all going on about?" Ryan said with growing frustration. "Delivering a baby is something that any midwife can handle without much difficulty. It is nothing exceptional unless. . ." The room seemed to close in on him as his eyes flickered from one person to the next. "Good heavens, were there complications? Excessive bleeding, perhaps?"

"Well, the thing is, Ryan. . .Mr. Summersby, I mean. . .I did operate on Lady Arlington." Mary turned a steady eye on him.

"What!" Ryan exclaimed. Surely he must have misheard.

"She had puerperal eclampsia," Mary told him simply.

"So you decided to cut her open? Good Lord, woman, what were you thinking?"

Mary's eyes narrowed with sudden fury. "She would have died if I had not done so."

"She might very well have died because of you. You are not an authorized surgeon, and what you are doing sets a very dangerous precedent. It might make others who lack the necessary qualifications think that they can go about cutting into people instead of seeking professional help."

"My father taught me everything I know," Mary retaliated. "Together, he and I experienced fewer fatalities in our patients than anyone else in this country."

"That does not change the fact that you are practicing medicine. Hell, you are slicing people open without a license!"

Mary held her ground, staring back at Ryan with steel in her eyes. This was clearly not a battle that she intended to lose. "Let me ask you this," she countered. "During your studies at Oxford, how often did you actually study a physical body, whether it be dead or alive?"

"That is not the issue here."

"I think it is precisely the issue. The universities pack your heads full of information that is completely useless unless they also show you how to apply it. There is a big difference in having the organs described to you by a lecturer and actually taking an up close look at them."

"That is what an apprenticeship is for," Ryan snapped. His blood was beginning to boil; another moment and he'd probably see red. Heaven help him if she wasn't the most infuriating woman he'd ever come across.

"But such apprenticeships hold no promise of a universal standard. In addition, most physicians and surgeons are reluctant to teach their future competitors, extending the period it takes a student to acquire the necessary skills to an indefinite amount of time."

Seeing that Mary wasn't about to give in, Ryan turned to Lady Arlington instead. "I would like to take a look at Lady Steepleton's work, if I may."

Lady Arlington nodded and placed her book on the table next to her bed. "You should not be too hard on her, Summersby." She looked to Mary, who seemed ready to explode. "She did the right thing, you know. Even Dr. Helmsley, the physician I have been using for the duration of my pregnancy, has told us how rare it is for a woman to survive this kind of surgery."

"Your physician condoned this?" Ryan could scarcely believe his ears. This was madness, complete and utter madness.

"He is the one who sent for Lady Steepleton in the first place," Lord Arlington replied. "In fact, he explicitly told me that she was our best option."

Ryan eyed Mary with a great degree of reluctance. Clearly, the fact that an actual physician had backed her up had only encouraged her to think that she had the right to operate. Did she have any idea of the danger in which she'd put Lady Arlington?

He watched as Lady Arlington folded down the covers and pulled up her nightgown enough to show her abdomen. There, a couple of inches below her navel, was a small scar, still graced by a neat row of stitches, but looking otherwise healthy and clear of any infection.

Ryan stared at it. It looked perfect. He frowned. This

wasn't at all the way in which a cesarean had been described in the books he'd read. He looked at Mary, who in turn was watching him with much interest. "I thought the incision should have been made just below the navel and in a downward motion—not across, the way that you have done it."

Mary nodded. "Yes, I know. The lengthwise incision is the traditional way of performing the procedure, the one that is practiced by the majority of surgeons in this country. However, a variety of methods have been recorded, and would you know, this method, where a transverse incision is made, will result in far less bleeding in the patient than the other, more popular method, will. It makes you wonder why, after Lebas, Dunker, and Lauverjat all claimed success with the transverse incisions more than twenty-five years ago, the lengthwise incision is still so eagerly applied."

Ryan could say nothing to that. He'd never even heard of these men before, but he had to admit that Mary had given him a great deal to think about. "It seems that there are a lot of contradictory opinions out there. I am surprised I never heard of this method before."

Mary sighed as she came to stand next to him. "Yes, there are many differing opinions," she said. "However, a procedure is either successful or it is not, and if it is not, then it is the physician's and the surgeon's job to apply a method that has been proven to be better. Unfortunately, these men of medicine are terrified of admitting that they may have been wrong, which implementing new methods is bound to suggest. Instead, they muddle on, without their patient's best interest at heart and with only their own, personal gain in mind.

"Now, if you are ready, I believe that we have taken up

enough of the Arlingtons' time with our discussion. After all, the whole purpose of our visit here this evening is to remove Lady Arlington's stitches." She looked at her patient. "I am sure you must be quite eager to have them out."

They sat in silence on their way back to Brook Street. Ryan waited in the carriage while Mary ran inside to change. When she returned, he gave her a faint smile. "I must say that you clean up rather well, Mary."

"Thank you," she said as she settled herself onto the seat across from him for the brief remainder of the ride back to Trenton House. After a moment's silence, she looked at him very directly. "I hope that what you have witnessed this evening has made you understand how important my work is to me."

"It certainly has, and I must admit that there is absolutely nothing that I can say to discredit you. You did an extraordinary job."

Mary beamed with delight. "I am so pleased that you think so, Ryan. In fact, your opinion matters a great deal to me."

"Then I am just as pleased as you, since you will no doubt listen to what I have to say." He fixed Mary with a steady gaze that made her instantly uneasy. "This unruly behavior of yours has got to stop. Not only are you breaking the law by practicing without a license, but you are soon to be a married lady of the *ton*. It would be preposterous for you to continue doing what you do. If you need a hobby, then perhaps you can think of something a little more ladylike, such as miniature painting or botany."

By the time Ryan was done, Mary was seething with rage. *How dare he!* The arrogance and patronizing male superiority! So angry was she that she had to clasp her hands in her lap to keep them from trembling. "I have no intention of doing any such thing," she told him icily.

"Be reasonable, Mary, and stop acting like a child," he all but shouted, then lowered his voice to a more moderate tone. "Of course you cannot keep up this charade. You have had a good run of it, I will give you that, but it is time to end it and accept the role that awaits you as a wife and mother."

Mary's jaw dropped. "Damn you, Ryan Summersby! I have saved seventy-three of the seventy-six patients I have ever treated. Do you have any idea what that means? I am not a green girl who cannot tell the difference between the spleen and the appendix, for heaven's sake. Any person will be safer in my hands than in any other's—save for my father, who was just as reliable as I, if not more so. Yet you would rather refer a patient to a licensed professional who will likely kill them instead of save them, just because he happens to have a piece of paper allowing him to practice?"

"I am sorry, Mary, but this is your own doing. You have ventured into an area of expertise exclusively reserved for men, and as my wife, I simply will not have it. Do you understand?"

The carriage came to a sudden halt. They'd arrived at Berkeley Square. Mary gathered what little self-control she had left and turned to him with a heavy heart. "Then I will not have you, Mr. Summersby."

"I have told you already, my lady, that there is no undoing it—the entire *ton* knows about our engagement."

"And whose fault is that?" she flared. "You and I are completely wrong for one another, yet for some absurd reason you are determined not to see that. So I suggest that you find a way to undo our engagement this instant, or God help me I shall cause a scandal far worse than any you have ever conceived off: I shall say no at the altar."

Without another word, she stepped down from the carriage and made her way to the front door of Alexandra's home, cursing the day she met Ryan Summersby as she went.

CHAPTER FOURTEEN

For the next five days, Mary buried herself in her father's journals. Whenever Ryan came to call on her, she sent him away. She was determined now, more so than ever, to solve the puzzle about her father, and while Ryan had offered to help in that regard, their recent argument had brought Mary crashing back to reality. She knew now that they would never see eye to eye, and though the fact that he would not accept her for who she was pained her, she was now too busy to give it much thought.

It wasn't until Alexandra grew thoroughly exasperated with her solitary confinement that Mary even realized how many days had passed by.

"You need to get out," Alexandra told her firmly one early afternoon. "Staying cooped up like this for days on end cannot be good for you."

"It is raining again," Mary told her, unwilling to give up her reading.

"Yes, I know. But that does not mean that we cannot go to Gunter's for tea. If you like, we could visit the Hunterian first."

Mary looked up. "Really? You wouldn't mind? I should hate to subject you to an endless display of surgical instruments for my benefit alone."

Alexandra grinned. "I think it might be interesting. Shall we agree to meet downstairs in fifteen minutes? That should allow you enough time to finish up and get yourself ready."

Mary nodded enthusiastically. "Yes, thank you, Alexandra. I shall just get my spencer and reticule."

"So tell me, what happened between you and my brother?" Alexandra asked a short while later as they rolled along Oxford Street in Alexandra's carriage. "He seemed a bit put out when I spoke with him yesterday, and every time he has tried to call on you, you have turned him away. Did you have another disagreement?"

"You could say that." Mary sighed. "He insisted that I give up practicing surgery, and I disagreed. In fact, he told me quite plainly that he would not allow me to jeopardize my reputation or his, to which I replied that if that were the case, then I would not have him."

"You called off the engagement?"

"Not exactly; I gave him an ultimatum. Either he can accept me for who I am, or I shall publically refuse him at the altar."

"Good heavens," Alexandra muttered. "No wonder he was in a foul mood."

She studied Mary for a long moment before continuing. "You do know that he cares a great deal for you?"

"I am not at all sure that he does, Alexandra. If he did, he would not try to take the one thing that I am truly passionate about away from me. He would not suggest that it is merely a hobby to me and that I might easily replace it with painting or botany."

"He said that?" Alexandra might have laughed if it weren't so tragic. Mary, who was looking quite glum, merely nodded. "I am sure he is only trying to protect you."

"Well, he will not have to worry about that anymore. As far as I am concerned, there is nothing left to be said about the matter. We are of two different opinions, and neither one of us is willing to budge."

Alexandra chose not to pursue the issue any further, but she decided that it was time for her to have another talk with her brother. Clearly, he was in desperate need of some pointers on how to handle a woman like Mary. One thing was for certain: he wouldn't get anywhere by threatening her freedom.

After paying a penny to view the exhibit, the two women walked alongside the display cases together, stopping every few feet to admire the contents.

"Oh, would you look at that," Mary remarked as she pointed to a tiny lizard that had been suspended in a jar of alcohol. "Fascinating how life has evolved so differently in different parts of the world, is it not?"

"Yes," Alexandra agreed. "I should love to travel as far as Australia one day and see one of those bouncing animals that I have heard so much about, or fish larger than a carriage. Can you imagine?"

Mary nodded her head thoughtfully. She'd been as far as Istanbul with her father. He'd given her a taste of what the world had to offer and an eagerness to see more. She sighed, wondering if that would be yet another dream she'd have to sacrifice if she chose to marry Ryan.

"I don't want to rush you, but I must confess that I'm terribly eager to see the Irish giant they have on display. Would you mind if I go and have a look? I'll only be a moment."

Mary grinned, acknowledging that few people were as interested in reptiles and insects as she was. "Not at all," she said, upon which Alexandra left Mary's side.

Mary moved on to a collection of butterflies. It was almost as if they'd simply paused for a moment, their bodies suspended in midair. In fact, she half expected them to flap their wings at any moment. But as fascinating as all of these things were, what she'd really come to see was the vast collection of surgical instruments.

She was just about to turn and follow Alexandra when she felt herself grabbed firmly by the arm and shoved through a narrow archway. A door banged shut behind her, leaving her in complete darkness.

Her pulse raced, and her breath came quickly as she reached for something, anything at all, that might allow her to get her bearings.

"You have an unfortunate habit of being too inquisitive for your own good, Lady Steepleton," a deep voice told her. It was not one that she recognized, though she suspected that the speaker was attempting to mask himself by lowering his tone.

She backed away from it, hitting the wall and knocking something metallic over in the process. It clanged loudly against the stone floor. "Who is there?" she asked in a voice far calmer than she felt. "What do you want?"

"Excellent questions, my lady," the voice drawled. "As for the first one, I cannot tell you the answer to that. If I did, you would have to meet the same fate as your father much sooner than we had intended."

"We?"

"Hm. . .yes, I would keep an eye on my back at all times if I were you. I am not the only one who wants your father's journals, you know."

Mary clenched her jaw tightly shut and took a deep breath to stop her voice from quivering. "The only one I had was stolen from me. I do not know where the rest of them are."

"And I do not believe you," the voice purred. "You see, I think you have them with you at Trenton House, where you have been staying for this past week."

Mary gasped.

"Oh, come now, you didn't seriously think that we wouldn't figure that much out, did you?" He sighed. "A smart move, though, on your part—placing yourself under the protection of the Summersbys and Lord Trenton. But we will get to you eventually, and those journals *will* be ours sooner or later, Lady Steepleton, no matter what you do to try and stop us. The only question is, how much are you willing to sacrifice?"

There was a clicking sound, followed by complete silence. Mary waited, her arms wrapped tightly about her torso to stop herself from shivering, but eventually she realized that whoever had spoken to her just now was no longer there. Feeling her way along the rough edges of the brick wall, she eventually found a door handle. She pushed down hard on it and gave the door a shove. It met with a bit of resistance, but when she put her full weight behind it, it finally gave way with a squeak.

Stumbling back out into the museum, she leaned against the wall and began taking deep breaths to steady her hammering heart. She felt like vomiting.

"Mary, where on earth have you been? I couldn't find you anywhere and. . .good heavens, are you all right? You look terrible." Alexandra put her arm around Mary's shoulders and led her toward a bench. "Please sit down and tell me what has happened." She then watched Mary with great concern as Mary told her about her encounter. "Was there anything at all familiar about this man?" Alexandra asked. "Did you recognize his voice?"

Mary shook her head feebly. "No." She met Alexandra's eyes. "I am sorry, but I just want to go home."

"All right," Alexandra agreed, feeling quite miserable herself. She'd failed to protect her friend when she'd needed her the most. Clearly, something had to be done; they had to get to the bottom of this.

Having returned from their eventful excursion in town, Alexandra and Mary were quietly enjoying their tea together in the conservatory, where several of the plants were already in full bloom, when Alexandra's butler appeared. "Mr. Summersby is here to see you, my lady," he announced in his typically affected tone.

"Thank you, Collins," Alexandra replied. "You may show him into the study."

Alexandra turned to Mary as soon as Collins had gone.

"It appears as though I have a guest. I don't suppose that I can convince you to join us."

Mary gave her a sad smile. "Thank you, but no. I think I will just wait for you here, if you don't mind."

"Not at all," Alexandra said, accepting her friend's need for solitude. "Feel free to water the roses if you like. I think they might be feeling a bit neglected."

Leaving Mary to look at the flowers, Alexandra made her way to the study, where she found Ryan waiting for her. He was dressed in a smart pair of light beige trousers and a dark brown velvet frock coat with a matching waistcoat beneath it. His cravat was tied to perfection as always.

"Ah, I am so glad that you were able to see me," Ryan remarked rather jovially as Alexandra came toward him. "Considering all the times I have been shown the door here recently, I was not at all sure of my success."

"Well, you can hardly blame Mary for not wanting to see you anymore after what you said to her—painting and botany, indeed—and in spite of the advice I gave you," Alexandra admonished, shaking her head with a great deal of disapproval. "You really do have a talent for mucking things up."

"I should have known that you would be the last person to understand. Hell, you probably think it would be a wonderful idea for my wife to be the instigator of the greatest scandal this country has ever seen. Can you imagine? A female surgeon without the right to practice, riding off in the dead of night, disguised as a man. . .the papers will have a field day, Alex, and I shall have my work cut out for me, keeping her out of Newgate, or worse even, Bedlam."

Alexandra rolled her eyes heavenward and sighed with clear exasperation before slumping down onto a caramel-colored velvet armchair. "Look, I know that Mary's occupation is not exactly acceptable, but you need to show a little understanding if you hope to have any future with her whatsoever. Think of a way in which to compromise, Ryan, and while you are at it, try to consider this: do you want to retain the fiery, carefree nature that you fell in love with, or do you wish to demoralize her in every way possible?"

There was a short moment of silence as Alexandra let that sink in before she continued. "I suggest you think very carefully about how you handle the situation, Ryan. You have found a unique individual who stands out from the crowd, but if you would prefer a more sedate woman who will jump at your every command, then I suggest you leave Mary and pick one of the typical brides this season has to offer."

Ryan stared at his sister before chuckling somewhat nervously. "Alex, I think you are reading far too much into this. Mary and I have not known each other for more than, what, three weeks at most? And for the majority of that time, it seems I scarcely knew her at all. Really, Alex, I am not at all in love with her." He shook his head in open frustration, while Alexandra raised a dubious eyebrow.

"Oh, Ryan, I do believe that you are." She smiled warmly. "But you must not despair just yet. I have a strong feeling that in spite of her fierce determination to thwart your charms, Mary is very much in love with you too."

Ryan's eyes brightened instantly. "Do you really think so?"

Alexandra giggled as she nodded her head. "I wouldn't have said so if I didn't." She turned serious once again. "Still, I don't think that she has admitted that much to herself yet, so it might be best not to say anything."

"Then what do you suggest I do?" Ryan asked, raking his fingers through his hair and walking across to the window. He stared out into the rainy street beyond. "The last thing she told me was that she would never have me, no matter what."

"Yes, well, I have been thinking. Perhaps it is time for us all to get away for a bit. As it is, Mary was practically attacked this morning on our visit to the Hunterian."

"What?" Ryan spun away from the window. "Why the hell didn't you say so before? Is she all right? What happened?"

"She is fine, but it was a nasty shock." She told him everything that she knew about the incident, while he stared back at her in horror. "So I was thinking that a house party at Whickham Hall might be just the thing."

"That does sound like an excellent idea," he muttered as he took a seat in one of the armchairs across from where Alexandra was sitting. "Any thoughts on whom you plan to invite?"

"Michael's parents perhaps, Papa, Michael's sisters—if any of them would care to join us—you, of course. . ."

"If you invite me, then I am afraid that Mary will not agree to go. I fear that you shall have to leave me out."

"Nonsense, Ryan. This is the perfect opportunity for you and Mary to patch things up a bit." She gave her brother a mischievous smile. "And since my memory has not been too good of late, I think that I may simply forget to tell Mary that you plan on attending."

"Why, Lady Trenton, you truly are a scoundrel of the worst possible kind," Ryan said and grinned. "But if your little scheme works, then I shall do my best to convince Mary to name our firstborn in honor of you."

CHAPTER FIFTEEN

With a great deal of cajoling, Alexandra finally managed to put together an acceptable guest list. Bryce would be attending, together with both of his sons, since William had just returned from his assignment the previous day. Michael's parents had also accepted the invitation, while their daughter Cassandra was the only one of Michael's sisters who'd been eager enough to escape to the country in the middle of the season. But then, just like last year and the year before that, she hadn't been a very big success. As it happened, she'd been quite gloomy since her friend Judith's marriage to Lord Barton, whom she'd been very confident about forming an attachment with herself.

And then, of course, there was Alexandra, her husband, Michael, and their one-year-old son, Richard, and finally Mary, who was looking quite forward to a country retreat.

"Oh look, the Summersbys are here already," Michael remarked as their carriage rolled up the graveled driveway to the sound of crunching pebbles. The space had been a bit tight for the duration of the journey since Richard's nurse had also joined them. Needless to say, they were all relieved to have finally made it to Whickham Hall so they could alight and stretch their legs.

"The Summersbys?" Mary asked warily as she narrowed her eyes. "Ryan is here too?"

"Yes and William, whom I am sure you will like immensely," Alexandra remarked, glancing at anything else but Mary.

"Not if he shares the same opinions as his brother." Mary lowered her voice to a whisper. "Why did you not tell me that Ryan would be here?"

"Because you never would have agreed to come if I had," Alexandra told her plainly.

"And as it is, I have a good mind to head straight back to London."

"It. . .er. . .it seems I must have put my foot in my mouth," Michael lamented. Neither woman responded to that. "I shall go and see how our guests are settling in."

"I did not peg you for a coward, Mary," Alexandra told her sternly as soon as her husband was out of earshot.

Mary froze. No, if there was one thing she'd never been, then that was truly it. "I shall stay," she acquiesced. "But I cannot promise that I will speak with Ryan, even if he addresses me. In fact, I am likely to be quite uncivil. Do you understand?"

Alexandra grinned as she took Mary's arm and began steering her toward the front entrance of Whickham Hall. "I would not have it any other way," she told her.

Alexandra's housekeeper, Mrs. Copplestone, practically swooped down on both ladies the minute they walked through the door. Naturally, since her master and mistress hadn't visited the place since early March, she had a whole string of issues she wanted to go over as soon as possible.

"I am afraid that all of this will have to wait, at least until tomorrow," Alexandra told the eager woman. "Right now I have guests to attend to. Tell me, where are my father and my brothers?"

"In the library, my lady," Mrs. Copplestone replied cheerily. "I think your father wanted to take a walk about the grounds, but now that it has begun to rain. . .honestly, I do not recall a worse summer in my life."

"Quite right, Mrs. Copplestone. Thank you, that will be all." She turned to Mary. "Well, now that we know where *not* to go, I will show you to your room and then give you a quick tour of the house before dinner."

"But I thought. . ." Mrs. Copplestone looked quite confused at Alexandra's determination to avoid her family.

"Once again," Alexandra said, "that will be all."

"Yes, my lady," the befuddled housekeeper replied as she bustled away to attend to her duties.

"This way, Mary," Alexandra said as she walked across to the stairs. "I thought you might like to have a room with a view of the gardens, so I have put you on the north side, if that is all right with you."

"Oh, I am sure that I shall be quite happy with whichever room you give me," Mary replied as she gazed up at the intricate woodwork adorning the ceiling.

They walked down a long corridor that had been tastefully decorated with occasional landscape paintings done in bright and cheerful colors.

"I was always of the impression that these types of homes were full of ancestral portraits," Mary remarked as she stopped to admire a cornfield dotted with poppies.

"Oh, they usually are," Alexandra agreed. "And Whickham Hall was no exception, you know, but Michael thought his ancestors looked like such a miserable bunch that he had them all carted away to the attic. I have to say that he made the right decision."

They continued onward until Alexandra opened the door to a large bedroom that had been decorated in various tones of blue. The bed had a heavy four-poster canopy with billowy white silk curtains. There was a vanity table with a mirror, a chest of drawers, and a wardrobe that must have been ten feet high. In one corner, between two armchairs, stood a round table with a vase that was overflowing with hydrangeas.

Mary gasped. "Oh, Alexandra, this is beautiful! It is so light and airy in here, so peaceful and tranquil. Thank you."

"It is my pleasure," Alexandra told her with a smile.

"And the view!" Mary exclaimed as she rushed over to the window and drew back the white voile that was meant to shade against the sun. "I have never seen anything quite like it."

"Yes. A pity that it is raining right now. On a clear day you can see for miles, but right now you can barely see the church steeple in the nearest village." She took Mary by the arm. "Come, let me show you the other parts of the house."

It took them about an hour to complete the tour. Mary made a mental note of the rooms she'd like to spend more time exploring later. So far, she'd managed to avoid seeing Ryan since he was no longer in the library by the time she and

Alexandra arrived there. Mary caught her breath at the sight of all the books lining the shelves.

"You may borrow whichever books you like," Alexandra told her. "In fact, I believe there is a small collection of medical books right over there in the corner."

Mary walked over to the shelves that Alexandra had singled out, running her fingers reverently along the spine of one of them. Picking it carefully up, she leafed through it. "Al-Zahrawi's book about surgical instruments, translated into Latin. Do you have any idea how much this single book must be worth?"

Alexandra grinned. "I take it that you will not be bored."

Mary stared at her as if she might be mad. "Certainly not. My only concern is that I will not have enough time to read everything during the few days that I shall be staying."

"Well, we shall just have to invite you back then, shan't we?"

Alexandra headed for the door, stopped, and turned to wait for Mary. "Come along," she told her with a smile. "The books will wait, but I am afraid that the dinner is best enjoyed while it is still warm."

With a longing look at all the wonderful books she hoped to browse through during her visit, Mary reluctantly followed Alexandra from the room.

"I will meet you in the dining room in an hour," Alexandra told Mary once they were back by the grand staircase. "You can ring for a maid to help you dress."

"Thank you," Mary told her before rushing upstairs. If she hurried, she might just manage to return to the library for a quick read before sitting down to dinner.

"Alex told me that I might find you here."

Mary, who stood hunched over a large book, looked up, her eyes meeting Ryan's as soon as he spoke. He'd been watching her quietly for a moment from the doorway, captivated by her apparent enthusiasm for whatever it was she was reading. To his delight, she gave him a dazzling smile. "I am sorry," she said, "but I simply could not resist. Have you read this? I saw a copy of it once, a long time ago, but it is the first time that I have truly had an opportunity to study it. Oh, Ryan; the man was a genius, an absolute genius! What he achieved. . .and at that time. . .dear me, it is almost beyond comprehension."

Ryan was speechless. He'd never known anyone other than himself to be so passionate about a subject. And the smile she'd given him: Was it possible? Dare he even hope?

He closed the distance between them in order to see the book that she was so enraptured by. "Ah yes, the famous al-Zahrawi." Leaning closer, he caught a whiff of her scent— hyacinths, he reckoned. Whatever the case, it ignited that fierce desire he felt whenever he was near her.

Clenching his fists, he straightened himself and moved away. He'd already made a mess of things twice. It was time for him to think carefully and to calculate his every move if he still intended to make her his wife. He looked out of the window at the pouring rain. "I have only read a few parts of it, not the entire thing."

"I don't know how you could possibly put the book down once you started reading," Mary muttered. "He describes here, for instance, a procedure that he developed: litigating the temporal artery to prevent migraines." Mary looked up from the book with a puzzled expression. "I always thought Paré developed the litigation of arteries, but apparently al-Zahrawi came up with it six hundred years earlier."

She leafed through the pages to another section. "And here," she said, pointing to a diagram. "Look at that: forceps to help in delivering a baby."

"It is quite remarkable," Ryan said, unable to take his eyes off Mary and hoping to keep up the amicable conversation. Her sudden interest in the book had made her forget how angry she was with him.

"It is more than that. There are roughly two hundred surgical instruments illustrated here that al-Zahrawi invented. His contribution to medicine is profound, Ryan. You must read this book if you have any interest in becoming a physician; promise me that you will."

"I promise," he told her sincerely. "But for now, it will have to wait, I'm afraid, unless we want Alex to come looking for us."

"Oh dear," Mary said, putting the book back on the shelf. "I completely forgot."

"Yes, it rather seems as though you did," he said with a grin. "But I must admit that you never looked more fetching than when you were standing there in your evening gown and white gloves, your head completely immersed in that book."

Mary frowned. "I was trying to concentrate," she replied in an irritated tone.

Ryan sighed. "I didn't mean. . ." He gave up trying to explain himself. What was the point if the woman was bent on being contrary? Perhaps he should just concede and acknowledge defeat. At least then he could start looking at all the women who would be more than eager to marry him—Lady Stephanie, for instance. His head reeled at the thought of it. As pretty as she was, she was nothing but an empty shell, with a venomous streak to her that ought to send any young man running for the hills.

No, he had to have Lady Steepleton; there simply wasn't any other way around it. His mind was made up, and so help him God if he wasn't going to do everything in his power to make it happen.

"I was just telling Lord Willowbrook about your father," Alexandra said to Mary from across the table a short while later.

Mary looked up somewhat flustered from her plate. The truth was that she hadn't been paying the least bit of attention to the conversations around her. She'd been thinking about Lady Warwick instead and wondering how she might be faring now that she had her displeased son to contend with.

"I remember your father quite well, Lady Steepleton," Lord Trenton's father told her. "I cannot say that we were close friends or anything like that, but I did go to him once for treatment."

That got Mary's attention. "Really?" she asked. "For what,, if you do not mind my asking?"

"Not at all," Lord Willowbrook told her with a smile. "As it happens, I had a cataract on my right eye, it must be at least five years ago by now. Your father operated on me, and, I must say, he did a mighty good job."

Mary stared at Lord Willowbrook. She remembered her father telling her about it at the time, how angry she'd been that he hadn't allowed her to attend. Apparently, she was now sitting down to dinner with the patient himself. "Did it hurt a lot?" she asked.

Lord Willowbrook nodded. "Like the devil. But I knew I was in capable hands. Your father came highly recommended, you know, from the Regent himself."

The Regent?

Mary had always felt so close to her father, had loved him with all her heart, and had blindly trusted everything he'd ever told her to be the truth. Yet there were clearly two sides to the man she'd known, and he'd worked very hard at keeping one of those sides hidden from her. "I had no idea," she muttered, feeling suddenly quite faint and unwell. "I am terribly sorry," she said. "Would you please excuse me?"

"Are you quite all right?" Alexandra asked anxiously.

"Yes, I will be fine," Mary told her, almost knocking over her wine glass in her haste to leave the room. "I believe the wine may have disagreed with me. I just need some fresh air."

"Perhaps I should—" William said as they all watched Mary escape through the dining room door.

"I will go," Ryan cut in, pushing his chair back and hurrying after her.

"Our brother has certainly set his cap," William remarked as he caught Alexandra's eye.

"Yes. . .I do believe he has," she replied. "But whether or not she will have him still remains to be seen."

"What?" chimed in. "I thought the matter was settled. After all, he did propose in front of the entire *ton.*"

"Yes, Papa," Alexandra said with a sigh, taking a sip of her wine and then licking her lips. "But he did so without Mary's consent, and since then he has not exactly been very good at persuading her to accept his impromptu proposal."

"What the devil is that supposed to mean?" Bryce demanded to know.

"Just that Ryan will not allow Mary to continue doing what she does when she becomes his wife, and Mary refuses to give it up. Things were said and, well, to cut a long story short, Ryan is doing his best to patch things up again."

"He is the one who will need patching up again if he mucks this up," Bryce fumed. "I want that woman for my daughter-in-law. So what if she is a bit eccentric? This family is comprised entirely of eccentric people."

"And what exactly is so eccentric about Lady Steepleton, Lord Moorland?" Michael's mother, Isabella, asked. "She seems perfectly respectable to me—not as flamboyant as one might expect, considering her title, but I find that rather refreshing."

"She is a surgeon," William said simply.

"*Madre mia!*" Isabella exclaimed. She looked about cautiously, then lowered her voice to a whisper. "Is that even allowed?"

"No," Alexandra told her. "She doesn't have a license, and it is also unlikely that she will ever get one as a woman. But she was taught by her father since she was fourteen years of age and had assisted him on his surgeries. And at Waterloo, where nobody cared one way or the other about who did the cutting and suturing as long as it just got done, she lost only three of the eighty or so men that she treated."

"Blimey," Lord Willowbrook muttered. "Those numbers are nothing short of astounding."

"That practically makes her the best surgeon in the country," Cassandra piped in. "What a pity it would be for such talent to go to waste—and when you think of all the people whom she might still save. . ."

"Here, here," William and Bryce concurred in unison.

"Perhaps if we were to back her up," Isabella suggested. "We could speak to Lord Woodbridge. Surely he must have some influence as the Master of the Royal College of Surgeons."

"All he can do is put it to a vote," Michael told her. "And even then it may need to be sanctioned by Parliament."

"Good luck with that," Alexandra grumbled, taking a slow sip of her wine. It had begun to dawn on her just how difficult it would be for Mary and Ryan to find happiness together.

CHAPTER SIXTEEN

"Mind if I join you?" Ryan asked as he walked out onto the terrace. It had stopped raining, leaving the air fresh and the hydrangeas dripping wet.

Mary sighed. "I thought I knew him," she murmured as Ryan stepped closer. "He was my father and my only parent for so many years. We never kept secrets from one another—at least, I did not think so. But as it turns out, everything about him was one big lie. I didn't really know him at all."

She squeezed her eyes shut to stifle the tears that were already threatening to trickle down her cheeks. Ryan offered her a handkerchief, but she shook her head and turned away. "I am sorry," she said. "I must look a frightful mess."

Ryan shrugged. "You look no worse than I did when Mama died."

She nodded with understanding. "That must have been a terrible blow to your family."

"It was, in a way. But in a sense it was also a relief; she suffered quite badly toward the end, you see. Alexandra was most affected by it, I suppose. Not only was she the youngest, but she was also there during Mama's final moments. Papa's reaction had a great impact on her. I must admit that I did shed a great deal of tears myself, but the pain does get easier to bear with time—even if it doesn't feel that way right now."

"You are right; it doesn't feel that way at all. In fact, it rather feels as though a knot has been tied around my heart, squeezing it so tightly that it aches with pain." She turned away from him and looked out over the drenched garden, the branches on both trees and bushes hanging limply under the strain of the newly fallen rain.

"You know," Ryan told her softly, moving one step closer to her, "it is possible that, in spite of all the secrets he kept, you *did* know the real Lord Steepleton after all. I cannot help but think that every moment you spent with him was genuine. And the person that he truly was the man that you knew him to be: an excellent surgeon who never gave a wit for his title or his fortune."

"But why would he keep it from me? What right did he have to do that?" she sniffed, turning around to face him.

"Think about it, Mary," he quietly urged her. "You have never told me about your mother. Was she from a wealthy family?"

"The truth is I scarcely remember her," she told him. Her voice grew distant. "I was six when she died, and though I still recall the pain of losing her, I cannot seem to picture her face. But as far as I recollect, her father was a blacksmith in Stepney, where we lived."

"It seems, then, that in order for them to marry, your father was forced to move down a few steps on the social ladder, because he knew it would be difficult for her to move up. He set up his practice in the small house that you grew up in, and when your mother passed. . .well, he made the decision to pursue his dream: the accumulation of medical knowledge.

"It may be true that he swept a few details under the rug, but he gave you an education that many society women would be green with envy over. And while you may be hurting now, in time I do think that you will come to realize that your father did what was best for you in the long run. He loved you dearly, and he held you in the highest regard. If he had not, he never would have trusted you with his life's work."

Mary stared at Ryan in astonishment. She'd been so caught up in her own little rift with him that she'd failed to realize what a great judge of character he actually was. He'd seen something that she hadn't: that it was the man she'd traveled Europe with, the one who'd struggled to teach her French and Latin and who'd opened her eyes to the wonder of medicine, that defined her father. He was precisely the person she'd known him to be, because all the rest of it—the title, the estates, and the vast fortune—was something he'd turned his back on before she was even born.

She nodded numbly. "You are absolutely right," she told him with an edge of disbelief to her words. "Thank you."

Ryan hesitated for a brief second, then coughed somewhat awkwardly before proceeding again. "I realize that this may be a sore topic with you, but I was hoping that you might have given our recent conversation a bit more thought, especially in light of the threats you've been getting. You must realize that you cannot continue to practice medicine."

Mary's gaze cooled dramatically at that statement. "I have realized no such thing," she told him in a tight voice.

"For Christ's sake, Mary, be reasonable! Not only is it against the law, what you're doing, but you're also putting people's lives at risk."

"I'm a very competent surgeon," she argued. She could feel the anger building inside her. How could she have been so foolish as to think he could ever understand?

"I'm not disputing that, Mary, but you must consider the fact that if Lady Stephanie was able to discover that you'd operated on Lady Warwick, then it's only a matter of time before word of your illicit behavior begins to spread. Once it does, you won't be able to help anyone."

"You have a valid point, I'll give you that. I shall simply have to take greater precaution next time." She knew that she was being stubborn, but she couldn't help it; it vexed her that he was being so unsupportive of her.

"Is there no reasoning with you?" Ryan said, highly agitated.

Mary stared back at him. It didn't seem to matter how much they liked one another or enjoyed each other's company. Her need to continue with her work, regardless of the risk involved, and his opposition to it would always stand between them. She let out a slow breath in an attempt to calm herself. "Perhaps one day, when you receive your license to practice, and a desperate man or woman turns to you for help, you will understand that turning your back on them is not an option, no matter what others might think. And I will say this much: as far as morality goes, I know that I am doing the right thing. Indeed, I have no choice."

A long silence followed. She couldn't tell if her words had affected him in any way, but she hoped they had. If he was going to be the successful physician that she hoped he'd one day become, then he was going to have to start caring a little more about doing what was right for the patient and a little less about public scrutiny.

"On a different note," Ryan suddenly said, bringing her back to the present. He was eager to change the subject, but then again, so was she. "May I ask if you have had the opportunity to uncover any information in your father's journals that might be of use to us, something that might shed some light on the threats that you have been getting?"

Mary slumped her shoulders and shook her head. "I'm afraid not. I keep searching for some sort of surgical or medical breakthrough—something incredible that might justify why these people, whoever they may be, might want to get their hands on it. But I keep reading, and nothing seems to stand out."

"Would you mind if I took a look?" Ryan asked carefully.

"No; maybe you will see something that I have missed," Mary told him with a crooked smile. "In any case, I am absolutely freezing, so if we could please go back inside, I would be most grateful."

"Yes, of course, right away," he said as he stepped forward to open the door for her.

"Would you like me to bring the journals downstairs?" Mary asked. "We could take a look at them in the library."

"The men will be in there enjoying their after-dinner drinks," Ryan told her, "and the parlor will be occupied by the ladies."

"Then where do you suggest we go?"

"I think we ought to finish the evening with our host and

hostess in an appropriate fashion; we have already stayed away for much too long."

Mary nodded. "Yes, you are probably right about that."

She began to walk toward the parlor, but Ryan caught her by the arm and held her back a moment longer. "I will come to your room once everyone else has gone to bed," he told her softly.

A pulse of nervous energy whipped through Mary at the thought of her and Ryan being alone together in her bedroom. Her stomach clenched as a wave of heat snaked its way along her spine. "That is not only a terrible idea, but a very improper one as well," she told him uncertainly. Her earlier annoyance had worn off a little at his willingness to help her, but she still felt that they had a great deal of issues to resolve. Being alone together in her bedroom would not be the best way to go about doing that.

"Mary, if anyone happens to discover us, then there really won't be much for them to say, short of shaking their heads disapprovingly. We are already engaged, remember? Besides, the sole purpose of my visit will be to look at your father's journals. I promise you that I will be on my best behavior."

"Have you not told me so before?" she asked, recalling a similar statement made at Glendale House only minutes before he'd kissed her.

He appeared to consider that for a moment. "I suppose I have." He grinned. "But this time, I really mean it." He waggled his eyebrows teasingly.

Mary couldn't help but laugh. "All right," she conceded. "But if you try to kiss me or touch me in any inappropriate fashion whatsoever, I will most assuredly scream. Do not make the error of presuming that I will not."

"Very well then," he chuckled. "We have an agreement."

It was just past midnight by the time Mary returned to her room. No sooner had she closed the door, than she heard a soft rapping against the wall. *That's odd*, she thought, as she followed the sound toward the far right corner of the room. She stopped and listened. As far as she could tell, it sounded as if someone was knocking.

Picking up an oil lamp, she moved closer until she was able to discern the faint outline of a door carved directly into the wall. She stared at it blankly for a moment until she heard her name spoken from the other side of it.

"Mary? Are you there?"

"Yes," she said, recognizing Ryan's voice. "Yes, I am here."

"Pull the latch."

Once again Mary studied the door, this time a little more closely. She finally spotted the tiny latch, partially hidden by the wood molding. She pulled it, and the door swung open. Ryan stepped through. He'd discarded his jacket and waistcoat and removed his cravat. He undid the first couple of buttons on his shirt and began rolling up the sleeves as he walked over to one of the armchairs. "Mind if I sit?" he asked.

Mary frowned at him in an attempt to conceal the way in which his scruffy appearance made her heart go pitter-patter. "Is your room just through there?" she asked instead, ignoring his question while she pointed at the open doorway.

"Well, yes; it would be rather odd for me to come that way if it were not."

"And did you know about our rooms being next to one another all along?" Her eyes narrowed even further as she searched his face for the answer.

"Of course. After all, I specifically asked Alex to arrange it that way. After everything that has happened and considering that Sir. Percy did ask me to protect you, I thought it best if I were close enough to come running should something happen."

"I see," Mary replied somewhat tightly. "Alexandra conveniently omitted that little detail when she showed me the room earlier in the day."

"She probably forgot," Ryan suggested.

"I somehow doubt that. In fact, I rather suspect that your sister is up to no good."

Ryan chuckled. "It wouldn't be the first time," he told her brightly. "But to reassure you, there is, as you have just seen, a lock on the door. I cannot come in unless you invite me. The same goes for you."

"I see," Mary remarked, still wary of the idea of Ryan's having access to her room at any given hour of the day without the knowledge of anyone else in the house.

Part of the problem was that, even now, sitting there so casually with his hair and clothes in disarray, he made her stomach flip uncontrollably, her heart race like a rabbit chased by a hound, and her knees turn to mush. In short, she could barely function when he was in such close proximity to her. And the last thing she wanted, the thing that just about horrified her the most, was the prospect of him finding out, because once he did, there'd be no stopping him; of that she was quite certain.

Turning stiffly about, Mary walked over to the trunk she'd brought with her. She opened it and lifted out the box that held her father's journals. Carrying it carefully across the room to where Ryan was sitting, watching her with intense interest and a crooked smile that forced her to catch her breath, she placed the box carefully on the table where the vase of hydrangeas stood. "Here they are," she said, pushing the box gently toward him.

Ryan sat perfectly still for a moment, just staring at the contents of the box. He almost appeared to be too afraid to touch them.

"Go ahead," Mary urged him. "Take a look. I am practically dying to know what you make of them."

"I don't even know which one to start with," he said. "Should I start at the beginning or at the end? What do you suggest?"

Mary shrugged. "I am not entirely sure. I have gotten as far as Volume 7 myself without finding anything. Perhaps you ought to work your way backward."

"What if we start on Volume 8 together?" he suggested instead.

Mary agreed, even though that would mean pulling her chair around so she could sit right next to him in order to see the book at the same time. With a small sigh, she prayed she wouldn't make a complete fool of herself before the night was out. Instead, she sat down, leaned a bit closer, and tried desperately to ignore his scent, a rich perfume of sandalwood.

For the next couple of hours they poured over John Croyden's notes. They varied from describing surgical procedures he'd performed to documenting all the information that he'd gathered on his travels and which he'd considered to be, in some way or another, medical breakthroughs.

"Did you happen to read this?" Ryan asked suddenly, pointing to the paragraph he'd just been reading. "He mentions something called ethereal spirits. Did your father ever talk to you about that?"

"The liquid Paracelsus wrote about?" she asked with a pensive frown.

Ryan nodded as he looked at Mary in wonder. "Apparently, he conducted some experiments and determined it to have a sleep-inducing effect on chickens."

Mary smiled slightly. She knew precisely where this was going and only waited for Ryan to continue.

"But here is the crux of the matter: Paracelsus discovered this more than 250years ago. Since then, there have been no further developments. I mean—and your father makes the same point as I am about to—this might be the very key to providing painless surgery for patients. Mary, this could be huge!"

"I know," Mary told him quietly. "And there are so many other examples just like this. Unfortunately, you practically have to scream to get anyone to pay attention. It is exhausting to say the least, and quite disheartening when the majority of the people you talk to dismiss what you say as nonsense."

"Do you think this might be the reason why these people are so eager to get their hands on the journals?" Ryan asked as he turned the next page. "They could probably make a fortune with all the information your father has gathered in here."

"I suppose it is possible," Mary told him. "I just—"

"Well, this is odd," Ryan remarked, interrupting Mary. He leafed through the rest of the pages in the journal as if searching for something.

"What is it?"

"I am not entirely sure. Let me see the last two volumes, please."

Mary handed them to him and watched silently as Ryan leafed through those as well. When he was done, he looked at her with a puzzled expression on his face. "From this point on," he told her pensively, as he pointed to a segment in Volume 8, "there is nothing but detailed accounts of surgeries."

Mary laughed lightly. "What is so strange about that? So he stopped writing about his discoveries and decided to focus on his own work instead. He was probably so frustrated by his peers' unwillingness to listen to him that he simply gave up on trying to make them."

"You don't understand," Ryan told her hesitantly. "Your father, from what I have heard, was one of the best surgeons of our time, but all of the patients listed here. . .they all died."

Mary sat for a moment in baffled silence. She leaned forward to peer down at her father's neat handwriting. "That is not possible," she finally said. "My father held the lowest fatality rate of any surgeon I have ever known. None of his patients died—at least not very often."

"Well, I don't understand it either, but it is all documented in here, written in his own hand. One hundred and thirty-four deaths, to be exact," Ryan muttered as he turned to the last account in Volume 10. "He numbered them."

"Good Lord," Mary gasped, sinking back against her chair. "That is completely impossible, Ryan. There. . .there has to be an explanation for this, it. . .No, I do not believe it."

Ryan turned a sympathetic gaze on her. "Perhaps we ought to take a break for the night," he suggested. "It is almost two in the morning and, well, I think it might be wise for us to get some rest."

"Rest? Do you honestly think that I will be able to sleep now after you just dropped this in my lap?"

"Well, I—"

"Absolutely not," Mary told him. "I intend to read about each of those cases until I make some sense of it all."

"You will do no such thing," Ryan clipped. "You will go to bed and sleep; you look exhausted." He began piling the journals back into their box. "And just to make sure that you do not hop out of bed and stay up all night, I am taking these with me."

"You cannot do that!" Mary exclaimed. "You have no right!"

"Sleep well, Lady Steepleton," Ryan told her jovially as he made his escape, closing and locking the door behind him before she could have another say in the matter.

Mary stood for a long time staring after him. She wanted to pummel the insufferable man until he was black and blue all over. The audacity of him to think that he could tell her what to do was enough to make her blood boil.

With a disgruntled moan, she eventually decided that there was nothing to do but change into her nightgown and climb into bed. Besides, she was likely to catch a chill if she continued standing there. Her feet were already freezing through the thin soles of her slippers. When had the month of July ever been so cold? By the time she'd finished combing out her hair, she had to admit that she was feeling a tad bit tired. Five minutes later, having snuggled down beneath the wonderfully fluffy down comforter, her head nestled in the soft folds of her pillow, Mary fell fast asleep.

Earlier that evening, in a private room of one of the most opulent homes in Mayfair, the Raven swiveled his brandy as he glared across at his companion. "You had no right to defy me," he muttered grimly. "You have forced my hand by doing what you did."

"Something had to be done to knock some genuine fear into that woman, to make her understand how serious of a matter this is."

"And you thought that threatening her at the Hunterian was the way to go about it? All you have done is make her more aware of the importance of her father's journals in all of this. Don't you see? She will be much more possessive of them now than she ever was before. Honestly, I cannot begin to imagine what you must have been thinking."

"What I was thinking is that the longer she holds onto them, the greater the risk of us all ending up at the end of a rope."

"I promise you that it will not come to that," the Raven remarked. "And if you would have exercised just a little patience, we might have been able to resolve this differently and without anyone's getting hurt. However, you have forced my hand with your foolishness. I am sending the Messenger tomorrow. He will retrieve the journals and, if need be, will deal with her just as he dealt with her father."

"You mean. . .?"

The Raven raised a mocking eyebrow. "What? Don't tell me that you don't have the stomach for sending the lovely young marchioness to an early grave." The other man stared back in horror. "Better her than us. Is that not so?"

"I only meant to frighten her."

"I understand." The Raven smiled sardonically. "And if she is fortunate, then perhaps that is all that will happen to her. But I should warn you about getting cold feet, my friend—unless, of course, you intend for them to stay cold, if you understand my meaning."

The other man had begun to tremble ever so slightly, but it was enough for the Raven to take notice. He couldn't be happier; after all, fear could be a most powerful weapon. His eyes gleamed with pleasure as the man before him nodded, stammering an almost incoherent apology. "Now, be off with you," the Raven said, dismissing the coward with an air of bored superiority. "You have caused enough trouble already to make my head spin."

Chapter Seventeen

"Care to join me for a morning ride?" Alexandra asked Mary as she wandered into the breakfast room, where Mary was enjoying her morning tea together with Cassandra and Isabella.

Mary looked up and almost choked at the sight of her friend brazenly standing there in the doorway, dressed in her snug breeches and loose-fitting shirt, her riding crop held firmly in her hand. "I. . .er. . ." She nodded slowly. "Yes, I think I should like that a great deal, actually."

"Good. I have an extra pair of breeches that you can borrow if you like."

Mary blushed all the way to the roots of her hair. "I must admit that I did bring my own pair—just in case."

"Wonderful!" Alexandra exclaimed. "Hurry up and get changed so we can be off. The weather is quite good at the moment, but who knows how long it will last."

Mary cast a glance at Cassandra and Isabella before turning back to Alexandra. "But won't. . .I mean, what will everyone think if I. . .Oh dear."

Alexandra grinned. "Nobody around here will care one way or the other about your choice in clothes; they have all been subjected to me for so long now that I think their sensibilities will withstand your antics as well. Is that not so, Isabella?"

The duchess, who'd been following the conversation with keen interest, smiled brightly. "Certainly, my dear. In fact, if I were a few years younger, I would not mind joining in the fun."

Cassandra's head snapped around to stare at her mother with a great deal of surprise. "Really?"

"Oh, yes," Isabella said. "I may look the part of a well-bred lady, but in my youth I was just as unruly as Alexandra."

"Oh, you must tell me all about it, Mama," Cassandra gushed with great enthusiasm.

Completely forgotten by the duchess and her daughter, Mary turned to Alexandra. "Give me fifteen minutes to ready myself," she said.

Alexandra nodded. "I will ask the grooms to saddle our horses in the meantime. Meet me by the stables?"

Mary quickly agreed before hurrying off upstairs to get changed. Turning a sharp corner at the top of the landing, she practically collided with Ryan, who was just then leaving his room. "Oh, I do beg your pardon," she gasped after skidding to a sudden halt.

"No need," Ryan said with a grin, moving swiftly out of her way. "I was actually coming to look for you. I thought perhaps you might like to go for a walk since the weather appears to have improved a bit."

"Thank you, but I have just agreed to go for a ride with

your sister." She paused for a moment while he looked back at her somewhat expectantly. She'd been looking forward to getting away from him for a little while—heaven knew he had a knack for confusing her mind, which she otherwise prided herself on being quite sound. But now it seemed as though it would be terribly rude of her not to suggest that he come along. Deigning a most ladylike facade, she said, "You are welcome to join us, if you like."

"What an excellent idea." There was a cheekiness to the immediate smile that graced his lips, and it made her question whether or not she'd made the right decision. "Perhaps I should ask William to come along too. It has been a long time since the three of us have raced one another."

"Well, then you had better hurry," she told him as she slipped past him on the way to her own room. "I told Alexandra that I would meet her by the stables in fifteen minutes, and that was already five minutes ago. Now, if you will please excuse me, I really must get ready."

Having practically torn off her gown and left it in a heap on the bed for the maid to deal with later, Mary threw on her shirt, breeches, and Hessians before grabbing her jacket on her way out the door. As she made her way toward the stables with long, brisk steps, she adjusted her shirt, which in her rush to be punctual, she'd neglected to tuck in completely.

Rounding the corner of the house, she caught sight of two grooms holding the reins of four magnificent horses. Alexandra and her brothers, who were in the middle of some sort of animated discussion, all turned to stare at her as she strode toward them.

"Well, you certainly do look sharp," Alexandra remarked. She nudged Ryan in the ribs. "Don't you agree?"

Ryan did his best to stop his eyes from straying to the perfect outline of Mary's thighs that her snug breeches offered. Instead he concentrated himself on her face. "I. . .I actually quite liked the way Lady Steepleton looked in a gown," he confessed, adding a note of disapproval that he hoped would sound convincing. It would have been a plausible statement if it weren't for the fact that his cheeks had turned bright red.

"Is that so?" Alexandra asked wryly. "Michael always said the same thing to me, yet there was no disputing the fact that he always loved the look of my backside in a pair of breeches."

"Alex," William cut in. "That is quite enough of that; there is no need to be vulgar."

"I had no idea that it was," she muttered, casting a quick glance over her shoulder to study her own rear end.

Mary choked back a laugh, while Ryan felt about ready to expire from their sister's lack of decent behavior. William appeared to fare no better. "Still the feisty hoyden that you always were," he muttered critically.

"Oh, William," Alexandra continued on a sigh. "Haven't you realized yet that I merely enjoy watching you suffer? It is such fun."

William glowered as he turned toward his horse, placed his foot in the stirrup, and swung himself up into the saddle.

Alexandra merely grinned while Ryan hid a smile. He knew she enjoyed scandalizing him and William. "Shall we get going?" she asked, grasping the reins of her own horse. "Mary, you can take the brown mare over there. Walk her for a bit so you get a feel for her, see if you like her."

As soon as Mary was out of earshot, Alexandra turned to Ryan with a crooked smile. "You have to admit," she whispered, "that your marchioness certainly has an exquisite figure."

Ryan coughed to mask his embarrassment. For a man who wasn't prone to blushing, he could scarcely believe how often he'd been doing so lately. And he hated being put on the spot, especially by Alexandra's outrageous remarks. "I scarcely noticed," he told her as he took the reins that the groom handed to him.

"The hell you didn't," Alexandra chuckled as she swung herself up into the saddle of a gray stallion. "Your jaw practically hit the ground when you saw her coming."

"She is right, you know," William muttered. He'd come up alongside Alexandra and had caught the last bit of her previous comment. "You can continue on toward that gate over there," he called to Mary. "We will be along in just a second."

Ryan simply raked his fingers through his hair in frustration. "If you as much as—"

"Easy does it," Alexandra told him blithely. "We are both on your side, aren't we, William?"

William nodded with great conviction before turning his horse about and heading after Mary.

"There, you see?" Alexandra reassured him. "You have absolutely nothing to worry about." And with that, she rode off after the others, while Ryan was left to wonder how Michael had ever managed to handle his sister. Clearly, the man was a genius.

"We are going to race from here on back," Ryan told Mary when they arrived at the remains of an old farmhouse. "It is about five miles or so. If you would like, you can ride back at a slower pace."

Mary looked as though he'd just punched her in the face. "Have you learned nothing about me over these past few weeks?" she asked. "I do everything to the best of my abilities. I despise failure, especially in myself. So if there is to be a race, then I am not only going to participate; I am also going to do my damnedest to win it."

"Good Lord! They *are* two of a kind," William exclaimed. "Where the devil do these women come from?"

"Well, as a recent mother of one child, William, I should be more than delighted to explain that little mystery to you anytime you like," Alexandra replied coyly.

"I shall get you for that!" William yelled, kicking his horse into a gallop and taking off at a maddening pace that sent dirt flying in all directions. The rest of them followed quickly behind him, racing with the wind beating against their faces until they could barely see where they were going.

Mary had taken the rear, but the minute she spotted Whickham Hall in the distance, she urged her mare forward, dashing ahead of both Ryan and William until she was neck and neck with Alexandra. The two women grinned victoriously at one another as they closed the space between them, barring the men from passing with too much ease.

They were just coming over a rise in the meadow when a flash of movement off to the left caught Mary's attention. She tilted her head to look. It almost seemed as though someone were thrashing about in. . .*was that a lake?*

Without a moment's hesitation, she abandoned the race and veered off to the side. The closer she got, the clearer the scene before her became. A young boy was flailing about in the water, while his friend looked on in horror from the embankment. He turned when he heard Mary's approach.

"Help him!" the boy yelled with fear in his voice. "He can't swim, and I—"

"How long has he been in there?" Mary asked, leaping from the saddle before her mare had come to a complete stop.

"I'm not sure," the boy muttered, shaking his head in despair. "Enough to know he won't be capable of treading water for much longer."

"Hold this," Mary told him firmly as she handed him the reins as well as her jacket. She stepped out of her boots and before considering how cold the water was likely to be, she dove in and began swimming as though hell were on her heels.

Ryan and William arrived at the scene shortly after Mary since they'd both been alarmed by her sudden change in direction. Alexandra, on the other hand, had been forced to turn back when she discovered that she'd lost all of her competitors. Ryan had immediately waded out into the water to help Mary get back to the shore, while William stood waiting to help at the very edge of the embankment.

With even strokes, Mary reached Ryan. She was dragging the limp body of a twelve-year-old boy behind her, while she herself gasped for breath. Together, they made it back to the shore, their feet struggling with the muddy lakebed as they went. "Put him on his back," Mary wheezed as William scooped the slight figure up into his arms. Exhausted from her efforts, she grabbed onto Ryan for support. "Make sure his head is lower than his body, if you can."

By the time Mary and Ryan scrambled out of the water together, William had already laid the boy on the embankment, just as Mary had told him to do. Mary rushed to the boy's side and felt for his pulse. There was still a small flutter, but they had to hurry if they wanted to save him. Mary turned a steady gaze on Ryan. "Do you want to save this boy's life?" she asked.

"I. . .I think it might be best if you—"

"Do you want to be a physician, yes or no?" she demanded. "And tell me quickly before we run out of time."

"Yes," he told her immediately.

"Then stop dallying and get over here," she said. "Be quick about it, or he will most assuredly die."

Ryan didn't need to be told twice. He got down on his knees across from Mary so that the boy was lying between them.

"Handkerchief?" Mary asked.

William thrust one into her outstretched hand. She tilted the boy's head backward, opened his mouth, and placed the handkerchief over it. "Now, lean forward and breathe into his mouth," she told Ryan.

He looked as if he might protest, but the firm look on Mary's face had him following her command in a second. He took a deep breath and exhaled it into the boy's mouth.

"Now press down here," she said, pointing to the boy's chest.

Ryan did as she asked, but nothing seemed to happen.

"Keep at it," she told him sharply. "You must not stop. Repeat the process. Come on Ryan, you can do it."

After three more attempts, the boy finally moved. It appeared as though he were choking at first until he suddenly began coughing up water, sputtering and gasping for air.

"Come on, let's sit him up," Mary suggested. She looked at Ryan and smiled. "That was very nicely done, Dr. Summersby."

"I. . .I did it," he muttered in utter disbelief. "I can't believe that I actually did it."

"Thank you, sir," the other boy exclaimed. "Thank you so very much for saving him."

"It was my absolute pleasure," Ryan muttered with a loopy smile. With a nudge from Mary, his mind cleared, returning to the severity of the moment. He jumped up and pulled a saddle blanket from one of the horses. It wasn't much, but it would warm the wet child until he was able to get some dry clothes.

"No more playing near that lake," William warned the boys. "At least not until both of you learn how to swim."

"William, what if you and I escort the lads home?" Alexandra suggested in a more soothing voice. "I think Mary needs to get back to Whickham Hall before she catches cold."

Ryan grabbed Mary's jacket and held it for her so she could put it on. The fact that her corset was showing through her white shirt as the fabric clung against her skin wasn't lost on him. William had noticed the same thing and was doing his very best to look at anything other than directly at Mary.

"I will take her back to the house and see that she gets a warm bath," Ryan said as he lifted her up onto her horse. "And I will also make sure that there is a hot cup of tea waiting for the two of you when you get back."

"We shall see you in a little bit then," Alexandra said, waving them off.

"I would like to thank you," Ryan said as he followed Mary into her room a short while later. Two maids were shuffling about, busy filling a large white tub with steaming hot water. They'd added some scented oils that filled the air with the smell of roses.

Mary turned to Ryan with a smile as she shrugged out of her jacket. He drew a ragged breath at the sight of her creamy white skin teasing him from beneath her wet shirt. The swell of her breasts was clearly visible, while her breeches hugged her hips and thighs so tightly he could barely breathe from just looking at her.

God help him how he longed to rip those clothes right off her and. . .He squeezed his eyes shut and tried to focus.

"It feels great, doesn't it?" she asked.

"Hm?"

"Saving that boy's life. Didn't it feel wonderful?"

Oh, right, the boy. Ryan dragged his mind away from the visions he was having of Mary lying naked on her bed. "Yes," he said. "It made me understand, in a way that nothing else ever would have, why it is that you are so reluctant to stop doing this. Saving that boy's life. . .I cannot explain it, it just. . ." Words failed him. It was impossible for him to describe what he felt right now, and seeing the way she was watching him, he knew she understood. There was no denying that this was one of those moments that would leave a deep mark on the rest of his life.

"Mary," he continued, "I know you will not marry me unless I allow you to continue your surgical work. I just. . .there's too much risk involved. Do you understand?"

She nodded slightly, wishing she could have it all and knowing that she would have regrets, regardless of which choice she made.

"I have an idea," he told her seriously. "You may not like it at first, but I hope that you will at least consider it." He stepped forward, taking her hand in his. "We could build a hospital together, for the women and children of London—a teaching hospital even. You won't be able to practice, but you will have a huge effect on health care nonetheless. And if you teach me everything you know, then together we can save thousands of lives."

Mary stared at Ryan in stunned silence. She was dumbfounded. Her initial reaction was to reject the idea. After all, if she couldn't practice, then what was the point? But pushing her own selfish goals aside and looking at the bigger picture, she caught a glimpse of what Ryan envisioned. If they could pull it off, it could be revolutionary. She would have full control over cleanliness and how each procedure was to be carried out. She would be able to promote research that centered on all of her father's findings. And the number of lives that would be saved as a result would far outnumber those she might save on her own. It was a compromise, but if she wished to marry Ryan, then it was the best offer she could hope to get.

She nodded slowly in agreement. "You have a deal," she told him hesitantly. After all, she'd need a man by her side if she wished to accomplish such a feat, and as new as the idea was to her, she was suddenly very set on realizing it. But it wasn't that simple. There were other matters to be discussed. "But on one condition. I would like to retain my independence. Therefore, if you wish to marry me, you will have to sign a settlement agreement."

Ryan frowned at that. "It is generally not customary for a wife to—"

"Do you mean to tell me that you are marrying me for my money?" she asked, fearful of what his answer might be. She knew she wasn't much to look at and couldn't help but be skeptical.

But something flickered behind Ryan's eyes that instantly made her regret asking such a question. His jaw tightened before it once again relaxed. He sighed deeply as he regarded her, and she found herself holding her breath. "No," he told her. "I have no interest in your money. So if you wish for us to have a settlement drawn up, then, by all means, I shall be happy to sign it."

Mary couldn't have been more surprised if a pink sheep had suddenly trotted by, dressed in a pinafore and a blue bonnet. She took a moment to compose herself before saying what she was certain would surprise Ryan in turn, "It has always been my greatest wish that if I were to marry, my marriage would be one of equality, a partnership between the best of friends. Naturally, we are still in the early stages of our relationship, you and I, but I do hope that we will one day feel quite strongly for one another." She had no desire to talk of love and was now forced to look away, horrified that he might think that that was what she'd just alluded to. She moved on quickly in order to change the topic. "So, as your friend, I should hate to see you subjected to a marriage wherein you have no control over the finances. If anyone were to find out, I daresay that you would find yourself quite humiliated."

Ryan appeared to consider this quite seriously for a moment. "I am sure that I will manage," he finally told her optimistically.

"Nevertheless, I do feel that I would be most comfortable

if our settlement were to give us equal rights to my funds. If we are to marry, then we must trust one another just as true friends ought to."

He frowned as once again something indecipherable passed behind his eyes. It was impossible for Mary to discern the meaning of it, much less what he might be thinking. He suddenly smiled. "Very well, my lady, I agree to your terms. Shall we seal it with a kiss?"

"The maids," Mary whispered, looking about nervously only to discover that both had completely vanished.

It suddenly hit her: she was alone in her bedroom with Ryan Summersby, and when she turned back to face him, there was no mistaking the hunger that shone in his eyes. He stared at her as he moved toward the door, nudged it shut with the heel of his boot, and turned the lock until it clicked firmly in place.

Her stomach fluttered with expectation, for in spite of all their recent arguing, she hadn't been able to forget the way he'd touched her in the carriage. Heat now flooded her veins as he walked toward her. She was still dripping wet and cold, but she didn't care. All she wanted right now was for Ryan to kiss her senseless.

Reaching out, he placed his hand against her cheek. She sighed and leaned into him, edging slowly toward him as he invited her closer. Her eyes closed on a deep sigh of contentment as she reveled in his caress. Placing her hands against his chest, she felt him stiffen for a moment. His heart was hammering wildly, and she couldn't help but smile at the knowledge that he was as affected by their closeness as she was. A moment later, she felt him relax, and he finally pulled her against him, wrapping her tightly in his embrace as he lowered his head and placed his lips against hers.

For a long moment, they remained quite still, just standing there in the silence, enjoying the closeness. But when he moved his hand against her back and she pressed herself closer, his movements grew more determined. Abandoning her mouth, he pressed soft kisses along her cheeks, one upon each of her closed eyelids, and finally upon the very tip of her nose. "Thank you," he whispered, drawing his fingers through the dark locks of hair that had somehow managed to escape their pins.

Mary's eyes shot open. She looked back at him in utter befuddlement. *Thank you?* "What on earth for?" she asked.

He smiled back at her with genuine adoration. "For doing me the honor of becoming my wife. And for this. . ." He kissed her again with such tenderness that it was not at all impossible for Mary to imagine that he might one day grow to love her.

If only.

Her thoughts on the subject soon vanished, however, at the feel of his hands reaching beneath her shirt and the warmth of his fingers as they traced their way along her spine. She shivered involuntarily.

"We really ought to get you out of these wet clothes," he told her in a husky tone, his breath brushing ever so gently against her ear. Another shiver shot through her, but this time it was not brought on by the cold.

His mouth closed over hers again, his tongue sweeping inside her mouth, tasting her as a soft purr of pleasure erupted from her throat. He was still as strong as she remembered, his chest more firm than she'd ever imagined. And her eager fingers seemed to have taken on a life of their own, for they now ran their way up his sides. How they'd made their way beneath his shirt she couldn't recall.

She gasped when he tightened his hold on her even further, for she could now feel him pressing against her, hard and insistent. There was no doubt about where they were heading, but she no longer cared. She wanted this—all of it—until they both cried out with pleasure. God help her, but she'd never thought herself a wanton, yet now, with the thoughts that were presently attacking her mind, she suddenly knew that she must be quite wicked indeed. Again, she did not care, although she did briefly wonder how she would ever be able to sit down to tea again with other respectable ladies of the *ton* without looking the part of a sinner.

Then, without warning, her wet shirt was pulled away from her, and she felt Ryan's hands roaming over her stomach. Liquid heat poured through her, pooling between her thighs, where it began to pulse with desire. She tugged at his shirt, working on the buttons with a sudden frenzy that she'd never before possessed.

By the time she finally managed to get his shirt off, he'd already undone her corset and sent it tumbling to the floor. He hugged her against him, and she reveled in the feel of her skin against his as he dipped his head to press smoldering kisses against the tops of her breasts. When she moaned her response and dug her fingers into his back, he let out a guttural groan.

Easing back, his eyes met hers, and she quickly noted the seriousness behind them. "Are you quite certain that this is what you want?" He seemed reluctant to ask, but clearly, as a true gentleman, he wanted to give her the chance to change her mind. "We can't undo it later or pretend that it never happened."

As much as she appreciated his gallantry, she'd never wanted anything more. "Yes," she whispered. "I want this. . .I want you."

There was a brief pause as he devoured her words. Then, with a suddenness that caught her completely unaware, he swung her up into his arms and carried her across to the bed, where he set her down gently. "In that case, I think that it is high time we removed these," he told her cheekily as he waggled his eyebrows.

"I could not agree more," she replied with a coquettish smile, lifting her legs so he could pull off her boots.

Her breeches followed soon after, leaving her entirely naked upon the bed and uncomfortably self-aware as his eyes slid over her from head to toe. He sighed with satisfaction, and she relaxed a little, her eyes locked with his, as he quickly removed the rest of his own clothing.

Mary simply stared. She'd seen her fair share of naked male bodies because of her profession, but none would ever be able to match that of Ryan's. It was enough to make her weep from sheer admiration. Heaven help her if she wasn't the luckiest woman alive: she was about to make love to Adonis.

"This will probably hurt a little," he told her soothingly as he climbed up next to her. "But it will only be for a moment, and I promise you that I will be as gentle as possible."

Mary grinned as she wrapped her arms about him, pulling him down toward her. "That sounds like the exact sort of thing I tell my patients before I make the first incision."

"Well," Ryan told her with a smile, "in this case, the pain will be followed by endless amounts of pleasure. Something like this..." He kissed her neck, while his fingers trailed down over her navel to caress her between her thighs. She purred in response to the sudden rush of fire bursting through her.

"And this," Ryan murmured, pushing a finger carefully inside her, "is only the beginning."

"Ryan," Mary gasped, bucking helplessly against his touch. "Stop...no, don't stop, I mean...oh God!"

Pulling back, Ryan placed a tender kiss upon her forehead. "Well, you are more than ready for me," he told her, running his fingers lightly through the soft curls that covered her womanhood. "Now, tell me once again that you want this."

"I want this," she whispered, gazing into the depths of those wondrously blue eyes. "More than anything."

"Because if you have any doubts whatsoever about marrying me, now is the time for you to walk away."

Mary held his gaze. "I know, but I'm not going anywhere. I want this. I want you, Ryan. Please don't torture me any further—I need you inside me."

"You have no idea how much I have longed to hear you say that, Mary," he murmured as he rolled on top of her, pressing her firmly against the mattress and kissing her lightly on the lips. Dipping his head lower still, his tongue found the tip of her right nipple. He circled the dark pink bud and growled with approval when she arched against him, her fingers spreading their way across the bed to grasp at the sheets. But it wasn't enough; she wanted more, and she wanted it now.

Wrapping her legs around his waist, she pulled him

toward her. His lips met hers, and a moment later, she let out a deep sigh of satisfaction at the feel of him entering her body. Heaven—she was in absolute heaven.

He moved carefully, deepening his kiss as he eased his way further inside her, his hands wandering over every part of her, caressing her and igniting her senses to a point where her need for him was almost too painful to bear. When he paused, she wanted to scream with frustration. Instead she writhed beneath him, clutching at him as if doing so might force him closer. Yet he lingered for an infuriating stretch of time, nibbling on her earlobe, kissing his way along her chest to suckle her perky nipples until she was driven mad with wanting. Then, when she feared she could stand it no longer, he plunged forward, burying himself completely within her soft, supple warmth, and as he did so, Mary yelled. It wasn't a quiet sort of yell that might have been intended to convey some minor displeasure. No, it was a loud scream of complete and utter agony, the sort of scream that was likely to bring people running from near and far, expecting to find a catastrophe.

Ryan froze. "Are you all right?" he whispered.

"How can you possibly think that I might be all right," Mary whimpered. "I have just discovered what a devilish liar you are. You said it would only hurt a little. Well, it hurt like bloody hell, I will have you know."

"I am sorry," Ryan whispered as he kissed her softly on her cheek. "I—"

There was a loud knock on the door. "Mary? Are you all right?"

"Damn," Ryan muttered. "It's Alex."

Alexandra knocked again, even louder this time.

"You had better answer her before she decides to kick down the door," Ryan suggested.

Mary stared at the door, momentarily stupefied, then pulled herself together. "I am all right," she called out. "I. . .I stubbed my toe, that is all."

"Well, I also brought some towels for you. The maids apparently forgot, so if you could please open the door, I will just—"

"No!" Mary blurted out in wide-eyed horror. She looked at Ryan, who appeared to be one second away from erupting into a fit of laughter.

"I am not really in a position to do that right now," she called back.

"I bet she would be quite shocked by the position you are actually in," Ryan chuckled, his eyes swimming with mirth.

Mary had to bite down hard on her own lip to stop herself from laughing. "Please leave them by the door, and I will get them in a minute."

"Very well," she heard Alexandra say. "But do try to be quick about it; we have guests waiting."

"I will, er. . .I will do my very best," Mary replied, desperately struggling to keep her voice steady.

There was a soft thump on the other side of the door as Alexandra dropped the towels. This was followed by a brief pause and then the sound of retreating footsteps as she continued down the hall. As soon as she was completely gone, Mary slapped Ryan hard across his arm. "You and your. . .your. . ."

"My what?" Ryan asked as he gazed down at her, his eyes filled with merriment.

"Your. . ."

"This?" He pulled out slightly, then drove back in.

Mary moaned at the unexpected tingles that rose through her body.

"Or," Ryan said, repeating the motion with increased speed and pressure, "this?"

Lord help her if this was not the most exquisite feeling in the world. She dug her fingers into Ryan's back, arching against him as she clenched her muscles and followed his rhythm. "Yes," she groaned as she felt herself carried away on a burst of energy. "Oh God, Ryan. . .I. . .I am. . ."

"Let yourself go, Mary," he urged her, teasing her nipples while he thrust himself back inside her.

And then it happened. On a cry of elation, she quivered around him, her muscles contracting as she soared upward on wings of extraordinary pleasure. And as she fell back to earth, she brought him tumbling with her, breathless, and truly gratified.

For several minutes after, they just lay there, wrapped in each other's arms, spent and sated. Ryan's hand trailed lazily over Mary's thighs in a swirling motion that made her skin tickle. His eyes were half closed, and he looked immeasurably pleased.

"Ryan?" she asked suddenly. "When we are married, can we do this all the time?"

Ryan grinned. "I take it that you enjoyed it?" he said with a cheeky smile.

She cast him a sidelong smirk. "You know I did, you fiend. In fact, I was surprised by just how much I liked it."

"Is that so? Well, you can count on doing it very, very

often indeed," he told her as his fingers crept down between her legs once more.

"Ryan," she gasped. "What about Alexandra?" But her legs had already fallen helplessly open in response to his touch.

"She can wait—and so can the guests, whoever they may be. In fact, the whole damn world can bloody well wait, because I am not even close to being done with you yet."

And before Mary could manage a reply, all of her thoughts flew out the proverbial window the instant Ryan kissed her.

CHAPTER EIGHTEEN

"Who do you suppose is here?" Mary asked a half hour later as they made their way downstairs. Having made love a second time, they'd finally managed to remove themselves to the awaiting bathtub, only to have made love once more there. Mary wasn't quite sure what the maids would think of the sopping wet carpet, but she was so giddy with joy that she barely even cared.

"I cannot begin to imagine," Ryan told her, stopping them both in front of the parlor door. "But I know what I will be thinking about while I watch you sip your tea."

Mary blushed. "I had no idea that you were such a naughty boy, Mr. Summersby," she told him sternly. But her heart was already hammering ridiculously hard at the thought of falling back into bed with him.

"My dear woman," he whispered. "you have no idea just how naughty I can be. After all, we have only just begun."

And with that, he opened the door to the parlor to find his father, Lord Willowbrook, and William entertaining Sir Percy and another gentleman whom he did not recognize, while Alexandra was seated on the sofa with Isabella and Cassandra. Everyone turned their heads at the sound of the door opening.

"Ryan!" Percy exclaimed cheerfully, breaking the hush that had fallen over the room. "Good to see you again."

"And you, Percy." Ryan nodded politely in greeting.

"I take it that this must be the lovely marchioness that I have heard so much about," Percy remarked.

"It certainly is," Bryce said as he sent Mary a pleasant smile. "May I present to you Lady Steepleton. Lady Steepleton, this is Sir Percy, an old friend of the family's."

"It is a pleasure to meet you," Mary said as she glanced quickly at Ryan. "Mr. Summersby here has told me so very much about you."

Percy grinned. "Yes, I am sure that he has, though you must forgive him; I was the one who suggested that he keep his assignment under wraps. After all, women never seem to care much for being under surveillance."

"They certainly do not," Mary remarked, her voice hitching a little with annoyance. Her remark did little to aggravate Percy's countenance, however. Instead, he looked surprisingly amused.

"What brings you all the way out here, anyway?" Ryan asked Percy, trying to smooth things over before his fiancée and his father's friend came to blows. "You never leave the city."

"Well, I suppose that is true, but then I happened to meet this gentleman at my club the other evening," Percy said, gesturing to the man on his right. "This is Mr. Alistair Croyden, Lady Steepleton's uncle."

"What?" Mary blurted out, turning her attention to the man Percy had just introduced.

"It is a pleasure to make your acquaintance," Ryan said, hoping his gallantry might overshadow Mary's sudden lack of good manners.

Mr. Croyden smiled kindly at both of them. "I imagine that this must come as quite a surprise."

Mary shook her head in disbelief. "But this is impossible," she said. "My father didn't have any siblings."

"He had two, as it happens," Mr. Croyden told her. "Although I regret to say that our sister, Fiona, passed away about three years ago."

"Good Lord," Mary murmured as she did her best to come to terms with this additional bit of information. "But he. . .he never mentioned you, not even once."

"I know," Mr. Croyden replied. "But perhaps you will understand why once I explain it all to you."

"But for now," Bryce cut in, "I think you might be well served with a warm cup of tea. After all, you have had a great many surprises to deal with lately, Lady Steepleton."

Mary simply nodded as she sank down onto a nearby chair, all the while wondering how many more secrets her father might have had that she had yet to uncover.

CHAPTER NINETEEN

"Lady Steepleton!" a voice called out. It was followed by the sound of quickening footsteps.

Mary turned to see her newfound uncle hurrying after her. She'd been strolling alongside Cassandra and Isabella after Ryan had suggested that they all go for a walk together, even though the sky was a bit gray and held the promise of rain.

"Would you mind if I walked with you for a while?" Mr. Croyden asked Mary, as he eyed the other two ladies. "Not to be rude, but my niece and I have much to discuss."

"Do you mind?" Mary asked Isabella and Cassandra.

"No, not at all," Isabella told her with a gentle smile. "We completely understand, don't we, Cass?"

Cassandra gave a sheepish nod as she pulled the hem of her gown out of a puddle with a sigh of despair. Isabella appeared not to notice, or perhaps she simply chose to ignore the mess her daughter was in. "Oh, look," she said. "Alexandra is showing Michael the roses. Come, let's join them." And with a firm hold on her daughter's arm, she dragged her away in the direction of the others.

Mary and her uncle watched them go before resuming their walk.

"I understand that you have had a trying few weeks," Mr. Croyden said with a wistful smile. "And I am sure that my unexpected appearance has done little to improve upon that."

"You are quite right," Mary told him, looking over her shoulder and noting that Ryan and William were talking to Lord Moorland and Sir Percy. "I cannot deny that I was a bit taken aback by your sudden arrival."

"Well, I suppose that it is a lot to take in all at once: family members you've never even heard of before, a title you never knew your father had, and a fortune that, I take it, is quite substantial."

Mary narrowed her eyes on Mr. Croyden. Funny that he should mention the money. "Tell me," she said, popping open the umbrella that she'd brought along. It might not be raining yet, but she wasn't comfortable with Mr. Croyden's proximity to her and hoped that the umbrella would keep him at a reasonable distance. "Why did my father never mention you or your sister, and why did he turn his back on his family? After all, he must have had a good reason."

Mr. Croyden would have had to be an idiot not to catch her meaning. He nodded thoughtfully. "I understand your concern," he told her. "You see, when your father fell in love with Harriet, your mother that is, he kept it from the family for a long time. He knew your grandfather would never allow him to marry her, especially not since he was the elder son and future heir. When your grandfather refused to stop pressuring your father into marrying a certain young lady who would have brought a great deal of money with her into the family, your father made his decision. He and Harriet eloped; they ran off to Scotland and got married in secret.

"Shortly after, when your grandfather found out about it, he was naturally furious." Mr. Croyden grinned. "In truth, I have never seen a man so livid before in all my life. For over a week, he and your father fought until our father eventually gave John an ultimatum: it was either Harriet or his inheritance. He could not have both."

Mary stopped in her tracks. "You do not paint a very pretty picture of your father," she said grimly.

"Well, you have to understand, nobility doesn't have the luxury of marrying just anyone they please. They have obligations, obligations that every man in our family has always honored. . .until John met Harriet, that is. Your grandfather, however, was not capable of accepting that his firstborn son would pick a woman over everything that he and all the previous generations had worked so hard to achieve."

"But surely your father could just have let you inherit his title instead. If he had two sons, then I don't quite see why it would be such a big issue if the elder decided to follow another course."

"No, it is probably quite difficult for you to understand," Mr. Croyden told her, but he didn't patronize. Instead, there was kindness in his voice. "John was the apple of our father's eye, you see. He doted on him since the very day that he was born, preparing him for the position he would one day fill. And even so, he never stopped him from studying medicine; he understood that John was passionate about that and that taking it away from him would do more harm than good. But he always thought that the day would come when John would face his responsibilities, take his seat in Parliament, and honor his family name.

"In the meantime, I decided to study law. After all, I always supposed that John would inherit everything and that I would have to make my own way in the world."

"And did you succeed?" Mary asked him. "Did you become a lawyer?"

"I did," Mr. Croyden told her thoughtfully. "And a good thing too, as it turns out, because in spite of what Father had told John about cutting him out of the will, the old man was never able to follow through. I think he always imagined that John would return to pick up the reins, but as you have probably concluded, he never did."

"But the estate and the house in London—somebody must have taken care of those places after your father passed away," Mary said, baffled by the oddity of it all.

"Oh, yes, there were caretakers, housekeepers, and butlers, all of them put in place by your father to keep things running just enough to stop them from falling into disrepair." Mr. Croyden stopped to look at Mary, studying her for a moment. "He didn't want any of it for himself, but he kept it all for you."

They walked on in silence for a while, just listening to the sound of the gravel crunching beneath their feet. Blackbirds swirled across the sky in a flurry of dark feathers before disappearing into a tree.

"I am curious, though," Mr. Croyden suddenly told her. "As a young man, your father always kept a journal."

Mary's head snapped around to stare at the man who claimed to be her uncle, but whom in reality she didn't really know from a hole in the wall. What on earth did he know about the journals, and why the sudden interest?

"I was wondering if he might have continued to do so," Mr. Croyden said, looking completely undeterred by Mary's reaction to his question.

"Why do you ask?" She did her best to sound completely dispassionate.

"Because if there is one thing that I remember about your father, it is how meticulous he always was. Even during his apprenticeships, he always questioned his superiors at every turn; drove them mad, you know. He would compare procedures, as I recall, always striving to find the best method instead of just following along like a sheep. I admired him for it, and, well, the thing is that I was hoping that he might still be able to help me."

The slightest frown appeared on Mary's forehead as she turned her head to look at her uncle. "I am sorry, Mr. Croyden, you must forgive me, but I am completely lost now. Would you please explain yourself to me?"

"Yes, of course," Mr. Croyden replied with a tight smile. "As it happens, I have recently been diagnosed with a sarcoma. The last three surgeons I spoke to have advised me to have my leg amputated, but I was hoping that there might be another option. In fact, I was hoping that if my brother did continue to keep his journals, that there might be something in them that I might be able to use."

Mary stared at him. "You have a sarcoma on your leg?"

Staring straight ahead and into the distance, Mr. Croyden grimly nodded his head.

"How big is it?"

"About the size of an egg," he muttered.

"Good heavens," Mary said softly. There was grave concern in her eyes now as she reached out to take her uncle's arm, squeezing it gently as a mark of comfort. "I will have to discuss this with Mr. Summersby since. . ." She saw the look of desperation on Mr. Croyden's face and forced herself to give him a reassuring smile. "I promise that we will do what we can; I don't have much experience with such things, but I do know that amputating can worsen your condition. In fact, I once saw a patient who had chosen that exact same course of action, hoping to rid himself of a sarcoma in his arm. The cancer metastasized, and the man died." Perhaps not the most positive thing she could tell a sick man, but he deserved to know the truth.

"Oh, dear," Mr. Croyden groaned, looking more miserable than ever, then turned his head to look at her with a hint of curiosity. "Would you by any chance care to tell me how you managed to see such a thing? I know that my brother enjoyed breaking the rules, but I cannot imagine that he would have allowed his daughter to. . ."

His words died at the stony look in Mary's eyes. "Most people would disapprove," she told him calmly, waiting to gauge his reaction. "But my father taught me everything he knew about medicine. He trained me to be quite a skilled surgeon."

"Really? How very. . .unusual." There was a lack of astonishment in his voice, however, that put Mary on guard once again. Why would such an outrageous admission not shock him more?

"But what about the journals?" Mr. Croyden pressed.

"Doesn't John suggest any form of treatment that might prevent me from having to cut off a limb?"

Mary sighed, her momentary suspicions set aside in light of a medically related challenge. "If I am not mistaken, he does mention a type of treatment that he came across once in Paris. He never tried it, though, and, to be honest, it would probably take a while for me to perfect it."

"But it might work? There might be a slight possibility that I can be cured?" Mr. Croyden asked hopefully.

Mary hated having to tell the man that it was very unlikely that she would be able to do anything other than what the other surgeons had offered to do. "I shall have another look at my father's journals as soon as we return to the house," she said. "Depending on what I find, we will try to determine the best course of action. I shall have to examine you, though."

"Yes, of course," her uncle said, breathing a sigh of relief. "And I can help you if you like—with the journals, I mean. I am quite curious to see what else my brother might have written about over the years."

Mary cast him a sidelong glance. She couldn't help but wonder if everything Mr. Croyden had just told her was true. Once again, Ryan's words rang loudly in her head: *Don't trust anyone.*

CHAPTER TWENTY

"Mary, I was wondering if I might be able to have a word with you in private," Ryan whispered as he followed her from the dining room after dinner that evening.

"Yes, of course," she said. She looked about hesitantly as the rest of the party wandered off toward the parlor. "I need to speak with you too. Where can we. . .?"

"This way," he told her, taking her by the arm and pulling her through a wide archway.

He led her toward the conservatory, where the humid air was filled with the scent of wet soil. Mary stared up at the glass dome covering the room as she took Ryan's hand and followed him along a tiled walkway toward a small seating area that looked out over the gardens.

"Mary," Ryan said gravely, releasing his hold on her so that he could arrange one of the rattan chairs for her, "I was looking through your father's journals again, just before dinner, and something stood out, something that I hadn't noticed before."

"Oh?" Mary asked with mounting curiosity as she sat

down. Her eyes trailed after Ryan as he moved to the opposite side of the table.

"Remember all of those surgical cases your father mentioned? The ones where all the patients died?" He took the seat across from her and then leaned forward to rest his elbows on his thighs.

Mary nodded. Of course she remembered; she'd scarcely been able to think of anything else since Ryan had pointed it out.

"Well, at the end of each of those entries, there are always a couple of letters: MH, MC, SB, VR, MT, I think. There are a few more, but I don't recall what they are right now." He frowned. "The interesting part is that these letters keep being repeated. I believe I counted roughly thirty VR's alone."

Mary looked off into the distance as she mulled this over. "Initials perhaps?" she finally suggested.

"I thought about that too," Ryan told her. "But if they are, then they don't belong to anybody that I've ever heard of."

Mary had to agree with that. Though she hadn't met all of her father's friends and colleagues, she was quite certain that she knew the names of most of them. None of these initials— if that was what they were—matched.

"So, even with this new discovery, we haven't really made any progress at all in terms of figuring out what this is all about."

"Well, I'm not so sure about that," Ryan told her with a smile. "You see, I had to read every single bit of information to find it, but eventually I did. One entry actually lists the date of the surgery and the hospital in which it was performed. When we get back to London in another couple of days, we can go to that hospital, ask them to pull the records, and see if a name matching those initials pops up."

"Oh, Ryan!" Mary exclaimed with an edge of excitement, "I could absolutely kiss you right now."

"Then by all means," he told her with a devilish grin, "go right ahead. I certainly won't be stopping you."

She looked nervously about the room, confident that someone would jump out from behind one of the ferns the minute her lips touched Ryan's. "I, er. . .I don't think. . ."

"Then I shall have to kiss *you*," he said as he leaned across the table between them to place a tender kiss upon her lips. "After all, I've been able to think of very little else since earlier in the day when we—"

"Ryan," she muttered, cutting him off, "someone might hear you."

"Unfortunately for you," he told her mischievously, "I really don't care. In fact, I don't mind if the whole world knows that all I can think of is you, lying naked beneath me on the bed while I—"

"Stop," Mary laughed, almost chokingly. "Please stop; it is hot enough in here as it is without your steaming up the windows by saying such indecent things. Besides, there is another matter that we need to discuss, so I really would appreciate it if you could be serious for just a moment longer."

"Only if you promise me that such an effort will be greatly rewarded upstairs in your bedroom later this evening," he murmured as he waggled his eyebrows with exaggerated fervor.

"I shall look forward to it," Mary told him with a playful smile, while a slow heat made its way toward her cheeks.

"Excellent," he said. He leaned back against his chair and folded his hands patiently in his lap. "Then by all means tell me. What is on your mind?"

She told Ryan about her conversation with her uncle and how she'd assured him that she'd check the journals for a way in which to treat his sarcoma. "I didn't get a chance to do it yet, so perhaps we could do it together and save some time. I know that my father mentioned a cancer patient in there somewhere, a woman who was treated by a Parisian surgeon, I believe. As far as I recall, her situation was quite different from what my uncle is now faced with, but maybe we can try to apply a similar cure."

Ryan looked at her skeptically. "That isn't all, though, is it? Something else is bothering you; I can tell."

"Well, with everything that has happened so far, I just don't feel very comfortable about this man whom I really do not know showing up out of nowhere and declaring to be my long-lost uncle. He mentioned the journals a couple of times and has asked me to see them under the pretext that he wants to understand his brother's reasons for leaving, and. . .Oh, I do not know, something about it just doesn't feel right."

"Well, I am quite sure that he is who he claims to be Mary, or Percy would not have brought him all the way out here. I can guarantee that a thorough background check was done to make sure that he is not an imposter, especially because of everything that has happened.

"However, it is not for me to say if he is somehow involved in the threats against you. I suppose it might make sense that a man who is as sick as he is would want to get his hands on your father's journals, where he might discover other possible treatment options that physicians in this country are otherwise ignorant of." Ryan paused for a moment, as if considering the possibility of Alistair Croyden's being the very culprit they'd been seeking. "Of course, we would need something more solid to go on than just a hunch, but I have to admit that he would also have a compelling reason to resent both you and your father."

Mary stared at Ryan, her brow furrowing into a deep frown. "Because of the inheritance?"

"Well, of course, Mary. Your grandfather snubbed Mr. Croyden in the worst possible way. When your father left, declaring he wanted nothing more to do with the family, your grandfather still left everything to him, even though your uncle stuck around, waiting and hoping, I would imagine, that just a small bit of your grandfather's fortune might go to him. But it did not. Your father was your grandfather's favorite, and your grandfather could not possibly have made that fact any clearer. It would be strange if Mr. Croyden did not hold some sort of grudge against him—and now you."

Mary leaned back against her chair. She was silent as she considered everything Ryan had said. "What should I do?" she finally asked.

"I think you should do what you can to help him with his sarcoma. Just be cautious; act under the assumption that he cannot be trusted. After all, we know very little about him aside from what he has told you."

"Very well then," Mary agreed, rising to her feet. Ryan got up as well and came toward her, offering her his arm. "I will examine him in the morning once I have gone over my father's notes." Turning her head to gaze out of the tall windows that surrounded them, Mary caught her breath. "Good heavens, Ryan, it is snowing!"

Sure enough, large plump flakes were drifting lazily toward the ground. "And this in the middle of July," Ryan muttered, sounding just as astonished as Mary. Wrapping one arm about her shoulders, they remained there for a long while, quietly watching the ground vanish beneath a smooth blanket of white.

The following morning, Mary got up early, even though she'd sat up late trying to devise a plan by which to help her uncle. The method that her father had suggested in his notes would require a bit of planning if they were to carry it out successfully, but she did believe that it might be possible.

"Mr. Croyden," she said as she took a seat across from her father's brother in the library, "my father did make an entry in one of his journals that just might be of use to us."

Mr. Croyden looked at her expectantly, almost unable to contain his enthusiasm. He was clearly eager to find out what Mary had in mind.

"He mentions a physician in Paris who, roughly forty years ago, cured a woman of cancer by applying a septic dressing. I cannot guarantee that such a treatment will work for you, but I do believe that it is worth a try."

Mr. Croyden looked mildly perplexed. "I do not even understand why something like that might work," he said.

"Well, I suppose that the infection brought on by the dressing might have somehow stimulated the woman's immune system." Mary paused for a moment as she regarded her uncle quite thoughtfully. "You have to understand that this woman went through many bouts of severe fever as a result of this, before she was finally cured."

"But she *was* cured?" Mr. Croyden asked hopefully. "Completely?"

Mary nodded. "Yes," she said. "It appears so."

"Excellent," Mr. Croyden remarked with a satisfied nod. "I must say that I am very pleased with your efforts."

"Well, don't thank me just yet; we still have a long way ahead of us. I shall need to examine you first, as I mentioned to you before, but I do think that—"

Mr. Croyden grinned as he waved his hands dismissively. "There will be no need for that," he said, cutting her off. "While I am immensely grateful for your efforts, I am not entirely sure that I would be very comfortable with a. . .ahem. . .a woman taking a peek at me."

Mary gaped at her uncle as if he were a complete lunatic. "I see," she told him drily as she got up and walked across to the window. The ground was still white from last night's snow. "You didn't seem to mind it in the slightest when I mentioned it yesterday."

"Please don't take offense. This is a delicate matter for me, and I. . .well, I am just not comfortable with a young woman such as yourself..." He looked at her pleadingly. "I was hoping that I might be able to borrow the journal that mentions this particular case so that I can show it to my physician in London. I will give you full credit, of course, and—"

Mary turned to him with frost in her eyes. "No," she told him sharply.

"No?" Her uncle spread his hands in exasperation. "But

surely you would not deny a dying man the means by which to recover."

"You are right. I will not. But if you want to make use of the information my father gave me, then you will have to put your welfare into my hands. If not, you are welcome to return to your London physician and tell him everything that I have just told you. But the journals will remain here with me."

Mr. Croyden narrowed his eyes as he met her gaze. "You are a stubborn woman, Lady Steepleton," he told her coolly, but a second later a warm smile creased the corners of his eyes. It was enough to strengthen Mary's resolve. There was something about this man that unnerved her.

"Never mind," he told her gently, his demeanor completely changed from that which he'd shown her a moment earlier. "I completely understand. No hard feelings, ay? Come, let us join the others in the parlor. I believe the men are having a game of faro, and I would love to see how they are getting on."

"Yes, of course," Mary replied, though somewhat brusquely. She regretted the way in which she'd handled the situation, particularly since Mr. Croyden was her only relative. It hadn't been her intention to tell him that she didn't trust him, yet that was precisely what had happened anyway. And now he'd probably resent her forever.

What could she do, though, short of letting him take her father's journals with him to London, and that was out of the question. Those journals were clearly very important to somebody other than her. She had no intention of letting them out of her sight until that little mystery had been solved. With a heavy heart, she accepted the arm that her uncle offered her and allowed him to lead her down the hall and toward the parlor.

Chapter Twenty-one

Mary awoke with a start that night. Sitting bolt upright in bed, she glanced steadily around the shadowy room. Slowly, her eyes adjusted to the faint outlines of the furniture that stood tucked away in the darkness. Everything seemed perfectly still, save for the faint ticking of the clock that sat upon the chest of drawers. Exhaling a breath of air, she was just about to settle back down again when a slight creaking caught her ears. Stiffening, she turned her head toward the bedroom door. She hadn't noticed it before, but now that she focused her eyes on that spot, she was able to see that the door stood slightly ajar. Another creak sounded, followed by the low thud of footsteps along the hallway runner.

With her heart thumping furiously in her chest, she leaped out of bed, crouching onto her knees to retrieve the box she'd hidden underneath it earlier that evening. Her fingers fumbled helplessly around the dusty space, unwilling to accept that the box was no longer there. It was gone. All of her father's work—her most precious possession—had been stolen.

She jumped to her feet, flinging her robe over her shoulders and casting a quick glance at the panel door that led to Ryan's room. There was no time to lose on waking him. Whoever had taken her father's journals would already be well on their way. She had to hurry.

Grabbing the pistol that Alexandra had given her, she raced out of the room in her bare feet, her robe and nightgown billowing out behind her in the chilly hallway as she ran.

At the sound of neighing, she quickened her pace, bounding down the stairs in a desperate attempt to catch the thief before he got away. She was almost there. Her hand reached out to grasp the handle of the large front door. It swung open quickly on a gust of wind, pulling her along with it and swirling her flimsy garments about her legs while her hair whipped across her face. Steadying herself, she looked out into the night, spotting the horse, just as a hand clad in a black leather glove pressed itself over her mouth and pulled her forcefully against the frame of a sturdy figure.

"You should have stayed in bed, Lady Steepleton," a thick voice told her leeringly. "It is not safe for a woman such as yourself to be running about at this hour, *unchaperoned.*"

A menacing laugh erupted from somewhere deep within the stranger's chest as his free arm snaked its way around her waist. Mary struggled against him, but he was stronger than her and held her in a firm grip that rendered her desperate attempts at escape completely useless. "The more you fight me, the more likely I shall be to lose my patience and serve you the same fate as your father. I must say, nothing has ever given me more pleasure than the sound of his neck snapping like a twig. And just so you know, my orders are to acquire his journals at all cost."

Mary froze. Her breath was coming in rapid bursts, while she tried to calm her pounding heart.

"That is better," her captor said. "Now, if you please, hand me that pistol before you cause an accident with it." He pried the gun out of her hand and tossed it aside. "Good; now, if I might make a suggestion, run back inside the house and do your best to pretend that this never happened." Her assailant came around to face her. He was dressed entirely in black, with a scarf covering his mouth and nose. A pair of dark eyes glistened with contemptuous delight as they swept over her. "Remember, we know who you are and all that you have done. We will ruin you without a moment's pause, my lady. So if I were you, I would forget that these journals ever existed. Go on with your life, or I promise you that you will live to regret it."

"Who. . .who are you?" Mary stammered "Who sent you, and what do they want with my father's journals?"

"You certainly have a lot of questions, don't you?" he sneered. "In answer to your first question, however, I am the Messenger. Be thankful that I will not answer the rest, for the answers would cost you your life."

With an overstated salute, the Messenger swung himself up onto his horse. The agitated creature snorted, sending clouds of hot breath out into the chilly air. He struggled a moment against the command of his master but finally surrendered to the pull of the reins, turning about and breaking into a fast gallop.

Hands hanging limply at her sides, Mary watched as the

darkness closed behind them, impervious to the cold that clawed at her flesh. After several minutes, she brushed her hair away from her face, then stooped down to pick up her discarded pistol as she wiped the onset of tears from her eyes with a shaky hand. She'd lost the only worldly possession that mattered: a lifetime's worth of medical research that had been entrusted into her care. Choking back a cry of anguish, she crept slowly back inside Whickham Hall on trembling legs.

"Mary?" Ryan implored, his voice a ghostly echo in the dimly lit corridor. The candle he'd brought along with him sent flickering shadows along the walls that stretched themselves until they reached across the ceiling. Occasionally, a few scattered puffs of smoke would rise from the melting wax, obscuring his vision for the briefest of moments. He paused at the top of the stairs, sweeping the candle in a wide arc, but he could see nothing but depths of infinite blackness below. With slow, deliberate steps, he made his descent toward the front hall. Filled with an ever increasing sense of concern, he called out her name once more, his voice resonating against the stone walls of the grand entrance.

A soft whimper caught his attention. "Mary?" he asked again, this time in a softer tone.

He held his candle out at arm's length and circled the room, the soft glow spreading outward from the center of the twitching flame before blending with the shadowy darkness. He turned back and suddenly paused. There, huddled against one corner, was a small hunched figure. "Mary," Ryan murmured with a mixture of relief and despair. Never in a million years would he have imagined that she could look like this, so fragile and utterly defeated.

He hurried over to her, kneeling at her side as he placed the candle on the floor beside them. Reaching out, he set his hands upon her shoulders and started to pull her toward him, but she flinched at his touch and instantly pushed him away, arms flailing to ward off the attacker that she thought him to be.

"Mary," he whispered. "It is only me, Ryan. It is all right; you are safe now." He reached for her again, and though her body remained tense, she allowed him to wrap his arms around her in a tight embrace. A moment later, he felt her shoulders tremble, and she began to sob, burying her face against his chest and dampening his shirt in the process.

He let her cry until her breathing had steadied, running his fingers through her hair and over her head in long, soothing strokes. "Come," he told her at last, as he took her hand in his and helped her to her feet. "We cannot remain here on these cold stone slabs, or we'll catch a chill. Let us go upstairs instead, and you can tell me what happened."

Mary wiped away her tears with the handkerchief he offered her and nodded so slightly that he barely noticed her response. Then, taking her by the arm, he guided her back up the winding stairs and down the hallway toward her room, all the while alarmingly aware of how cold she felt beneath his touch.

"Is everything all right?" a voice asked from behind them just as they reached Mary's door. They both turned to find Michael standing in the doorway of his bedroom.

"There has been an incident," Ryan told him gravely as he

met Mary's red-rimmed eyes. "Give me a few minutes to get Mary settled back into bed, and I will meet you in the library to tell you what happened."

Michael nodded, ignoring the impropriety of a genteel young lady being escorted unchaperoned to her bedchamber by a man whose eyes had held a roguish gleam for the past few days. Instead, he merely closed his bedroom door behind him and started off in the direction of the stairs. "I will get the claret ready," he muttered, disappearing into the darkness and thus out of sight.

"Now then," Ryan said as he eased Mary's robe off her shoulders and lifted her onto her bed, tucking the blankets around her. He brushed a few strands of stray hair from her face and gently lifted her chin so he could meet her gaze. "What exactly happened? I heard a horse ride off. Who was it? Who frightened you like this?"

Mary shrank back against her pillows and clutched his hand in hers. She closed her eyes briefly, only to find her mind flooded by visions of a dark figure mocking her with his venomous glare. "The Messenger," she whispered, meeting Ryan's eyes with a dead stare. She saw the flicker of overwhelming anger in them and caught her breath, quite unwillingly.

Swallowing hard, she forced herself to go on while Ryan listened quietly to her every word. "He took the journals," she told him in a small voice at the end. "Every last one of them. Those books meant the world to me, Ryan."

"I know," he said as he wiped a tear from her cheek with the pad of his thumb. His eyes filled with regret. "But he did not take them all, Mary; we still have one left."

Mary stared at Ryan in puzzlement while she waited for

him to explain. The box was gone; the journals had all been in there.

"Earlier today, while you were speaking with your uncle in the library, I took the liberty of borrowing the last volume of your father's journals, hoping to perhaps discover something more in it. It is still on my bedside table."

Mary closed her eyes against the fresh onset of tears and breathed a huge sigh of relief. "Thank you," she said, gently squeezing his hand.

"In a way, it is the most important one," he added. "It is the one that lists the hospital where one of the many fatal surgeries took place. It is also the one that lists all of the initials. If we can work out what they stand for, we might be able to find the people who took the journals."

"You don't think that this is the doing of just one man?"

"I don't know, but I do think that the Messenger is just that: a messenger." *Not to mention a cold-blooded killer.* "I believe there is someone else behind him pulling the strings and telling him when to jump. I intend to find out who that somebody might be."

Mary nodded thoughtfully. "And I thought my uncle might have had a part in this," she said. "I treated him quite badly, I'm afraid, but the man I saw this evening—I couldn't see much of him—I could tell that he was no more than thirty years of age."

"I had the same impression when I met him in London," Ryan told her. "But you still ought to tread lightly. There is no harm in being cautious." He ran his hand carefully along her cheek. He couldn't read her expression in the dim light, but he knew that she'd had a terrible fright, and he was prepared to do bloody murder because of it. If something had happened to her. . .His jaw tightened at the very thought of it.

"You are right," Mary agreed as he lowered his head, kissing her briefly on the forehead. "Please be sure you put the journal somewhere safe before going downstairs to meet Trenton. I would hate for something to happen to it."

"You have my word," he told her softly as he tucked the blankets around her once more and headed toward the door. He turned for a moment to look at her, his hand resting on the handle. "I will be back to check on you before I go to bed." But Mary didn't offer a reply; she was already fast asleep.

"You say that somebody came into Lady Steepleton's room while she was sleeping and stole her father's medical journals?" Michael asked in shock. His forehead was creased in an angry frown as he paced about the library, the brandy in his glass sloshing from side to side.

Ryan sipped his claret. "That is correct."

"And she confronted this man alone?" Michael asked in even greater disbelief.

"She had a pistol," Ryan explained. He would have laughed at the absurdity of it all if it weren't so damn serious. "Your wife gave it to her, I believe."

"Of course she did," Michael muttered as he took a large gulp of his drink. "That woman has probably handed out weapons to half the women in England. A pity that Lady Steepleton did not have the opportunity to use it, or the man would be hanging from the stable rafters by now and receiving a good whipping."

"I agree," Ryan told him. "But I intend to find the instigator behind all of this and put an end to it once and for all."

"If you need help, Ryan, I hope you know that you can count on me." There was fire in Michael's eyes. A young lady had been accosted in his home: Ryan knew that it was enough to make him lust for revenge.

"Yes, of course. Thank you," Ryan told him sincerely before emptying his glass.

"You know," Michael said after a moment's silence, "you might do well not to trust anybody. I checked the doors myself before going to bed; they were all firmly locked. And our intruder did not make use of a window."

"Are you suggesting that—"

"I am merely stating the facts," Michael told him, placing his empty glass on the sideboard. "For whatever reason, the front door was opened after we had all retired. If anything, it certainly makes you wonder."

"I hear that there was quite a stir last night," Mr. Croyden remarked as he sat down to breakfast the following morning and proceeded to fork a large slice of ham onto his plate.

"Yes!" Cassandra exclaimed. "It is all very exciting."

"That will do, Cassie," Isabella chided her daughter. "Mary could have been seriously injured."

"But she was not, Mama," Cassandra countered. "She is perfectly fine, a bit pale perhaps but. . .oh, I wish something like that would happen to me. My life is perfectly dull, you know."

Isabella gave her daughter an admonishing look. "I think

perhaps you ought to worry more about your shawl, my dear; the tip of it is trailing in your coffee."

With an exasperated grimace, Cassandra began dabbing at the stain that was rapidly spreading its way along the edge of her silk wrap.

"I hope you know that we are all eager to support you in whatever way possible, Lady Steepleton," Lord Willowbrook said as he caught Mary's eye from across the table. "To think that this villain had the audacity to enter your bedchamber while you were sleeping. . .Well, I certainly hope that he is apprehended as soon as possible."

"Here, here," Bryce chimed in. "I would like to see the bastard swing for this."

"Well," Percy remarked, "I am not sure if that is likely to happen, old chap. After all, he did not hurt anyone. However, I am confident that Ryan will do his best to sort out this mess. Is that not so, Ryan?"

Ryan glanced across at Percy in annoyance. He knew that he'd made an unforgivable mistake and that the Messenger should never have been able to gain access to Mary's bedroom. But he hadn't thought that they might actually be followed all the way to Whickham Hall. "Considering that there are no fewer than two agents from the Foreign Office under this very roof, not to mention the foreign secretary himself, I must agree with your assessment of the situation, Percy. It certainly is quite a mess."

"Hm, I suppose you are right," Percy conceded with a tight smile. "None of us expected this to happen. We were not at all prepared."

"And the journals?" Mr. Croyden asked, adding some

cheese and a couple of sausages to his ham. "Were all of them taken?"

"I am afraid so," Mary lied. She still had the one that Ryan had taken to his room, but nobody was going to know about that except for the two of them.

"Well"—Mr. Croyden sighed with a large measure of regret—"I don't suppose there is much to be done then."

"Not to worry," Mary reassured him. "We do not need the journals in order to help you. If you like, I can even have a word with the surgeon you decide on using and explain the procedure to him."

"Thank you," Mr. Croyden muttered. "That is very kind of you."

"Well, it is the least I can do after everything that has happened. I am sorry I did not trust you when you asked to look at the journals yourself, If I ever find them, you will be the first to know."

Her uncle nodded in appreciation. "I would be most grateful for that. I know my brother and I were not particularly close in later years, but he *was* my older brother, and I. . .well. . .I hope you understand how important those journals are to me."

"I believe I do," Mary said as she met his gaze. "Because I feel precisely the same way."

procedure when ...

Chapter Twenty-two

"Any luck?" Mary asked as she watched Ryan leaf through yet another volume of Westminster Hospital's medical records. They'd already spent the last few hours going over each of the fat books that now lay stacked on one side of the table, a compilation of every surgical procedure the hospital had performed over the past decade.

"Not yet," Ryan replied as he turned the page. The top right corner stuck, so he carefully pried it loose with his fingers. "And we have already gone back seven years. Maybe we should just start from the beginning; we must have missed it."

"No," Mary told him stubbornly. "Let us continue until we have gone as far back as 1806. Then we can start over."

Ryan sighed as he continued scanning the text. Most of it appeared to have been scrawled in a hurry with little attention to graceful handwriting. That was part of the reason it was taking so long: most of the notes were almost impossible to discern.

Ryan turned the pages a few more times, his sense of hope diminishing a little more with each time. But then, suddenly, there it was, the entry he'd been searching for. "I found it," he gasped.

Mary rushed to his side, looking over his shoulder at the book that was laid out on the table in front of Ryan. She peered down at the text: "1808: Eliza Blackburn arrived at the hospital," she remarked. "She was pregnant, just as my father's entry says. Apparently, she was concerned about the welfare of her baby, said she had not felt it move in a couple of days. A physician examined her. . .let me see. . ."

"Dr. Nigel Clemens," Ryan muttered. "I know him quite well; in fact, I spoke with him just recently at the Glendale ball."

"So did I," Mary told him. "Lord Woodbridge introduced us. I was with your father at the time, after our. . .well. . .after our falling out." She placed her hand on Ryan's shoulder as her thoughts returned to the evening they'd spent at Glendale House. "Your father seemed to be well acquainted with him," she said before returning her attention to the text. "According to this, Clemens dismissed Eliza after examining her, recommending that she return home and get plenty of rest. She died a week later. . .from puerperal fever."

Ryan looked at Mary in bewilderment. "How is that even possible?" he asked. "I thought puerperal fever was contracted only after the onset of labor."

"Hm. . .go back one page," Mary told him. "Who did Clemens treat before he treated Eliza?"

"A Georgina Hilton. . .she arrived at the hospital earlier in the day. She was in labor, and Clemens helped her deliver her baby. She too developed puerperal fever and died a few days later."

"And before that?" Mary asked with growing excitement.

"Before that it seems he carried out a postmortem on a woman who'd died the previous evening from. . .puerperal fever."

"I knew it!" Mary exclaimed. "No wonder my father was compelled to make a note of it: Clemens caused the death of both of these women. He probably failed to wash his hands after handling the corpse, and—"

"Hold on," Ryan told her. "How would the fact that he performed a postmortem have anything to do with the deaths of Georgina and Eliza?"

Mary stared at him for a moment. "They really don't teach you much in medical school, do they?" she said. "Remind me to lend you my copy of William Buchan's *Domestic Medicine*. There is a whole chapter in there on the importance of cleanliness, especially after handling the sick or that which may convey infection. My father was a huge advocate for his work and continuously tried to make the rest of the medical community see the truth in it."

Mary sighed as she slumped back down onto her chair. "They mostly chose to disregard his advice, though, claiming that Buchan's work was for housewives who were willing to believe anything. If I am not mistaken, one colleague of his argued that if washing your hands between each patient was so vital, then the medical schools would place more emphasis on it. And since they do not, then it really could not be of much importance at all."

Ryan frowned as he pushed the medical records aside and opened John Croyden's journal once more. He studied a few of the entries before looking up at Mary. "I think I have an idea as to what this is all about," he told her. Mary looked at him expectantly. "It seems to me that your father was conducting an investigation. He was cataloguing malpractice cases, and judging by this, some of these physicians have a lot to answer for. He paused. "If a good lawyer were to take them to court, some of them might very well hang for murder—the level of negligence is simply astounding."

Mary's mouth fell open. She stared at Ryan as she considered the implication of what he'd just said. It made perfect sense.

"That would certainly explain the threats," she told him quietly. "If some of the physicians my father was investigating found out about this. . .of course they would want to stop him from making his findings public."

Ryan nodded. "They want to destroy the evidence, Mary, all the records your father spent so many years compiling."

"But why would my father take on such a huge task on his own? To what end? So he could blackmail these people, threaten them in some way or cause a scandal? My father was not the sort of man who would do something like that."

"Perhaps not, but from what you have told me, he *was* the sort of man who would want to improve the survival rate of anyone in need of medical attention. So then, don't you think he just wanted to draw attention to the physicians and surgeons who were doing a careless job? He may simply have been hoping to have their licenses revoked." Ryan paused for a moment before continuing. "There are roughly ten men listed in here. If all the evidence against them were to be brought to light all at once, it might be enough to bring about a scandal that results in significant changes not only in patient care but in medical learning altogether."

"Then there is only one thing for us to do," Mary told him resolutely. "We have to figure out who the rest of these men are, and then we have to take our findings to the *Mayfair Chronicle*."

"Have you completely lost your mind, Mary? You will be stirring up a hornet's nest if you do that. Let us not forget that these men killed your father. They have pretty much threatened to do the same to you. I am sorry, but I cannot allow you to do this. You have to let this go."

"You cannot allow this?" Mary asked harshly, accepting the fight that Ryan offered her.

"Can't you see? You will be putting yourself in terrible danger—hell, you are already in terrible danger!"

"Exactly," she shot back. "And if I do not find these men, if I do not see justice served, I will always be looking over my shoulder, wondering if I am safe—if our children are safe." She pouted her lips and gave him a sulky look.

"Oh, bloody hell!" Ryan exclaimed. "Why the blazes did you have to bring our unborn children into this?"

"Because I cannot let this go. I am sorry, Ryan, but this is of enormous importance, not only to me, but to all the people who will one day end up under the knife of one of these butchers. Why, there are physicians and surgeons out there ordinary citizens trust with their lives, but who, it seems, are doing more harm than good. It is a doctor's duty to ensure that everything in his power is being done to help his patient; there is no room for arrogance or for denying that a mistake has been made. A surgeon's mistake is inexcusable. Refusing to fix it is unforgivable, and I will not stand silently by while these men continue to kill off their patients because they are too damn stubborn to listen to reason.

."Besides," Mary added with a crooked smile, "if you do not help me, you know that I will try to work this out on my own, and to be honest, I am really not that good with a pistol, regardless of all the efforts your sister made to teach me."

He studied her for a moment as if he hoped to read her mind. "You are right," he finally told her. "As much as I hate to admit it, you are absolutely right: something has to be done, and there is no way that you are doing it on your own. But you have to promise me that you will be careful. Do not tell anyone about this, Mary; it could cost you your life."

"I understand," she said quietly as she reached for his hand. She gave it a light squeeze. "Thank you for helping."

"I will help you in any way that I can, Mary. After all, I. . ."

He was just about to open his heart to her but thought better of it. A more appropriate time would present itself once all of this was over. For now, they had a lot of work to do. "You have my word," he told her instead, before turning his attention back to the open journal in front of him. He wondered if she'd noticed that he'd been about to tell her something else, but she seemed too caught up in the situation at hand to have given it much thought. And since he very much doubted that she reciprocated his feelings, he'd just stopped from making a complete idiot of himself. After all, her reasons for marrying him were purely practical: she'd made that abundantly clear when he'd proposed.

Skimming his fingers along the open pages of the journal, Ryan pointed to a segment of the text. "Now, looking at this," he continued, "it appears as though your father referred to Dr. Clemens as Mr. Clemens when he added the initials at the end of his entry, perhaps in the hopes that nobody would make the connection."

"What are the other initials again?" Mary asked as she glanced down at her father's carefully written notes.

"Well, LT and SB seem to stand out quite a bit. In fact, each of them is mentioned about forty times."

"Good heavens, that is a lot. Do you suppose. . ." Mary stared at Ryan as if she suffered from amnesia and had just recalled her own name. "At the Glendale ball, when Woodbridge introduced me to Clemens, there was another gentleman there, a Sir Boswick, I believe."

"I think you mean Sir Bosworth," Ryan said, folding his arms on the top of the table and turning his head to look directly at her.

"Yes, that is right. Well, your father mentioned that he was involved in quite a scandal a few years back—something about a malpractice suit. Apparently, the whole thing was hushed up, and he eventually regained his reputation, but do you suppose that he might be the SB to whom my father is referring?"

"It is possible, I suppose, though I would have a difficult time believing it. I know the man quite well; he is a good friend of the family's. To think that he might have—"

"Ryan," Mary told him calmly as she cut him off, "Clemens seems equally unlikely, and yet we already know that he caused the death of at least two patients through his own negligence. We do not know enough about the rest of the patients that died at his hands, though I doubt my father would have mentioned them unless he was just as responsible for those. So we are looking for men who have gone to great lengths to hide their mistakes. They are not going to stand out among the crowd, I'm afraid."

"I believe you are right," Ryan said and sighed. "As for LT and VR, I am not sure who they might be; nothing really comes to mind. And then, of course, there is MH, who pops up just a couple of times. . .I"

"Oh, no," Mary gasped, looking suddenly quite ill. "Let me see that."

Ryan passed her the journal and watched while Mary flipped back a few pages. Her index finger skimmed the writing until she found the date she was looking for. She read the entry in silence before sinking back against her chair. "It's Helmsley," she whispered on a breath of defeat. "MH is Mr. Helmsley, my father's closest friend. How could he. . ."

Ryan watched as her eyes began to glisten. He understood her feeling of betrayal, for she had known the man her whole life. "They were like brothers," Mary whispered. "I always thought he was a good physician, but. . ."

She glanced at the open page of her father's journal. "I remember the argument that he and my father once had about that very case." She nodded toward the book. "My father insisted that Jack was to blame for that man's death, a farmer who lost his leg after having it crushed beneath an overturned cart. Jack denied it, of course. He claimed that he did everything he could and that the farmer's family was to blame for not alerting him when the wound became infected. I just cannot believe that he might have had something to do with my father's death."

"Perhaps he didn't," Ryan told her in an attempt to offer comfort. "His initials only appear a few times when compared to the others, and you must not forget, you told me yourself that when Lady Arlington needed help, he called for you because he recognized his own limitations. It is possible that he has learned his lesson and has nothing to do with the threats against you."

"I'm not so sure," Mary muttered, her voice more miserable than ever. "But you can be quite certain that I intend to find out. Don't forget that I was repeatedly warned against continuing my practice—that I was told not to follow in my father's footsteps. Helmsley is the only physician I can think of who knew that I performed a cesarean on Lady Arlington. He cannot be trusted."

"Then don't trust him. But you still ought to consider the other names, because someone like Sir Bosworth, for instance, who, as unlikely as it seems, apparently caused an astonishing amount of fatalities, would have much more reason to see the journals destroyed. And let us not forget Mr. Clemens and whoever VR and LT might be."

"Perhaps you are right," Mary muttered.

She appeared to be considering something. "Do you know—I promised Lord Woodbridge that I would have him over for tea one day. He is the master of the Royal College of Surgeons; perhaps he can shed some light on who the rest of these men are."

"I think that might be a very good idea. In the meantime, I shall have a word with my father and Percy. With a little luck, all of this will be resolved within the next few days."

A short while later, as clouds obscured the afternoon sun, a large carriage pulled into a clearing just outside Gerrards

Cross, drawn by four great horses. A gentleman wearing a black greatcoat got out, his booted feet leaving imprints in the spongy wet grass. Placing his beaver hat on top of his head, he strode brusquely toward the two men who awaited him.

"Mr. Croyden," the Raven remarked as he leaned his heavy frame against his cane. "I must say that I was very pleased to hear of your success. Your endeavors, and those of your son, are greatly appreciated."

"Thank you, my lord," Alistair replied as he handed over the box containing John Croyden's precious journals. He cast a nervous glance in his son's direction.

The tall, sturdy figure of the Messenger responded with a slight frown. His lips were drawn in a tight line, while his coal black eyes met those of the Raven's. "Unfortunately, one of the journals appears to be missing," he said, keeping his eyes trained on the man who'd employed him a little over a year ago. He didn't trust him further than he could throw him, no matter how highly his father spoke of him. The Messenger was no fool: he knew a callous villain when he saw one, and the orders he'd received from him until now spoke of a man who was ruthless enough to stab his own mother in the back. There was no telling what he might do, now that he knew they had failed him.

"And which volume is it that has gone missing, precisely?" the Raven asked them from between clenched teeth.

"The last one, my lord," Alistair replied with an excessive amount of regret.

The Messenger winced. He hated seeing his father reduced to a sniveling coward before this man. Still, the look of anger that shifted behind the Raven's murky eyes was far from lost on him. He braced himself for the onslaught he expected, but it never came.

Instead, the Raven merely glared at both of the men before him. "I see," he finally muttered. "What a pity."

"My sincere apologies, my lord," Alistair groveled. "I know how unacceptable this is, but you must not worry; we can easily retrieve the tenth volume for you. Right, Matthew?"

The Messenger said nothing in response to his father's claims. He merely nodded.

The Raven held up his hand. "That will not be necessary," he said with mild amusement flickering behind his dark gray eyes. "In fact, I would rather like to thank you for your assistance. You have been most helpful, both of you, but I think it is time for me to take matters into my own hands."

"But. . ." Alistair sputtered, a look of desperation creeping over his face. "I believe Lady Steepleton trusts me now. She doesn't think I had anything to do with the theft. I am sure she will let her guard down and—"

"And how do you plan to explain the sudden disappearance of your sarcoma?"

"That. . .that was your idea. . .I merely. . ." His voice trailed off as realization kicked in.

"She is a smart woman, Mr. Croyden. She will hardly be fooled by you forever, you know." The Raven began walking back toward his carriage, his boots sending a spray of water in all directions as he went. "Sooner or later, she will discover what you have been up to."

He stepped up and took his seat on the bench, placing the box beside him as he closed the door, locking it firmly in place. "And once she does," he told Alistair through the open window, "I have no desire for anything or anyone to lead her back to me."

A flock of birds in a nearby tree scattered at the sound of the two deafening shots that followed. Matthew and Alistair fell to the ground in quick succession, their bodies pressed firmly into the soggy ground, their startled eyes staring upward toward a heaven that neither man was likely to see.

Returning his pistol to the inside pocket of his coat with slow precision, the Raven tapped the roof of the carriage with his cane. His visit to Gerrards Cross had lasted long enough. It was time for him to return to London.

CHAPTER TWENTY-THREE

"Lady Stephanie, as delighted as I am for your enthusiasm in regards to this subject, I simply do not think that—"

"Perhaps I did not make myself completely clear," Stephanie snapped. She took a sharp breath and stared directly at Mr. Dunn. The anxious editor was quickly taking on the likeness of a cornered animal, trapped by a merciless hunter.

"There is a lady out there," she said and pointed toward the window with a stiff finger, while her lips drew together in a tight line, "who believes that it is perfectly all right to go around cutting people open willy-nilly. Well, I for one will not stand for it."

Oh, how she'd gloated when she'd discovered that Lady Arlington had undergone surgery at the hands of Lady Steepleton. The information hadn't been easy to come by, but after seeing Lady Steepleton and Ryan Summersby dance together on the terrace of Richmond House a few weeks earlier, she'd enlisted the help of her maid, offering her a bonus if she could uncover anything unsavory about the marchioness. It had taken both time and patience on her part, not to mention that she'd spent a full week's allowance on bribes. Apparently, the Warwick servants had been especially reluctant to comply, but the promise of a rather substantial reward had eventually loosened the tongue of one maid. And it had been worth it: this was precisely the sort of juicy detail that would put the presumptuous woman's name to shame forever. It was a priceless piece of information, the sort with enough meat on it to keep the gossipmongers busy for the remainder of the season.

She'd initially planned only to take Lady Warwick's and Lady Arlington's cases to the press, but she'd changed her mind at the last minute and conjured up an additional story. After all, Lady Arlington's surgery had been a great success, as had Lady Warwick's, and while these accounts would add the necessary credulity Stephanie needed, they just weren't dramatic enough.

If a scandal were to ruin Lady Steepleton's reputation for good, as Stephanie hoped it would, then something a little more shocking, like a failed surgery, would have to be contrived. Besides, it was just a small fib to a man she didn't even know or care about. While Lord Warwick's warning had given her pause, she'd eventually decided that the prospect of seeing Lady Steepleton ruined was undoubtedly worth the risk.

Stephanie stopped herself from smirking, a difficult feat when she could practically see the promise of victory staring her straight in the face in the form of a thin, little man with receding hair and a pair of spectacles perched precariously upon his skinny nose.

And once Lady Steepleton had been publically humiliated, it would be impossible for Ryan to continue to associate with her. He'd be forced to cast her aside like a dirty dishcloth, leaving just enough space for Stephanie to swoop in and offer comfort. If she had to fudge the truth a bit in order to add some drama, then so be it. In the end, it was all for a good cause.

She returned her attention to the man in front of her.

"Now, I have written an article about a rather unpleasant experience that a close friend of mine recently had to endure at the hands of this. . .this charlatan. You see, this poor woman—Miss Charlotte Hayworth, to be precise—who recently took ill, was under the impression that this woman knew what she was doing. Well, what can I say; she's a bit naive, I suppose. If she would only have come to me for advice first, I would have strongly advised her to seek proper medical attention."

Mr. Dunn leaned forward, placing his elbows on his cluttered desk as he stared back at Stephanie from behind his spectacles. "Tell me more about Miss Hayworth's experience," he encouraged her.

"Very well, though I do not see why you cannot simply read the article. All the details are there, you know, and I did go to great pains in order to write them down."

Mr. Dunn exhaled an exasperated gush of air. This woman was clearly of the more spoiled variety. Still, if what she said was true, then he would gladly endure it with as much grace as he was capable of, for it would make a wonderful story. "I understand," he told her drily. "But I would still appreciate it if you would tell me in your own words."

Lady Stephanie twisted her mouth as if considering how

best to begin. "From what my friend has told me, she began experiencing pain in the lower right side of her abdomen about two weeks ago. This pain quickly accelerated, becoming so severe, in fact, that she could neither sit nor stand. Her mother noticed her discomfort, of course, but since she had little desire to be examined by their family physician in such an intimate place, she merely declared that it was nothing more than her monthly courses giving her trouble."

"I see," the Mr. Dunn remarked, trying not to roll his eyes. He was not the sort to blush or stammer at the mention of such things. "So, then what happened?"

"Well, Miss Hayworth had heard from a mutual friend of ours—Lady Arlington, to be precise—that there is a lady who has recently returned from the continent, a woman who is taking it upon herself to perform some minor surgeries for a few ladies in need."

"Good Lord!" the Mr. Dunn exclaimed, grabbing a piece of paper and dipping his quill in his inkwell. A few globs of the black liquid splattered across his desk, spraying a stack of papers with dark specks. Ignoring it, he began taking notes immediately.

"Lady Arlington, you say? And just what exactly did this. . .lady physician, for lack of a better term. . .what did she do for Lady Arlington, if I might ask?"

"Oh, have you not heard?" Lady Stephanie donned a look of unblemished innocence. "I thought that something as juicy as this would surely have reached your office by now. Judging from your expression, however, I daresay that it has not. Well, sir, let me enlighten you, for it is certainly quite intriguing. You see, she performed a cesarean for Lady Arlington."

"A what?" The poor editor felt certain that he might expire from the horror of it all.

"You know, when they cut the woman open and—"

"Yes, thank you, I know what it is." He put his quill down carefully in front of him and straightened his jacket. "But that, Lady Stephanie, is hardly something that one might dismiss as minor surgery."

"Well, I suppose not." She tilted her head and delivered a practiced smile. "Lady Arlington was fortunate, you know; her procedure went rather well. As for my friend, however. . .well, after the surgery—"

"And what surgery was that again?" Mr. Dunn scribbled furiously on the piece of paper in front of him.

"How forgetful of me." Her smile widened marginally to show her brilliant white teeth. "She had her appendix removed."

The editor's jaw dropped.

Lady Stephanie nodded to confirm that he'd heard her right. "She tells me it was quite painful. And when it became infected. . .well, she had no other choice but to have another surgeon fix that stupid woman's mistake. She was so careless, you see. Poor Miss Hayworth is very lucky to still be alive."

"How awful for her," Mr. Dunn muttered, for lack of anything better to say.

As difficult as it was for him to believe what the woman before him had just said, the promise of such a scandalous story filling the front page of the newspaper was too great a temptation to pass up. He brushed his misgivings aside.

"Yes, it was rather." Lady Stephanie's eyes met his in a

steady gaze. "So you see, I would very much like to prevent another innocent woman from suffering at this lady's hands."

Mr. Dunn nodded with sympathy. "Yes, I can understand that."

"And that is not all," she added.

"It is not?"

"Oh, no," Lady Stephanie said, brushing a bit of lint from her skirt. "She also removed a kidney stone from Lady Warwick."

Mr. Dunn raked his fingers through his thinning hair as he sank back against his chair with a loud sigh. He wasn't at all sure how much more of this he could take; it was simply too outrageous.

"You mean the Dowager Countess?" he asked.

"Why, yes. Do you know her?"

Of course he knew her; *everybody* did.

"I have heard her name mentioned on occasion," he lied. He made a few more notes before pausing. He'd just realized that he'd missed one very vital detail.

"And what is the name of this lady, the one who seems to think herself a surgeon?"

"Oh, did I not say? Why it is the Marchioness of Steepleton—Lady Steepleton, to be exact."

Bloody hell!

"And you are quite certain that all of the details you have just given me are accurate? The *Mayfair Chronicle* does have a name to uphold, and—"

"I completely understand," she told him. Her gaze drifted toward the window, where raindrops were steadily gathering on the glass. She was silent for a moment before turning her attention back to Mr. Dunn. She told him simply, "You have my word on it."

Given the limited time that remained before the deadline, this would have to do if he wanted to run the article. Besides, he very much doubted that a lady would put her own reputation at risk by fabricating such information. "You understand that once your story goes into print, the repercussions could be quite severe. Lady Steepleton might very well find herself dragged to court, perhaps even to prison. Are you prepared to let that happen?"

"Why, of course; I would not have come here otherwise." Lady Stephanie gave the editor a frosty stare that sent a shiver down his spine. "Lady Steepleton has overstepped her boundaries. She has acted rather despicably, to say the least, and I simply feel that it is my duty to stop her before someone else gets hurt—or dies."

The editor nodded slowly. She had a point, though he couldn't help but wonder if there wasn't a far more personal reason behind this attack. Still, a woman practicing medicine without a license. . .the public needed to know about it.

"Well then," he told her after a short sigh, "you may look forward to seeing your article in the paper no later than tomorrow morning. After all, we cannot allow for such disgraceful behavior to carry on any longer than it already has."

"I could not agree more," Lady Stephanie told him as she picked up her reticule and rose from her seat. "I shall look forward to reading it."

Across the street, William Summersby was having a dinner jacket fitted by his tailor. It wasn't something he particularly enjoyed, rather a chore that his father had given him upon seeing how worn the fabric was on the ones he had. His longtime friend, Col. Conrad Jennings, waited impatiently for him to finish.

"I would like to make it to White's by five," Conrad remarked as he picked up a random hat from one of the shelves. He turned it over in his hands, glanced at the price, and then put it carelessly aside, feigning disinterest.

"Why the sudden hurry?" William couldn't help but ask. Conrad had told him earlier of course, but William had always enjoyed twisting the knife whenever Conrad was concerned.

Conrad flapped his arms in annoyance. "You know perfectly well that I want to place a wager against Cummings before the deadline, which happens to be three o'clock, in case you need reminding."

Oh, dear; it was already quarter to.

"I am surprised that you have not done so already," William told him. "Why the devil would you wait until the very last minute?"

He knew this too, of course. Again, the knife. . .

"Well, I was hoping to discover if the poor sod might, by some miracle, be able to escape his fate, though it does seem that he will be married before the month is out."

"Miss Huxley certainly did her damnedest to trap him. It would be quite the scandal if he were to refuse her now, especially if she were to start showing."

"Dear me, I had not thought of that possibility. Do you think she might be—"

"Who knows? But if she is, then there is even more reason for him to settle the matter expediently."

"You are absolutely right, and that is precisely why. . .Good Lord, who on earth is that?"

William turned his head and leaned forward to peer out of the shop window. At first he couldn't tell whom Conrad might be referring to, but then he saw her: Stephanie Maplewood with her head held high under a straw bonnet trimmed with yellow ribbons.

"What an exquisite creature," Conrad murmured, mostly to himself, but loud enough for William to hear.

Exquisitely venomous, William thought.

To Conrad he said, "If you pursue that woman, then I shall be the one placing bets at White's as to how long you will manage to survive your marriage before she does you in."

"Oh, don't be daft," Conrad told him as his eyes followed Lady Stephanie. "A woman such as that, with a face so pretty and a figure so shapely—a man would be a fool *not* to pursue her."

"Is that so?" It was becoming increasingly difficult for William to keep a straight face at the sight of Conrad drooling over Lady Stephanie. Conrad was generally fierce in his demeanor—a military man who didn't take nonsense from anyone. He was tough too in his bearing, the sort of man who instilled fear in his opponents. Yet here he was, ogling a woman as if she were a plum pudding he might be ready to devour.

"Trust me on this," William told him seriously. "That woman is nothing but trouble. In fact. . ."

Damnation. Was that the office of the *Mayfair Chronicle* that she was leaving just now? What the devil was she up to this time? William was beginning to think he'd rather not know.

"You were saying?" Conrad asked in a dreamy voice.

William eyed his friend with a grim smile. "Only that she very nearly ruined the reputation of my future sister-in-law intentionally, I will have you know."

"Why on earth would she do that?"

"Beats me, although I do suspect it has a lot to do with her affection for my brother."

"You don't say," Conrad muttered wryly.

He waved his hand as if to brush aside this last piece of information as though it held no significance whatsoever. "No matter," he said. "I shall have her all the same."

"Then you are either a fool, Jennings, or some sort of masochist—perhaps even both—because *that* woman will give you nothing but a headache, and I will happily wager that it will be from the frying pan she uses to hit you over the head."

"Feisty, is she?"

"No, not exactly; more like vicious and vile."

"So I take it you will not be visiting me much once I marry her?"

Once, not if?

"Only if I can bring a pistol with me so I can protect myself when she tries to stab me in the back."

"Have a little faith, will you?" Conrad turned to William with a grin. "Did I tell you that I recently started breeding dogs in my spare time?"

Bloody hell. Don't tell me.

"I shall look forward with great pleasure to putting a

muzzle on that little vixen and making her heel." He winked at William. "You will see; I shall promptly put her in her place and have her whispering sweet nothings in my ear before you know it. You can bet on *that* at White's if you like."

"I will be sure that I do," William said and grinned.

He shrugged out of his jacket and handed it back to the tailor. "Let me have this in navy as well," he said. "Now then, I do believe we had best be on our way if you still want to place that bet against Cummings; we have only five minutes to spare."

CHAPTER TWENTY-FOUR

White fluffy clouds sped across the sky as Mary entered Hyde Park at a brisk pace that afternoon. She'd sent an invitation for tea to Lord Woodbridge earlier in the day, but before he arrived, she simply needed to get out of her house for a while.

She'd returned there yesterday, against Ryan's recommendations, but the fact of the matter was that she wasn't comfortable with continuously imposing herself on Alexandra when she had a perfectly good house of her own. After all, Alexandra had a husband and a child to see to, and though Mary liked her immensely and valued her friendship, she knew that if something were to threaten that friendship, it would likely be a houseguest who got in the way—as all houseguests eventually did if they overstayed their welcome.

So, having engaged in yet another lengthy argument with Ryan, she'd eventually gotten her way, though he had made it quite clear that he thought her a fool—a careless fool at that.

Now, as she left the footpath behind her and marched hastily across the grass, she considered all the horrible things she'd said to him in anger. Ignoble cad and numbskull had certainly come up at some point, but she was perhaps slightly less proud of malodorous milksop, in response to which he had called her a jingle-brained harridan. Needless to say, they'd parted on less than amicable terms.

Jingle-brained harridan, indeed. Insufferable man!

Well, Mary had to admit that the insult she'd thrown at him with as much vigor as a spectator might apply in tossing rotten tomatoes at a poor performance in the East End had been grossly misplaced and merely a depiction of her own furious temper, which generally escalated with alarming haste whenever Ryan Summersby opened his mouth to speak.

She now wondered if she ought to apologize. After all, he *did* have a point, but then again, so did she. She breathed a sigh of frustration. When would he come to realize that she loved her freedom and independence and that she had no intention of sacrificing it—not for anyone.

But Ryan was already trying to dictate where she was allowed to go and for how long she was allowed to go there. He'd insisted that if he were otherwise occupied, she take Emma along with her at all times, and he'd even had the audacity to direct Thornton about, informing the aging butler that the security at her house was not up to scratch and needed seeing to immediately. The poor man had been left with no choice but to start adding locks to her bedroom door and boarding up her windows—a wise decision, considering that she was feeling increasingly compelled to jump out of one of them. In truth, Ryan was treating her like the helpless woman he clearly considered her to be, with need for constant guidance from a level-headed man, a position he'd quickly claimed without as much as asking for her acceptance.

Not that she would have given it. She couldn't deny that there were people with an incomprehensible desire to frighten her, perhaps even harm her, but even if she did find herself in the face of danger, she certainly didn't want Ryan to be lurching behind her at every turn, ready to jump in and rescue her.

And *if* she were to marry him—and there was still that big *if* in her mind, regardless of what she had told him—then she wanted the kind of partnership she'd spoken of at Whickham Hall. She didn't want to be considered weak or inferior by anyone, least of all by her husband. She didn't want to be brushed aside or treated like a child. And she especially didn't want him to think that if he left her side for a minute, she'd fall prey to only Lord knew what.

If that were truly the case, then she could just as well wave good-bye to her independence forever and acknowledge that she might as well remain home in bed. Her life as she knew it would be well and truly over.

The sound of twigs snapping among the trees caught her attention. She'd been so caught up in her own thoughts and the dialogue she planned to have with Ryan the next time she saw him that she'd failed to notice where she was going. She'd left the most popular area of the park behind and was now quite alone, surrounded by trees. Nobody could see her.

Her heart quickened as another twig snapped. A rustling sound followed. It was probably just a small animal—a squirrel perhaps, or a mouse.

"Mary?"

She gasped at the sound of that voice. Her heart leaped

into her throat. She stiffened, paused, and turned around very, very slowly.

"I hope I am not intruding." It was Jack Helmsley, dressed rather casually in a beige jacket and brown trousers. "But I saw you walking and decided to follow. I must say, you certainly keep a brisk pace." He was breathing heavily from the effort of chasing after her.

Mary stared at him. She took a small step backward. "What do you want?" she asked in a strained voice.

"Not exactly the warm welcome I was expecting." He studied her for a moment.

"Well, you startled me," she said, willing her voice to stay calm. "I was deep in thought about a rather serious matter."

"I see." He wiped his brow with a white handkerchief, then looked at her much like a father might at a child he was concerned about. "There is something you ought to know, something I have not yet told you." He took a step forward. "I am afraid that I have not been very honest with you."

Mary took a sharp breath and held it. Her heart was still drumming vigorously against her chest.

"You see, your father. . .How do I put this? I. . .well, you see, the thing is that—"

"Oh, for heaven's sake, I already know that you killed him." The words were out before she could stop them. And once they were out, there was no taking them back. Mary clapped her hand over her mouth and stared at Jack.

Oh, hell!

"Is that what you think?" He gaped at her in astonishment. "How did you even. . .? Never mind; I know that you have been making inquiries."

He took another step in her direction, and she consequently tensed so much that she thought she might snap in two. "I have actually made a lot of interesting discoveries lately."

Dear God, why would I tell him that?

"I see." Jack frowned at her while he considered this. "And would these discoveries have anything to do with your father's journals, by any chance?"

"You are the worst kind of scoundrel I have ever met in my entire life," she flared as a sudden wave of anger assailed her. The last of her fear was swept away as she leaned toward him. "My father loved you like a brother; he trusted you, respected you, helped you, and this is how you repay him, by having him killed?"

"You have to listen to me," Jack told her carefully. "I—"

"No, you listen to me, Jack," Mary sneered as she pulled the pistol that Alexandra had given her from her reticule.

"What are you. . .?" Jack held up his hands in surrender. "Look, I realize how this must seem. I know your father mentioned me in the course of his investigation, but I did not sanction his death."

The laugh that Mary gave him was a mocking one. She tightened her hold on the pistol. "And why should I trust anything that you have to say? Because you told me that my life was in danger? Or perhaps because you informed me about my father's investigation? Oh, wait; you did neither of those things, did you, Jack? Instead you deliberately kept it from me."

"I am sorry, Mary," Jack told her as he stepped toward her once more. "You have every right to be suspicious of my actions."

"Stop right there," she warned. "I will shoot you—do not make the mistake of thinking I will not."

Jack sighed. He dropped his gaze to the ground. "The truth is that I was just as worried as everyone else about what might happen if the journals were not destroyed. My whole livelihood is at stake, Mary. You have to understand that I could lose everything if my errors were brought to light."

"And I am supposed to feel sorry for you?" The sneer was back in her voice again. "You had my father killed, Jack. For that I can never forgive you."

"Have you not been listening to a single word that I have said?" He looked back up at her, his eyes full of desperation. "I did not—" But just then he made the irrevocable error of reaching out toward her. It was an impulsive plea for forgiveness on Helmsley's part, a plea that Mary completely misread as a sign of aggression.

Reflex rushed into her fingers, forcing her to squeeze the trigger. She closed her eyes, just as the gun went off with a loud bang, propelling her backward against the trunk of a tree. Silence followed. Her eyes remained firmly shut for one second, two seconds, three seconds. . .She opened them slowly.

Jesus, Mary, and Joseph and all the apostles—I have killed him!

Mary peered down at the heap of limbs that lay sprawled at her feet. How curious; she couldn't seem to find the point of impact. And there wasn't much blood either. In fact, there wasn't any as far as she could tell. It had to be on the other side of him then, the side she couldn't see. She looked at her hands, still clutching the pistol. As if it had just scorched her flesh, she tossed it aside, into the bushes.

What now?

She leaned forward to take a closer look at Helmsley's body.

Closer and closer. . .

A hand reached out and grabbed her. Mary screamed, her voice shrill with startled fright.

"Mary. . ." Jack groaned, his eyes fluttering open. "What the blazes were you thinking?" His fist clutched the fabric of her skirt.

Pulling away, Mary tried to run but fell instead, her knees hitting the ground with a thud. "Help me, Mary; my shoulder hurts like the devil."

"Unhand me, you ill-begotten scoundrel!" she cried, her hands reaching for something, anything, that might help her pull herself away from him.

"For the love of Christ, Mary," Jack muttered as he rolled over onto his side. "You shot me; you could have bloody well killed me, you little idiot."

Mary scrambled about in the dirt, desperate to get away from him. She'd tossed away her only weapon and now. . .*Oh God*. . .Her dress caught on some brambles and tore. Her hand curled around the root of a tree. She tried to pull herself up, but Helmsley latched onto her ankle. Kicking with all her might, she did her best to be rid of him. It was of no use.

"Is that it, then?" he asked her angrily. "Are you just going to leave me here like this?"

"What do you think? After everything you have done?"

With a pained sigh, he fell back against the undergrowth.

"You do not know what you have gotten yourself into." He winced with pain as he clasped his shoulder. "You have the wrong man."

"I hardly think so," she hissed. "You have done nothing but lie to me these past few weeks—perhaps longer than that even; who knows? And of all the initials mentioned in my father's journals, you are the only one I actually knew. Yes, I have met Clemens and Bosworth recently, but they were not friends of mine. You, on the other hand, you were like family."

Grabbing onto a nearby tree for support, she lifted her free foot and stomped down as hard as she could on Helmsley's wounded shoulder. With a cry of sheer agony he released her. "Mary, please," he croaked, but she didn't stop to listen to what he might have had to say; she was running as fast as her feet could carry her, toward the corner of the park that would put her closest to Brook Street and home.

CHAPTER TWENTY-FIVE

In his father's town house on Grosvenor Square, Ryan was quietly enjoying a cup of tea in the parlor while he waited for his father and brother to arrive. Percy had also been called to attend, though he was expected to be late; his brother and his father, however, were not.

Ryan tapped his fingers restlessly on the table next to him. He sighed, got up, walked to the window, and sighed again before returning to his chair. Where the devil were they? He'd told them earlier that it was a matter of great importance.

He decided to take another sip of his tea.

A few minutes later, the sound of the front door opening and closing could be heard. Hutchins's voice rang out loud and clear, there was a pause, and then the soft tread of approaching footsteps. The parlor door opened.

"So sorry," William exclaimed upon his arrival. "I was out with Jennings—had to hurry over to White's so he could place his bet against Cummings."

"Ah, yes, I had forgotten about that poor devil," Ryan muttered.

"Mmm. . .better he than I—that is all I can say," William said and chuckled.

"Still not ready to set up that nursery of yours, I take it?"

"No, especially not now that you have clearly snagged the only available woman worth having."

Ryan laughed. "That may well be, though I have to say, the tongue on that woman leaves much to be desired."

"Oh, come now; it cannot possibly be any worse than Alex's."

"She called me a malodorous milksop, right in the middle of Oxford Street, for all the world to hear."

"Well, you must have done something to deserve it," William told him, jumping valiantly to Mary's defense.

"I shall remember that when you find yourself carted off to the altar by a willful chit with a mouth more foul than a Covent Garden nun," Ryan said, glowering at his brother for good measure.

"Speaking of which, you will never guess who I saw this afternoon," William remarked, directing the subject smoothly away from himself and the topic of marriage.

"Who?"

"Stephanie Maplewood. It appeared as though she was leaving the office of the *Mayfair Chronicle*."

Christ!

"Jennings was quite taken with her, you know," William added.

"The man is a damn fool if he falls into that trap," Ryan muttered.

"I thought exactly the same thing; told him so too, in fact. Yet, upon further consideration, I am not so sure about which of them would be the one getting trapped—if they were to wed, that is."

"What do you mean?" Ryan asked for the sake of asking. He really couldn't care less about Jennings or Stephanie Maplewood, least of all now when he was trying to focus on helping Mary.

Where the hell were Bryce and Percy anyway?

"He breeds dogs, you see," William said and snorted as if he'd just said the funniest of things.

Ryan served him a blank stare. "Who?"

"Jennings, of course. Have you not been listening? I told him about Lady Stephanie's transgressions, I warned him of her conniving nature, and do you know what he told me?" William chuckled with glee. "That he would like to *put a muzzle on that vixen and make her heel*."

Ryan's lips began to twitch. A moment later, both men were in stitches at the prospect of Lady Stephanie being bound by marriage to a man who would treat her precisely as she deserved.

They were so amused with themselves, in fact, that it took a while before they noticed Bryce and Percy standing in the doorway, staring at them as if they'd just escaped from Bedlam.

"Oh, there you are." Ryan grinned as he strode toward Percy to shake his hand. He gave his father a warm smile. "William was just telling me about Colonel Jennings's plans to woo Stephanie Maplewood."

"Well, if there is a man in all of creation who might be able to discipline that woman, then he is certainly the one." Bryce smirked. "He has one very simple rule: reward the good behavior and punish the bad."

"And you think that will work with Lady Stephanie?" William asked.

Percy was the one to answer that question. "She has been spoiled in every which way imaginable since the day she first opened her eyes on the world—a common mistake made by parents with only one child, I'm afraid. But really, she has been allowed to get away with far too much, and her recent behavior has been quite despicable, to say the least. She needs a firm hand to guide her and someone to tell her *no* every once in a while.

"I know Jennings well; he is tough as nails. She will not be able to wind him around her little finger, and in the end, he will be doing her a favor—if she will have him, that is. . .there is, of course, that little detail to consider."

"And while we are on the topic of Lady Stephanie," Ryan added, "William saw her earlier this afternoon leaving the office of the *Mayfair Chronicle*."

"What the devil is that woman doing, going to the press?" Bryce barked.

"Not sure," William told him. "But I doubt that she was merely paying a social visit."

Ryan shuddered. "Perhaps we ought to go over there ourselves and try to discover what she has been up to."

"An excellent idea," Bryce said as he sat down in one of the chairs. "But first, why don't you tell us why you have asked us all here to meet you."

Ryan lifted the teapot from the table in front of him. "Tea, anyone?" he asked.

"Do I look like a woman to you?" Bryce growled. It was a known fact that he hadn't had a cup of tea since his wife's death. He'd taken great pleasure in watching her pour, but he'd never been particularly fond of the drink itself. Now that she was gone, he really didn't see any point in the British custom of afternoon tea, which was, in his opinion, highly overrated. "Give me a brandy instead," he said as he pulled a cigar from his pocket.

"Percy?" Ryan asked, his hand still on the teapot.

"Go ahead and pour me a cup," Percy told him.

"Me too," William added.

"Right then," Ryan remarked once he was done. "You all know about the threats against Mary and that there are men out there who want to get their hands on her father's journals."

Everyone nodded.

"Well, I believe that we may have determined why." Ryan took a sip of his tea; it was already cold. He winced. "Her father was conducting an investigation into what he considered to be medical malpractice cases."

"That would certainly explain a lot," Percy muttered.

"Yes. In fact, the findings are rather astounding." Ryan eyed his father. "Apparently, Mr. Clemens and Sir Bosworth were both very much involved. Each was responsible for roughly thirty or so unnecessary deaths."

"Good Lord," Bryce murmured as he stared at Ryan in disbelief. "Are you quite certain of this? It is a rather large accusation to make if. . .I mean, both of these men are very well respected and—"

"I am sorry. I know that Bosworth in particular is a good friend of yours. Unfortunately, it is true: the evidence is all in Lord Steepleton's writing."

Ryan went on to tell them about his and Mary's visit to the hospital, the records they'd found, and the initials that matched each of these men.

"Now, there are still a few initials that I have not been able to decipher. That is why I have asked you to come. I was hoping that you might be able to help me discover who they are."

"Very well," William told him. "Let us hear them."

Ryan pulled a piece of paper from his jacket pocket and cleared his throat. "There is *MH*, whom we have discerned to be Dr. Jack Helmsley, a close friend of Mary's father." He paused for a moment before moving on. "*MT* appears quite frequently, as do a few others, but the most prominent initial of all is *VR*."

"And the first letter of each initial denotes the man's title?" William asked with mounting interest.

"I presume so, judging from the fact that *MC* stands for Mr. Clemens, while *SB* stands for Sir Bosworth. If Lord Steepleton was consistent, as I believe he was, judging from his meticulous notes, then, yes, the first letter denotes the title."

"The *MT* could be Mr. Thornfield." Percy's voice was distant when he spoke. "I hate to think it; the man is a good friend of mine, but he must be considered. He is one of London's most prominent surgeons, after all."

"And *VR*?" Ryan asked expectantly.

Bryce and Percy glanced at one another knowingly. Neither of them said anything, though, as if they each hoped the other might embark upon that topic.

"Well?" Ryan persisted.

"It seems that Lady Steepleton has been stirring up quite

the hornet's nest." It was Bryce who'd finally decided to enlighten his son. "Not only does she have spirit, but she has tremendous courage to take on the most prominent physicians and surgeons this city has to offer."

"Who is he?" Ryan asked with growing concern. His voice was low and quiet as he stared across at his father.

"Only one man comes to mind, I am afraid: the Viscount of Ravenwood."

"Who?" Ryan and William voiced the question simultaneously.

Percy looked as though he'd much rather be elsewhere, while Bryce merely took another sip of his brandy, smacking his lips together as he swallowed. Concern marked his aging eyes.

"You probably know him better as the Earl of Woodbridge—the master of the College of Surgeons himself."

Bloody hell!

Ryan and William both stared at their father in dumbfounded disbelief. They didn't move—they simply couldn't. They just sat there while they tried to absorb the enormity of what he'd just told them.

"That is not possible," Ryan eventually managed to say. "He is the Earl of Woodbridge; you just said so yourself. It doesn't make sense for Lord Steepleton to refer to him as *VR*."

"It does if that is how he remembered him," Percy said. "You must not forget, Woodbridge and Croyden were friends for years—since they were lads, in fact, and long before Croyden decided to spurn his heritage. And though both of you are too young to recall, Robert Finley was known as the Viscount of Ravenwood in his youth. He did not inherit the title of Earl of Woodbridge until his uncle passed away about twenty years ago."

Ryan was nothing short of stunned.

Dear God—Mary!

"William, come with me this instant." Ryan was out of his seat and across the floor in two bounds. He paused at the drawing room door while he waited for William to follow. "Mary is having tea with Lord Woodbridge as we speak," he explained. "I think it might do rather well if we hightailed on over there to see what the blazes is going on and more to the point, make sure that she is all right."

CHAPTER TWENTY-SIX

After the incident in the park, Mary went straight home. She'd considered stopping by Summersby House to tell Ryan about what had happened but had thought better of it. After all, this was precisely the sort of thing that would prove his point and have him hover over her like a mother hen in no time at all.

Instead, she hurried upstairs to her room with Emma on her heels and a troubled Thornton staring after her. Emma at least had the decency not to inquire as to why her mistress's gown had been torn and covered in dirt. She quietly helped her wash up instead and change into a clean dress so she would look respectable once her guest arrived. The Earl of Woodbridge would be coming for tea at any moment.

Mary now waited anxiously in the parlor for Robert to arrive. She'd asked Thornton to ensure that some tea and cucumber sandwiches would be made ready, but now she wondered whether she ought to have added some crumpets with jam since Robert had always been fond of sweets.

She sighed as she placed her hands loosely in her lap.

Her encounter with Helmsley had rattled her more than she cared to admit. She'd actually tried to shoot him. No, she *had* shot him; what she'd *tried* to do was kill him. And what now? He was still alive and would almost certainly come after her again. She wasn't safe, not even in her own home.

Her thoughts went to Ryan and everything he'd told her. Damn it if he hadn't been right. She wasn't able to protect herself as well as she'd thought she could—Helmsley had just proven that.

But was she going to run crying into Ryan's arms like the stereotypically feeble female? Not bloody likely. Her stubborn pride would never allow her to follow that course of action, even though it was exactly what she wanted to do most. No, she'd argued with him and insulted him on the basis that she was strong enough to take care of herself, and so she would.

"My lady," Thornton remarked in a drier voice than usual, "Lord Woodbridge has arrived. Shall I show him in?"

"Yes, please do," Mary replied. "And please ask one of the maids to bring us the tea."

Thornton raised an eyebrow as if to say, "Do you seriously think I need reminding?" Instead he merely nodded and backed out of the door.

"Robert!" Mary exclaimed as her father's longtime friend strode into the room, his cane thumping loudly against the floor as he went. "It is so good to see you again. Thank you for coming."

"Thank *you* for inviting me," Robert told her with a cheerful smile. He remained standing until she'd sat down again, then took his seat in the pale blue armchair that stood next to the fireplace. A maid entered carrying a tray with a teapot and two cups. She placed it on the table, bobbed a curtsy, and left.

"I would have invited you sooner, but Lady Trenton and her husband were kind enough to let me join them in the country for a few days."

"I completely understand," Robert told her smoothly. "Did you have a good time?"

"Oh, yes. It was lovely to get away from the city for a while, especially with everything that has been happening lately."

Robert took a sip of the tea that Mary had just poured for him and frowned. "Yes, I understand that you have been quite busy since your return. And with Lady Stephanie so intent on seeing you ruined. . .well, I can only imagine how difficult it must have been for you."

"I was rather hoping that nobody would have heard about that little incident."

"What can I say?" Robert spread his arms wide as he leaned back against his chair. He crossed his legs and smiled. "Gossip has a remarkable way of reaching those who are interested in it, and I must admit that I have been very interested in keeping my eye on you and everything that you have been up to."

Mary felt her cheeks flush from embarrassment. "I do not suppose that you have also heard that I have an uncle I never knew existed."

"Hm. . .come to think of it, your father did have a brother and a sister, I believe, though I have not heard any news about either one of them in years."

"Well, my uncle showed up a few days ago. He is terribly

ill, I'm afraid, and in dire need of immediate medical attention. He wanted to know if my father might have come across an alternative treatment for a sarcoma than the one his surgeon is currently suggesting: amputation."

"I see. That does sound rather serious."

"Unfortunately, he will not allow me to help him any further. He insisted that a man attend to him."

Robert chuckled. "You must try to understand that for a gentleman—an older one, in particular—well, it really would be quiet unseemly to allow a young woman to perform any sort of examination requiring the patient's state of undress." He seemed to consider his next words with great care. "That is not to say that you are not perfectly capable; I know that you are, Mary. Your father trained you very well."

"You are right, of course," she said. "I just wish that there was something more I could do for him. He seemed so desperate."

"I imagine he would be if he had a sarcoma."

Mary nodded ruefully. "He wanted to see my father's journals, but I wouldn't let him. I did not trust him, Robert. He showed up so unexpectedly, and with everything that has happened, the threats and the thefts. . ."

Robert frowned, leaning closer as if he expected her to explain.

"I have not told you, have I?" He shook his head, his dark eyes filled with interest. Considering his longtime friendship with her father, Mary was confident that he would do whatever he could to help her. "Since my arrival in London, I have received multiple threats to abandon my practice. My bedroom has been broken into, both here and at Whickham Hall during my stay there. All of my father's work—every single one of his journals—stolen."

"That is very unfortunate," Robert murmured with a hint of gravity.

"To say the least." Mary sighed dejectedly. "Did you know that my father was murdered? No, of course you did not." Her eyes were beginning to burn. "The worst of it is that I know who did it."

"You do?" Robert shifted in his chair as if he weren't quite ready to hear what she had to say.

Mary slowly nodded. "It was a whole group of physicians and surgeons that my father had been investigating for malpractice. Mr. Clemens and Sir Bosworth, whom you introduced me to at Glendale House, are among them. So is Helmsley."

Robert's eyes widened, and Mary realized just how shocking this news must be for him. After all, these were all men whom he knew rather well— friends, in fact.

"And even though Helmsley does not appear to have been as involved as the rest," she continued, "I *know* that he is the one behind the threats, the thefts, and worst of all, my father's murder. He simply knew us too well for it to have been anyone else, and he took advantage of that knowledge in the worst possible way."

Robert frowned, giving Mary the impression that he was finding all of this quite difficult to digest. It was to be expected, considering that she'd just accused some very respectable members of society of murder. She watched as his expression eventually relaxed into one of sympathy. He let out a ragged sigh and slumped back against his seat. "I am so sorry," he told her. "I had no idea. It is. . .incomprehensible, to say the least."

They sat in silence for a while, contemplating the issue, before Robert eventually spoke again. "But if your father intended to make all of Helmsley's errors and careless mistakes public, then Helmsley could have not only lost his license, he could have gone to prison for a very long time."

For a brief second, it almost sounded as if Robert was defending Helmsley, but a moment later he sadly shook his head. No, he was just stating the facts to try to better understand the situation at hand. After all, she'd had some time now in which to come to terms with what had happened, while Robert was probably still in shock.

"I realize that," Mary told him. "But that does not excuse what he did or what he is still doing."

"It certainly is a rather damnable affair, if you'll excuse my language. Tell me, how may I be of assistance?" Robert asked.

"Actually, I was hoping that you might be able to help me discover who some of the other men involved might be."

His face brightened at that request; he was obviously eager to help, for which Mary was truly grateful. She explained how she and Ryan had worked out who the other physicians were, then reached for the burgundy, leather-bound book that was lying on the table next to her. As reluctant as she was to let it out of her grasp, she had no reason not to trust Robert with it. Besides, if he was going to help her as he said he would, then the least she could do was show a little faith in him. Leaning forward, she handed the book over to him without the least bit of hesitation, watching as a look of reverence came over his face. She knew that her father had done some remarkable work in his time and appreciated that a man as prominent as the Earl of Woodbridge would treat his journal with such care and admiration.

Discovering what Helmsley had done both saddened and angered her beyond compare, but at least she knew that she could still count on Robert. There was also Ryan, whom she knew she could depend upon. Thinking of him now, she briefly wondered if he'd uncovered any new pieces of information. Probably not, or he would have hurried over and told her at once, regardless of their earlier argument. Of that she was certain.

Robert flipped open the journal and ran his fingers across the text.

"Do you see the initials at the end of each paragraph?" Mary asked, observing Robert's fascinated appreciation of her father's work.

He nodded slowly, his eyes narrowing slightly as he scanned the page. "I don't believe that I know who those initials belong to," he told her regretfully, looking up and meeting her gaze.

"Oh," Mary muttered. The disappointment she felt was overwhelming. "I had rather hoped you would, considering your connections within the medical community."

"Yes, I suppose that is true. But let's not give up hope just yet." He gave her an optimistic smile. "I have a record at my home of all the physicians and surgeons who have worked in London within the past ten years. Perhaps if we look in it, we might discover something new."

"Oh, Robert, I knew you would do everything in your power to help, and this is certainly an excellent idea." She didn't want to abuse his willingness to help, but she also felt that time was of the essence. Consequently, she only stopped herself momentarily before adding, "I know it is rather late. I don't suppose you would want to—"

"I don't mind going over it right away if that is what you wish to do," he told her gently. "I know how important this is to you."

Relief washed over her. "Thank you," she said, hoping she'd think of an appropriate means by which to repay him later. "You have always been very kind to me, and this. . .this means a lot."

"It means a great deal to me too, Mary," Robert assured her. "More than you can possibly imagine. After you?"

With a quick nod, stopping only to pick up her spencer and reticule, Mary followed Robert without a moment's hesitation, only too eager to discover who else her father had been investigating.

"Is that not Woodbridge's carriage?" William asked, pointing to the landau that was pulling away from the curb in front of Mary's house. They'd gotten there as fast as they could, running the last hundred yards out of concern for Mary's safety.

Ryan frowned. "I think so." He turned and bolted up the stairs leading to the front door of Mary's home and began hammering at it so furiously that William feared the door might break.

"May I help you?" a perplexed Thornton asked upon opening the door. He looked questioningly from one brother to the other.

"I need to see Mary," Ryan told him on a gasp of air. "Lady Steepleton, I mean. I would like to ensure that nothing has happened to her."

"She was well when I last saw her," Thornton remarked. "A matter of minutes before you arrived."

Thank God!

Ryan breathed a sigh of relief. "May I speak to her, please? I know it is rather late, but there is a matter of great importance that I *must* discuss with her at once."

"Oh, I am afraid not," Thornton told him. "Her ladyship has gone out for the evening. You are welcome to wait, of course, but I really cannot say how long she will be."

Ryan's heart leaped back into action, quickening its pace to a perilous beat.

"Where did she go?" He could scarcely get the question out. He felt faint, as if the world were folding itself in on him.

"I am really not certain, but she did leave with the Earl of Woodbridge, so she is in very good hands."

Oh, dear God in heaven!

"He is going to kill her," Ryan murmured, turning his back on the startled butler. "I just know it."

"Then we have not a moment to lose," William said as he grabbed his pale-faced brother by the arm and began dragging him along in the direction of Lord Woodbridge's mansion. "Now, pull yourself together, Ryan; the woman you love is depending on you."

Love?

He'd almost told her he loved her yesterday, but he hadn't felt it as strongly as he did now that the words had actually been spoken, even if it *had* been by William. Hearing it made

it so much more real. Yes, he loved her, more dearly than he'd
ever loved any other, and he'd be damned if he was going to let
a villain like Woodbridge get in the way of that.

"You are quite right," he told William as he quickened his
pace to a run. "I am going to find that bastard, and when I do,
he will be sorry that he ever crossed me."

CHAPTER TWENTY-SEVEN

"I have always admired your home, Robert," Mary remarked as she stared up at the vaulted ceiling in the foyer of Wood-bridge House. "I remember visiting here as a child when my father would come to call on you, and I always dreamed of what it might be like to live in such a place."

"And now you know," he told her cheerfully.

"Oh, my house on Brook Street is nothing compared to this, though you are very kind to imply so."

"I was actually thinking of Steepleton House."

Mary looked momentarily confused.

"The estate in Northamptonshire?"

"Oh, yes, of course. Unfortunately, I have not had the time to visit it yet." She paused for a moment as she ran her eyes along the railing of the wide marble staircase. "But I take it you have been?"

"Once, as a child, when your grandfather was still alive. Your father invited me along one summer. It was quite splendid.

"Come, let us go this way," he said. With heels clicking

against the marble floor and his cane thumping loudly at his side, Robert led Mary through to his study.

"Now, before we get started, I would like to show you something rather special." He crossed the carpet to a door that stood between two bookcases and opened it.

Mary stepped forward. She walked past Robert, peered inside the room, and simply gaped at what she saw. "Heavens!" she exclaimed.

"Is it not marvelous?"

"It is certainly quite unusual," she told him as she glanced about the room that Robert had clearly spent much time on converting into his private operating theater.

"And yet it has served me rather well." His voice was strained with the early tones of annoyance. This room was his pride and joy, and all she had to say was how *unusual* it was? He wanted to slap her but stopped himself. It wouldn't do for her to lose faith in him just yet. There would be plenty of time for that later.

"Most members of the *ton* abhor having to venture into a hospital filled with diseased commoners," he explained. "Here, in the confines of this room, I am able to offer them absolute discretion with less chance of catching another contagious illness." He wouldn't tell her that the members of the gentry weren't the only ones who'd paid a visit here. After all, he could hardly kill off too many of them before drawing suspicion. Besides, they were the ones funding his rather elaborate lifestyle. That was not to say that he hadn't been tempted to botch up Lord Hornby's operation. He simply couldn't stomach the fool.

Now, the commoners, on the other hand, with all their

putrid afflictions—nobody cared if one of them didn't make it. Oh, the power of the surgeon! He was like a god, holding the life of his patients in the palm of his hand. How many times had he decided to save a life, and how many times had he decided to let the poor unworthy wretch just slip away? The feeling he felt when that vital decision was made was unlike any other. It gave him wings and sent him soaring, knowing that all men who came to him were putting their lives in his hands. And yet, before each surgery began, Robert had no idea which way things would go. That was what excited him the most. Sometimes, it was out of his hands, of course, but in most cases, it would come to him about halfway through, out of nowhere. He'd suddenly know if he was going to allow the person who lay before him to live or to die. And there was nothing in the world that could make him feel more alive. It was quite exhilarating.

As for Mary, her fate had already been determined, of course. He glanced at her now as she paced about the room, examining every little detail. His mouth twisted itself into a leering grin at the prospect of what was to come. If Mary would only have looked, she would have seen it for what it was: a warning to get the hell out of there. But she was too absorbed, too preoccupied, and too trustworthy, so she missed it, focusing her attention on the operating table instead.

"This is really quite something," she marveled as she ran her hand across one of the leather straps that were hanging from the side of the operating table in the center of the room.

"I must say it works splendidly well," he told her. "I added enough straps to keep the patient restrained at all times. You see, like this I only need to leave the straps in the area where the surgery is being performed undone. The rest will keep the patient firmly in place."

He watched her closely, saw her admiration, and decided to exploit it. "Here, how about if you climb up, and I will show you."

"I'm not exactly dressed for something like this," Mary told him hesitantly, but he could tell that she was wavering. She was just like her father, too eager to learn of the newest advances that medicine had to offer. How ironic that it would soon be her downfall.

"Come, it will only take a moment. Besides, I would like an honest opinion on the level of comfort this thing has to offer. I have tried it myself, of course, but I fear I am not as finicky as some of the ladies."

Mary grinned, rising to the challenge—and the bait. "Very well then, I will give it a go."

Excellent.

"Here, you can use this stool to climb up, then just lean back. . .there you go. . .comfortable?"

"As a matter of fact, I am actually," she admitted, sounding surprised.

But when she began to sit up again, Robert stopped her with his hand. "Come on, Mary; you cannot say that you have tried it unless you have *really* tried it. It will only take a moment." He forced a warm smile as he reached for one of the straps.

Mary hesitated. There was something in Robert's voice that she didn't like. It sent a cold chill through her, but she quickly dismissed it. His demeanor was, after all, just as charming as it had always been. Besides, she'd known him for as long as she could remember. He would never hurt her.

Her thoughts returned to Helmsley as Robert tightened the straps around her right arm. She'd known *him* her whole life too, and. . .what was it he'd said?

You have the wrong man.

Panic assailed her. The sudden fear of being rendered helpless in a room with just one man present, no matter who that man might be, had her heart thumping against her chest within seconds. She aimed for a calm voice. "I am sorry, Robert, but I am not feeling all that well. Please untie me."

"Not to worry, Mary, you will feel much better soon."

"Robert." She pulled at the restraints, but they wouldn't budge. "Please help me get down."

"In a minute." His voice was tight and suddenly cold.

Grabbing her left arm, he held it down to strap it in place. Mary flung her leg out sideways, kicking him as hard as she could against his head.

"You will pay for that," he sneered, holding his hand firmly against the bruise that was forming above his left eye.

And before Mary knew what hit her, Robert punched her solidly in the face, splitting her lip and knocking her out cold.

I cannot move. Why can't I move?

Mary's head was pounding. She tried to move her arms, but they wouldn't budge. Her legs seemed just as useless. Opening her eyes slowly, a blurry vision of an almost empty room greeted her.

Where am I?

Turning her head sideways, she spotted a figure. She

blinked a few times, allowing her eyes to focus, and then realized who it was.

"Robert?" her voice croaked. He leaned toward her, peering down at her anxious face. "What happened?"

"You honestly don't remember?" he asked mockingly. "You were being difficult, and I had no choice but to hit you."

The fear she'd felt earlier was upon her again. She struggled helplessly against her restraints. They wouldn't budge. Tears welled in her eyes, but she held them back. She'd be damned if she was going to let him watch her cry.

"Why are you doing this, Robert?"

"Because you refused to listen to me, Mary. I warned you repeatedly, but you simply would not follow my advice. You insisted on snooping around in matters that did not concern you—just as your father did."

Mary took in a sharp breath. *It was Robert then, not Helmsley.* "But how did you find out that I was practicing?"

"Oh, that was easy enough; Helmsley told me. He's not completely innocent, you know. But he didn't know about your father's murder until after the fact. He never would have agreed to it, you see."

Mary breathed a sigh of relief. Well, at least that was something.

"So *you* had him killed?"

"Of course; he'd gathered far too much incriminating evidence against me. I simply couldn't allow that, I'm afraid." The unaffected tone of his voice made her shudder; he might as well be discussing the weather.

"But he was your friend. I just don't understand—"

"He would have publicized information that would have

sentenced me to death, Mary. Friends don't do that to one another."

"But the initials," she muttered. "You don't match a single one of them."

"Of course I do, you silly little fool. I am VR, the Viscount of Ravenwood. I haven't used the title since my youth, but it is mine all the same."

Heaven help me.

"So, as you can see, you are in quite a bit of trouble, my lady."

"Will you at least tell me who my father's killer was?" she asked with a growing sense of hopelessness.

Robert's lips drew together in a wide and hideous smile. His eyes glistened. "It was your very own cousin, my dear."

"My cousin? What cousin?"

"Remember your dear uncle Alistair? Well, he had a son who hated you and your father as much, if not more than, his father did. His name was Matthew, by the way, but you probably know him better as the Messenger."

Mary gulped. She was related to that man—by blood? *Good grief.* She considered Robert's words carefully. "Was?" she asked quietly.

"Hm?"

"You said his name *was* Matthew."

"So I did," he murmured, dragging his words as though he was selecting each of them with great precision. "I shot him just outside Gerrards Cross, along with your uncle." Robert walked across to a small table with a tray on it. He picked up a scalpel, ran his finger along the edge, then smiled. He looked back at Mary. "It wasn't anything they did. In fact, they carried out their assignments rather well, although I was a bit disappointed when they left behind the last of your father's journals.

"But in the end, it boiled down to one simple thing: you would eventually discover that your uncle was *not* suffering from a fatal illness, and once you did, you would also realize that he was somehow involved. I couldn't allow for you or anyone else to go knocking at his door. He knew too much, and so did his son."

"So now you're—"

"Tying up loose ends, so to speak." He moved closer until he was standing right next to her. "Now, would you like me to tell you what I have in mind, or would you rather be surprised?"

Mary's heart sank. This was it, her final moment. Hot tears burned her eyes, but still she did not cry.

Stall for time.

"I would like for you to tell me," she managed to say on a faint whisper as her whole body began to tremble.

Ryan banged his fist relentlessly against the tough wooden door of Woodbridge House.

"Why the devil is nobody coming? Are there no servants in this place?"

"Should I perhaps try to find a battering ram?" William asked as he watched the little effect his brother was having on bringing down the door.

"Be serious, William." Ryan's tone was hard as steel. "That butcher in there might very well be carving up Mary as we speak."

"I know," William muttered. "But rather than hammering away at this blasted door while he does so, we might be better off if we try to find another way inside."

Ryan paused. "You have a point," he admitted.

"All right then," William said with renewed enthusiasm as he eyed the garden wall. "I will give you a leg up, and then you can pull me up after you. Agreed?"

This wasn't the time to argue, and in any event, Ryan knew that his brother had more experience with this sort of thing than he did. He would gladly follow his advice.

A few minutes later, they landed in the garden with a thump.

Ryan straightened himself, glanced about, and then headed across the lawn toward the terrace. William followed close behind him.

"These are locked too," Ryan growled as he pulled on the French doors with all his might.

"Not to worry." William picked up a sculpture of a garden fairy that had been placed decoratively in one of the flowerbeds. "This should do the trick." And without further ado, he sent the figurine crashing through the glass, reducing it to smithereens. Reaching through the gaping hole that now greeted them, and careful not to cut himself, Ryan turned the lock. A second later, the door swung open without a glitch. They stepped through into the ballroom, a vast open space with a wide marble staircase leading up to the foyer. Ryan and William hurried on, their heels clicking softly against the polished floor.

"It seems deserted," William remarked, commenting on the lack of servants that most homes such as this one would be teaming with.

"I know. It's eerily quiet." Ryan's voice echoed around them. He spotted an open door and marched toward it. "Woodbridge's study," he said as he popped his head inside to have a look. "It's empty."

He was just about to move, when a sliver of light caught his attention. It was coming from beneath a door he hadn't noticed before. Waving William over, he pointed toward it.

William arched an eyebrow. "I think we may have found our man," he whispered. "You had better pick a weapon."

Damn. Why hadn't he thought to bring a pistol along with him? He'd been in a dratted hurry and had arrived at the scene completely unprepared. Edging quietly forward with William right behind him, he moved across to Woodbridge's desk and opened the top drawer—nothing but sheets of paper.

"These will do," William whispered from the opposite corner. Ryan watched as his brother's shadowy figure reached up to remove something from above the fireplace. A moment later, William placed a large dagger in his brother's hand.

A shrill scream shook the air, and Ryan sprang into action. With his hand clasped firmly around the hilt of the dagger, he ran toward the door he'd seen and flung it open. The scene that greeted him was that of a nightmare. There was Mary, strapped to a long, wooden table, her gown slashed open down the middle to expose her entire chest and belly. Poised over her, with a scalpel grazing her creamy white skin, stood Woodbridge. He looked up the minute Ryan entered and served him a sinister smile. "I wasn't sure that you would make it in time," he muttered. "In fact, I'd quite given up on your playing the hero. But now that you have come, you will be able to enjoy the show."

"What the hell is wrong with you, Woodbridge?" Ryan's voice was tight with contempt. "Do you really think I will just stand idly by while you cut away at Lady Steepleton?"

Mary whimpered, her eyes huge with fear as they sought out Ryan's. The imploring look in them made his blood boil.

Woodbridge chuckled. "I suppose that might be too much to hope for. But let us not forget, that by the time you make it over here with that thing," he gestured idly toward the dagger, "Mary will be long dead."

"You bastard!" Ryan ground out, his words hovering around them. "I will send you to hell if you as much as touch a hair on her head."

"Now, now, let's not get carried away. As it happens, I have a much better idea." His smile was no different than the one he might have given if he were enjoying a nice cup of tea or a walk in the park. It couldn't have been more contradictory to the situation at hand. "You will do no such thing. I have a sharp scalpel here. One false move and Mary dies."

Ryan winced. He felt William stir beside him and eyed his brother with a grim expression.

"It seems as though we have little choice in the matter." William's tone was calm. In fact, it was completely devoid of emotion. It was impossible to tell what he might be thinking, but Ryan knew. Without a moment's hesitation and with a movement so swift that it was hard to follow, Ryan flung his dagger at Robert.

A muffled cry sounded, followed by a clatter and a loud thump as Robert stumbled backward and fell, the dagger protruding stiffly from the side of his neck.

"Well done!" William cheered as he rounded the table

on which Mary was strapped and peered down at the Earl of Woodbridge, who now lay sprawled across the floor. Blood was rapidly pooling around him. "I say, he does look rather pale."

"Is he dead?" Ryan asked as he hastened to unfasten the straps that held Mary.

"How the devil should I know?" William asked dejectedly. "I am not a physician, you know."

Ryan helped Mary to sit up, pulling her gown closed around her as best he could, and covered her with his jacket. "Are you all right?"

She gave a small nod. "Yes, thank you."

He kissed her forehead briefly, then met her gaze dead on. "Don't move," he told her. "I shall be right back."

Leaving her side, he strode over to where William was standing and looked down at the mess he'd made. "He will bleed to death unless we do something."

"I hope you are not suggesting that we save his life," William remarked.

"That is precisely what I am suggesting," Ryan told him brusquely as he pulled the dagger from Robert's neck, grabbed some linen towels, and jammed them down hard over the gaping wound. "If he dies now, he will not have suffered nearly as much as I would have hoped. Besides, I have no desire to be charged with murdering a member of the *ton*, no matter how much he might deserve it." He looked up at his shocked brother. "We are going to do whatever we can to save him, William, and then we are going to send him off to Newgate to rot while he awaits his trial and sentencing. There is no doubt that he will hang for what he has done, but he will do so with the public humiliation he deserves."

William nodded wryly. "Remind me never to cross you," he said, grinning. "You have a fiercer bite than you let on."

A loud banging caught their attention.

"I had better see who that might be," William said as he headed out the door. He returned a moment later with Bryce and Percy in tow, followed by two Bow Street runners.

"Well, well, well," Bryce remarked as he glance around the room. "I daresay Lord Woodbridge has been rather busy, has he not?"

"It certainly appears so," Percy concurred, looking equally astounded by what his longtime friend had been up to.

"We will take it from here," one of the runners remarked as he glanced over at Mary. "If one of you gentlemen would be so good as to see the lady home—I believe she might be in need of a change of clothes."

"I shall take her," Ryan said, "if one of you will take over from me."

William stepped forward to help. "I will do my best," he muttered.

Leaving everything in the capable hands of William, Bryce, and Percy, Ryan hailed a hackney. "Brook Street, if you please," he told the driver as he lifted Mary up and settled her on one of the benches.

He took the seat beside her and clasped her hand tightly in his. "I am so sorry that you had to endure that." His voice cracked with emotion as he squeezed her hand.

She leaned her head against his shoulder and tucked her other hand under his arm. What an ordeal. She felt drained.

"I just want to go home," she whispered, closing her eyes against the hot onset of tears. She couldn't stop them any longer. She felt a painful lump rise in her throat, and before she even knew how it had happened, Ryan was hugging her against him while she sobbed against his shoulder.

"Shh, he crooned, stroking his hand gently against her hair to soothe her. "It is over now. I will take you home so you can get a good night's rest, and in the morning, you will feel much, much better. I promise."

She sniffed loudly as she gasped for breath in an attempt to calm herself.

"Here." He offered her a handkerchief.

"I am so. . .sorry," she managed to choke out, accepting the white piece of fabric he held toward her. She dabbed at her eyes, which she knew must be red and puffy by now. Her hair was a tangled mess, and her lip where Robert had hit her hurt like blazes.

"There is nothing for you to be sorry about," Ryan told her firmly. "You did nothing wrong."

"I must look a fright, though." She gave him an awkward smile.

He kissed her lightly on the forehead. "You do," he said with a grin, squeezing her hand. "But not to worry; we can fix that. As for your height, however. . .now, that is a different issue altogether."

"My height?" She grimaced, completely caught off guard by such a backhanded statement.

"Surely you must have noticed that you are not that tall."

"I am petite," she cried.

He appeared to ponder that for a moment, and then shook

his head in disagreement. "No, you are not all that petite. Of course, it is not for me to say, but if it were, I would say that you are rather gnomish."

"Gnomish?" she squeaked. She narrowed her eyes, then whacked him firmly across the shoulder.

"Ouch!"

"Did that feel gnomish to you?"

"I think someone may have just pinched me," he moaned, looking about as he pretended to search for the culprit. His eyes found hers, and his smile widened into one of mischief. "Was it you, my little gnome?"

"Well," she huffed, "if I am a gnome, then you are a big oaf—the biggest I have ever seen, in fact."

"A big oaf, you say? As long as I am not a milksop, I really do not mind."

She pouted slightly before her stern facade began to crumble into one of apology. "I am sorry I called you a milksop," she said. "You really aren't one, but you made me so angry and—"

"I know," he told her. "I said some terrible things to you too."

"You called me a jingle-brained harridan."

"Not one of my proudest moments—I am sorry about that. I don't think that you are jingle-brained or a harridan."

"But you think that I look like a gnome?" Her question held an air of disbelief.

He smiled at her cheekily. "No, not really; your feet are too big—no respectable gnome would ever have feet that size."

"Ryan Summersby, I do believe that I despise you above

all others." But her eyes sparkled with the humor of it all, belying her outraged demeanor.

Thank you for the distraction, for making me forget.

"Do you really?" he asked her seriously.

"Oh, absolutely," she said.

"You don't—not really. I don't believe you," he insisted.

"Prove it," she challenged with a wry smile on her lips. "Prove that I don't detest you."

And with that he kissed her, more passionately than ever before, unleashing every emotion he'd felt for the past few hours: his fear, his pain, his love—all present in that one simple caress.

"You will make me the happiest man in the world when you become my wife," he whispered close to her ear.

She pulled back slightly in order to look him in the eye. "Why?" Her voice was quiet, full of hope, yet worried all at the same time.

It was a simple question, one that he certainly knew the answer to. But now that the moment had come for him to tell her, the words wouldn't come. Three little words of monumental importance were stuck in his throat as if they were glued together. He stared at her blankly.

What the devil is the matter with me? Just tell her.

And then it dawned on him. He was searching for something better, something more than those three little words, which in truth, seemed suddenly, completely inadequate when it came to the way he felt about her.

But he knew that wasn't what she saw, for the look of disappointment in her eyes spoke volumes. He'd let her down like the fool he was. He opened his mouth, hoping that words would come, but then the moment had passed. They'd arrived at her house, the steps were set down, and all Ryan could do was help her to the door.

"I apologize, I—" he told her sheepishly.

"No need to." There was pain in her eyes. "I prefer honesty to deceit. I always will."

And then she was gone, the door closing firmly behind her.

Ryan stood there for a long while. He felt like punching something, he'd never been so furious with himself in all his life. He considered knocking on the door and explaining himself to her, but he'd probably make a mess of that too. Instead, he walked back to the hackney, climbed aboard, and allowed the driver to take him the short distance to Grosvenor Square. Tomorrow he'd buy some flowers and a ring and make a proper effort to propose.

Chapter Twenty-eight

Ryan woke the following morning to the sound of incessant hammering at his bedroom door. There was no point in ignoring it; whoever it was was determined to get his attention one way or the other. Climbing out of bed, he pulled on his undergarments and walked groggily across the floor, opening the door to William, who was frantically waving a newspaper with a look of fury in his eyes.

"You are not going to believe this," William said as he pushed his way past Ryan. "Close the door; we need to talk."

"Can it wait until I'm properly dressed?" Ryan asked.

"Would I be here if it could?" William fumed.

"I suppose not." Ryan grabbed a shirt from a nearby chair and pulled it over his head. "What's the matter?" he asked.

"That. . .that despicable woman." William was so distressed he seemed unable to get the necessary words out of his mouth.

"Who on earth are you talking about?"

"Lady Stephanie, of course; who else?" He shoved the newspaper in Ryan's face. "Read this."

Ryan took the paper and unfolded it somewhat hesitantly,

casting his brother a sidelong glance as he did so. He looked just about ready to explode, and *that* worried him—especially after last night's events. His eyes scanned the front page.

"Well?" William prompted.

When Ryan looked up at his brother, there was murder in his eyes. "I am going to kill her," he told him softly, tossing the paper aside and reaching for his boots. "I am going to bloody kill her."

"And I am coming with you." William smiled wryly. "I've never been to Clayden House before."

Stephanie's father, Peter Maplewood, the Earl of Clayden, was in his study when his butler came to inform him that the Summersbys had come to call. He knew Lord Moorland, of course, but had never spoken more than one or two words to his sons. Naturally, he couldn't help but wonder why they might have come.

An idea struck him. Was it possible that one of them had come to offer for Stephanie? He'd heard that the younger of the two had developed an attachment to the Marchioness of Steepleton, so perhaps the elder was the one with an interest in his daughter. Peter considered this thought with growing excitement. If that was the case, his daughter would one day be the Countess of Moorland.

"Show them in," he said, without further hesitation. But when the two men strode into his study, Peter knew that a marriage proposal was the furthest thing from their minds.

"Lord Clayden, did you happen to see the *Mayfair Chronicle* this morning?" Mr. Summersby asked without preamble.

"I. . .I am afraid not," Peter stammered, surprised by the question. When he'd come down for breakfast that morning, Stephanie had already taken the paper up to her room. He hadn't had a chance to look at it since.

"Well, perhaps you would like to read it now." Mr. Summersby tossed the paper onto Peter's desk. It landed with a thud. "And then you can tell us what the devil your daughter thinks she is playing at."

Oh, no.

Peter read the fine print with growing concern. A shiver ran down his spine at the sight of his daughter's name. And there was Lady Arlington's name, together with Lady Warwick's. Lady Steepleton's was there too in big, bold letters, followed by more accusations than might be bestowed upon the worst kind of villain.

Dear God in heaven, what has she done?

"I can assure you, gentlemen, that I intend to have a very serious word with her about this the instant she gets home."

"So do I, Lord Clayden."

Mr. Summersby held Peter's gaze unflinchingly until the older man eventually acquiesced. "As you wish, though I must warn you that it might be a while."

"I am sure your butler can offer us a drink with which to pass the time," Lord Summersby declared, to which Peter could only nod. What a god-awful day this was turning out to be.

As it happened, Ryan and William were in for a two-hour wait. Ryan considered walking over to Mary's house a few times, just to see how she was doing. He could only imagine what she must be going through after reading the headline. But each time he got up to leave, he wondered if it wasn't best to stay and wait for Lady Stephanie. She wouldn't be getting off lightly this time—at least not if he had anything to say about it.

The front door eventually opened to the sound of chirping female voices. Lord Clayden, who'd joined Ryan and William in the parlor, got up and went to greet his wife and daughter. A moment later, the three members of the Maplewood family made their entrance.

"What a lovely surprise," Lady Clayden remarked. She practically pushed her daughter out in front of her, to be quite sure that she wouldn't go unnoticed. "Have you come to call on Stephanie?"

"Actually, my dear. . ." Lord Clayden's voice trailed off as he noticed the frosty looks the brothers were directing at his daughter.

Lady Clayden, caught up in her own little universe, missed it entirely. Lady Stephanie, on the other hand, didn't appear to do so, for she held a stubbornly arrogant tilt to her chin that made Ryan want to slap her. The urge increased when she offered both men a dazzling smile.

"We certainly have." Ryan's voice was full of disgust for the woman before him, with her fake smile and her pretentious attitude. "Indeed, there is a great deal for us to discuss."

"Well, perhaps we ought to leave you to it then," Lady Clayden chuckled before turning to her husband. "Come, let us go."

"I don't think—" Lord Clayden began.

He was interrupted by Ryan. "I am generally a patient

man, but it does seem as though my patience has run out. Now, please sit down, if you will."

His tone was curt to the point of rudeness. Lady Clayden looked at him in astonishment. She then looked at her daughter, who was suddenly quite pale. Then she looked at her husband, who nodded toward the chair closest to her. "Very well," she said, perching herself on the edge of her seat.

"You too, Lady Stephanie."

"I would rather remain standing, if you don't mind."

"Sit down this instant, or so help me God, I will shove you into that chair myself," Ryan barked.

Lady Stephanie shrank backward, practically stumbling into her seat as she began to acknowledge the severity of the situation. Lady Clayden gaped at Ryan as if they'd all been accosted by a madman, while her husband looked rather pleased with the way in which Ryan had taken charge of his unruly child. Well, it was about time that *somebody* did *something* to put the girl in her place.

"Must you really be so. . .undisciplined, Mr. Summersby?" Lady Clayden sought out William and met his gaze. "This really is quite inappropriate, you know."

"What your daughter has done is far more inappropriate, Lady Clayden," William told her in an even tone.

"I see." The countess stiffened slightly as she turned to her daughter with an imploring look in her eyes.

"Well?" Ryan stared at Lady Stephanie with all the vehemence in the world. "Aren't you going to tell your dear mama what you have done?"

"I cannot possibly imagine what you mean," Lady Stephanie mumbled.

Ryan leaned forward until his face was inches away from hers. "Listen to me, you conniving little witch. You have deliberately tried to ruin the reputation of one of the best women in England. She is above you in every conceivable way—in rank, intellect, kindness. . .In truth, she is a thousand times the woman that you will ever be. So for you, a little rat, to try to destroy her for your own personal and selfish gain is completely unacceptable."

He straightened himself and adjusted his jacket. "Your daughter, Lady Clayden, has published an article in today's paper, a slanderous article built on nothing but hate and envy. She has taken it upon herself to spread the most outrageous lies about the Marchioness of Steepleton, my betrothed."

Lady Clayden looked as if she would faint, while Lady Stephanie appeared as though she might actually spit at Ryan in response to this final declaration.

"It's not all lies," Lady Stephanie snarled. "Lady Arlington's cesarean and Lady Warwick's surgery—"

"Ah, yes, two other ladies whom you decided to drag through the mud as well." He stared at her coldly. "Unfortunately, you are mistaken, Lady Stephanie. Neither lady was ever treated by Lady Steepleton; it seems as though your source of information was quite wrong."

"But I. . .I know from both Lady Arlington's maid and Lady Warwick's, they—"

"But who will believe you when the most outrageous evidence of all was nothing but a figment of your own twisted imagination?"

Lady Stephanie gaped at him in horror as the meaning behind his words began to sink in.

"So here is what you are going to do, Lady Stephanie," Ryan continued. "You are going to renounce every single word in that article of yours, and you are going to do so by this afternoon so that it makes tomorrow's paper. Do I make myself clear?"

"But I will be thought the worst possible liar in all of England. Everyone will hate me."

"So then, it really won't make much difference to you, will it? You are already the worst possible liar in all of England, and from what I hear, you don't have very many friends either."

"She may face charges," Lord Clayden said, realizing the implications of his daughter's actions.

"It is more than likely that she will," Ryan agreed.

"Surely there is another way." Lady Clayden quickly jumped to her daughter's defense.

"I'm afraid not," Ryan told her grimly. "As it is, your daughter may already have caused irreparable damage." He turned toward Lord Clayden. "I trust that you will help her write a plausible retraction letter, my lord."

"You have my word on it, Mr. Summersby." He rose to his feet to see his visitors out. "As to the other matter that we have discussed. . ."

"I shall have a word with Jennings right away," William promised. "He was rather eager when we last spoke, and as I mentioned before, he will be very firm with her."

Lord Clayden nodded gratefully. "That's precisely what she needs—a bit of structure and discipline. Her mother and I have, unfortunately, let those slip." He allowed the butler to open the front door. "Thank you, gentlemen, for your visit.

I will do my best to ensure that Lady Steepleton's name is cleared by tomorrow morning."

"What now?" William asked once Lord Clayden's butler had closed the door behind them.

"I have to talk to Mary," Ryan told him. "It's time I made a proper proposal."

"You'll need a ring for that."

"And flowers too—roses, I believe, a big bouquet of red roses." Ryan sighed, his forehead creasing in a pensive frown. "And even with all of that I'm not entirely sure that she will still have me."

"Why the devil not? I thought the deal was as good as sealed, that the ring was just a formality."

"We didn't exactly part on the best of terms last night," Ryan admitted as he hailed a hackney to take them to Bond Street.

William waited for Ryan to get in, then jumped up onto the opposite bench. "It seems as if it's becoming quite a bad habit of yours, doesn't it?"

"What?"

"Well, every time you and Lady Steepleton part ways, you always manage to put your foot in your mouth and say something that undermines all of your other efforts to woo her."

Ryan raised a critical eyebrow.

"I don't suppose you'll tell me what happened this time."

There was a tense moment of silence, after which Ryan finally met his brother's curious gaze. He sighed heavily. "She wanted me to declare myself to her, and I froze."

"You froze?" There was a note of incredulity in William's voice.

"It was awful, William. I knew what to say—what she wanted me to say—but the words just wouldn't come, and before I knew it, she was gone, and I was left standing alone on her doorstep."

"It seems to me that you might be needing more than just a ring and some flowers." William's voice was most grave. "In fact, I would suggest you bring along a string quartet and a small pony. Tie a ribbon around its neck, and that just might do the trick."

Ryan rolled his eyes, but William persisted. "I don't think you realize just how serious this is." He studied his brother for a moment. "Do you love her?"

"Of course I bloody love her, William." His voice was tinged with annoyance. "I wouldn't be marrying her otherwise."

"All right," William said and grinned. "Then let's try to salvage this relationship before it turns into an even greater fiasco."

It was almost three by the time they made it to Brook Street, much later than Ryan had ever intended. He only hoped that the outrageously expensive square-cut emerald he'd bought for Mary would work in his favor.

"May I help you?" Thornton asked upon opening the door.

Ryan straightened his spine and squared his shoulders, ready to do battle. "I have come to call upon her ladyship. May I come in?"

"I am afraid her ladyship has left town," Thornton remarked somewhat affectedly.

Ryan's jaw dropped. *Left town?*

"Where has she gone, if I might ask?" He did his best to keep his voice casual, but the despair he suddenly felt seeped through all the same.

"I am afraid that it is not my place to say, particularly since she specifically asked me not to."

That wasn't exactly what Ryan was hoping to hear. She'd not just run away; she'd run away from *him*.

"What if we were to ask you where she has gone? Would you give us an honest answer?" William asked.

"I have never been prone to tell fibs," Thornton remarked. "But I am also loyal."

"Yes, of course; I wouldn't dream of suggesting otherwise." William pulled a wad of bank notes from his pocket. "However, I am presuming that she either will be back at some point or intends to send for you in the near future. If not, you would already be out looking for another place of employment. So logic decrees that she has not decided to leave the country. Now, if she were from a large family, I would say that she had gone to stay with one of her relatives. However, since these appear to be in short supply, I am more inclined to believe that she might have gone to Steepleton House in Northamptonshire instead. I am also willing to bet that this fifty-pound note is about to confirm that."

Thornton eyed the money with great interest. It was obvious that he wanted it, but he was also the sort of man who'd never forgive himself for betraying his mistress. So he hesitated until Ryan and William both felt as though they were turning old and gray with each passing second.

"Come now," Ryan urged him. "I merely wish to tell her ladyship how I feel about her." He pulled the small velvet box that the jeweler had given him from his pocket and showed Thornton the ring. "This is for her, if she will have me."

"Then by all means, you must go after her. Your brother is right. She is at Steepleton House. I will have the groom bring a couple of horses around from the mews so that you may go directly there."

"Splendid!" William exclaimed as he held the fifty-pound note toward Thornton.

The butler eyed it momentarily, then shook his head. "No," he said. "If I take that, then you will have bribed me, and I shall only feel rotten about telling you where she has gone. I would much rather believe that you managed to draw your own conclusions, which, as it happens, you did."

He looked at Ryan. "You are a good man, Mr. Summersby, and I know that her ladyship is very fond of you. I wish you all the best, and Godspeed."

CHAPTER TWENTY-NINE

Mary walked along the dark and dreary hallways of Steeple-ton House, her gown swishing about her legs as she went. The name had certainly misled her. It wasn't a house at all, but a magnificent castle.

She'd met the housekeeper immediately upon her arrival. The poor woman, whose name was Mrs. Thompson, had been in a clear state of panic over her mistress's unexpected visit. So Mary had decided to take a closer look at her property, while Emma unpacked her things and Mrs. Thompson made certain that clean linens were put on the beds.

Entering the long gallery, Mary regarded the various works of art with dejected interest, while her feet occasionally scraped against the herringbone parquet. The truth was that her thoughts were elsewhere—on Ryan Summersby, to be exact.

It certainly seemed as though Stephanie Maplewood had finally gotten her wish.

Mary sighed as she crossed to the full-length windows

that overlooked the countryside. It was raining again, the water distorting her view through the wavy glass.

The one thing that Ryan had insisted must never happen had come to pass anyway. Not only was her reputation now in tatters, but there was still the very real possibility that she might find herself arrested and forced to face charges. Any dream she'd ever had of marrying Ryan was gone forever. He'd always made it clear to her that he disapproved of her profession. Now that it had had such a dire effect on their lives, he'd never forgive her.

And then, of course, there was the matter of the way he felt about her. He hadn't been able to tell her he loved her, which could only mean that he didn't. Instead, he'd looked panicked and terrified as he'd fumbled about for something to say to her, something that didn't have that four-letter word in it. It was enough to break her heart.

With a heavy sigh, she settled down onto the window seat and pressed her forehead against the cold glass pane.

I have lost everything.

What reason did she really have for remaining in England? Nobody wanted her there, and the one man who possibly did would no longer be able to have her. Wouldn't it be better for everyone if she simply went back to the continent? She could seek out some of her father's friends in Paris perhaps and. . .and what? She was still a woman who nobody would allow within ten yards of a patient, unless they happened to be in the middle of a battlefield—in which case, nobody really seemed to care.

Hopeless; absolutely hopeless.

There was also America to consider, of course, or perhaps

somewhere like India, but both of these places just seemed so impossibly far away from the man she loved: Ryan.

Ryan?

Was that not him right now, riding as if hell were on his heels, and with William at his side? What the blazes were they thinking? Rain was pelting down, and there they were, galloping up the drive at full speed. She wrapped her shawl tightly about her shoulders and took off at a run toward the stairs.

"**M**ary!" Ryan's voice rang out loud and clear against the old stone walls.

"Mr.. . .may I help you?" the housekeeper asked, looking quite shaken by the sudden arrival of two unexpected visitors.

"I have come to see Lady Steepleton," Ryan told her with a wide smile, then lowered his voice to a whisper. "Tell me where she's hiding."

"I most certainly will not," the older woman declared. "If you like, you may wait right here while I see if she would like to receive you."

"Very well, then you may tell her that Mr. Summersby and his brother, Lord Summersby, have come to call on her, that we have gotten ourselves completely drenched, and that we would very much appreciate a warm bath before we catch our deaths."

"I will pass the message along," the housekeeper told him primly as she sashayed off in search of her mistress.

She didn't have far to go. In fact, she almost walked right into her as she turned the corner on her way toward her ladyship's bedroom. "I beg your pardon," she gasped.

"No need," Mary told her gently. She'd been standing there the whole while, plucking up her courage to face Ryan. "Would you please ask a couple of the maids to prepare the baths that our guests have requested. Then speak to cook about supper; it appears as though we are going to be a few more than she expected."

Mrs. Thompson didn't argue. She gave a quick nod of confirmation before hurrying off to see about her business.

Mary took a deep breath to calm her nerves. She then stepped forward to welcome her visitors, who were both standing in puddles of water by now. They were a sorry sight to behold, the two brothers. Their clothes were clinging to their bodies, and their hair was pasted against their foreheads, dripping wet from the rain. "I have to admit that I was not expecting you," she said as she walked toward them.

"You left without a single word of explanation. What did you think I was going to do?" Ryan's gaze was anxious as it found Mary's.

"Well, in light of everything that has happened, particularly after the article in this morning's paper, I rather thought you might like to pretend that you never met me."

Ryan stared at her in open astonishment. "Never met you?" he muttered. "Mary, you are the most extraordinary woman I have ever known. I could never dream of forgetting you."

She smiled slightly at that. "It was still foolish of you to ride through the rain like that—you might get very sick, both of you. You should at least have taken a carriage."

Ryan nodded thoughtfully. "I have always heard that love will make a fool of any man, though I must admit I never thought it would happen to me."

Mary's breath caught, her heart suddenly hammering frantically while her stomach began tying itself in knots. Before she could voice a response to his comment, though, Ryan was down on one knee before her—a very soggy suitor indeed. There was a look of desperation in his eyes that went straight to Mary's heart. *God, how she loved him!*

"I have asked you before, and you said yes. I know that a lot has happened since then, but I am hoping, praying, that you will give me the same answer now."

Her throat tightened, while tears pricked her eyes. "And what of Lady Stephanie's article in the paper? My name has been utterly and irrevocably besmirched. Think of your family, Ryan; you cannot do this to them."

"Is that why you ran?" His question was only a faint murmur, spoken on a breath of air. The look in his eyes told her that her answer was of the utmost importance to him.

Unable to speak for fear that she might burst into tears, she nodded her response.

"Mary," he told her seriously as he reached for her hand and held it in his, "I know I have been angry with you in the past for carrying on the way you did, but you must believe me when I tell you that I would never allow a malicious lie, posted in the *Mayfair Chronicle* by a venomous woman, to come between us."

"It is not all lies, Ryan; you know that." The tears were already beginning to flow—it was beyond her power to stop them.

"I know," he said softly. "But by tomorrow morning, London won't know that, though I daresay that Lady Stephanie will have a great deal to answer for; from what I understand, Lady Warwick was quite livid." He paused for a moment. "I also wanted you to know that your father's journals have been recovered—all ten of them."

Mary gasped as she choked back a sob, her hands trembling as they covered her face. *Thank God.* When she raised her head again, Ryan was looking her straight in the eye. "I have seen you work, Mary; you are by far the most skilled physician and surgeon that I have ever met. I know that I was against it to begin with, but I must admit that it would be a crime to force you to give up your practice.

"However, you must understand that you cannot continue to break the law. Practicing without a license, especially since you are a woman. . .it could have dire consequences, and I just don't wish for us to live with that kind of constant worry."

"I know," she said softly.

"That said, my suggestion to build that hospital we were talking about still stands. You could have an incredible influence on medicine this way." He paused, regarding her with all the love he felt for her. Hell, he would move heaven and earth if it would only make her happy. "And I promise that I will use my connections to the best of my abilities to obtain the permission we need for you to practice as a surgeon. Now, I cannot guarantee anything—"

He never got a chance to finish. She was suddenly on the floor with him, her arms about his neck, and she was kissing him as though her life depended on it.

"I. . .ahem. . .I think I will go and see if the housekeeper has gotten our baths ready," William muttered as he strode away with squelching boots.

"Mary," Ryan eventually said and grinned, easing slightly away from her. "I didn't finish my proposal."

Mary's eyes swam with merriment, and her lips edged upward into a warm smile. She didn't say anything, however; she just waited with what little patience she possessed for him to proceed.

He pulled a small velvet box out of his pocket and opened it. "Mary Croyden, Marchioness of Steepleton and the finest surgeon I have ever known, I love you more than words can say. Would you do me the tremendous honor of becoming my wife?"

"You might be an oaf," she said, laughing, "but you are my oaf, and I love you. So yes, a thousand times, yes."

"Do you know, you are quite outspoken for a little gnome," he chuckled as he slipped the ring onto her finger. "But I must admit that it is one of your finest qualities; I wouldn't have it any other way." And to prove it, he pulled her back in his arms and kissed her so thoroughly that she was sure never to forget it.

AUTHOR'S NOTE

My knowledge pertaining to nineteenth-century medicine was greatly improved during the course of writing this novel. What probably surprised me the most was discovering that oftentimes, the key to curing an ailment already existed, but that opening people's eyes to it could be an impossible undertaking.

Take William Buchan (1729–1805), for instance, whom Mary refers to on numerous occasions throughout the novel. When I was trying to find out when people initially became aware of the importance of hand washing and other antiseptic procedures, Ignaz Semmelweis (1818–1865), a Hungarian physician who demonstrated that the contagion of puerperal fever could be drastically reduced by routine hand washing, kept popping up. He made this discovery in 1847, and even then he failed to convince the rest of the medical community of the importance of his findings. But since 1847 didn't suit the period in which the story is set (namely, 1816), I decided to dig a little deeper until, lo and behold, William Buchan eventually surfaced, though he was by no means easy to find.

His book *Domestic Medicine* was written in 1769, almost 100 years before Semmelweis made his claim, and in it he writes that "were every person, for example, after visiting the sick, handling a dead body, or touching anything that might convey infection, to wash before he went into company, or sat down to meat, he would run less hazard either of catching the infection himself, or of communicating it to others."

In my opinion, this strongly suggests that the importance of cleanliness was known, even if the vast majority of people (including the medical community) were too stubborn to pay heed to the benefits.

At another point in the story, Mary's uncle Alistair mentions a sarcoma on his leg, which Mary hopes to cure by provoking an immune response to bacteria, a method she claims to have read about in her father's notes. Spontaneous regression for the cure of tumors did grow in popularity toward the end of the eighteenth century, though with varied amounts of success. In 1783 a Czech physician by the name of Wenzel Trnka von Krzowitz (1739–1791) observed the complete remission of breast cancer in a patient after the patient developed tertian malaria. Other physicians around that time noted similar cases and began encouraging fevers and inflammations in their patients through a number of different methods, discovering that the cancers would often regress after a few weeks. An actual treatment plan was eventually developed by Dr. William Coley (1862–1936).

In addition to these interesting facts, I was surprised to learn that ether was discovered roughly 200 years before it was ever used during surgery, and that the famous surgeon Abu al-Qasim al-Zahrawi (936–1013) not only performed operations for the removal of cataracts, but also invented a wide variety of surgical tools that have inspired many of the ones being used today.

For more information about this and other historical facts pertaining to my novels, please feel free to visit my research page at www.sophiebarnes.com.

Thank you so much for joining me on my adventures!

ACKNOWLEDGMENTS

So much work went into this book that I often found myself overwhelmed by all the detail, yet through it all, my husband never stopped encouraging me to keep on going. Thank you so much for your love and support—I'd be lost without it.

Monica, Vicky and Laura—When I asked for a favor, you were instantly there to help me out. Thank you so much for reading the draft of this book, for offering me advice on how to improve it, and for being such wonderful friends!

A big thank you to the rest of my family and friends for reading my previous books—I know you felt obligated, so I really appreciate your efforts (especially yours, Dad).

To my wonderful editor, Esi and the rest of the Avon Books team—thank you so much for your incredible assistance. It's a pleasure working with all of you!

And as always, a HUGE thank you to you, dear reader, for not only buying my book, but for making it all the way to the acknowledgments!

Dying to know if Lord William will
finally meet his match?
Keep reading for an excerpt from

THE SECRET LIFE OF LADY LUCINDA

Available November 2012

And don't miss these previous books by
Sophie Barnes

LADY ALEXANDRA'S
EXCELLENT ADVENTURE

and

HOW MISS RUTHERFORD
GOT HER GROOVE BACK

Available now

An Excerpt from

THE SECRET LIFE OF LADY LUCINDA

London, 1817

William Summersby stared into the darkness that surrounded the terrace of Trenton House. He'd stepped outside with his father in order to escape the squeeze inside the ballroom. Taking a sip from the glass of Champagne in his hand, he shot a quick glance in his father's direction. "I've made up my mind, Papa."

Bryce said nothing in response to this, but merely waited for his son to continue, the cigar he held in his hand seemingly forgotten for the moment.

"I've decided to marry."

"Oh?" His father's surprise was clear. "I suppose you must have some candidates in mind then?"

William turned away from the darkness to face his father, knowing that what he was about to say would probably be met with disapproval. "I have done far better than that, Papa. In fact, I have already proposed." He paused for a moment, allowing his father to digest this surprising piece of news. "It may please you to know that the lady in question has accepted, and that we hope to marry before the year is out."

"I. . .er. . .I see," his father muttered in a half-choked tone that did little to conceal how astonished he was. "I always imagined that you would consult me first when it came to choosing a bride. However, you're grown, undoubtedly capable of making such a decision on your own. What, if I may ask, is the name of the lady who has so suddenly captured your heart, William?"

"Lady Annabelle—Lord and Lady Forthright's daughter, if you recall."

An immediate frown appeared on his father's forehead. "Yes, I know her well enough, though it did not occur to me that you were so well acquainted with her."

William merely shrugged. "I'm hardly getting any younger, you know. It's bad enough that both of my siblings are now married. I'm your heir, and as such, I have a certain responsibility."

His father's frown deepened. "You aren't even thirty years of age."

"Perhaps not, but I've attended enough social gatherings by now to have met all the eligible young ladies available, and I am forced to admit that not one has made my heart beat faster. Thus, my decision has been based on logic. Lady Annabelle will make a most agreeable wife. She is from a very respectable family, she has a level head on her shoulders, and I daresay that her looks suggest that our children shall not be lacking in physical attributes."

Bryce stared back at his son with sad eyes. "I always hoped that you would marry for love, William. I was fortunate enough to do so, and it is quite clear that Alexandra and Ryan were as well."

"We can't all be that lucky, Papa. First comes duty, however unfortunate that may be. But I will not run from it. I've tried long and hard to make a match that would put Romeo and Juliet's love to shame but with no success. I see no point in wasting any more time. Lady Annabelle will suffice. She's quite pleasant, really."

"Well, if your mind is made up, then the least I can hope for is that you might, in time, find more appropriate words with which to describe your bride. 'Most agreeable' and 'quite pleasant' are rather lacking, if you ask me. And don't forget that if you both live long and healthy lives, you will be stuck with one another. Do you really wish to spend the remainder of your days with a woman who merely *suffices*?"

William let out a lengthy sigh. He'd always longed for the sort of happiness his father and mother had shared, but as time passed, he'd gradually been forced to acknowledge that he would be denied that sort of marriage. The woman he longed for didn't exist. "There's no one else. Besides, I've already proposed, and she has accepted. It would be badly done if I were to go back on my word now."

"Perhaps." His father patted him roughly on his shoulder. "But whatever you do, you have my full support. I hope you know that."

Lucy Blackwell's gaze swept across the ballroom, like a hawk seeking out its prey. She'd barely made it through the door before finding herself assaulted by a hoard of young gentlemen, all wishing to know her name and why they'd never seen or heard of her before. She'd favored each of them with a faint smile but had otherwise done little to enlighten them. She wasn't there to elaborate on her pedigree in the hopes that one of those young gentlemen might find her eligible enough to merit a courtship. No, she'd done her research as meticulously as any detective, and consequently, she already knew whom she planned to marry. All she had to do now was make his acquaintance.

Moving forward, she slowly made her way around the periphery of the room until she found her path blocked by a small gathering of women who appeared to be quite caught up in whatever subject it was that they were discussing. Lucy was just about to squeeze past them when one of these ladies, a lovely blonde with bright blue eyes, stopped her. "Please excuse my ignorance," the woman said, "but I don't believe that you and I have been formally introduced."

Lucy stared back at her, making an admirable attempt to hide her annoyance. How many people would delay her this evening?

"I am the Countess of Trenton, and these ladies who are presently in my company are the Marchioness of Steepleton and my sister-in-law, Lady Cassandra."

"It is a pleasure to make your acquaintances," Lucy told them, managing an even broader smile at the realization that the woman before her was not only her hostess, but also Lord Summersby's sister. "My name is Lucy Blackwell. I am Lady Ridgewood's ward."

"I had no idea that she had a ward," Lady Trenton said, looking to her companions as if to see if either of them had ever heard of such a thing. Both ladies shook their heads.

"As you may know, Lady Ridgewood favors the country," Lucy told them by way of explanation. "And since I have only recently turned eighteen, there hasn't been much reason for us to come to London until now. But her ladyship has most graciously agreed to grant me a season, so here I am."

"And not a moment too soon," Lady Cassandra blurted out. "One can never start scouring the masses quickly enough. Finding a good match can often take more than one season." She followed her statement with a nervous giggle, which led Lucy to believe that Lady Cassandra had probably been on the marriage mart for some time.

Lucy responded with an awkward smile. "I daresay that I hope it won't take more than this one."

"Have you perhaps set your sights on someone already?" the marchioness asked with a great deal of curiosity as she moved a little closer.

"I was practically stampeded on my way in here," Lucy remarked, unwilling to divulge any important details to these women, for fear that they might sabotage her plan. "Surely there must be a potential husband among them."

All three women nodded in agreement.

"But for now, I am actually searching for a certain Lord Summersby, for he and I are meant to dance the next set together, and with the crowd being as dense as it is, I'm finding it rather difficult to seek him out."

Lady Trenton served her a bright smile. "I would be delighted to be of service. Are you not aware that he is my brother?"

"Forgive me, my lady, but I really had no idea." It was a small lie perhaps, but one that Lucy deemed necessary.

"Well, he most certainly is. And if I am not entirely mistaken, I saw him not too long ago on the terrace with our father. Come; I will take you to him directly."

"That is most kind of you, my lady, but really quite unnecessary. I should hate to impose."

"First of all," Lady Trenton began, linking her arm with Lucy's, "you shall call me Alexandra from now on, for I am quite certain that the two of us shall be wonderful friends. Second of all, it is no imposition at all."

Lucy could think of nothing more to say. She was quite certain that she and Alexandra would be far from friends once she put her plan into motion, but she couldn't help but admit that she did need her, if for no other reason than to lead her to the right man.

"Shame on you, William," Alexandra teased moments later as she stepped out onto the terrace with Lucy in tow. "It seems that you've quite forgotten your dance partner— a bit out of character for you and rather ungentlemanly, I might add."

If Alexandra continued speaking, Lucy found it impossible to focus on what it was she was saying, for the man who presently turned toward her, the very one she planned to ensnare, would undoubtedly be capable of taking her breath away ten times over. In short, he was the most perfect, the most handsome, the most memorable of any man she'd ever set eyes upon before. That Mother Nature had taken it upon herself to create such a fine specimen must surely be a crime against all the other poor creatures who'd have to walk in his shadow. She drew a sharp breath.

"Lucy?" a distant voice from a far-off place seemed to ask.

Lucy's first instinct was to ignore it, but then she felt Alexandra's hand tugging gently on her arm, hurtling her with startling force right back to reality. "Hm?" She couldn't for the life of her imagine what she might be expected to say, much less overlook the puzzled expression on Lord Summersby's face.

"I don't believe we've ever met, Miss Blackwell."

Panic swept over her from head to toe until she realized that the words had been spoken, not by Lord Summersby, but by an older gentleman who stood to his right. He wasn't quite as tall as Lord Summersby, but he still had an imposing figure, and Lucy considered how terrifying he must be when he was angry. Thankfully, he looked rather cheerful at present. His eyes were a tone lighter than Lord Summersby's, his chin a little rounder around the edges, and his nose slightly bigger.

"Please allow me to introduce myself. I am the Earl of Moorland. It seems I must apologize for detaining my son from his prior engagement."

There was a flicker of something in the old man's eyes that was by no means lost on Lucy. Mischief, perhaps? *How odd.*

Lord Summersby, on the other hand, had taken on a rather stiff stance, his gray-blue eyes regarding Lucy with a mild degree of interest.

"It is a pleasure, my lord," Lucy responded, offering the earl a graceful curtsy.

"William, you've not said a single word to Miss Blackwell as of yet." Lord Moorland's voice was stern—the mark of a man who was used to being in command. "I daresay you'd do rather well to make your own apology. A lesser woman would already have had a fit of the vapors in response to your lack of attention."

There was a momentary pause. Lucy held her breath, wondering if Lord Summersby would act as a gentleman or declare her a liar before all. Her heart hammered, and her palms grew sweaty, but then, like her very own knight in shining armor, he gave a curt nod and took a step toward her, not only saving her from utter humiliation, but unwittingly helping her realize the next part of her plan.

"Forgive me, Miss Blackwell." His eyes bore into hers, holding her captive as he spoke. "It seems that I was so engrossed in the conversation I was having that I must have had a complete lapse in memory. Indeed, it is so severe that I might just as well not recall having asked you at all. I do apologize with the sincerest hope that you will still allow me to make good on my promise."

Lucy almost lost her nerve. Not in a million years would she have imagined that any man would make her feel so small and wretched. His tone had not been mocking, but his meaning had been clear. He thought her a charlatan, and why wouldn't he? After all, they'd only just met, and she'd hardly done anything to make him think highly of her. Quite the opposite, in fact. She groaned inwardly, knowing that what she planned to suggest would sound ludicrous to him. She hoped he'd accept without a fuss, however, for if he didn't, he'd likely hold a harlot in higher regard than he would her once the night was over.

Pushing all sympathy from her mind, she squared her shoulders and strengthened her resolve. "Nothing would please me more, my lord," she replied, allowing him to take her by the arm and lead her back inside the ballroom.

Taking up their respective positions for the start of the quadrille, Lucy shot a quick glance at Lord Summersby, who was standing right beside her. "Thank you," she whispered as the music started, and two other couples began their turn about the dance floor.

"I cannot say that you are welcome," he muttered in response, "for I despise deception."

"I'm sorry, my lord, but I saw no other way in which to make your acquaintance."

"Really?" Though his face remained fixed upon the other awaiting couple across from them, his irritation was quite apparent. "I'm not sure what game you're playing, Miss Blackwell, but I can assure you that I am far from amused."

Before Lucy could manage a response, he'd taken her by the arm and led her forward, turning her about before leading her in a wide circle while the other couples looked on. As soon as they were back in their places, Lucy pulled together every ounce of courage she possessed. This was the reason she'd come, and she would have only one chance at getting it right. "I have a proposal," she whispered. "Truly, I am in need of your service."

For a moment, she wasn't entirely sure if he'd heard her. Heart hammering in her chest, her legs growing weak with expectation, she feared she might suddenly collapse from sheer nerves.

"And what service might that be?" he finally asked, leading her forward once again.

"I've done my research, my lord, and am quite familiar with your career. In fact, you are regarded as the best foreign agent that England has to offer, and as it happens, I am in need of precisely such a man. I will pay you handsomely enough, of that

I promise you." She wondered if there would be enough money in the world to pay him for participating in her mad endeavor.

Lord Summersby shot her a sideways glance. "As *tempting* as your offer may be, I fear you must take your business elsewhere. You see, Miss Blackwell, I am soon to be married and have every intention of settling down to a peaceful family life in the country, away from all the excitement that the Foreign Office has to offer."

Lucy blanched.

Marry?

Apparently, she had far less time to set her plan in motion than she had hoped. If Lord Summersby married someone else, then. . .She had intended to let him in on her scheme, but if he'd already proposed to another woman, then she might have to resort to more desperate measures.

Her mind reeled as he steered her smoothly back toward their places. The music faded, and all the couples bowed and curtsied—all but Lucy. She was far too busy making a hasty change of plans.

"I take it that your so-called *research* didn't mention that I am betrothed?" He was leading her back toward the periphery of the ballroom.

"It did not."

"Well, it has been a rather hasty decision, I suppose."

Lucy stopped walking, forcing Lord Summersby to a halt as well. Staring up at him, she searched his eyes for the answer to a question that she dared not ask. Until that very moment, William had paid very little attention to the physical attributes of the woman with whom he'd been dancing. Not only had the lighting been quite poor outside on the terrace, but he'd also been so angry that she'd had the audacity to slither her way into his life through lies and deceit, that her looks had been the last thing on his mind.

Since then, he'd barely glanced in her direction, but now that he was given no choice but to take a good look at her, he couldn't help but feel his heart take an extra beat—a rather disconcerting feeling, given the fact that he intensely disliked her. However, as well as that might be, he could not dismiss her exceptional beauty. Her hair was fiery red, her eyes intensely green, and her bone structure so fine and delicate that she could have worn a sack and still looked elegant. But the gown that Miss Blackwell was wearing was by no means any sack. Instead, it showed off a figure that boasted of soft curves in all the right places.

Clenching his jaw, William swallowed hard and forced himself to ignore the temptation. He would marry Annabelle, and that would be that.

"Do you love her?" Miss Blackwell suddenly asked, her head tilted upward at a slight angle.

By deuce, even her voice was delightful to listen to. And those imploring eyes of hers. . . No, he'd be damned if he'd allow her to ensnare him with her womanly charms. She'd practically made a fool of both his sister and his father; she'd get no sympathy from him. Not now, not ever. "You and I are hardly well enough acquainted with one another for you to take such liberties in your questions, Miss Blackwell. My relationship to Lady Annabelle is of a personal nature, and certainly not one that I am about to discuss with you."

Miss Blackwell blinked. "Then you do not love her," she said simply.

Good grief, but the woman was insufferable. Had he at any point in time told her that he was not in love with his fiancée? Why the devil would she draw such a conclusion? It was maddening and quite beyond him to understand the workings of her mind. "I hold her in the highest regard," he said.

Miss Blackwell stared back at him with an increased measure of doubt in her eyes. "More reason for me to believe that you do not love her."

"Miss Blackwell, if I did not know any better, I should say that you are either mad or deaf—perhaps even both. At no point have I told you that I do not love her, yet you are quite insistent upon the matter."

"That is because, my lord, it is in everything you are saying and everything that you are not. If you truly love her, you would not have spent a moment's hesitation in professing it. It is therefore my belief that you do not love her but that you are marrying her simply out of obligation."

Why the blazes he was having this harebrained conversation with a woman he'd only just met, much less liked, was beyond him. But the beginnings of a smile that now played upon her lips did nothing short of make him catch his breath. With a sigh of resignation, he slowly nodded his head. "Well done, Miss Blackwell. You have found me out."

Her smile broadened. "Then it really doesn't matter whom you marry, as long as you marry. Is that not so?"

He frowned, immediately on guard at her sudden enthusiasm. "Not exactly, no. The woman I marry must be one of breeding, of a gentle nature and graceful bearing. Lady Annabelle fits all of those criteria rather nicely, and with time,

I am more than confident that we shall become quite fond of one another."

The impossible woman had the audacity to roll her eyes. "All I really wanted to know was whether or not anyone's heart might be jeopardized if you were persuaded to marry somebody else, That is all."

"Miss Blackwell, I can assure you that I have no intention of marrying anyone other than Lady Annabelle. She and I have a mutual agreement. We are both honorable people. Neither one of us would ever consider going back on our word."

"I didn't think as much," she mused, and before William had any time to consider what she might be about to do, she'd thrown her arms about his neck, pulled him toward her, and placed her lips against his.

About the Author

Born in Denmark, SOPHIE BARNES spent her youth traveling with her parents to wonderful places around the world. She has lived in five countries on three continents and speaks Danish, English, French, Spanish, and Romanian. She has studied design in Paris and New York and has a bachelor's degree from Parsons The New School For Design. Most impressive of all, she's been married to the same man three times, in three different countries and in three different dresses.

While living in Africa, Sophie turned to her lifelong passion: writing. When she's not busy dreaming up her next romance novel, Sophie enjoys spending time with her family, swimming, cooking, gardening, watching romantic comedies, and, of course, reading. She currently lives on the East Coast.

Visit Sophie Barnes's website at www.sophiebarnes.com. You can also find her on Facebook and follow her on Twitter at @BarnesSophie.

Visit www.AuthorTracker.com for exclusive information on your favorite HarperCollins authors.

ABOUT THE AUTHOR

Born in [...], SOPHIE HANNAH [...] publishes novels and a dog with [...] children in [...] places around the world. She has lived in [...] countries on three continents and speaks Danish, English, French, Spanish, and German. She has studied design in Paris and New York and has a [...] degree from [...]. The New School for [...] where she is a [...] professor. She has married [...] in three different [...] in three different continents but is not a [...] While living in Argentina she [...] became [...] the Pilates [...] at [...] university. [...] When she was studying [...] to write her debut novel, Sophie began a regular cure with her family, swimming pool, and [...] with her communities and [...] and currently teaching and culinary arts [...] at East Coast. [...]

Visit Sophie Hannah online at www.sophiehannah.com. You can also find her on Facebook and follow her on Twitter @sophiehannah.

Give in to your impulses . . .
Read on for a sneak peek at seven brand-new
e-book original tales of romance
from Avon Books.
Available now wherever e-books are sold.

THREE SCHEMES AND A SCANDAL
By Maya Rodale

SKIES OF STEEL
The Ether Chronicles
By Zoë Archer

FURTHER CONFESSIONS OF A SLIGHTLY NEUROTIC HITWOMAN
By JB Lynn

THE SECOND SEDUCTION OF A LADY
By Miranda Neville

TO HELL AND BACK
A LEAGUE OF GUARDIANS NOVELLA
By Juliana Stone

MIDNIGHT IN YOUR ARMS
By Morgan Kelly

SEDUCED BY A PIRATE
By Eloisa James

An Excerpt from

THREE SCHEMES AND A SCANDAL
by Maya Rodale

**Enter the Regency world of the Writing Girls
series in Maya Rodale's charming tale of a
scheming lady, a handsome second son, and
the trouble they get into when the perfect
scandal becomes an even more perfect match.**

Most young ladies spent their pin money on hats and hair
ribbons; Charlotte spent hers on bribery.

At precisely three o'clock, Charlotte sipped her lemonade
and watched as a footman dressed in royal blue livery approached James with the unfortunate news that something at
the folly needed his immediate attention.

James raked his fingers through his hair—she thought it
best described as the color of wheat at sunset on harvest day.

He scowled. It did nothing to diminish his good looks. Combined with that scar, it made him appear only more brooding, more dangerous, more rakish.

She hadn't seen him in an age . . . Not since George Coney's funeral.

Even though the memory brought on a wave of sadness and rage, Charlotte couldn't help it: she smiled broadly when James set off for the folly at a brisk walk. Her heart began to pound. The plan was in effect.

Just a few minutes later, the rest of the garden party gathered 'round Lord Hastings as he began an ambling tour of his gardens, including the vegetables, his collection of flowering shrubs, and a series of pea gravel paths that meandered through groves of trees and other landscaped "moments."

Charlotte and Harriet were to be found skulking toward the back of the group, studiously avoiding relatives—such as Charlotte's brother, Brandon, and his wife, Sophie, who had been watching Charlotte a little too closely for comfort ever since The Scheme That Had Gone Horribly Awry. Harriet's mother was deep in conversation with her bosom friend, Lady Newport.

A few steps ahead was Miss Swan Lucy Feathers herself. Today she was decked in a pale muslin gown and an enormous bonnet that had been decorated with what seemed to be a shrubbery. Upon closer inspection, it was a variety of fresh flowers and garden clippings. Even a little bird (fake, one hoped) had been nestled into the arrangement. Two wide, fawn-colored ribbons tied the millinery event to her head.

Charlotte felt another pang, and then—Lord above—she suffered *second thoughts*. First the swan bonnet, and now this!

James had once broken her heart horribly, but could he really marry someone with such atrocious taste in bonnets? And, if not, should the scheme progress?

"Lovely day for a garden party, is it not?" Harriet said brightly to Miss Swan Lucy.

"Oh, indeed it is a lovely day," Lucy replied. "Though it would be so much better if I weren't so vexed by these bonnet strings. This taffeta ribbon is just adorable, but immensely itchy against my skin."

"What a ghastly problem. Try loosening the strings?" Charlotte suggested. Her other thought she kept to herself: *Or remove the monstrous thing entirely.*

"It's a bit windy. I shan't wish it to blow away," Lucy said nervously. Indeed, the wind had picked up, bending the hat brim. On such a warm summer day as this, no one complained.

"A gentle summer breeze. The sun is glorious, though," Harriet replied.

"This breeze is threatening to send off my bonnet, and I shall freckle terribly without it in this sun. Alas!" Lucy cried, her fingers tugging at her bonnet strings.

"What is wrong with freckles?" Harriet asked. The correct answer was *nothing* since Harriet possessed a smattering of freckles across her nose and rosy cheeks.

"We should find you some shade," Charlotte declared. "Shouldn't we, Harriet?"

"Yes. Shade. Just the thing," Harriet echoed. She was frowning, probably in vexation over the comment about freckles. Charlotte thought there were worse things, such as being a feather-brain like Lucy.

Charlotte suffered another pang. She loathed second thoughts and generally avoided them. She reminded herself that while James had once been her favorite person in England, he had since become the sort of man who brooded endlessly and flirted heartlessly.

Never mind what he had done to George Coney . . .

An Excerpt from

SKIES OF STEEL
THE ETHER CHRONICLES
by Zoë Archer

In the world of The Ether Chronicles,
the Mechanical War rages on, and
appearances are almost always deceiving
. . . Read on for a glimpse of Zoë Archer's
latest addition to this riveting series.

He *had* to be here. His airship, *Bielyi Voron*, had been spotted nearby. Through the judicious use of bribery, she had learned that he frequented this tavern. If he wasn't here, she would have to come up with a whole new plan, but that would take costly time. Every hour, every day that passed meant the danger only increased.

She walked past another room, then halted abruptly when she heard a deep voice inside the chamber speaking in

Russian. Cautiously, she peered around the doorway. A man sat in a booth against the far wall. The man she sought. Of that she had no doubt.

Captain Mikhail Mikhailovich Denisov. Rogue Man O' War.

Like most people, Daphne had heard of the Man O' Wars, but she'd never seen one in person. Not until this moment. Newspaper reports and even cinemagraphs could not fully do justice to this amalgam of man and machine. The telumium implants that all Man O' Wars possessed gave them incredible might and speed, and heightened senses. Those same implants also created a symbiotic relationship between Man O' Wars and their airships. They both captained and powered these airborne vessels. The implants fed off of and engendered the Man O' Wars' natural strength of will and courage.

Even standing at the far end of the room, Daphne felt Denisov's energy—invisible, silent waves of power that resonated in her very bones. As a scholar, she found the phenomenon fascinating. As a woman, she was . . . troubled.

Hard angles comprised his face: a boldly square jaw, high cheekbones, a decidedly Slavic nose. The slightly almond shape of his eyes revealed distant Tartar blood, while his curved, full mouth was all voluptuary, framed by a trimmed, dark goatee. An arresting face that spoke of a life fully lived. She would have looked twice at him under any circumstances, but it was his hair that truly made her gape.

He'd shaved most of his head to dark stubble, but down the center he'd let his hair grow longer, and it stood up in a dramatic crest, the tip colored crimson. Dimly, she remembered reading about the American Indians called Mohawks, who wore their hair in just such a fashion. Never before had she seen it on a non-Indian.

By rights, the style ought to look outlandish, or even ludicrous. Yet on Denisov, it was precisely right—dangerous, unexpected, and surprisingly alluring. Rings of graduated sizes ran along the edge of one ear, and a dagger-shaped pendant hung from the lobe of his other ear.

Though Denisov sat in a corner booth, his size was evident. His arms stretched out along the back of the booth, and he sprawled in a seemingly casual pose, his long legs sticking out from beneath the table. A small child could have fit inside each of his tall, buckled boots. He wore what must have been his Russian Imperial Aerial Navy long coat, but he'd torn off the sleeves, and the once-somber gray wool now sported a motley assortment of chains, medals, ribbons, and bits of clockwork. A deliberate show of defiance. His coat proclaimed: *I'm no longer under any government's control.*

If he wore a shirt beneath his coat, she couldn't tell. His arms were bare, save for a thick leather gauntlet adorned with more buckles on one wrist.

Despite her years of fieldwork in the world's faraway places, Daphne could confidently say Denisov was by far the most extraordinary-looking individual she'd ever seen. She barely noticed the two men sitting with him, all three of them laughing boisterously over something Denisov said.

His laugh stopped abruptly. He trained his quartz blue gaze right on her.

As if filled with ether, her heart immediately soared into her throat. She felt as though she'd been targeted by a predator. Nowhere to turn, nowhere to run.

I'm not here to run.

When he crooked his finger, motioning for her to come toward him, she fought her impulse to flee. Instead, she put one foot in front of the other, approaching his booth until she stood before him. Even with the table separating them, she didn't feel protected. One sweep of his thickly muscled arm could have tossed the heavy oak aside as if it were paper.

"Your search has ended, *zaika*." His voice was heavily accented, deep as a cavern. "Here I am."

An Excerpt from

FURTHER CONFESSIONS OF A SLIGHTLY NEUROTIC HITWOMAN

by JB Lynn

Knocking off a drug kingpin was the last thing
on Maggie Lee's to-do list . . . Take three
wacky aunts, two talking animals, one nervous
bride, and an upcoming hit, and you've got
the follow-up to JB Lynn's wickedly funny
Confessions of a Slightly Neurotic Hitwoman.

"I see a disco ball in your future." Armani Vasquez, the closest thing I had to a friend at Insuring the Future, delivered
this pronouncement right after she sprinkled a handful of
candy corn into her Caesar salad.

Disgusted by her food combination, I pushed my own
peanut butter and jelly sandwich away. "Really? A disco ball?"

If you'd told me a month ago that I'd be leaning over a table in the lunchroom, paying close attention to the bizarre premonitions of my half-crippled, wannabe-psychic coworker, I would have said you were crazy.

But I'd had one hell of a month.

First there had been the car accident. My sister Theresa and her husband, Dirk, were killed; my three-year-old niece, Katie, wound up in a coma; and I ended up with the ability to talk to animals. Trust me, I know exactly how crazy that sounds, but it's true . . . I think.

On top of everything else, I inadvertently found myself hurtling down a career path I never could have imagined.

I'm now a hitwoman for hire. Yes, I kill people for money . . . but just so you know, I don't go around killing just anyone. I've got standards. The two men I killed were bad men, very bad men.

Before I could press Armani for more details about the mysterious disco ball, another man I wanted to kill sauntered into my line of vision. I hate my job at Insuring the Future. I hate taking automobile claims from idiot drivers who have no business getting behind the wheel. But most of all I hate my boss, Harry. It's not the fact that he's a stickler for enforcing company policy or even that he always smells like week-old pepperoni. No, I hate him because Harry "likes" me. A lot. He's always looking over my shoulder (and peering down my shirt) and calling me into his office for one-on-one "motivational chats" to improve my performance.

I know what you're thinking. I should report his sexual harassment to human resources, or, if I deplore the idea of workplace conflict (and what self-respecting hitwoman wouldn't?), I should quit and find another job.

I was getting ready to do just that, report his lecherous ass and then quit (because I really do despise "helping" the general public), but then the accident happened. And then the paid assassin gig.

So now I need this crappy, unfulfilling, frustrating-as-hell clerical employment because it provides a cover for my second job. It's not like I can put HITWOMAN on my next tax return. Besides, if I didn't keep this job, my meddling aunts would wonder what the hell I'm doing with my life.

An Excerpt from

THE SECOND SEDUCTION
OF A LADY

by Miranda Neville

**Enter the thrilling, sexy world of Georgian
England in this splendid Miranda Neville
novella—and catch a glimpse of Caro, the
heroine of the upcoming *The Importance of
Being Wicked*, on sale December 2012.**

"Eleanor!" She looked up. He stepped forward to meet her
on the bridge. "Eleanor!" He should ask her how she was, why
she was there. But he didn't care why she was there. All he
wanted to do was take her into his arms and tease her stern
mouth into returning his kisses.

His outstretched arms were welcomed with a hearty
shove, and he landed on his back in cold water.

"What—"

She looked down at him, grim satisfaction on her elegant features. "I beg your pardon, Mr. Quinton, but you were in my way. I have things to attend to."

As he struggled upright in the thigh-deep water, she completed her crossing. Cold soaked through every garment, chilling his skin, his ardor, and his heart. "Wait! You are trespassing," he called, a surge of rage making him petty. He'd been wrong, yes, but his intentions had ultimately been honorable. She had sent him about his business with a cold rebuke. And returned all his letters unread.

"Oh? Is this your land?" she said with a haughty brow, knowing well that his home was over a hundred miles away, near Newmarket.

"Effectively, yes," he said, clambering up the bank. "I have control of the Townsend estate for another three weeks, until my ward reaches his majority."

"In that case," she replied, "I'll collect *my* charge and be off."

Ignoring the squelching in his boots, he reached for her again. In the bare second his wet hand rested on her lower arm, warm under his chilled fingers, longing flooded his veins. "Eleanor," he whispered.

"Get your wet hands off my gown." She shook him off.

"Won't you forgive me?"

Her grey eyes held his. He'd seen them bright with affection and wild with ecstasy. Now they contained polished steel.

"I think, Mr. Quinton, it would be better if we both forget that there is anything to forgive."

Max deliberately mistook her meaning. "Good," he said. She watched him unbutton his clammy, clinging waistcoat with the outrage of a dowager. Yet she'd seen him wearing even less. Or felt him, rather. It had been dark at the time.

The garment slid down his arms. "I'm ready to apologize again, but I'd like it even better if we could begin a new chapter. Can we start again? Please, Eleanor."

Eleanor watched Max Quinton drape his wet waistcoat over a branch, in fascinated disbelief that, meeting her after five years, he should be stripping off his clothes. She trusted he wouldn't be removing all of them. The entreaty in his voice affected her, but only for an instant. Giving him a dunking had blunted the edge of anger that his appearance provoked, that was all. Nothing else had changed.

"I made it clear in the past," she said coldly, "that our acquaintance was over. Forever. Should we meet again, which I trust won't be necessary, you may call me Miss Hardwick."

"Don't you think that's absurd, given what we once were to each other?"

She stepped farther away from this unpleasantly damp man. Never mind that his figure was displayed to advantage beneath clinging linen, fine enough to limn the contours of his chest and reveal an intriguing dark shadow descending to the waist. It was true that his thick, wavy hair looked quite good wet, but she no longer responded to the lilt of laughter in his deep voice. "Our past relationship was founded on falsehood and meant nothing. I never think of you, and I'd like to keep it that way. We meet as indifferent strangers."

A smile tugged on his lips. It was one of the first things she'd noticed about him, that hint of humor in an otherwise grave face. "Do you often push strangers into rivers?"

"You deserved it."

An Excerpt from

TO HELL AND BACK
A LEAGUE OF GUARDIANS NOVELLA
by Juliana Stone

**All Logan Winters wants is to be left alone with
the woman he loves. But fate isn't on his side . . .
Logan and Kira are back in the latest League
of Guardians novella from Juliana Stone.**

Priest knew he was in trouble about two seconds after they exited the bed-and-breakfast. Up ahead, just past the giant pumpkin display, stood a pack of blood demons. They'd donned their human guise, of course, but it did nothing to hide the menace they projected. A family of five gave them a wide berth as they traversed the sidewalk, and he watched as the mother hustled her children past.

Smart humans.

The damn things looked like a bunch of thugs—all of

them well over six feet in height, with thick necks, tree trunks for legs, and shoulders as wide as a Mack truck.

They were mean and strong, but dumb. Bottom feeders who kissed the asses of most of the underworld. He wondered who they called boss.

Normally, Priest wouldn't have blinked. As an immortal knight of the Templar, he was used to dealing with all sorts of otherworld scum. In fact, it had been a few months since he'd flexed his muscles and connected his fists with demon hide. Normally he looked forward to this kind of shit because life, such as it was, gave him only a few moments to feel truly alive. Making love to a hot-blooded woman did that. Waking up to the smell of fresh rain did that. Killing a bunch of punk-ass demons did that. He glanced to his side.

But normally he worked alone.

Casually he leaned his tall frame against the brick façade of the coffee shop to his right and kept Kira out of view. The woman didn't say anything—she didn't have to. Her pale features and large, exotic eyes couldn't hide her fear. But there was something else there, and it was that something else that was going to make all the difference in the world. Anger.

He reached his hand forward, as if to caress her cheek. All the while, his eyes scanned the immediate area looking for demons. To anyone glancing their way, they appeared to be a couple deeply involved in each other. Lovers.

Priest ignored both her flinch and her quick recovery as his gaze swept along the street behind him. His liege—the Seraphim Bill—hadn't told him much of this assignment, but he knew enough. He knew where Kira Dove had been.

The gray realm.

It was a place he was all too familiar with, and he had to give it to her, the little lady had spunk. Anyone who escaped purgatory in one piece was strong. He'd never met the hellhound, Logan Winters, but his woman had guts.

His eyes hardened when he spied a second pack of blood demons hunkered down near the bed-and-breakfast they'd just left. When he felt the unmistakable shift in the air that spelled real trouble, his insides twisted.

Lilith's crew.

Just fucking great. His Harley was nowhere near where he needed the damn thing to be. He was surrounded by demons, in the middle of a large crowd of innocents and this little bit of woman had the very bowels of hell on her trail.

A new scent drifted up his nostrils. Lilith's pack hounds were here somewhere, and their human disguises would be hard to penetrate. Those guys were pros.

Priest straightened and dropped his hand from her cheek until he drew her delicate fist into his large palm. Damned if he was gonna let the queen bitch of hell get to Kira Dove. Strong white teeth flashed as he smiled and looked down at her.

"You ready to rock and roll?"

Huge eyes stared up at him, their dark depths hiding a hell of a lot more than pain and fear. There was strength there . . . determination, and—he smiled—a fuck-you attitude.

She nodded and then whispered, "Let's do this."

An Excerpt from

MIDNIGHT IN YOUR ARMS

by Morgan Kelly

**For fans of *Downton Abbey* and readers
of Jude Deveraux and Teresa Medeiros
comes the brand-new tale of a love
that crosses the boundaries of time . . .
from debut author Morgan Kelly.**

Laura collapsed on top of him with a weak moan that he sucked from her lips as he withdrew and coiled himself around her, face to face, his arm cradled along her spine. They were both slick with sweat, drenched in the only substance that quenched what it had ignited.

"One doesn't learn *that* in finishing school," he murmured appreciatively into her ear, when he could speak. She giggled, hiding her face in his shoulder.

"I suppose you think me utterly wanton?" she said. "Isn't that a word you use these days, to describe women like me?"

"There are no women like you," he said, tucking a damp curl behind her ear.

"Not here," she agreed, snuggling against him.

"Not anywhere," he said.

Laura smiled and pressed her lips to his chest. He ran his fingernails slowly up and down her back, and she nearly purred. He loved the way their skin stuck together, as though they were truly fusing into one person. His eyes grew heavy, and he blinked, afraid that if he fell asleep, she would simply disappear. He didn't know the rules. He didn't know if there were any. They seemed to be making them up as they went along.

"In this time," he said, "are you truly not yet born?"

"Not for years and years."

"Then how is it you can exist, here and now, with me?"

She looked up at him, her head arched against the pillow. "I really don't know, Alaric. I only know that I do, and that I have never felt more alive than when I'm with you."

"If you . . . stayed, here, with me, what would happen when you *are* born?"

Laura rolled onto her back, her leg still hooked around him and her body pressed alongside his. She cradled her head on her arm, the sinuous curve of her underarm upraised. Tiny beads of sweat pearled her collarbone, a necklace of her own making. "I don't know. But my time isn't a good one, Alaric. It's a dangerous time, when the whole world has been at war with itself. I've seen things I can't erase from my mind. People have done things that take away their humanity—and now they are expected to carry on like decent citizens."

"I know what war is," Alaric said.

"Not war like this," Laura said quietly. "We can never be the same, any of us. Being here with you makes me feel like none of that could ever happen."

"Maybe it won't," he said gently, running his palm over her sweet flesh.

"Oh, it will," she said. "And then it will happen again. Time isn't the only endless cycle."

An Excerpt from

SEDUCED BY A PIRATE

by Eloisa James

In Eloisa James's companion story to
The Ugly Duchess, Sir Griffin Barry, captain
of the infamous pirate ship *The Poppy*, is back
in England to claim the wife he hasn't seen
since their wedding day . . . but this is one
treasure that will not be so easy to capture.

"You're married to a *pirate*?"

Phoebe Eleanor Barry—wife to Sir Griffin Barry, pirate—nearly smiled at the shocked expression on her friend Amelia Howell-Barth's face. But not quite. Not given the sharp pinch she felt in the general area of her chest. "His lordship has been engaged in that occupation for years, as I understand it."

"A pirate. A real, live pirate?" Amelia's teacup froze, halfway to her mouth. "That's so romantic!"

Phoebe had rejected that notion long ago. "Pirates walk people down the plank." She put her own teacup down so sharply that it clattered against the saucer.

Her friend's eyes grew round, and tea sloshed on the tablecloth as she set her cup down. "The *plank*? Your husband really—"

"By all accounts, pirates regularly send people to the briny deep, not to mention plundering jewels and the like."

Amelia swallowed, and Phoebe could tell that she was rapidly rethinking the romantic aspects of having a pirate within the immediate family. Amelia was a dear little matron, with a rosebud mouth and brown fly-away curls. Mr. Howell-Barth was an eminent goldsmith in Bath, and likely wouldn't permit Amelia to pay any more visits once he learned how Sir Griffin was amusing himself abroad.

"Mind you," Phoebe added, "we haven't spoken in years, but that is my understanding. His man of business offers me patent untruths."

"Such as?"

"The last time I saw him, he told me that Sir Griffin was exporting timber from the Americas."

Amelia brightened. "Perhaps he is! Mr. Howell-Barth told me just this morning that men shipping lumber from Canada are making a fortune. Why on earth do you think your husband is a pirate, if he hasn't told you so himself?"

"Several years ago, he wrote his father, who took it upon himself to inform me. I gather he is considered quite fearsome on the high seas."

"Goodness me, Phoebe. I thought your husband simply chose to live abroad."

"Well, he does choose it. Can you imagine the scandal if I had informed people that Sir Griffin was a pirate? I think the viscount rather expected that his son would die at sea."

"I suppose it could be worse," Amelia offered.

"How could it *possibly* be worse?"

"You could be married to a highwayman."

"Is there a significant difference?" Phoebe shrugged inelegantly. "Either way, I am married to a criminal who stands to be hanged. Hanged, Amelia. Or thrown into prison."

"His father will never allow that. You know how powerful the viscount is, Phoebe. There's talk that Lord Moncrieff might be awarded an earldom."

"Not after it is revealed that his son is a pirate."

"But Sir Griffin is a baronet in his own right! They don't hang people with titles."

"Yes, they do."

"Actually, I think they behead them."

Phoebe shuddered. "That's a terrible fate."

"Come to think of it, why is your husband a baronet, if his father is a viscount and still living?" Amelia asked, knitting her brow. Being a goldsmith's wife, she had never been schooled in the intricacies of this sort of thing.

"It's a courtesy title," Phoebe explained. "Viscount Moncrieff inherited the title of baronet as well as that of viscount, so his heir claims the title of baronet during the current viscount's life."

Amelia digested that. Then, "Mrs. Crimp would be mad with glee if she found out."

"She *will* be mad with glee," Phoebe said, nausea returning.

"What do you mean?"

"He's back," Phoebe said helplessly. "Oh, Amelia, he's back in England."